SIX OF SWORDS

CELESTIAL EMPIRE : ONE

T·A·MILES

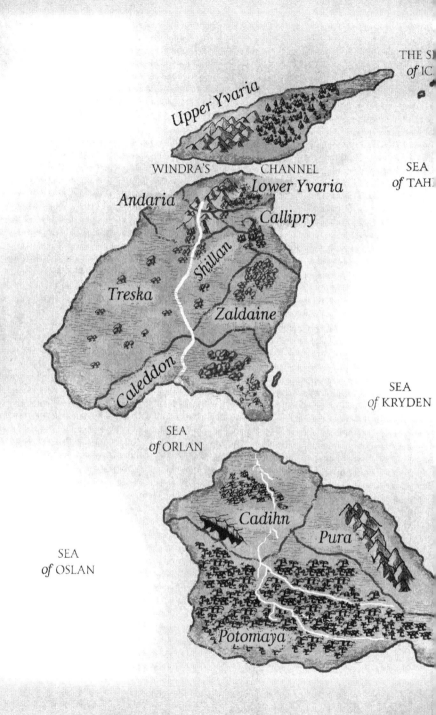

THE S[...]
of IC[...]

Upper Yvaria

WINDRA'S   CHANNEL   SEA
                                of TAH[...]
Andaria   *Lower Yvaria*

Callipry

Shillan

Treska

Zaldaine

Caleddon

SEA
of KRYDEN

SEA
of ORLAN

SEA
of OSLAN

Cadihn   Pura

Potomaya

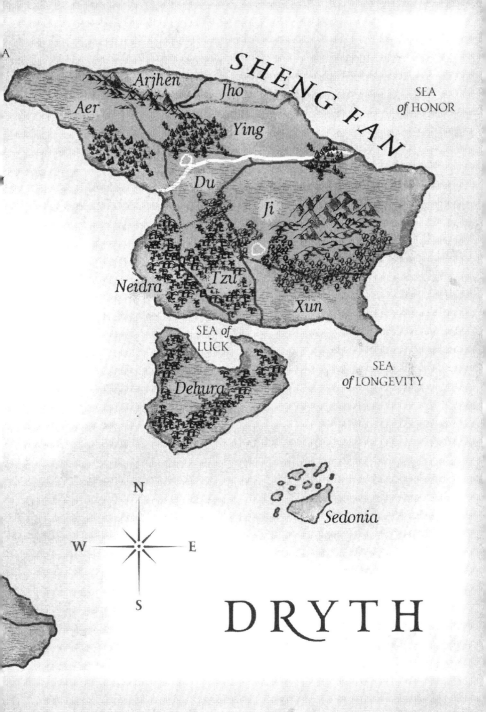

SHENG FAN

A

Arjhen

Jho

Aer

Ying

SEA
of HONOR

Du

Ji

Neidra

Tzu

Xun

SEA of
LUCK

SEA
of LONGEVITY

Dehura

N

Sedonia

W — E

S

DRYTH

SHENG FAN

THE IMPERIAL CITY

FA LENG

BEIXO CASTLE

Xun

YAN XING

Ji

YAT'ZEN

LI TING

Jung Ho Bridge

ZHI PING

HUI FANG

TANG BAI

Du

Ying

Jho

Arjhen

DHONG CASTLE

LU'BAN

SHIMAO BAY

Jung River

HE JUNG

Tzu

Neidra

Aer

SKRIMM'S HARBOR

N E S W

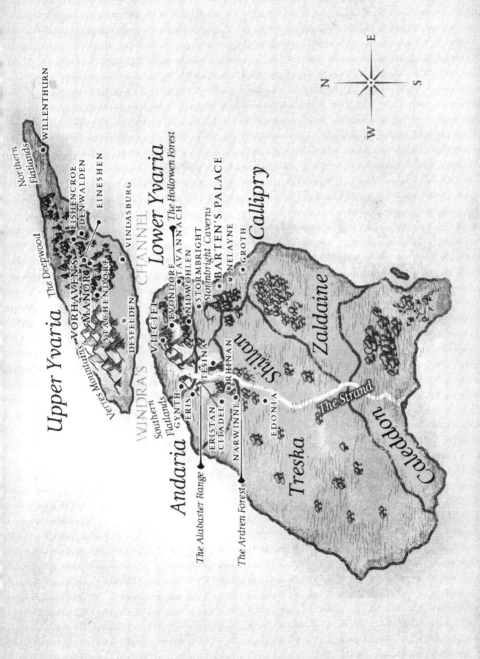

A RAVENTIDE BOOKS PUBLICATION
AMES, IA

Copyright © T.A. Miles 2012, 2016

Map © T.A. Miles 2016, map elements by Ignacio Portilla M.
(eragon2589.deviantart.com/)

Cover illustration by Charlie Creber
(creberart@gmail.com)

Ebook design & formatting by Write Dream Repeat Book Design LLC
(wdrbookdesign.com)

ISBN-13: 978-0692694916 (Raventide Books)
ISBN-10: 0692694919

VISIT RAVENTIDE BOOKS AT
RaventideBooks.com

CHASE THE UNICORN
for free ebook opportunities
and to be the first to know about
giveaways, releases, and promotions

RaventideBooks.com/

10 9 8 7 6 5 4 3 2
Second Edition

For Mom and Dad, who raised me in fantasy worlds.

♦ ♦ ♦ ♦ ♦

SIX CELESTIAL
SWORDS

CHAOS

The Sleeping Dragon

IN THE TIME before man's first breath the Celestial Dragons swam the heavens, the warmth of their souls glistening in the vast skies above the Throne of Heaven. The Spirit Dragons came into being soon afterward, as dark as the Celestial Dragons were radiant. Unlike their fair kin, who served a purpose simply by shining their light throughout the heavens, these creatures were given a duty. They were charged to become the guardians of the Infernal Regions, the curious oblivion where the Celestial Dragons could not cast their light. At once discontented with their role and resentful of the Celestial Dragons, the Spirit Dragons emerged from the depthless void beneath the Throne of Heaven, like shadows come to life. They warred with their cousins, seeking dominance, blackening the heavens with their presence as the terror and confusion of the dark pool from whence they'd risen followed them into the skies.

The battle soon drew the attention of the Ancient Gods, creators and protectors of all things. However, the involvement of the gods did not bring resolution, as they were reluctant to destroy their own children. After a fruitless effort to restore order through reason, the gods withdrew and the dragons' numbers diminished as the terrible struggle continued.

Before long, victory seemed to be in the Spirit Dragons' favor. Slowly, the remaining Celestial Dragons retreated from the Throne of Heaven, whereupon the largest of the Spirit Dragons, calling itself Chaos, killed all but two of its fellows and set itself upon the

Throne. There it sprawled triumphantly, in open defiance of the gods, who seemed impotent against such transgression. Secure in its victory, the Spirit Dragon coiled its serpentine body upon the throne and gradually drifted to sleep, relying on its two companions to alert it to any intrusion.

A timeless darkness passed while Chaos occupied the center of the heavens and eventually the other Spirit Dragons slept as well. It was then that the gods acted.

The great warrior Cheng Yu, wielder of the Jade Emperor's flaming blade and the Emperor's personal guard, attacked one of the sleeping dragons with his great spear and set it afire where it lay, leaving it to burn forever in eternal flames. Another was embraced by the pearlescent arms of Mei Qiao and wrapped forever in the soft, iridescent splendor of her robes, never to wake again. Chaos, the third dragon, was simply touched by the Jade Emperor himself and as it slept, the world formed around its curled body.

Sensing that something was happening to it, the dragon stirred, but it was too late. An imprisoning crust had already formed over its scales and along its spine, vast mountains had cropped up. At first the beast wept in its anguish, and thus were formed the oceans. Then, enraged, it tried to burn its way to freedom, causing the seas to boil and the mountains to erupt as the dragon's flames turned much of its prison molten. It struggled in the overheated quagmire that suddenly surrounded it, but the surface quickly cooled and hardened, and the world continued to grow.

Gradually, the dragon calmed and—lulled by the songs of the first birds—it slept once again. Those destroyed by Chaos were given to the Infernal Regions. Light returned to the heavens with the Celestial Dragons and the Jade Emperor was proud as balance came to be restored. However, in his great wisdom the Emperor foresaw a danger. As life continued to flourish in the throne become cradle and man was born, he feared what might happen if Chaos were to awaken yet again. The mortals would have no defense and not even the gods could watch over the sleeping dragon indefinitely. Moved by his emperor's compassion, Cheng Yu immediately offered his spear. Mei Qiao, inspired by her lover, whom she could never hold again so long as she held the lesser Spirit Dragon, sacrificed her ceremonial sword, known as the most beautiful weapon ever to be forged. Two servants of each god followed suit, giving their awesome weapons to mortal warriors, who were charged to become the guardians of their own world, protectors against the rise of Chaos.

PROLOGUE
Sun Goddess

SONG DA-XIAO, Empress of Sheng Fan, sat centered upon a rug of intricate weave lain over polished stone at the far end of the Palace of Imperial Peace. Her face was immaculately painted in the full ceremonial splendor befitting her divine station above her people while her form was draped in layers of yellow brocade robes. Her feet were tucked beneath the elegant silk garments as she maintained a straight posture, her head just bowed so that her forehead nearly touched the steeple of her fingers while she held her hands together in prayer. She held herself steady in spite of the weight of the elaborate headdress of iridescent beads and gold filigree interwoven with her long black hair while she extended her concentration beyond the physical world.

Enormous silk tapestries draped the walls of the chamber around her, depicting images of celestial spirits and symbols which granted power and bestowed luck upon the Empire and its sovereign. Song Da-Xiao needed the blessing of her ancestors now, more than ever. She wanted only to protect the land and its people. That she could not do so troubled her deeply, inspiring tears she determined she would never shed. It was not her place to display weakness or fear. It was her duty to shield Sheng Fan and its people from evil at any cost. She would die for them. If her sacrifice would preserve the land and the people, then it would be made so. Sadly, it would not be so simple.

In light of a recent and unexpected onslaught she had but one option, and that was to stay alive. She had retreated to the one place in the Imperial City where she could summon all of the strength inside of her and fortify it. Sequestered under armed and constant guard, she sat alone in the temple and prayed to the celestial spirits, that they and her people would grant her this strength.

She did not eat, for fear of poisoning and did not sleep, for fear of treachery. She simply sat, meditating while the fasting purified her soul and otherwise emphatically projected her prayers beyond the temple, to the farthest reaches of Sheng Fan, to the one man she had always trusted and never doubted.

Xu Liang… come back to me safely, my brother.

ONE

The Peacock Departs

A T THE EDGE of the civilized world, Xu Liang opened his eyes. For an instant, the orbs glistened an almost pearlescent shade of blue behind the sheen of unshed tears viewable in the reflective surface of a nearby box. As the afterglow of magic faded, his eyes returned to their natural brown color. The tears were yet held and, in the stillness of his surroundings, they gradually dissipated.

Xu Liang lifted his head. He sat cross-legged at the center of a circular tent, his slim physique draped in elegantly cut layers of silk. Lush shades of indigo, lavender, and jade were enhanced with embroidered images of long-tailed birds, crescent moons, and delicate blossoms. The fashionable tapestry he wore was interrupted only by his sash and the straight flow of his night-black hair, the ends of which were folded on the floor along with the excess silk while he sat down in meditation.

Once again, he was leaving Sheng Fan for the 'barbarian' outer realms. He might have smiled, if not for the dread weighing in his heart. As it was, his eyebrows drew gradually together across the plane of his brow and his mouth formed a frown.

Her unhappiness was also his.

The thought was not permitted to linger. He looked to the tent's entrance a full second before a man dressed in the colorful, laminated armor of a guard came inside and knelt before him.

"My lord, the arrangements have been made," the man said. "We board the Swimming Dragon tonight."

Xu Liang nodded once and the guard left. In the resumed solitude, Xu Liang glanced to his right, at a black lacquer wooden box almost four feet in length resting beside his bedroll. He studied the intricate gold and silver filigree that decorated much of the box and then turned his face away, and closed his eyes again.

Do not worry, my Empress. I will find the others.

◆ ◆ ◆ ◆ ◆

HA MING JIN all but leapt out of his seat, his fist curled triumphantly. There were times when his youth carried him away—he was no boy, but much younger than the previous leader of the Xun Kingdom—and this was such a time. News of his longtime rival's absence from the battlefield—that at times seemed to exist privately between the two of them—was just about more than he could handle without savage laughter. He'd been waiting years for his opponent to make such a dire error.

Xu Liang was frequently away from the Empress' side, but never had he failed to stand by her during truly important occasions. Especially early into her young rule, when more than Xun had been unable to accept a mere girl child as their sovereign.

Without Xu Liang, who had diligently served her father in the past, Song Da-Xiao would have been banished by now or assassinated, like her birth brother Song Lu. Somehow the scholar she had taken as a sibling by oath, who also served as Imperial Tactician, had been able to convince the Imperial Court of her charismatic virtue and her right to ascension through blood connection with the late Emperor Song Bao. Afterward she was a cautious ruler, following in her late father's footsteps with exacting efforts and many of the people grew to love her.

It went without saying that Xu Liang's tutelage and guidance attributed largely to Song Da-Xiao's success as a ruler. He had hand-selected the Empress' bodyguards and personally seen to the banishment, imprisonment—or executions, if necessary—of any and all recalcitrant court officers. Some believed that he had done this for his own comfort, so that he could move on with his physical and magical research of Sheng Fan. Yet, for all of his effort, he seemed never to be too far away. He could be absent from the court for a year only to suddenly return if something threatened the Empress' security.

For almost six years Xu Liang's presence alone had thwarted nearly every rebellion before it truly began. And now, with the threat against the Song Dynasty greater than ever, he had left his beloved Empress. Why? Had he gone to gather military reinforcement from another kingdom—from Ying perhaps, who could still be considered a firm Song loyalist? Or was this simply another of his useless expeditions?

Ha Ming Jin had never faltered in his belief that Xu Liang would one day expose his true love, not of the Empire but of his magic, and in so doing he would expose the unworthy child he had vainly been protecting. It seemed that day had arrived. Still, it was almost too good to be true.

Ha Ming Jin looked down at the messenger kneeling before him. "Xu Liang has left the Imperial City? You're sure?"

"Yes, Lord Ha. Scouts reported having sighted him in the Yatzen district of Ying just ten nights ago. Heading west, my lord."

Ha Ming Jin considered this information aloud. "He's going to overshoot Dhong Castle if he hasn't already turned north. Perhaps it is not the Empress' intent to summon reinforcements from the Northern Kingdom, then." His lips curled into an ambitious smile before he could truly begin to wonder about Xu Liang's destination. "Ah, a foolish child. The time to seize control of Sheng Fan has never been better." He focused again on the messenger. "Send word to the troops at Fa Leng to press the attack. We will continue our northern advance. Finally, the Imperial City will fall and Sheng Fan will unite under the banner of Xun."

The messenger pressed his fist loosely against his open hand, nodded obediently, then departed. Alone, Ha Ming Jin carefully allowed a chuckle to escape him.

Xu Liang ... always fanning your feathers for all to see, like the vain peacock you are. You'll regret your arrogance this time. You will see that your confidence is misplaced in that child.

◆ ◆ ◆ ◆ ◆

LI TING WAS a small fishing community. It provided almost solely for itself. On occasion a few junks made the journey up or down the Tunghui river to barter with another village that specialized in something else, such as raising oxen or growing rice. These small places existed as siblings sharing responsibilities, with the head of their household naturally being the Empress. If there was discord among them, she would resolve it. When there was harmony, the villages prospered and the Empress was proud. Her pride showed now through Xu Liang's quiet smile as he rode along the riverbank and looked out at the last boats on the water taking advantage of what light remained as the sun set.

"It's beautiful, isn't it?" Xu Liang said to the man riding beside him, one of eight bodyguards assigned to him by the Empress. Under Emperor Song Bao he had frequently traveled with half as many, but Song Da-Xiao was young yet and worried overmuch for those who fancied themselves her protectors.

The addressed bodyguard looked briefly out at the water and the darkening sky. All too quickly his eyes were back on the open ground to the other side of their small caravan, which led to a thick stand of trees. "Perhaps we should have waited for full cover of darkness, Master Xu. This area feels too open with the tree line so near."

"Lord Xu Liang has asked you a question," someone else said. The elder bodyguard had traveled with Xu Liang in the past.

The reprehensive tone the senior guard used—if not the words themselves—brought an abrupt look of apology to the younger guard's features.

Before the youth could speak, Xu Liang said, "Perhaps you're right." He waited just long enough for his young guard to agonize over how he should respond to such a statement coming from his superior, then continued in quiet, nonabrasive tones. "Maybe there is some measure of carelessness to my actions. However, this journey is not of leisure, nor of stealth, but one of haste. We must accept some measure of risk in order to achieve our goal."

The young guard inclined his head a bit nervously, clearly wanting to look elsewhere—either at the nearby forest to watch for assassins or simply away from his master altogether, though he dared not before he'd been excused to do so.

He was so young, Xu Liang thought; easily upset, in spite of his skill and training. True youth too often inspired recklessness.

"We must all be on our guard," Xu Liang concluded.

The young man went back to scanning the open land preceding the village and the relative quiet of the caravan resumed.

At that time, Xu Liang closed his eyes in concentration. Sensing nothing out of the ordinary, he opened them again and looked to the upcoming village. Small wooden buildings dotted the riverside. Lamplight glowed within many of them while torches lit the docks.

Among the four fishing junks floating idle beside the village was the *Swimming Dragon*, whose captain had graciously agreed to charter the Empress' envoy all the way to Ti Lao Bay for minor compensation, considering that he did not realize precisely who he'd agreed to charter. It may have been obvious that Xu Liang was no commoner, nor a typical lord for that matter, but this far from the Imperial City there were very few who recognized him by his face alone. No one, in fact, who didn't belong to the immediate presiding family in Du—the territory Xu Liang's company would shortly be entering once they began their journey along the Tunghui.

Naturally, every part of Sheng Fan belonged to the Empire, but years ago a certain distribution of power became necessary in order to ensure that the people were properly governed and that the land was better defended. The decision had been made before Xu Liang's services began in the Imperial Court. It had been made, in fact, before his birth. Had he been able to serve at the time he would have strongly advised against the Five Kingdoms Resolution. In his opinion it was no resolution, but a prelude to disaster. He blamed the Kingdoms for the Song family's current struggle.

Since the lords of the outer regions of Sheng Fan had been given a taste of the Dynasty's power, it seemed they now wanted more of it. Or as if they'd like to spit it back and create something new that they would force all of Sheng Fan to swallow—under a new banner and a new emperor, of course.

An example came to mind: Du—residing on the farthest western border of Sheng Fan—harbored steadily evolving ambitions of becoming a separate nation in and of itself. It would not be so, not so long as at least one member of the Song family remained who could be placed and kept upon the throne of the Empire, offering enough stability to the land to hold such ambitions at bay. However, posing a more urgent threat was the Xun Kingdom, to the south of the Imperial City, who wanted simply to bring down the Song and begin a new dynasty of its own. It was a constant struggle to keep the rebellious governors mollified or beaten back and, unfortunately, it was too late to revoke power that had already been given without provoking costlier civil battles.

And now the Empress was under attack from another source as well. One whose roots carried back to the very creation of Sheng

Fan and whom no one, including Xu Liang, expected to see in their lifetime.

The oldest of the bodyguards, Gai Ping, positioned his horse alongside Xu Liang's, placing himself between his master and the young guard he'd previously reprimanded. "My lord," he beckoned with respect. When Xu Liang looked at him, silently inviting him to speak further, he said, "I know that you can see things as other men cannot, but the air disturbs me. The others are uneasy as well. Should we quicken our pace?"

"No," Xu Liang replied quietly. He looked away from the man and again caught a spectacular view of the sky gleaming orange over the river as the sun departed from the sky. "Moving at a rushed pace would only attract attention. If there is someone here to be concerned with, they are going to be a concern regardless of how quickly we arrive at the inevitable conflict."

"You sense something, then?"

Xu Liang shook his head. "I sense nothing here, but I trust your instinct, which leads me to believe that the disturbance awaits us in the village, or will come from there. In fact, ... here it comes now."

As he was speaking, Xu Liang returned his gaze to the upcoming river settlement, where a well-armored man on horseback rode out to meet them.

The stranger stopped at the edge of the village, wearing a grim smile on his broad, bearded countenance while no less than ten armed men scrambled to catch up with him on foot. As the peons arrived they took up a defensive stance in front of their evident commander.

Xu Liang drew his mount to an eventual halt and held his arm out, silently instructing his bodyguards to do the same. Xu Liang studied the men on the ground and assessed by their common appearance that they were little more than bandits, men paid for the use of their sword arms.

Paid by whom?

"The famed Xu Liang of the Imperial City," the man on horseback said with tremendous confidence and very little respect. Perhaps it had not yet been earned in his eyes. "Can it be?"

Xu Liang looked to the speaker on horseback. The man bore no symbols or colors anywhere on his person that would readily indicate his lord, if he served one. The man's attire appeared mostly blue, a shade too pale to belong to the Blue Dragon of the Ji Kingdom. Besides, Ji housed the Imperial City, or had rather been formed around it, like armor for the breast to protect the heart. No one of Ji's military would dare impose so vile and flagrant an act of treachery before one of the Imperial Court. Xu Liang knew this not so much through personal pride, as through the pride of others. He knew that one who disagreed with Ji this strongly would not impersonate the Blue Dragon, as it would embarrass and dishonor them to in any way bear the flag of an opponent. A warrior this bold would, without question, speak openly against his enemies, with his appearance as well as his words and actions. Xu Liang thus concluded that this man was a rogue, and not one to be taken lightly. The size of his pole-axe and how easily he balanced it while mounted suggested tremendous strength.

The rogue's eyes narrowed coolly in Xu Liang's appraising silence. "I've heard rumors that you are very wise and also quite beautiful. It pleases me to see that the rumors were only half true."

Unmoved, Xu Liang said, "Really? And which half would you be referring to?"

The stranger laughed. It was a deep sound that could easily put fear into the hearts of defenseless peasants. "You're nothing more than the Empress' ornamental bird." He lifted his pole-mounted blade. "I have nothing against birds, Xu Liang, but I must strike you down!"

"We do what we must," Xu Liang answered.

He had no sooner done so when the men on foot charged. The bodyguards responded in turn, spurring their horses forward to intercept. That left the nameless rogue and Xu Liang facing each other across several yards of open ground.

Xu Liang detested violence, particularly at this level, but he understood that in some instances it proved necessary. In this instance, the rogue was barring his passage into the village and more importantly, to the vessel he needed to board in order to carry out his duties to his Empress. He held steady and watched his opponent approach at a full charge.

We do what we must.

The rogue spun his blade once above his head, then drew his arm back, preparing to swipe Xu Liang from his own mount as the gap between them drew smaller. It would not be so easy.

Xu Liang closed his left hand, leaving two fingers raised, and held it just in front of him at chest level. Then he closed his eyes, extended his right arm, and whispered a brief phrase.

"None of your magic!" the rogue cried out, but too late.

The wind was already lifting strands of Xu Liang's long hair and it lifted the stranger's blade when he struck against the spell, curbing the pole-axe at an awkward arc above the intended victim's head. The rogue managed to hold onto the shaft of his weapon, but he was forced to charge past his opponent and circle back for another attempt.

Xu Liang opened his eyes to the clash ahead of him, taking the time only to note that all of his bodyguards were still mounted, except for one, and that that one appeared uninjured, fending off two opponents at once. A member of the rogue's gang of bandits already lay motionless in the short grass.

Such a foolish waste, Xu Liang thought, then turned his mount around to confront his own attacker, who was coming back. Xu Liang crossed his arms in front of himself, then drew them apart not too slowly, and thrust both hands outward. The air shimmered faintly, and a soft blue radiance preceded the sudden, brief eruption of wind that shot across the grass, pushing both the oncoming horse and its rider backwards.

The rogue took the brunt of the spell while the alarmed horse reared back, effectively spilling its rider onto the ground. The man was forced to let go or be dragged by the frightened animal as it turned and fled. The rogue landed on his back, but didn't stay there for long. On his feet once more, he wielded the pole-axe with two hands. After cursing Xu Liang, he charged again, impressing him. Many would have given up after being struck from their horse, assuming that every attack would be countered as effortlessly as the first two. But then, maybe this man knew that the attacks hadn't been countered effortlessly.

Xu Liang closed his eyes and his left hand again. He uttered a soft chant, pointing his right hand at his opponent, who found himself caught in a sudden updraft of magical force and lifted several feet off the ground. The rogue cried out as the ground abandoned him, grunting when it returned more quickly than he'd been raised from it as Xu Liang's spell-casting hand lowered. Xu Liang heard his victim hit with a thud that at least took the air out of his lungs if it didn't break anything. He opened his eyes to see the man slowly rising, coughing as he tried to recapture his breath.

Xu Liang couldn't help but to smile just a little. "You are beginning to intrigue me. I am rapidly losing interest in defeating you at all. Perhaps we can cross words instead?"

"No words can save you, sorcerer," the rogue growled. He took a step forward, cutting the air between them with his blade. "Now, fight me!"

"You will fight me!" someone else decreed. Less than a second after the words were issued, the young bodyguard dashed past Xu Liang, toward the rogue.

In the suddenness of the moment, Xu Liang recalled the youth's name, and called out to him. "Guang Ci!"

The guard did not listen. With the cruel smile of a wolf, his opponent waited for him, and swung. Red clashed against the evening sky as the young man was flung aside.

Xu Liang replied to this offense without warning. He performed the wind thrust spell again, but rather than using it to jolt the man as he had before, he channeled much more strength into it— the same strength he might have exerted physically in weapons' combat—drawn from the mind and spirit rather than muscle. Disks of soft, colorful light surrounded Xu Liang, seeming to radiate from him and then fall away as the powerful magic stored within him began to show itself. The wind responded at once, found its aim, and sent the rogue skidding and somersaulting over the grassy earth. Xu Liang expected the man was dead when he finally came to a stop out of view in the distant grayness of evening, but he did not bother to investigate.

Xu Liang's immediate concerns were for his fallen guard. He did not go to him, but closed his eyes and found the man's heartbeat. He followed its rhythm through the wounded guard's blood, to every pulse point and knew that death would not be the outcome. The rogue's blade had cut under his armor, but not in a vital area. More than anything it was the shock of the blow keeping the young guard down. Like Xu Liang, he was now also impressed with the man's strength.

Gai Ping approached and knelt down just behind Xu Liang. "Nine of them fell to our blades, my lord. The last one fled."

"Who do you suppose they were?" Xu Liang wondered aloud, recovering quickly from his exertion, and from the brief rise of panic and anger that had inspired it.

The elder bodyguard gave an easy reply. "They were foolish men, bandits who made the mistake of underestimating you, my lord."

Xu Liang refrained from smiling. He asked, "Are there many bandits known to this region? One would think that the villagers would complain. A small community such as this could ill afford to be frequently, or even infrequently, troubled by such destructive men."

"Perhaps that was the reason they came," the older guard suggested. "Because the village would be unclaimed and unsuspecting."

"Perhaps," Xu Liang allowed, but he would not satisfy himself with so simple an explanation. The bandits' leader knew him. At least, he knew who to expect—who he was waiting for, at the behest of an unknown enemy.

"My lord," someone else said, speaking in a low, strained voice. It was not strained as a result of weakness or injury, so much as with shame.

Xu Liang looked down at Guang Ci kneeling before him and realized with a glance toward the river that the young guard had lifted himself and walked without assistance from the place where he had been violently flung. Xu Liang would have sent another man to aid him. The guard's injury may not have been mortal, but surely the attack had taken something from him. However, Guang Ci showed no sign of being in pain, in spite of the dark stain spreading over his armor, just beneath his left arm.

"I have disgraced you," the reckless youth admitted. "And I have proven that I cannot perform my duty to protect you. I accept my punishment."

"Don't you think that being swatted to the ground by a very large blade is punishment enough?"

Positioned above the kneeling guard, Xu Liang could just see the young man's appalled expression at the words. Either he was confused by his master's forgiveness or dismayed by his attempt to shame him further by making fun of his defeat.

Xu Liang was neither forgiving nor making fun of his impetuous underling. He said, "I have no intentions of executing you for overreaching yourself in an attempt to perform your duty, however thoughtless and rushed the attempt may have been. Even if it would be in my best interest to return one so careless to the Empress, we know that at least one of those bandits left here alive. There may be others. I would exact your execution myself before I would see you ambushed and killed by men without honor. And as I've already stated that such is not my intent, you will proceed on this journey with the rest of us.

Now rise, Guang Ci, and assist the others in building a pyre for the bodies. We will not leave their corpses to defile such beautiful land as this."

◆ ◆ ◆ ◆ ◆

THE WORLD CAME back slowly. Xiadao Lu sat up against the tree that ended his unexpected flight and shook his head. His ears were ringing and his back ached through to his chest. Even his teeth hurt, but nothing appeared to be broken. He moved his limbs experimentally and thanked the enchantment on his armor. Then he looked at the rift he was sitting in, that had followed him on his swift and forced dash across open land. Were it not for the solitary tree fortuitously in his path he might still have been going.

He rubbed his undamaged but aching wrist that he had twisted when his pole-axe caught on the earth and was ripped from his grasp, and a satisfied grin split across his jaw. "You're more powerful than I've heard, Xu Liang."

Xiadao Lu suddenly laughed and stood, jogging along the rut until he came to his weapon, still intact; they'd both survived the mystic's assault.

He seized the weapon and tore it free from the earth, then glared through the blanketing darkness of nightfall toward the village. "We'll meet again!"

On that vow, Xiadao Lu turned and fled the area.

◆ ◆ ◆ ◆ ◆

THE MOON SHONE silver over the night-blackened Tunghui. Xu Liang stood at the railing of the *Swimming Dragon*, looking back toward land and the village that glowed with calm lamplight in the near distance. It appeared that there would be no immediate retaliation for the bandits' defeat. Their main forces must not have been camped nearby, or perhaps what Xu Liang had seen amounted to all of them. All of them save for the individual who was funding them, who knew Xu Liang would arrive at that village when he did, because the village itself was not the target.

Several at the Imperial City had known of Xu Liang's departure, but few had been made aware of his destination. Regardless, it seemed that someone did not want him to proceed. Whoever they were, they had failed in this attempt to stop him, but he would have to be more prepared for the next.

TWO ⊙
The Barbarian Ship

TI LAO WAS a merchant community and also a fishing industry on a much grander scale than the village further up the Tunghui River. The city itself was walled, containing at least ten thousand households along with the magistrate and his family while outside, a flourishing settlement had cropped up. These were the peasants, peasants who were also fishermen and artisans. They wore hemp-linen instead of silk and their sons learned the skills of their fathers and grandfathers, rather than studying for military or civil service.

Xu Liang had never known such a life, but he had grown to admire it. A child prodigy, he had passed his first test for a raw officer status at the age of fourteen. By sixteen, he was excelling in the ranks and by seventeen, he had Emperor Song Bao's attention. Through rigorous and constant study, Xu Liang—now thirty-two—had secured his path in life, though he knew well that it was the wealth and status of his family that had opened that path up for him to begin with.

Born to Lord Xu Hong of Du in the nearby city of He Jung, Xu Liang was the second son behind one already a man, and thus became the center of much attention from the start. However, such attention came with less admiration and more suspicion as people quickly began to wonder how the Xu family—known for its men of large physical stature, who were roughly handsome and possessed of fiery tempers—had acquired one such as Xu Liang. At first considered a sickly child, he rapidly bloomed into what some had labeled a creature of astonishing beauty and mesmerizing grace. Of course Xu Hong's wife was a most charming and attractive woman, but in all of Sheng Fan only one family was famed for its abundant fairness of form and manner.

The Xiang family, who ruled the northern kingdom of Ying, had long been referred to as the Peacock of the Empire. As well Xu Hong's wife had in the past been suspected of carrying on with none other than the head of the Xiang household, Lord Xiang Wu. In Xu Liang it seemed confirmed. In spite of that, it was not mentioned outside of the family that the highest household under the banner of the Green Dragon had a Peacock in its midst, masquerading as one of its own. Xu Hong may have been a gruff, temperamental man, but he was no fool and he saw the efflorescing child's potential. In Xu Liang, the Lord of Du saw an opportunity not only to acquire greater fame throughout the Empire, but to enact an uncharacteristically subtle revenge against his rival.

Rather than accuse his wife publicly and expose her illegitimate child, which would have required him to deliver some form of punishment before 'grudgingly' adopting her son, Xu Hong kept the matter a family secret. He decided that he would not sponsor an adopted son along the path to imperial office, but his own natural child. As Xu Liang continued to blossom mentally as well as physically, Xu Hong's scheme quickly saw success. Not only was his eldest son a strong and capable heir to his kingdom under the Empress, but his second son was among the highest ranked in the Empire, above even the governor of Ying, who had thought to shame him in secret by luring his wife to dishonorable acts. While unquestionably it was Xu Hong's foresight in this matter that spared his wife execution, it may have had something to do with his mercy in light of her crimes that he later procured two more sons by her, both strong and burning with his warrior's blood. It did not take them long to excel in the Empire's military ranks. And, unfortunately, there was no prouder man in all of Sheng Fan than Xu Hong, the most difficult to reason with of all the Kingdoms' governors.

In spite of this, Xu Liang felt remiss for not stopping to pay his respects to his parents—either in Du or Ying. He had sent a message to Xu Hong, letting him know that he would be passing through his territory—not as a requirement but as a courtesy. Even though Xu Hong had been disdainful, insensitive, and even vicious innumerable times throughout Xu Liang's childhood, concerning whose blood was to blame for any weaknesses he might have displayed, the

Officer of the Imperial Court would not repay the wrongs committed against the son. If there had been time to go to He Jung himself, he would have. While he didn't often look forward to lengthy visits with Lord Xu or his half-brothers, Xu Liang enjoyed spending time with his mother. As well he longed to spend meaningful time with the man who had sired him.

Even though their first meeting occurred when Xu Liang was already a man and the blood shared between them had never been spoken of, he still felt the connection to his natural father. Xiang Wu seemed aloof, but it was understandable. He had lost two sons without including Xu Liang, both stillbirths. His fourth son was still a boy and no one to carry on his position as Lord of Ying yet, if he should be somehow removed from that position. Unlike Xu Hong, he had earned all of his fame within the Empire on his own and the strength of Ying rested solely on his shoulders. Somehow he maintained the northern region and also his position as its governor. Xu Liang, who was aware of but not imbided of his rank above both his natural and adoptive fathers, couldn't help but to respect Xiang Wu and to feel some pride in succeeding as his son. He felt pride and at the same time he regretted that he could not sometimes be recognized as a son of Ying.

The foolishness of the notion made him smile inwardly. What did it matter whether he was recognized as a son of Ying or of Du? Ultimately they were all children of Sheng Fan. He served his Empress above all. Immediately beneath Sheng Fan's sovereign, he had no choice but to serve his recognized paternal family. He always felt sentimental before leaving his homeland. He would recover once the river had carried him out to sea, delivering him to a land where he would be surrounded by people who didn't try or care to understand the structure of family and government in Sheng Fan.

Unfortunately, he was having some difficulty convincing any of the boats lining Ti Lao Bay to leave on such short notice for such a lengthy journey. He hated to resort to using his station with the Empress in this instance, but if he must he would present the seal of imperial office and commandeer a vessel.

For his previous expeditions there had always been much more time to plan, to arrange the necessary accommodations. Haste juxtaposed against caution made such planning impossible now. It would be imprudent to present a trail of communication and contracts or imperial orders for an enemy to follow ahead of him. Although now, in light of the previous assault his company had suffered, the effort seemed futile.

An old woman selling bowls of rice with portions of fresh fish put the dilemma momentarily aside. Xu Liang moved through the crowded outer streets near the docks, unconsciously following her sales pitch. He had not eaten for several days, but that was not the reason he was drawn to the stand. The growling stomachs of his bodyguards actually threatened to break his concentration.

"Fish!" the elder called out. "Caught this morning!" She noticed Xu Liang approaching and made quick eye contact. Her smile broadened. "Fresh fish," she encouraged. "You're hungry, yes? Have some."

She was already serving. She scooped the rice into a generous bowl and began selecting recently cut portions of fish. There were the remains of older fish lying close by on the same table, but she had undoubtedly noticed the lavish dress and courtly manner of her customer, and didn't dare to offend with less than what she'd advertised.

"You're handsome, but you're thin." She handed him the bowl and Xu Liang paid her. "You eat more, okay?"

He smiled. "Thank you, madam. You are a woman of ineffable wisdom." She nodded pleasantly and Xu Liang added, "Might I trouble you for seven more?"

Her smile faded briefly. She watched him hand the first bowl back to one of his men and her confusion ended. The enormous grin returned and she bowed informally. "Seven more. Yes."

The food was delivered. Xu Liang paid the woman and thanked her, then waited while his men stood in the general vicinity of the stand and ate their afternoon meal. It was much more convenient to buy food in a place such as Ti Lao than to trouble with the rations, and it would also save the rations for when they might truly need them. There was no telling precisely where this journey would set them and under what conditions. Xu Liang knew there were mountains to cross after crossing the ocean. They were cold mountains. Life was sparse and they would not be able to rely on hunting.

"The woman is right," came the voice of his eldest guard.

Xu Liang looked at the older man attentively. "About what, Gai Ping?"

The man swallowed a mouthful of rice. "You should eat more."

"I'll note your concern," Xu Liang answered, smiling faintly. He knew that Gai Ping was not making a comment about his slender frame, which appeared thinner due to his height—a trait he owed to his Xiang heritage. Rather, he understood that the man was making verbal note of the fact that he had not seen his master eat since they'd left the Imperial City. Xu Liang had neglected to inform his guards that he would be fasting throughout their journey. Strange as it seemed, not eating would be necessary to maintain his strength on this journey—not physically but spiritually. He would tax his magic to its limits in this effort and it would require much meditation and a level of inner pureness that one could not achieve through any form of indulgence. Even if that were not so, he wouldn't feel right eating while she could not. So long as his empress suffered, so would he.

Fortunately, there were ways to preserve the body under such conditions, strong meditation being the most effective of them. He was lucky to have found the time for it for the duration of their journey aboard the *Swimming Dragon* and he hoped to be able to do the same while crossing the Sea of Tahn.

When the men were finished eating, the bowls were deposited in a basket beside the old woman's stand. Xu Liang led them back toward the ships, determined to have one chartered and underway before sunset. The disturbance along the docks didn't make the task any easier.

Xu Liang stopped when he heard the shouting. Whatever went on, it was enough to have attracted the local law enforcement. The guardsmen were not having an easy time regaining control of the situation. That was made all the more obvious with the abrupt tossing of a guard into the observing crowd of civilians. When a second one came sailing toward Xu Liang, Xu Liang lifted his hand and discreetly enforced just enough of an invisible barrier to stop the body short of colliding with him and his men. The guardsman sat for a moment, stunned and possibly wondering what he'd hit, but he was too eager to return to the fight to debate the matter.

"We will go around them," Xu Liang decided, changing his mind when he heard a very familiar laugh.

♦ ♦ ♦ ♦ ♦

FU RAN HEFTED his huge two-handed sword again and swung wide. More guards flew, most of them landing harmlessly in the open space provided by the cautiously distant crowd. The blade wasn't actually hitting any of them, else they'd all be dead by now.

An enchantment he'd grown pleasantly accustomed to provided his weapon with a bit of extra reach, an unseen force that broke the air like the wake of a ship on the water and very efficiently spread an unwelcome crowd.

It was amusing when persistent men like Ti Lao's guards kept coming back. It made Fu Ran laugh out loud, and probably had a lot to do with the stubbornness of his opponents. However, he was having too much fun to care about their persistence or their pride.

"To the infernal regions with all of you!" he shouted. "You're a pathetic lot! Do you think I'd allow myself to be defeated by such as you! Are there no men among you?"

The guards were finally getting weary. It probably wouldn't be long before someone decided to draw a bow.

A giant among men, Fu Ran made for an easy target. He'd grown naturally taller and stronger than most and trained to be stronger still. His sleeveless jerkin boasted the thickness of his arms. The size of his body—along with the size of his sword—his wild grin, and bold laughter put fear into enemy and ally alike. He'd shaven his head and tattooed dragons down the length of each arm to worsen his appearance. In some places he was known as the Laughing Devil. He would hate to have his reputation besmirched by a well-aimed arrow and so decided to put an end to the afternoon's play. "I'll take one more before taking my leave! Who dares?"

He expected a handful of guards again, in which case he would toss them a bit farther this time and be on his way. He was shocked when someone said softly, "I will dare it … if you will."

Fu Ran was prepared to laugh at the effete creature standing before him, until he took a second look, and recalled that only fools judged Xu Liang by his appearance. He smiled anyway and readied his sword. "This is going to hurt," he warned.

Xu Liang inclined his head almost imperceptibly. "One of us, perhaps."

Fu Ran laughed, and charged. Xu Liang stood idle, his hands pressed lightly together, as if prayer would save him. It might have, but Fu Ran carried no ordinary sword. The mystic closed his eyes and waited for the strike. Fu Ran lifted his weapon high and delivered it, somehow not surprised when Xu Liang quickly parted his hands and clapped them together again, trapping the blade between them. Fu Ran leaned all of his weight into his attack, but to no avail. Neither the sword nor the sorcerer holding it at bay would budge.

"You've gotten better," Fu Ran said through his teeth. "I might actually work up a sweat!"

"It is not my wish to fight you, Fu Ran," Xu Liang answered quietly. "I require but a moment of your time."

Fu Ran was still pushing. "About another second is all you're going to get!"

"Then I shall be quick. Do you still sail aboard the *Cloud Runner*?"

The question took Fu Ran off guard. "What?"

Xu Liang spread his hands apart so that they still touched at the heels. Fu Ran and his sword were pushed backward by an invisible force—the wind itself, as guided by a mystic of Sheng Fan ... an aeromancer, specifically. Several steps came between Fu Ran and Xu Liang, but Fu Ran managed to keep his balance and his weapon, though it pulled awkwardly at his arm as the spell and the blade's own immense weight tried to carry it still further back.

He got the weapon under his control once again and frowned this time after he laughed. The sound was more reflexive now, but still inspiring fear in most of his audience, he was certain. "Are you telling me that you can't find a ship?"

"Are you saying that you have one?" the delicate man asked calmly.

Fu Ran answered with his blade, this time swinging wide rather than cutting down.

Xu Liang held his right hand out and drove the blade into the wood underfoot.

Fu Ran followed through with the swing anyway and spun out of it, facing his imperturbable opponent with a wicked grin on his face while a trail of plank shavings settled onto the scored walkway. "Sorcerous tricks! Would you dare to face me without your magic?"

Xu Liang stared a moment, revealing nothing with his tranquil expression. Then he took a disappointing step back.

So the years had changed him. The student-official Fu Ran had known never backed away from a challenge, even if it seemed too great for one of his fragile nature to overcome. He may not have charged at anything headlong, but he never fled. Imperial office must have finally been getting to him. He didn't look any older, but maybe he was beginning to feel the weight of his position at last. Youth couldn't be easy to hold onto, surrounded by scrolls and otherwise pinned beneath the heel of an over privileged, overbearing ruler. One had to flex his sword arm in order to keep it strong and Fu Ran doubted that Sheng Fan's Imperial Tactician did much of that these days.

Fu Ran sighed and almost turned to leave. Almost, except that Xu Liang never took his eyes off of him and when he reached his hand back to one of his evident bodyguards, a sword was placed in it.

The mystic held the weapon as if it were as light as a paper fan. He said, "Would you dare to face me without *your* magic?"

Fu Ran's grin returned. He untied the red tassel from his sword's hilt and tucked it into his belt. "Scholars taking up arms in public brawls? What is the Empire coming to, I wonder?"

"Yes. I'm sure you do," Xu Liang sighed.

Fu Ran took his sword in both hands and stalked his prey. "Maybe there is some of Xu Hong in you after all."

"Xu Hong would have killed you already. I am still hoping to negotiate."

Fu Ran chuckled and stepped into his attack, stopping short when someone cried out nearby. He looked as the Ti Lao guard fell on his face with a bolt from a crossbow sunk into his back. "Damn..." Fu Ran looked to Xu Liang to call off their match and saw that the man was already surrounded by his bodyguards. Instinct took over. "What are you idiots planning to do, stand around and get shot? Xu Liang! Come with me!"

The mystic didn't look at him as he scanned the nearby rooftops. Fu Ran moved quickly behind the bodyguards while the civilian crowd scattered and the Ti Lao guards delayed any action, appearing too confused to do anything but gawk at their fallen man.

"Who would attack the Ti Lao guard?" Xu Liang pondered. He added softly, but with no humor, "Other than you?"

"That's for the magistrate to find out," Fu Ran decided, grabbing the mystic by the shoulder of his robe. "This way!"

The mystic's intelligent brown eyes moved from one starkly angled roof to the next, and then narrowed. He suddenly pressed his hands together and began softly chanting.

"There's no time!" Fu Ran wheeled the smaller man around, lowered somewhat, then bent him over his shoulder.

One of Xu Liang's bodyguards protested at once. "Take your hands off my lord!"

Fu Ran elbowed the man in the face. "Get out of my way!"

The young guard fumbled back and Fu Ran dashed past him. Xu Liang was still chanting as he was hauled down the dock like a sack of grain. Fu Ran noted silently that even the smallest sack of grain might have weighed more than the Imperial official.

Footsteps indicated that Xu Liang's bodyguards were following. Fu Ran began to wonder himself who would fire on the Ti Lao guard. Maybe Ti Lao was under siege. That seemed unlikely, considering the direction of the attack. Barring a peasant uprising, an assault should have come from the river, or the fields farther out, not from within the city itself. At any rate, it was foolish to stand around and make a target out of oneself. If they wanted the Ti Lao guards, let them have them, Fu Ran thought.

A sudden wind came in from the across the water. Banners that had been relatively still in the previous breeze began to billow actively. Fu Ran had no sooner taken notice of the abrupt change in weather when a white horse strode into his path, carrying a man who was neither guard nor peasant. A handful of armed men jogged up to join the rider.

"Where do you think you're going with that parcel?" the rider asked. His dyed yellow hair was tightly raveled behind him, looking like a long golden tail against his fanciful red silks. Several small charms hung off his tasseled belt, which almost made Fu Ran swallow his automatic laughter.

As it was part of his fierce image, he grinned anyway, holding his sword out in defiance.

The newcomer smiled back. It was an expression that chilled Fu Ran to his bones. "We'll play ... if you insist."

The man started making telltale hand gestures and Fu Ran recalled that his enchanted tassel was currently tucked into his sash. "Damn! Is there nowhere in Sheng Fan a man can go without running into sorcerers?"

"You may put me down now," Xu Liang suddenly said, and Fu Ran didn't hesitate, reaching quickly for his only thread of magic and pressing it against the hilt of his sword as he took up the weapon in both hands. He lifted the sword just as the stranger was finishing his spell and hurling it in the form of a tumbling cloud of flame toward him. The enchantment allowed Fu Ran to deflect the assault and bat it harmlessly into the river.

The sorcerer seemed surprised.

Fu Ran laughed loudly. "Ha! Not as easy a game as you thought!"

The other's dark eyes narrowed indignantly. "We'll see." He pointed dramatically at Fu Ran and the entourage he'd gained in abducting Xu Liang. "Kill all of them! At once!"

The armed strangers came. Xu Liang's bodyguards began to respond.

"Stay back!" Fu Ran warned. Then he took a single step forward and swept his blade out in front of him. The sorcerer's handful of men flew, one of them colliding into the sorcerer before he could do anything to defend himself.

Fu Ran drew back, grinning triumphantly as the man gave a muffled cry and fell off his horse.

"Impressive," Xu Liang said, and Fu Ran couldn't tell if he was being sarcastic. The mystic added, "About my inquiry concerning your ship..."

"All of you follow me," Fu Ran said quickly. He led them onto the nearest pier, toward a ship much taller and broader than the dragon boats Ti Lao Bay was used to having lined along its docks. If he didn't know better, he would have guessed that Xu Liang had planned this wild departure. How better to avoid assassination than to draw attention, and a hell of a lot of it? However, he knew that the mystic was adamantly opposed to recklessness.

Fu Ran stopped halfway down the pier, ushering Xu Liang's men past him, realizing belatedly that four of them were leading horses. In the crowd he hadn't even noticed just how many guards the mystic had, let alone the horses. If that wasn't enough, Xu Liang was walking, unconcerned, his hands tucked into the sleeves of his robes. The wind swept his hair behind him, where it seemed to float like a thousand glistening strands cast by caterpillars that spun black silk.

"Hurry!" Fu Ran urged, noticing that the blond sorcerer's men were drawing bows.

"Do not worry," Xu Liang said. "The wind will not let the arrows carry this far."

Fu Ran watched the bowmen try anyway, tensing as he fought the urge to run to Xu Liang and shield him from the deadly rain. The arrows faltered and veered everywhere but at their aim. Fu Ran grinned broadly and railed at them. Their leader was back on his horse and, after a moment of glaring in the face of Fu Ran's deliberate insolence, decided to retreat.

"Cowards!" Fu Ran shouted, and he continued to jeer at them until Xu Liang stopped him.

"That will do," the mystic said, lightly touching Fu Ran's arm.

Fu Ran eventually calmed down, then harnessed his sword at his back, and looked at Xu Liang. He studied the official of the Empire in his layers of fancy silk with his ankle-length hair drawn back from his smooth face with two small beaded combs, his girlish mouth vaguely frowning. He didn't know whether to kneel before him, embrace him, or strike him to the pier. Deciding that the last two options would probably kill the mystic if he wasn't prepared for such assault, Fu Ran performed a variation of the first. He put his fist into his hand and bowed slightly. The simple gesture stirred more memories and emotions than he was prepared for, and he meant it when he said, "My lord, I'm pleased to see you in good health."

The frown slowly lifted from Xu Liang's expression. He smoothed the rumpled silk at his shoulder and said, "Old habits do indeed die with difficulty."

Fu Ran smiled irresistibly. As usual, Xu Liang was right. Even though it had been several years since he'd acted as the slightly younger man's bodyguard he'd never quite shaken his sense of loyalty toward him, and seeing him in danger had renewed his old duty full force. Abandoning Sheng Fan and becoming a landless sailor hadn't changed him as much as he would have thought that morning.

He shook his head and changed the subject. Gesturing to the large ship, he said, "If you're wanting to leave Sheng Fan, you'll find no ship better suited for it than the *Pride of Celestia*."

◆ ◆ ◆ ◆ ◆

XU LIANG LOOKED to the vessel waiting at the end of the pier. His men were already gathered at the edge of the gangway with the horses, waiting for instructions. "It's much larger than the *Cloud Runner*, and not built in Sheng Fan. Are you still seeking your place in the world, Fu Ran?"

The large man ignored the second question, but in answer to the first comment said, "It's an Aeran vessel, captained by an Aeran woman, who has an incurable fascination with everything that has anything to do with Sheng Fan. I'm sure I don't even have to ask if you and your men can board."

"Then there should be no trouble arranging a contract," Xu Liang said thoughtfully, and he started to walk toward the ship. "Perhaps now my journey can truly begin."

It had been purely luck to find Fu Ran at Ti Lao. Xu Liang never would have expected to meet him there. The captain of the *Cloud*

Runner had been even more disenchanted with the Empire than Fu Ran. The man rarely returned to Sheng Fan's ports for any reason, least of all to be badgered into taking aboard servants of the Empire by one who couldn't seem to forget that he no longer served it. Perhaps that was why Fu Ran had come aboard a new ship, both to shake his former captain's lectures about what anchored him to Sheng Fan and to make a better attempt to pull up that anchor himself. Whatever the reason, it turned out to be fortuitous for Xu Liang, and the Empress.

"Does she speak Fanese?" Xu Liang asked his former guard as the large man led him aboard and ultimately below deck.

Fu Ran laughed. "Don't you speak Aeran?"

"It has been some time since I've had to utilize that language. My studies recently have revolved mostly around certain far-western tongues. I would hate to carry on an awkward conversation."

"I can't imagine you doing anything awkwardly, Xu Liang, least of all speaking."

Xu Liang smiled only a little. "I rode on your shoulder like a sack of rice but moments ago."

"And still managed to cast a spell," Fu Ran noted. "That's something to be proud of."

Xu Liang didn't agree, but he opted not to argue. He thought back on the incident and the sorcerer who was evidently looking to halt his passing, just as the rogue at Li Ting had been. "I apologize, Fu Ran, for any trouble this may cause you."

The former guard waved the notion away with one large hand. "I cause myself trouble."

"That may be true, but the Ti Lao guard can be reasoned with and would likely not be inclined to attack your ship unannounced."

Fu Ran looked at him seriously. "Do you think those assassins will try something like that?"

Xu Liang shook his head. "I do not know them, so I cannot say for certain. But I will inform you that there was an incident further up the Tunghui as well. It was someone else, but I suspect both parties are working for the same individual."

Fu Ran sighed, "I guess it's just not safe for your kind outside of your imperial cage."

"It is not safe there either," Xu Liang reflected.

Fu Ran glanced at him, silently curious, and Xu Liang expounded.

"The Five Kingdoms Resolution is gradually becoming a rebellion," he said. "Xun is being more difficult than ever, and I fear that

Tzu's silence as it sits all but unnoticed in the southwest may be indicative of its intent to follow suit. I left the kingdom of Ji just as Xun attacked it on its southern border, at Fa Leng. I fear that Governor Ha Ming Jin will not rest until he has sated his ambitions."

"I remember him," Fu Ran said. "His ambitions were the primary cause of Ha Sheng's death, weren't they?"

"That is only hearsay," Xu Liang replied impartially. "It was unfortunate, however, to lose Ha Sheng. He was a rational man, even if discontent."

Fu Ran shrugged, as if unconcerned. "Shouldn't you be with the Emperor in his hour of need, then?"

Xu Liang fell briefly quiet. He disguised his pain with a neutral tone. "I wasn't. And now Emperor Song Bao is no longer with us. I hope that I will not repeat my past error."

"Song Lu can take care of himself," Fu Ran said, shrugging again.

A twinge of anger followed by a sting of pain made Xu Liang's words and tone abrupt. "Perhaps you would like to visit his tomb, Fu Ran, and ask him why he did not."

Fu Ran stopped in the narrow wooden corridor and for several moments didn't move or speak. When he finally pressed his hands together and bowed his head, Xu Liang understood and he deeply appreciated Fu Ran's respect, even though it was belated. He wished that same respect existed for the Empress, but he knew better than to expect so much.

"Fu Ran," someone said, and they both looked to a slim, but strongly built woman with pale orange hair and intensely green eyes walking toward them. She was dressed in the hodgepodge of leathers that was often worn by 'barbarians' and carried a sword at her hip. When she saw Xu Liang, she studied him with unexpected but understandable concern. In a diplomatic attempt to include him in the following discussion she began speaking Fanese to her crewman. "What did you bring me?"

"An officer of Sheng Fan's Imperial Court," Fu Ran answered. "His name is Xu Liang."

Xu Liang bowed in respectful greeting.

The Aeran woman had yet to take her eyes off him and did not look away when she said to Fu Ran, "I'm assuming that if he wanted taxes or something of that nature from us you wouldn't have let him onboard?"

"He's not that kind of officer, Yvain. He's a scholar."

Again, Xu Liang inclined his head. "What I seek aboard your vessel, madam, is passage from Sheng Fan."

The woman still seemed skeptical. "To where?"

"I must cross the Sea of Tahn," Xu Liang replied. "If you are not prepared to sail that far at this time, then I would be grateful for passage to another port where I might negotiate for the longer journey with someone willing."

The woman stared at him for a moment longer, indicating nothing with her firm expression. Finally, she said, "Your god of luck is with you, Xu Liang. It just so happens that the *Pride of Celestia* sets sail for Callipry in only a few hours. Just as soon as we finish purchasing supplies, in fact."

She came forward and finally smiled, then bowed as was customary in Sheng Fan. "You're welcome to ride along for a modest fee and moderate tolerance for the many questions I'm liable to have for you once I'm not quite so busy. It isn't often that we have someone onboard who can read." After saying that, she smiled slyly at Fu Ran and departed.

The large man's face reddened like a ripening plum and Xu Liang smiled quietly.

♦ ♦ ♦ ♦ ♦

"XU LIANG MUST not be permitted to leave Sheng Fan!"

Ma Shou sighed languidly, slouching forward on the back of his horse. A part of him wished to be done with the entire affair of pursuing the Imperial Tactician. The rest of him remembered what he had to gain in carrying on with it.

"He's with the barbarians now," he said to his companion—a man of great strength and perhaps greater foolishness. "A ship full of them. Perhaps you would like to go retrieve him, Xiadao Lu."

The larger man glared at Ma Shou without actually turning his face while they observed Ti Lao's waterfront from a hill overlooking the city. "Perhaps you'd like to explain your failure to retrieve him yourself to our lord."

"And your failure as well," Ma Shou reminded coolly. "It would be an unpleasant scene, wouldn't it?"

Xiadao Lu's fists tightened audibly around the reins of his mount. "You are a fool to underestimate me, Xu Liang!" he growled. "Before this is over, you will wish you had finished me at Li Ting!"

THREE
Messengers of Fate

THE IMPERIAL CITY was a myriad of complex open spaces. The flagstone aisles were wide, marked with low walls or structures built at dramatic yet concise angles. Many of the roofs were red and adorned with figurines of the legendary beasts of Sheng Fan. Marble and bronze statues guarded gateways and the low, wide staircases adjoining levels of the enormous sacred grounds. Activity was constant, but orderly and pleasurable to watch as life moved tranquilly beneath slender trees and graceful eaves.

It was absurd to Jiao Ren that he could look at such a scene and feel anger. He would have turned away and taken in a view of the green mountains in the distance, but he would have felt worse daring to turn his back on the city that was the glory of Sheng Fan and the sanctum as well as the throne of the Empress. So he stood upon the outer west wall with the moat and the Gate of Heavenly Protection behind him, returning the glare of a fierce dog statue below, in front of the Temple of Divine Tranquility.

He felt like there was nothing he could do here and nothing that could be done with Xu Liang gone. It was not right to think that. This was not a battle the Imperial Tactician needed to be present for, but it was one he had planned for just the same. And it was Jiao Ren's duty to remain at what would all too soon be the forefront of a struggle fiercer than any Sheng Fan had known before.

"Such a bold look of anger," someone observed. "You are troubled, young general?"

Jiao Ren glanced at the slender man suddenly beside him, dressed, as he was, in the fanciful blue and gold silk of an officer under the banner of the Imperial City and the Blue Dragon of Ji. The newcomer was older than Jiao Ren, old enough for his hair to have turned white. His face was narrow, somewhat hollow at the cheeks and looking even more pointed with his thin, sharp beard. The brocade robes of his station as a scholar-mystic, woven with images of bats and symbols of good fortune around the large coiled dragon at his back, were no more elaborate than Jiao Ren's attire, but more flowing, as tended to be the preference among scholars. Jiao Ren, an officer of the Imperial Army, wore a long tunic cut to expose his pants and boots and to allow for more freedom of movement. There were dragons at his shoulders and one also winding down the front panel of his gold-trimmed tunic. He wore soft leather boots as well as a green sash at the waist and a blue silk headband to keep his past-the-shoulder hair out of his face. Though he was still considered quite young at just twenty years, he was glad to have some maturity about him, to not be known for brash behavior.

"I am not troubled, Lord Han Quan," he finally said to the elder. "I am mired in foolish doubts."

"To doubt is to question, and to question is not foolish."

In a respectful tone, Jiao Ren said, "It is if Lord Xu Liang's tactics are the matter of debate." He felt his fists closing involuntarily as the frustration mounted. *This waiting!* He liked to consider himself a temperate and patient man—one who was hasty and easily agitated could never last long on any battlefield—but he usually knew what he was waiting for. The Imperial Tactician's instructions had been explicit, but his plans unclear.

"Xu Liang is an educated and intelligent man," Han Quan admitted. He pulled his hands out of the draping sleeves of his robe and added sternly, "However, he is young for his station, like the Empress. It presents an uncomfortable imbalance to have two such fledgling individuals at the summit of the vast mountain Sheng Fan is to the rest of the world."

Jiao Ren looked at the mystic again and his dark eyes lingered this time. At length, he returned his gaze to the inner wards of the Imperial City and said evenly, "Xu Liang is no fledgling, Lord Han. He has served the Empire for almost two decades now. I was a mere child when our late Emperor Song Bao saw promise in the mighty Lord Xu Hong's second son."

Han Quan's narrow eyes glimpsed Jiao Ren in his peripheral vision. He said calmly, "And in comparison to a man of my years you are a mere child still. The Empress is but an infant. And the Imperial Tactician, who has also assumed the role of Imperial Tutor, in spite of his frequent absence from the court, is a very young and very restless man. How can he know what is best for Sheng Fan when he cannot even decide what is best for himself?"

Jiao Ren frowned involuntarily. "Master Han Quan, his thorough study of the land and its history helps him to perceive its future. He does nothing against the Empress' wishes."

"General Jiao Ren, you misinterpret me. I am not criticizing, but stating fact. And the fact remains that there is a terrible conflict facing the Empress and the people, and the land of Sheng Fan. In his haste to research the matter, Lord Xu Liang has hidden our empress from us. It is as snatching the sun from the sky. The people see only the looming shadow of a storm and they grow concerned, some fearful."

"A storm is nothing to fear."

"Not to one who watches it from the safety of higher ground."

Jiao Ren turned to look at Han Quan once more, but the ancient mystic was already departing. He decided not to holler after him, but turned back to the wall and placed his hands upon the railing. He stared out over the Imperial City and its residents out of doors, and wondered if they were fearful. They did not look it, nor did they act it, but perhaps…

At that moment he felt a tremor in his hands. It was nothing violent and nothing that came from him. He felt it beneath his hands, in the stone itself as the minor quake reverberated up from the earth. He severed contact with the wall and looked closely at the Imperial City's residents still moving about below him. No one reacted to the tremor and in the still air not even a leaf trembled. He looked to the guards stationed on the walls, all of them seeming not to notice. It must have been very weak and therefore—he lightly touched the wall again and felt no vibration—nothing to be concerned with.

◆ ◆ ◆ ◆ ◆

SONG DA-XIAO opened her eyes, not alertly but almost as a reflex to the tremors in the air. Since their beginning, they had been growing steadily more insistent, like an assault ram hammering against stubborn gates. Stubborn and sturdy as they may have been, even the gates of the Imperial City would weaken without reinforcement.

The Empress' eyes, gleaming golden with magic, fell shut, as if she'd fallen back asleep after being stirred by a sudden noise in the night without actually having regained consciousness. Her prayers continued uninterrupted. And then, for no apparent reason, her spirit and prayers strengthened.

◆ ◆ ◆ ◆ ◆

WE HAVE SET out to sea, my empress. We are unharmed. Remain strong and remember that you are the life essence of Sheng Fan.

Xu Liang withdrew from his meditation with a pang of dread in his heart. Though he hid his concern from the Empress, he could tell, through her, that time was moving rapidly against them. A heavy thump drew his attention to the door of the narrow cabin Captain Yvain had been gracious enough to lend him for the journey across the Sea of Tahn. The first noise was followed by a second. Feet scuffled and voices rose.

"Get out of my way! Worthless peons!"

"You will not interrupt our lord!"

"I told you to get out of my way!"

Xu Liang sighed, then calmly stood and made his way to the door. He reached for the latch, then thought better of the action and stepped aside.

The door burst open and Guang Ci stumbled backward into the room. He managed to stay on his feet, glaring at the one who'd pushed him. The young guard reached for his sword.

Xu Liang stopped him. "We are guests, remember."

"My lord!" Guang Ci stepped out of his fighting stance and dropped onto his knee. "My apologies. I did not realize—*mmmh!*"

One of his fellow guards staggered with momentum into the room and rolled over him.

Xu Liang sighed once again. "Fu Ran, you are a menace."

The former guard stepped into the cabin, shoving back the man who followed him. He grinned with satisfaction that was just beginning to nettle Xu Liang. "This is the best these drones can do? It's a wonder you haven't been killed."

With no humor in his tone, Xu Liang said, "It is a wonder, yes, with you so carelessly flinging them about. At any rate, that is their concern and not one that they will easily discard, as you can see."

Fu Ran glanced at the bodyguards surrounding him, who were waiting for the order to dispatch him. There was not a trace of fear in the brute, but his features darkened noticeably. "The captain wants to see you," he said to Xu Liang.

Xu Liang inclined his head in agreement to the invitation, instructed his men to stay behind, and went with Fu Ran. No words were exchanged between them as they passed through the narrow corridors. There was nothing to be said. Fu Ran had abandoned the Empire. Nothing would come of an argument between them, except the same conclusion that had been drawn fourteen years ago. In Fu Ran's mind, there was no place left for him in the Empire; no place he would accept, Xu Liang would argue. Until now they had managed to accept each other's positions whenever they infrequently met. It irritated Xu Liang that Fu Ran would dare to imply that those who had taken his place were incompetent, years after it had voluntarily ceased to be his concern. Of course, Fu Ran's pride had always been his greatest weakness. A weakness Guang Ci seemed to share. Fortunately—and ironically—that shared trait would not enable Guang Ci to follow Fu Ran's example, for now.

On the deck of the *Pride of Celestia*, Xu Liang was led abaft, where he found Captain Yvain standing at the railing, looking out at a sea blanketed with low-lying clouds. She glanced back at Xu Liang as he arrived and motioned him closer. Fu Ran stayed back.

"I apologize if I disrupted your meditation, Master Xu," the captain said. "But I've got a splinter in my mind and I think you just might be able to remove it."

Xu Liang decided not to mention the scuffle below decks between one of her men and all eight of his. He said cooperatively, "How may I help?"

With her eyes on the fog behind her ship, Yvain said, "Fu Ran tells me you're more than just an official of Sheng Fan's court. He mentioned to me that you're a sorcerer. Is that true?"

"I have studied magic for many years," Xu Liang admitted. "I have acquired an adequate understanding of it."

The Aeran woman smiled without looking at him. "Is there any way you can see through that fog?"

Xu Liang closed his eyes. "What should I be looking for?"

"These clouds settled in three days ago, just after a lookout spotted another ship in the area. No one's seen anything since. I thought we'd try looking at it from a fresh perspective, if you catch my meaning."

"Give me a moment," Xu Liang replied, and he began pulling in the unseen details of the air and the water around them. He opened his eyes more quickly than he expected, jostled from his scan by the passage of a very large presence. Not another ship in the fog, but a ...

"Dragon!" came a voice from above.

All eyes went skyward, except for Xu Liang's. Before the lookout in the crow's nest reiterated, he knew what the man would say. "Serpent! Beneath the ship!"

Yvain cursed in her own language and began barking commands at her crew, at once distracted from the mysterious patch of fog.

Xu Liang discerned enough words to understand that the Aerans had encountered a sea dragon before and knew how to defend the ship against their unpredictable nature. That surprised him. Dragons, as a race, were often reclusive creatures, phantoms of the ancient past that haunted more stories than populated areas. Xu Liang had never seen one before—of land or sea—outside of artistic interpretation. He found himself curious and fearful, fearful for the dragon, even as it slid beneath the *Pride of Celestia* and rocked it severely.

Fu Ran rested his hand on Xu Liang's shoulder as Xu Liang took hold of the railing. "It might be safer for you below decks. These beasts can make for some pretty rough seas when they pass ... and when they don't."

Xu Liang shook his head. "Thank you for your concern, but I might be of some assistance up here."

"Dragons are resilient against magic," Fu Ran informed urgently.

Xu Liang shelved the new information at the back of his mind, and then said, "Perhaps, Fu Ran, but ships generally are not." The big man looked confused until Xu Liang added, "Please inform your captain that I intend to conjure a southeastern wind. We will evade both the dragon and the ship in pursuit at the same time."

Fu Ran looked down into the water, then out to sea, and back at Xu Liang. He gave a crooked smile before jogging across the deck toward Yvain. He passed eight familiar men, who had clearly felt the assault on the ship and responded in the only way ingrained upon them. Without acknowledging his guards, Xu Liang positioned himself for prayer.

◆ ◆ ◆ ◆ ◆

FROM THE HIGH deck of the *Jade Carp,* Xiadao Lu glowered at the clouded sea ahead of them. Surprisingly, it was not as easy to track a man on water as it was on land. Nothing but open space with nowhere to hide ... and yet it had taken several days to finally catch sight of the barbarian ship that had swept Xu Liang away from Sheng Fan. The mystic's destination was a mystery, but Xiadao Lu had sworn to his lord that he would not reach it. His fist tightened unconsciously as his thoughts darkened.

I shall not fail.

A whiff of foulness suddenly assailed the warrior's nostrils. His expression lightened with amusement. He'd only come across the odor once before, along the Chang River near his boyhood home. He watched a magnificent beast rise from the water then, as mighty and splendorous to behold as the legends told. It was as looking upon a god and to this day, Xiadao Lu wondered what had inspired the creature to show itself. His grandmother had told him that it was the spirit of one of their ancestors speaking to him and, out of respect, Xiadao Lu immediately began wearing colors to match the beast's scales. He believed that the gesture brought the dragon's luck upon him and gave him an advantage over his enemies. He welcomed a second encounter with such a creature, and that reflected in his tone when he said, "I smell a dragon!"

In his voice that was either incessantly bored or incessantly mocking, Ma Shou said, "And all this time I've been crediting that stink to the 'captain' of this vessel. It's a pity that pirates are the only men willing to take to sea upon a moment's notice."

"Better pirates than barbarians," Xiadao Lu answered. Then he glanced over his shoulder at the sorcerer sitting cross-legged on the deck floor. "Tell me what you see through this mist of yours."

"The barbarian ship remains on a western course. They don't seem suspicious. Of course, that's too good to be true."

Xiadao Lu agreed. "Xu Liang knows. He can be fooled, but he is no fool. We were able to surprise him at the Tunghui River and at

Ti Lao, but as you have seen, he does not live on his guard because he does not have to. Luck is with him."

"A greater luck than your dragon ancestor?" Ma Shou wondered aloud, and if Xiadao Lu had known for certain that he was mocking, he'd have struck the sorcerer down in the very instant. Forgiving the man his strangeness and recalling that he was also useful, Xiadao Lu let him be.

"He has charm perhaps," Ma Shou added. "And a great deal of it, but charm and luck do not always go hand-in-hand. Take away the charm of the Empress and the charm of Sheng Fan and you are left with what the barbarians will see."

"What do you mean?" Xiadao Lu wanted to know. He disliked the sorcerer's cryptic manner of speech.

Ma Shou sighed. "A man without his fame, in the eyes of an ignorant stranger, is nothing more than a man. Among strangers, one must earn his allies."

"Or buy them," someone added.

Xiadao Lu watched the captain of the *Jade Carp* make his way up the wide stairs of the high deck. He was a wiry man but solid. Xiadao Lu did not doubt that he knew how to use the sword slung at his belt.

A crooked smile captured the pirate's lips. "Don't worry. Your money wasn't wasted. Let us catch the ship you're following and I'll prove it to you."

Xiadao Lu laughed welcomingly at the man's enthusiasm and confidence. "I've heard the rumors about you, Zhen Yu."

"The rumors don't do me justice."

"You'll get your chance," Xiadao Lu assured. His features gradually firmed and he added, "When you do just remember one thing. I will destroy Xu Liang myself."

Zhen Yu nodded, but his lopsided smile remained. Xiadao Lu didn't trust the captain, but for now he had his purpose, just as the sorcerer did.

"The wind has shifted," Ma Shou informed suddenly.

Zhen Yu lifted his face to the sky. "Yes. Now it's southeastern." He frowned. "It feels southeastern, but we're still moving due west, at the same pace."

"So is our fog," Ma Shou added.

Xiadao Lu glowered. "Xu Liang!" He turned toward his own sorcerer. "Ma Shou, can you compensate?"

The other closed his eyes and placed his hands together. "Of course," he mumbled. "But I will need time to meditate. Wind is not my area of expertise and conjuring this fog has required much of my attention. We will lose them for a brief span."

"Unnatural fog, phantom winds that defy the true wind…" Zhen Yu shook his head. "I'll advise you mystics to be cautious. Nature doesn't like to be toyed with."

"Neither do I," Xiadao Lu snapped. "We will catch that ship and we will kill everyone onboard!" He nodded to Ma Shou. "I leave it to you, sorcerer"

Ma Shou fell utterly still.

Zhen Yu watched him for a moment, then said, "And what about the dragon? There are more of them out at sea than on land. More that are seen by men, at least. They can be dangerous."

Xiadao Lu turned to face the sea with confidence. "Dragons are messengers," he decided. "Be it good or ill, this one will deliver us our fate this day."

◆ ◆ ◆ ◆ ◆

FU RAN TOOK up a long spear as it was issued to him. He felt the ship moving as the steersman directed the *Pride of Celestia* into Xu Liang's wind. They were moving much quicker than before, but not nearly quick enough to outrun a dragon if it meant to catch them. Fu Ran glanced toward his former lord and saw the eight armored men surrounding him.

Idiots! You can't defend him from a dragon or the waves it'll stir! We have the wind. You should be hauling him below decks.

They didn't and, of course, they wouldn't. They were too accustomed to 'duty', too inured in their station beneath their master. They didn't dare to touch him. It never occurred to them that they could be protecting a friend and sometimes friends had to be handled roughly in order to be kept safe. But that was the trouble with life in Sheng Fan; 'a place for everyone, and everyone in their place'. Those who existed outside of the system designated long ago by the very first emperor Sheng Fan had ever known were considered rogues, bandits, pirates, and worst of all, barbarians. Barbarians worst of all because they could never fit into the system, even if they wanted to. They were uncivilized, sharing the scruples of wild beasts, cruel and without virtue. Fu Ran was a son of Sheng Fan. He could go back if he wanted to and restore his 'honor'. He wouldn't, not even for a friend.

The ship swayed. A finned spine crested above the water, above the railing of the ship, momentarily shadowing the deck before the beast descended again and sent a minor wave crashing down on it. The brine-smelling water rushed beneath Fu Ran's feet and tried to pull them out from under him. He maintained his balance and, with a glance, saw that the wave didn't quite reach the stern, where Xu Liang remained in his meditative stance. Perhaps the wind would die too quickly if he stopped. Still, Fu Ran couldn't help worrying that he would look back after the next wave and find that the mystic had been swept away.

◆ ◆ ◆ ◆ ◆

"NOT YET!" YVAIN hollered to her crew from the helm. The beast rose again as it undulated through the sea, showing more of its lustrous scales this time, gleaming green and gold in the sunlight directly overhead. The strange fog was slowly falling behind them, along with whomever it concealed. The dragon stayed with them, more playfully than persistently. Dragons seemed more curious than malicious. However, their curiosity—because of their size— often proved deadly to sailors. Time would tell the outcome of this encounter.

Yvain's gaze flitted toward the sorcerer aboard her ship, who'd maintained the presence of a specter throughout the journey thus far. Everyone knew he was there, but the days had gone by without so much as a glimpse of him as he holed himself in the tiny guest cabin and proceeded to pray.

As Yvain understood it, the Fanese people held their gods and ancestors in the same respect, believing that many of the gods began life as ordinary humans who, through leading extraordinary lives, were later deified. It was not that way in Aer. To the Aerans, heaven was known as Celestia and the 'People of the Stars' governed the lives beneath them. Sometimes they elected to show themselves through the eyes of mortals—one such as Yvain, whose eyes were considered several shades too brilliant to be anything but Celestian. It granted her no special talents, nor any powers—so far as she could tell—but many attributed her strong leadership skills to the star who'd given her its grace. She was the second child of her bloodline to have such eyes, a bloodline that was not purely Aeran, but crossed through an unprecedented marriage between her Aeran great-grandmother and a Neidran man.

In Neidra—the sweltering green land to the southwest of Sheng Fan—people believed in multiple gods and also worshipped their ancestors, the greatest of whom supposedly went to live among those deities after death. Yvain respected all religions and thus believed that whomever or whatever Xu Liang prayed to was listening and answering. His 'wind god', if such were the case, may turn out to be the salvation of her crew this day, and of the dragon, who she did not wish to harm.

The beast rose and flashed its glistening scales again. The sheen was so bright as the sunlight played off the dragon's iridescent hide that Yvain had to close her eyes. At that precise moment she experienced a vision so sudden and so vivid that it was as if she hadn't shielded her eyes at all from the blinding splendor of the dragon. She saw the sun rise over a cold, barren landscape. The trees were as skeletal fingers, grasping for the unreachable warmth. The land they were rooted in was as broken, unhealed skin, shrouded in an ill mist. A human figure stood alone, a silhouette against the red-orange brilliance of the ascending sun. Man or woman, child or elder, Yvain could not tell, but the sight of the individual made her instantly sad. There were tears in her eyes when she opened them again.

The dragon was gone.

The crew relaxed slowly, hesitant to release the collective breath everyone had been holding until they were certain the beast had returned to the depths of the ocean.

Fu Ran joined Yvain at the helm. The Fanese giant laughed, but he couldn't conceal his relief. "Maybe we should consider keeping a sorcerer onboard for moments like that."

Yvain's moist eyes traveled past Fu Ran and stopped once again at Xu Liang. He was still in prayer, oblivious to the dragon's departure. "I want to talk to him when he's finished. Send him to my cabin."

Fu Ran's smile left him and he nodded once. Yvain realized then that her tone might have been unduly abrupt, but she did not make amends. She left the helm, determined not to let anyone see Yvain of the *Pride of Celestia* in tears.

FOUR
The Moon Blade

T HE DAY HAD nearly gone when Xu Liang felt a safe distance had been put between the Aeran vessel and the Fanese ship in pursuit. The dragon had been no real threat and left of its own volition. Or so it would seem.

A conference with Yvain revealed that the dragon may have had a purpose in its appearance after all. Xu Liang was not about to question the captain's claim, not openly or privately. He saw no reason for her to lie. She seemed quite sane and, though it wasn't readily apparent to look at her, he understood by talking to Yvain that she was a deeply spiritual woman. Her experience had been real, whether or not anyone else could feel or understand it. Xu Liang did feel the vision somewhat himself as she related it to him, sparing no detail, not even the tears that rimmed her spectacularly green eyes. It was in evidence that she'd intended to overlook that part of her story when she began hastily wiping at the moisture that was renewed with the telling.

Xu Liang stood in the middle of her large cabin, observing her respectfully as she sat at a modest table beneath the room's only window. He had listened and thus far not spoken.

When it became clear that Yvain had nothing more to say, he selected his words carefully. "Dragons are ancient creatures," he said. "Not only as a race, but as individuals as well. They are among the oldest sentient beings known to the world and they are very wise. Their wisdom inspires us and sometimes enables us to see what we would otherwise have spent our entire lives blind to."

Yvain issued a weakly cynical smile. "That's very touching, and very diplomatic." Her gaze wandered out the window. "However…"

"However?" Xu Liang prompted.

She glanced at him, then said to the sea, "I don't think it was the dragon. I think it's hereditary."

In that moment, Xu Liang felt like an eavesdropper on words that may have been somehow intended to be private. He did not allow that to delay his response for long. "How so?"

"My great-grandfather used to have visions," Yvain replied after a pause. "Anything could trigger them. A word, a touch, a flower kissed by a summer breeze … anything. He kept record of them in his poetry. I've been told that I have his eyes."

"And you are only now learning that you have his 'sight'," Xu Liang presumed.

Yvain looked at him and slowly nodded. "I've never dreamed so vividly while I was awake as I did when I saw that dragon."

Xu Liang decided not to mention his own visions, as they were a practiced craft, certainly not an inherited clairvoyance. In a meditative state he could extend his senses beyond his physical self. He could detect things that way, but he could not foresee events.

"I wanted to tell you," Yvain added, "because I don't think the vision pertained to me beyond my experiencing it. My ship is going to dock in Nelayne, a port city which doesn't look anything like the terrain I saw in the vision. We'll spend a few days there at most, conducting our business. And then we'll head back out to sea. Unless you plan to tour the northern trade routes, you'll be traveling the land. There are regions like what I saw along the edges of Callipry, toward Lower Yvaria and into Andaria. I don't know what any of what I saw means, but maybe you will, if you see it."

Xu Liang understood, and inclined his head respectfully. "I thank you."

Yvain waved the words away. "Don't. I've yet to deliver you safely to your destination. Sharing eerie visions isn't part of the contract, Master Xu Liang." He smiled and she stood. "However, answering a few questions for me was part of our original bargain, if I recall correctly."

Xu Liang nodded. "You do, yes."

He watched her walk toward a long chest at the end of the room's bed. She pushed up the lid and began sorting through the box's contents, soon pulling out a wooden scroll case. She stood again, brushed the glossed, engraved container off, and carried it to Xu Liang.

He frowned with instant curiosity. "What is this?"

"A small treasure of Fanese origin," Yvain answered proudly, insisting that Xu Liang take it. "You're the first person I've met from Sheng Fan educated enough to understand it."

"Am I?" Xu Liang wondered aloud, carefully taking the casing into his hands. He studied the object, fingering the characters that had been carved and then painted onto the wood before being lacquered over. He read the inscription aloud. "Cai Shi-meng. It's dated spring, in the year 184 of the Celestial Calendar. This is almost one hundred years old."

"Significant?" Yvain queried.

Xu Liang felt a chill as history settled in his grasp and suddenly felt too heavy to hold. He managed by pulling the scroll case close to his body and taking a moment to recover himself. At length, he said, "Cai Shi-meng was an Imperial Scholar, during the reign of Emperor Ganzan Li, whose assassination at the hands of his own brother-in-law paved the way for the first Song Emperor. For a time after Ganzan Li's death, Cai Shi-meng disappeared. During the year 184 he would have been absent from the Imperial Court. There were several rumors as to his fate—some insisted he'd gone mad—but many who respected him believed that he simply refused to serve another master.

"He resurfaced many years later, allied with the governor of a strong rebellious province and wielding a weapon of Heaven, it was said. How it came to him, no one was certain, but after heading several successful military campaigns against the late Ganzan Li's brother-in-law, who'd named himself emperor, he was known as the 'Scholar General'. It was a young Song Dai, grandfather of the Empress Song Da-Xiao, who defeated the brilliant Cai Shi-meng in battle and made off with the blessed weapon. Impressed, the sonless ruler adopted Song Dai and named him his successor. Even though he later had sons—some of whom would protest Song Dai's position—the Song Dynasty came into being and the weapon wielded against the Empire, called the *Spear of Heaven*', remains in the hands of the Song family to this day."

Yvain held a child's glimmer of wonder in her bright eyes. She indicated the scroll case and asked, "Do you think this might detail how Cai Shi-meng found the weapon?"

"It may," Xu Liang answered, looking at the ancient encasement once again. "More importantly, it may indicate whether or not he knew of the others."

The Aeran woman blinked. "Others?"

"Since the time of the 'Scholar General', another blessed weapon has been found. The '*Pearl Moon*', a keen sword of mysterious origin, believed to have been wielded by Liu Dan, the God of poetry and song. As a man, he was a great warrior, renowned for his awareness of the battlefield and his graceful fighting style. It was said that his enemies were felled in a 'dance of death'. The legends speak of the blade and how it glowed in the company of its siblings."

"Siblings?" Yvain breathed. "Is that … are you looking for the others? Is that why you left Sheng Fan?"

"Yes," Xu Liang answered quietly. "I have cause to believe that such weapons as these would not all be found in the same place."

"But if the legends speak of them being together…"

"The legends refer to them as siblings. Born of the same source, perhaps, but drifted apart as many siblings do and drawn together in times of need, as many siblings are."

Yvain might have had more questions, but Xu Liang held up his hand.

"Please" he said. "That is all I feel comfortable saying on the matter. I do not yet understand all of it." He lifted the scroll case. "But perhaps this will help. Would you mind if I took this to my cabin to study?"

Yvain shrugged then shook her head. "No, of course not. That's why I showed it to you. I'd like to hear more about it, though. I adore Fanese myth and lore."

Xu Liang bowed. "It would be my honor and my pleasure, madam. I thank you for your trust and generosity."

Yvain bowed in return and Xu Liang took his leave.

◆ ◆ ◆ ◆ ◆

THERE WERE two scrolls in the case. At first it seemed nothing more than a detailed accounting of Ganzan Li's '*execution on behalf of the people of Sheng Fan whom he'd come to tyrannize, and for the sake of the land, which he'd come to neglect*'. Of course, Cai Shi-meng called it rather bluntly murder, '*a heinous assassination motivated by jealousy, hatred, and a desire for power, committed by immoral parties who will bring ruin to the Celestial Kingdom'.*

The Celestial Kingdom. Sheng Fan had not been referred to in that way since the Five Kingdoms Resolution came into effect. Perhaps it never would be again.

Xu Liang found it easy to sympathize with Cai Shi-meng. However, the bitterness and displacement the Scholar General felt read through clearly in his words and while it was understandable, it was not to be taken as anything more than that. Xu Liang belonged to the Song Dynasty. Their enemies were his enemies and their allies were under constant scrutiny to ensure that no such removal as what Ganzan Li experienced would be enacted upon them.

It was a difficult struggle. There were many who did not agree with Song policy or the Song themselves, but Xu Liang had seen their virtue and he had vowed to uphold the rights of those mandated by Heaven to guide and govern the people of Sheng Fan. Fate had not been with Ganzan Li, who might have impressed virtue upon Cai Shi-meng, but who also weakened the Celestial Kingdom with his vain palace-building campaigns and his lack of attention to the invasive ambitions of outsiders. It was because of his neglect that the Five Kingdoms Resolution became necessary.

Xu Liang could never forgive him that, as it had also led to the struggle the Song family currently faced, and to the death of his beloved prince, intended heir to Emperor Song Bao, slain by bandits while away from the Imperial City. It was no random attack and it was no expedition that had kept Xu Liang from the heir's side then.

A few short months after the Emperor's passing to illness, an assault on both the southern and western territories of Ji commanded their separation. Song Lu had always been too headstrong and insisted that Xu Liang go to the south to make battle plans against the sophisticated forces of the rebellious Xun Kingdom while he went west to put down the impudence of a band of rogues. He intended the action to bolster his favor among the people, saddened and confused as they were by the Emperor's sudden demise. Xu Liang shared his misgivings with Song Lu, but the young heir would not have them and, with a confident smile, he promised that he would return to the Imperial City before his trusted counsel and friend had completed his own task in the south. Song Lu was unable to keep that promise.

Xu Liang had returned from another success against the persistently defiant Southern Kingdom just in time to shield Song Lu's young sister from a fate similar.

Unworthy men had surrounded the princess, and browbeaten her in Xu Liang and Song Lu's absence nearly to the point of a self-imposed exile. Officials who were not so bold against Song Bao had suddenly revealed their treacherous nature and tried to force Song Da-Xiao away from the throne of Sheng Fan. They had failed and it was a difficult task in the following years to ensure her safety.

With her confidence and purpose renewed, the princess-become-empress would not abandon the Imperial City or her duty. Thus her enemies began to consider assassination. Xu Liang's service to the Songs had never been so demanding. It continued to tax him, but he would not rest until the Song Dynasty was secure. He would certainly not have expected the late Cai Shi-meng to be of any assistance.

And yet, not only had the Scholar General found the *Spear of Heaven* to begin with, but he had mentioned it in his writings.

'*The Song will pay for their treachery. I shall destroy those who killed my lord and all who support them. I have been given the tool necessary to exact my revenge and to restore order to the land. At last I have discovered one of the Celestial Blades that Ganzan Li had long sought. The Spear of Heaven, the blade wielded by the mighty Sun God Cheng Yu, forged in the blazing heat of the Celestial Dragons' breath, a weapon against the chaos of the land. As the Emperor is the life essence, the scholars the mind, the warriors the armor, and the commoners the backbone, the Celestial Blades are as the sword arm of the land, cutting back all intruders and opposition. Only they can still the chaos that has been stirring since man's first step upon the land. This blade coming to me is an order I cannot ignore, a command given to me by the gods to expel the unworthy and restore peace. I shall fulfill this task and welcome the others to it, should our paths cross. Though the Blades have traveled in their time, I do not believe that I wield one alone.*'

Indeed, Cai Shi-meng had not. The sword *Pearl Moon* had come to Xu Liang from the quick and deadly hands of an opponent who very nearly killed him and impressed him a great deal in so doing.

After years planning the siege of Jang Bai—a Ji stronghold annexed by none other than Xu Hong of Du—there were still imperfections. Perhaps it had something to do with the enemy being the very man who'd raised Xu Liang—who had earned no mercy for that in this instance, but who understood well just who would be opposing him. The soldier wielding *Pearl Moon* had found a way to penetrate Xu Liang's frontline and the main defenses with only a small troop. He cut his way across the battlefield and struck down two of Xu Liang's bodyguards before Xu Liang fully realized what had happened. With unforgettable resolve in his dark eyes, the warrior announced himself and struck out.

Even with a wind barrier, the force of the blow felled Xu Liang from his mount. He saw a glimmer of blue on his way to the ground. The remaining bodyguards attacked the enemy warrior. Only two survived, and they had not been the victors that day. Xu Liang had the belated awareness of a stand of bowmen to thank for his survival. The would-be assassin fell at his feet with multiple arrows stuck in him. He relinquished the blade only after informing Xu Liang that fate had chosen him. Fate had selected Xu Liang to live and, he slowly realized, to take up the Celestial Blade that had been delivered to him, though perhaps its delivery did not turn out quite as the enemy had intended.

Jang Bai was eventually taken, the ambitions of Du and Xu Hong were again smothered, and *Pearl Moon* was acquired. More than the victory, Xu Liang cherished the blade, which enabled him to further the research he had been conducting since very early into his service under the Song. It was only recently, however, that he understood its significance.

Upon the second scroll of Cai Shi-meng, battle plans had been drawn. Xu Liang studied them with fascination, admiring the complex tactics that had earned Cai Shi-meng's forces a stunning victory at Yan Xing; the historic battle was said to have lasted only a few weeks.

Xu Liang had known little of swift victory. The commander Xu Hong had placed at Jang Bai held out for eight months before being overwhelmed by Ji's larger forces, which Xu Liang had hesitated to reveal in order to lull the enemy with false hopes. What were then the Emperor's troops had arrived in stages from the base camp hidden in the tall emerald hills overlooking the river valley and in amounts large enough to limit the mobility of the enemy, forcing them to concentrate almost solely on defense. Cai Shi-meng, driven by his anger, might have devised a quicker way, but Xu Liang was better known for his patience.

Xu Liang laid the second scroll flat on top of the first, upon the blanket he had spread over the hard wood of the cabin floor. Two candles were placed to either side of the blanket upon which he sat cross-legged, illuminating the small windowless room with a soft orange glow. The scrolls did not appear to say much of immediate interest pertaining to the Celestial Swords, but they spoke worlds to Xu Liang, who recognized the words' underlying meaning—meaning that Cai Shi-meng himself may have overlooked in writing them. Xu Liang felt as if the scrolls had been delivered to him, deliberately. It was otherwise a strange coincidence that the dragon should arrive and inspire Yvain's vision, which in turn reminded her of the scrolls.

Xu Liang sighed with a sense of accomplishment and closed his eyes. And that was when he felt the intruders.

♦ ♦ ♦ ♦ ♦

THE FANESE ship came out of the darkness like a wraith drifting over the water, enshrouded in lingering tendrils of mist. In the blackness of the night, no one had seen the fog encroaching until it was too late. The enemy was upon them and it was time now for the *Pride of Celestia* to live up to its name.

"Damn," Fu Ran cursed, grinding his fist unconsciously into his hand. "They caught up with us after all."

"And much sooner than I would have expected."

Fu Ran glanced back at the mystic as he arrived on deck. "You should stay below. This is no place for scholars."

Calmly, Xu Liang said, "You seem to forget that I have seen battle."

Fu Ran was forced to take a second look at his former master. Seen it, yes, but from the rear of hundreds of thousands of troops, safely out of the range of everything except for catapults…or from the seclusion of a hidden base camp, receiving reports and issuing orders or advice. Xu Liang himself was like a specter, an otherworldly being floating through the world with virtually no physical aspect to him save that others could see him and—if they dared—touch him. It was with touch that Fu Ran recalled that Xu Liang was no spirit, but human, and a particularly frail one at that. In spite of their rough reunion at Ti Lao, it seemed to Fu Ran that the wake of a blade alone, even if the weapon utterly missed the sorcerer, would deal him a mortal blow. It seemed that way, but he'd made the mistake of underestimating Xu Liang before and if he honestly believed him so defenseless he would never have sparred with him at Ti Lao.

Just as his confidence in the mystic was beginning its pendulum swing, Xu Liang touched his arm lightly. With the faintest smile, he said, "You must trust me, Fu Ran. I have not held my position at the Imperial Court this long through carelessness."

He was right, as always. Fu Ran nodded, swallowed his old sense of duty as it came up, and turned his attention to the Fanese vessel drawing too near. "Who are they?"

"I do not know," Xu Liang admitted. "But they are more persistent than I anticipated."

"Bastards," Fu Ran grumbled, and watched Aeran archers line up across the deck.

The pale northern men were skilled hunters, trained with a bow almost from the moment they could hold one. Tonight men would be their game. The shapes of the raiders were just visible in the trace light of Fanese-style mounted torches— 'fire baskets', the Aerans called them. The way the pirates were gathering made their intentions all too clear.

Fu Ran's lips curled upward. "I don't think a wind is going to carry us away from this fight."

"No," Xu Liang agreed, missing Fu Ran's sarcasm or ignoring it. "There isn't time and besides, with the ships this close, it would carry both."

Fu Ran nodded, though he was absent from one concern as another came up. "I know you can cast a quick spell when you have to, but I think I'd feel better if I knew you were carrying that fancy blade of yours."

"I have it," the mystic answered with no enthusiasm.

Fu Ran drew his great sword from the harness at his back and a grin peeled slowly across his face. "Let them come."

They did.

It began with grappling lines. Xu Liang forced two back with a quick burst of wind and one failed to reach on its own, but three were successful, their metal ends digging into the wooden railing of the *Pride of Celestia*. The ships drifted closer and the men aboard the Fanese vessel readied a wide plank to lay across the shrinking distance. The Aeran bowmen fired and were fired upon. Ensuing cries of pain indicated that they had hit their mark and also been hit themselves. The survivors on both sides continued, but it wasn't enough to prevent the plank coming down, clattering against the deck. The ruckus continued as the first wave of boarders trod over it.

Fu Ran was there to receive them, swinging his enchanted blade in wide arcs, sweeping several of the enemies overboard at once. Those that landed on *Pride's* deck were intercepted by others of the Aeran crew, including their captain, who wielded her light blade expertly against two slightly dazed but nonetheless dangerous Fanese bandits.

♦ ♦ ♦ ♦ ♦

XU LIANG LIFTED *Pearl Moon*, watching the pale, sleek blade glimmer along the edge, as if with anticipation. Somehow it knew when it was needed, and it was eager to answer the call to duty. Perhaps too eager, but there was no choice. Xu Liang was well aware that he had brought this danger upon the *Pride of Celestia*. He would defend her, by whatever means necessary.

The bodyguards shifted around Xu Liang, preparing to receive a handful of oncoming bandits that had evaded Fu Ran's welcome. Blades crossed. Xu Liang fell into an unnatural stance that somehow felt natural to him while he held *Pearl Moon* in his grasp. He had never been fond of fighting, not even in practice, but he had accepted his training as a youth because Xu Hong would have it no other way.

'*A brush and ink pot will not save you from an assailant,*' his father had said more than once, long before his frail, studious son had even considered taking up a study in magic. Even so, Xu Hong would not have been satisfied relying on any element other than iron or steel to shield one of his clan. Today, as so many days before it, Xu Hong's insistence proved worthwhile.

A bandit crept around the occupied bodyguards and came at Xu Liang. Xu Liang closed his hand tighter around the hilt of his sword and caught the green and blue tassels swinging in the corner of his vision as he blocked the high blow. The pale magic glow radiated from the edge of the blade and hummed as it deflected the common iron used by the bandit.

A space was put between combatants. Xu Liang took advantage as he saw another of the man's allies coming, cutting low before the bandit could strike again. The man fell to the deck and Xu Liang spun away from the next attacker, feeling the air separate with the bandit's fierce swing, just missing him. Xu Liang did what the moment commanded, then moved on to the next foe, giving himself to the blade's fervor, recalling a proverb inspired by the Goddess Mei Qiao: *When the Moon rises over darkness, she does so fiercely and without remorse.*

♦ ♦ ♦ ♦ ♦

SEVERAL FEET AWAY from Xu Liang, Fu Ran roared with laughter that put hesitation into the movements of his multiple opponents. He batted three more into the sea with the flat of his blade, hearing the crack of at least one ribcage. He elbowed the skull of another attacker who was attempting to jab his side while it was left momentarily unguarded by his swing. The man dropped to the deck and Fu Ran turned his head just in time to catch a blur of many colors rushing by him as a bandit leapt down from the deck railing.

"You missed!" Fu Ran gloated.

His grin became a frown when he felt warm moisture running down his arm. He wheeled around to face the man just rising behind him, dressed in green trousers decorated with many gold serpents and held at the waist with a wide belt. His arms and bare chest were home to several tattoos of scaly creatures. From head to toe, there was a wild look about him, bordering on crazed, enhanced with cunning. He carried a broad one-handed sword with a curved blade and a gold hilt, probably stolen.

"You must be the Laughing Devil," the bandit said with a smirk. He lifted his weapon. "They call me Zhen Yu."

"The River Master," Fu Ran recalled, his smile returning as he tasted the forthcoming challenge. "What brings you out to sea?"

"A lot of profit," the pirate answered and he came forward, performing a series of stark, precise slashes that threatened to pass Fu Ran's heavier blade.

The extra reach provided by the enchanted tassel spared Fu Ran the embarrassment. He stepped back and swung out.

Zhen Yu leapt out of harm's way and darted back in, again attacking almost faster than his larger opponent could block. Fu Ran paid attention to the man's timing, and surprised him by lunging forward when Zhen Yu pulled back to swing at the start of a fresh series of attacks. Fu Ran utilized his own momentum, ramming his large bald head square into the smaller man's tattooed chest.

Zhen Yu flew backwards with the assault, knocking over two other bodies in his path.

Fu Ran grinned and slowly let go the silk tassel dangling from his sword's hilt.

◆ ◆ ◆ ◆ ◆

WITH HIS BACK to the plank, the Laughing Devil missed the coming of several uninvited boarders, including Xiadao Lu, who'd spotted his quarry before even crossing between ships. Sorcerers made a bad habit of revealing themselves with their magic. He followed the erratically swelling blue light to the mystic, cutting down the opponent Xu Liang was engaged with to announce himself.

Xu Liang looked at him, eyes narrow and gleaming softly, like a pair of pallid moons in a heavy sky. Magic filled the Imperial Peacock, but that did not trouble the warrior come to destroy him.

Xiadao Lu held the shaft of his weapon in both hands. His stance was light and balanced, prepared for anything this time. "This is where your journey ends. I will kill you now!"

The mystic appeared undaunted. "Even if that were so, it would not be the end of my journey, but the beginning of a new one. However, I do not think that you will be the one to show me that path."

"We shall see!" Xiadao Lu retorted and lunged forward, into a series of strikes that were deflected and returned, and blocked again. The pattern continued for several moments with only brief pauses between the combatants during which one glared softly while the other issued a vicious scowl.

To say the least, Xiadao Lu was surprised. He had expected more sorcery from the official of the Imperial City, and would never have anticipated such swift, dexterous—and even aggressive—movement from one who looked as if he would break if he walked too heavily. Perhaps more than an ornament. Still he was no match for a warrior of Xiadao Lu's accomplishment and skill.

"What is it you hope to gain in this?" Xu Liang asked while their blades locked up.

"More glory than I anticipated, judging by your skill with a weapon," Xiadao Lu answered through his teeth.

"Is that all?" the mystic wondered with disappointment a student might expect from a tutor whose point he'd completely missed.

Xiadao Lu didn't care for the reproach and, with a growl, he unlocked their weapons and shoved the mystic back several steps.

Xu Liang caught himself and assumed a defensive stance. "Tell me. Who was it that interested you in this hunt for glory?"

Xiadao Lu answered with his blade, striking swift and sudden at the mystic. He failed to disarm the smaller man, but managed to send him reeling back, exposing his neck and chest as his sword arm flung back. Xiadao Lu chose a target and dove in for the kill.

He felt the jolt against his weapon before he saw the flash of steel that preceded it. Sparks shot off the momentarily fused blades and his sword-axe skipped off the unexpected obstruction, veering too high, but still drawing blood. Xu Liang went down. That was all Xiadao Lu had time to see before an armored man unleashed his fury on him in a vain attempt to right a situation that, in the guard's mind, had gone horribly wrong.

Xiadao Lu concentrated solely on protecting his vital areas as one bodyguard was joined by another, and another ... as if they all suddenly realized what had been going on behind them. Xiadao Lu waited for them to exhaust their immediate rage that was mixed with panic. Then he held his weapon across his body and lunged forward with an enormous surge of power, forcing them back far enough to hold them off balance and unable to attack for the few seconds he needed to make his escape. It would be far too risky to fight them all in their crazed state, even with the protective enchantment cast upon his armor. They could be dealt with later, if Xu Liang managed to survive.

♦ ♦ ♦ ♦ ♦

SORCERY HAD ITS PLACE, but in a confined battle aboard boats one who focused primarily in pyromancy was wise to resort to other methods of defense.

Ma Shou was not defenseless without his magic, and he proved that by blocking a random attack with his twin short blades crossed in front of him. Afterward, he pushed the assailant back and slid the sabers apart, cutting swiftly at two barbarian opponents nearby. His movements were calm and ordered, efficient and seemingly effortless to anyone watching, he believed. Some men would claim that they had never seen Ma Shou break a sweat, not even in the most heated of battles. Some would attribute that to the nature of his craft, concluding that he was immune to heat. He let them believe what they wished to believe, just as he allowed Xiadao Lu his disdain. He had not been put upon this world to impress the likes of him, an overgrown ox who knew nothing of grace or patience. Ma Shou had seen the fruits of that one's labor. He was currently up to his neck in it as dozens of ill-bred men tried to sever his head with their crude weapons and crude tactics.

The fighting had spread onto both ships, as barbarians trying to keep the pirates at bay pushed them back onto the deck of the *Jade Carp*. The smirking pirate captain had scrabbled over like an eager rat for a morsel of food when he heard the mad laughter of the giant who had succeeded in making Ma Shou look like a fool back at Ti Lao. He was still embarrassed by the whole affair, from the instant of shock he felt as his own man came flying at him, to the fall itself, and especially the pathetic muffled groan that emitted from his own throat as he went over. The art had been taken out of the battle. There was no choice left but to retreat.

This fight was rapidly getting ugly as well.

Ma Shou remained on the deck of the *Jade Carp*, helping the others to keep the wandering barbarians back. They were strong and there were a lot of them. Zhen Yu may finally have come upon a ship he couldn't take.

It was a stupid plan anyway. Pirates never considered subtlety, and men like Xiadao Lu were always too eager to rush headlong into any battle. Against an enemy they knew so very little about, it was doubly stupid. They should have taken Xu Liang in Sheng Fan. If not for the mystic's luck, they would have. And what were his chances for success anyway? Long centuries had passed since the Celestial Swords were last witnessed together. They could have strayed anywhere, to unexplored, uninhabited regions, to the bottom of the sea … the belly of a volcano …

It was an endeavor for fools.

But I am surely in the midst of foolish men, Ma Shou thought, and struck back another opponent. A bellow of laughter from the other ship made his spine shudder. There was a sound he wished to silence.

◆ ◆ ◆ ◆ ◆

"HA!" FU RAN roared as he knocked the pirate to the deck once again. "Is that the best you've got?"

Zhen Yu sprang up, then leapt into the air and slammed the pommel of his sword into Fu Ran's skull, sending his brain for a spin. The smaller man sneered like a malicious child. "Better still than what you've given!"

Fu Ran lifted his hand to his head to steady it. With the other hand still gripping his sword he managed to prevent the pirate's next attack from piercing his heart. And now he was angry. Still somewhat dazed, he stomped forward and brought his elbow down fast and heavy onto the pirate's unprotected shoulder.

Zhen Yu sank to the deck like a dropped sack of grain. In the instant that followed, Fu Ran heard someone shout and something struck him behind the knees, felling him like a great tree.

"We leave now!" someone shouted, and Zhen Yu scrambled to his feet.

The pirate grinned, still with his wild confidence. He looked over his shoulder and hollered, "Everyone! Back to the *Carp!*"

Those that were able backed out of their battles and headed for the Fanese vessel.

♦ ♦ ♦ ♦ ♦

YVAIN CAUGHT ONE of her men by the arm as the pirates departed. "Don't pursue. I think we gave them a second thought. Let them go lick their wounds. We'll be docked in Nelayne by the time they're bold enough to consider a second strike." She then gave the same command to stay put to the rest of *Pride's* crew, kicking the intruder's makeshift bridge into the water herself when enough of them had fled. The stragglers threw themselves overboard while individuals on both sides cut the grappling lines, allowing the ships to drift apart.

"What did they want?" Fu Ran asked, appearing beside her, pressing the ball of one hand to his temple.

Yvain watched the distance between the ships grow, then said, "I don't know. Apparently their aim wasn't to sink us. Maybe they wanted to steal something, though I couldn't guess as to what. It's not as if we're a treasure ship...if there is such a thing."

Fu Ran dropped his hand, suddenly forgetting about his head wound.

Yvain watched him step around her and jog toward a knot of people gathered not far away. He began immediately shoving people aside. She sighed and went to see what the matter was, stopping along the way to issue an order to a milling crewman. "Find Yendrick and bring him up here. Tell the healer he's got a long night ahead of him."

The crewman nodded and left, and Yvain went to join the others, where Fu Ran was on his knees beside Xu Liang, his head bowed in evident relief. The mystic wasn't standing but he was alive and upright, pain distorting his fair features while he clutched his hand to one slim shoulder. Blood seeped between his fingers, looking redder against his opalescent skin. He didn't look accustomed to pain, but he seemed to be handling it well enough. "How bad?" Yvain asked him.

Xu Liang's words came out strangled. "A mere scratch for some... a serious injury, I fear, for one such as myself."

"I don't understand," she said.

While the bodyguards looked at her with varying measures of disdain, Fu Ran lifted his head and explained. "He doesn't eat when he meditates. It strengthens his spirit, but it weakens him physically."

"Our healer will look at you," Yvain promised.

Xu Liang shut his eyes tightly for an instant and then shook his head. "I thank you, but no. I cannot allow it."

Yvain frowned at that idea. "If you think you're going to sit there and bleed to death on my deck..."

The mystic looked up at her suddenly. "You do not understand," he snapped, surprising everyone but his statuesque guards with the sudden edge in his tone. "No healer's hand or medicine must touch me! I can accept nothing from him, or anyone else." He relaxed somewhat and added softly, "I must be left alone and allowed to rest."

"He'll be fine," Fu Ran finally said, slowly standing. He wasn't convincing and didn't seem convinced himself.

He turned eventually and drew Yvain away from the others. "You can't interfere. He's entered a state—magical, spiritual, whatever you want to call it—that can't be corrupted. I've never seen him go this far before, but I can promise you that whatever inspired him to do so is serious to him, more important than life. He's probably been meditating at this level since he left the Imperial City. If we interrupt him now, he'll lose whatever focus he's been trying to hold onto and depending on what that is, it could be the same as killing him."

"So we let him die, then?" Yvain asked caustically.

Fu Ran shook his head with patience that was not typical for him, squeezing her arm gently in his large hand.

Yvain hadn't even noticed his touch until then. It was at moments like this that she thought deliberately about their long-standing friendship and the many near encounters they'd had with something more. And it was in the midst of a thought like that, that Yvain dismissed romance for common sense. She opened her mouth to continue her argument against letting a Fanese official die on her ship.

Fu Ran spoke first. "Just as his meditation has endangered him, it can save him. The meditation taxes him, but his magic sustains him. He'll be all right by morning." Fu Ran's hand slipped away as he looked over his shoulder at the mystic. In a moment, he added, "And if he isn't ... to the Thousand Hells with his magic. I spent too many years of my life protecting his to see it end now."

FIVE
The Price of Sorcery

XU LIANG'S BODYGUARDS patched up their own wounds, which were relatively few, and otherwise spent their time standing watch around their master, who'd yet to leave the deck where he'd fallen. At some point he shifted from his knees into a cross-legged position and held his hands together in front of himself. The torn sleeve of his robe—both the under and out layer—was heavily stained, defacing the elegance of the long-tailed birds embroidered into the silk, just as the minor ruination of his once perfect skin offended the mystic's gentle beauty. The blood appeared to have stopped flowing, but the skin was still broken and greatly bruised. It made Yvain's stomach turn to look at it, even though she'd seen far worse. The wound just seemed so out of place on Xu Liang. The pain he had shown after the battle had drained from his expression and he now looked like a delicate stone idol, marred by a blasphemous hand. Yvain understood the devotion of his guards... the same devotion Fu Ran evidently still felt, even years after abandoning Sheng Fan and his master.

"He is doing well," someone suddenly said, speaking Fanese.

Yvain's gaze darted to the bodyguard who'd spoken to her. He was an older man with black hair turning white, on his head as well as in his neat beard and mustache. She just noticed the way each of the bodyguards' hair was bunched at the top of their heads in a uniform fashion. They had taken their helmets off, but were otherwise fully armored in Fanese tradition, and probably roasting in the afternoon sun that was shining down on the deck. Their ages were indeterminable with the exception of two; the elder and one who looked to be just out of his teens. The latter sat rigidly, either trying to seem imposing or stay alert. Yvain couldn't decide which.

She approached the old one facing her. "It's all right to speak? We won't disturb him?" She indicated Xu Liang with her eyes.

"It takes more than simple talking to disturb my lord," the guard replied.

Yvain accepted that with a nod, then asked, "What happened the other night?" She hoped after speaking the question that she hadn't just offended the man by seeming to question his ability to protect the mystic. What she truly wondered was how the sorcerer had failed to protect himself, and she didn't necessarily mean from the attack.

The aging guard did not indicate umbrage. He said neutrally, "My lord suffered for his bravery and now he suffers for his sorcery."

Recalling what Fu Ran had said, Yvain asked, "Did you know he'd taken it this far?"

"No," the guard answered honestly. And then a smile crept into his aging features. "My lord knows that I worry about him."

Yvain returned his smile. "How long have you been with him?"

"Nine years." The man sighed. "Perhaps now my lord will think I'm getting too old."

"I doubt it," Yvain offered. "All of you fought well and bravely."

The bodyguard bowed his head in a manner that seemed more friendly than simply respectful.

"We'll be arriving at Nelayne soon," Yvain informed. "We only planned to stay docked for a few days, but we'll stay as long as you and Xu Liang need."

"My lord will be ready," the guard said with confidence and nodded again.

Yvain left him to his duty.

◆ ◆ ◆ ◆ ◆

NIGHT GREW DARKER as a storm approached.

From a balcony several stories up, Alere Shaederin watched the starless black mass encroach upon his home. A chill wind preceded it, billowing the observer's ivory-blond hair and snapping the fabric of his shirt.

It would be fierce this time. Worse than any of the other storms that had invaded the Lower Verres Mountains of Northern Yvaria this season. Soon the steep towers, grand balconies, and elaborate bridges of the castle would be glistening wet as the rain sheeted down and sporadic strands of lightning leapt across the sky, weaving webs among the clouds.

Once Alere had marveled at such spectacles of nature, particularly as the warmer storm season was so brief in this region. Recently, he had begun to fear them, as he wondered now at their source. They seemed only to herald misery, with a determination that could not have belonged to nature.

Alere closed his gray eyes and felt the oncoming force. The energy brushed over his fair skin and filtered into his flesh. He thought back, to a night such as this, and a beautiful young mother, who had sheltered her son from his fear of the beasts in his dreams.

"You must never fear them," his mother had said. And she said it again, years later when the nightmare creatures attacked their home and slew nearly all of the Shaederin household.

It should not have happened. They were elvenborn, descended of the highest of their kind. Morgen Shaederin was renowned for his prowess as a warrior and a slayer of demons. And yet, somehow, he fell to darkness. His wife took up his sword and fought the invaders with her own skill, but the elves were overwhelmed. Eria Shaederin returned to the place where her adolescent son had been charged with keeping the other children of the household hidden and safe. She was mortally wounded, but showed no fear and little pain as she issued Morgen Shaederin's blade to its rightful inheritor and said, *"You must never fear them, Alere. You must survive ... and defeat them."*

The voices of the past departed and one belonging to the present spoke softly. "It still looks the same. It constantly amazes me just how much."

Alere opened his eyes, but did not look back at his cousin. Aside from himself, Kailel was the oldest of the remaining Shaederins. He was just sixteen, and scarcely that, but it would have to be old enough.

"You're going to do it, aren't you?" Kailel said in a moment, and while his tone was calm, Alere could sense the distress building inside of his cousin. "You're going to leave us."

"I cannot stay here."

"I'll come with you," Kailel offered at once.

"One of us must remain. Our family must be rebuilt, and the rebuilding must take place here, in our home."

"But your father was the lord of our house. It is your place ... it is your responsibility to stay here!"

Unconsciously, Alere's hand strayed to the hilt of the sword at his belt. "I inherited what my father wished me to inherit. The house is yours, Kailel. I did my part by leading you from it six years ago and by bringing you back to it now."

"We would have died in those passages without you, Alere. I know that." Kailel spoke with deference now. However, he continued to argue, as it was his only defense against Alere's determination. "I know that well. I still have unsettling dreams about that night. I was not too young to understand why we'd been sent into the mountain corridors. It was you who kept us calm and safe. It was you who led us to Lord Doriel's land and negotiated our stay. You were the one who served him. You lent him your father's sword in becoming a guard in his army. I think that blade has done its task and you must do now what your father did when the fighting was over. You must put it away and turn your attentions to your family."

Alere lowered his gaze from the horizon and closed his eyes again. "It is for my family that I must leave this place again. What happened here was not random."

"Your father had many enemies," Kailel confirmed unhappily, as if he knew what Alere would say next.

Perhaps it was predictable, then, that Alere's answer would be, "They are my enemies now."

A long silence passed between the cousins. At length, the younger said, "I cannot stop you."

Kailel left and Alere opened his eyes once more to the coming storm. He watched the lightning tumbling from the sky until he could just hear the answer of thunder. Then he turned away and walked back into the bedroom that once belonged to his parents. He looked over the draping webs and layers of dust, and realized that it would take considerable effort to make the place livable again. Some of the others had already begun the cleaning since their arrival earlier in the season. Alere had spent much of that time searching the castle for unwanted residents and he would stay until the task was finished. Thus far he had discovered nothing but spiders and rats, and a few other small beasts that had strayed in from the surrounding wilderness, all of them mortal children of Ysis, the goddess of the sky and mother of all that lived beneath her ever changing veil. It was the goddess's immortal children that one had to be wary of, particularly her daughter Ceren, goddess of the earth and of the Void.

The offspring goddess, according to legend, had been charged to watch over the physical world and its inhabitants from a closer perspective and to maintain a balance between the World and the Void; life and oblivion. It seemed that she more enjoyed toying with the scales than keeping them in check. There were times when Alere believed that the goddess had gone mad. There had been far too much war carrying on throughout Dryth. War among men, war among men and demons, possibly war among the gods themselves as well.

Alere had seen the battlefield. He'd seen it littered with the bodies of thousands of men and beasts, killed by blade and by will, and sometimes by magic. He had seen his own blood flowing freely over his eyes from a terrible wound, the scar of which still traced his hairline. He had seen much for his young age, but nothing that troubled him so greatly as what he had not seen; the murder of his family at the hands of a legion of unnatural invaders.

He wondered what could be worse, the actual event, or his imagination's interpretation of it ... of the sounds and the smells, and the sensations while running through blackened passages that claws were ever close to tearing at his back. Even now, he shuddered inside thinking about it.

Outside, the storm had finally arrived, and the sound of the rainfall washed at once into the room. Alere stood in front of the fireplace and listened to it. He stared long at the healthy flame and eventually his gaze wandered to an item on the mantel, covered over in dust and abandoned webs.

He stepped forward and lifted his hand to the object, slowly sweeping away the layers of filth. When he'd exposed the wooden sword stand, he stared at it, visually tracing every delicate engraving. He fell almost into a trance-like state while studying the fascinating work until he came upon a word; a name. *Aerkiren*, the name given to his father's sword, which in the Northern Elvish tongue literally meant 'sky of evening', or more commonly, 'twilight'.

"It sings when darkness falls," Morgen Shaederin had said.

Alere drew the long elven blade at his hip and held it in both hands, studying the emblazoned symbols for several moments before finally setting the sword upon its mount. He hesitated to take his hands away from it at first, almost as if he believed it would vanish or as if somehow he would not be able to reclaim it. Eventually, he lifted his hands and stepped back … and watched.

The lighting in the room made it difficult, but soon enough Alere descried the faint glow along the edges of the engravings; a soft violet light that seemed to actively trace the symbols. Alere had seen them glow stronger, but he had never seen them fully brilliant, not even in the near pitch darkness of the mountain corridors he and his siblings had fled through. Perhaps then he had been too preoccupied to notice, but it seemed unlikely, since the enchanted glow should have lit their path and all any of them could remember was the absolute depth of the darkness in those passages. This blade, clearly a gift from the gods, was mystery to him. He knew little of its origin and almost nothing of its true purpose in the world of mortals. Morgen Shaederin did not live long enough to explain such things to his son, if he had ever known himself.

I will not tarnish your legacy, Father. I will do whatever I must to serve the power that was bestowed upon you.

Alere did not hope to master the enchanted blade. To attempt to do so would be to defy the gods, and only arrogance and foolishness set a mortal soul on such a campaign.

The twilight glow of the sword *Aerkiren* gleamed in Alere's eyes, as if the weapon itself were a sentient being and had read his thoughts, and understood them.

◆ ◆ ◆ ◆ ◆

EVEN THE OPEN corridors of the castle were dark. Months could not lift the gloom that had spent years settling. Even after the bodies of their relatives had at last been properly buried, the spirits of those savagely murdered still seemed to linger in the air. They seemed to linger, but not one ghost of the past had been found after a long and thorough search.

Alere stood idle for a moment upon a carpeted staircase between floors that was also a bridge across the center hall of the mountain fortress. Someone had been along to light the lamps. Not all of them, but many of the sleek, decorative iron posts had a fire glowing within the delicate glass shapes that topped them. It was not an entirely useless endeavor, as the bridge happened to be one of the easiest and quickest routes from one side of the main house to the other. Still, the light did little to penetrate the surrounding shadow and even less to uplift Alere's spirits.

He could justify passing charge of the house to Kailel. Not only was his cousin the son of Morgen Shaederin's closest brother, but he had a sound presence of mind about him and a natural skill at handling the affairs of the household. Already he had been to the treasury and tallied the remains of the Shaederin capital against the records and the evidence of thieves. Mostly artifacts and items throughout the castle appraised by the greedy eye to be of tremendous worth had been taken. The treasury itself had been ransacked, but apparently not by a large number of burglars and none who were inclined to return after filling their purses once. The remains belonged entirely to the Shaederins, without lien or attachment, as Alere had paid for their stay in another elven lord's domain with his sword arm and very nearly his life, on more than one occasion.

Kailel had trained with a sword as well and his skills were not lacking. Again, his placement as lord of the Shaederin household was justified. And yet, Alere couldn't help the misgivings he felt dropping such a burden in the lap of one so young.

And are you so old? He asked himself. *At just sixteen you set foot upon your first battlefield. Kailel is the same tender age and he has only to combat his emotions. He will do well here, with the others. It is where he belongs.*

"Alere?"

The tiny voice drew him out of his pause. He shifted his focus back to the steps and walked up a few more of them, stopping again when he saw the small girl in his path. He knelt to her height. "Edelyn, it is late. You should be in your bed, little one."

"I'm not tired," she said. "I'm never tired. I want to go with you."

He smiled at her gently and tucked strands of pale hair behind her ear. "And you may … when I have returned from my journey and you are old enough to be taught to ride."

Edelyn was the smallest of them—not seven years old yet, as she had been an infant when they fled from their home—and so, in her endearing innocence, accepted the terms without considering them. She did so with a firm nod.

Alere stood and lifted her into his arms. "My darling little one, I shall surely miss you."

"I love you, Alere," the child yawned, wrapping her arms around his neck.

"And I love you," he answered, but she did not hear as she had already fallen fast asleep upon his shoulder.

Kailel, however, standing at the top of the bridge of stairs, did hear. "How can you leave them?" he asked, and not argumentatively, so much as wonderingly.

Alere said softly, "With a heavy heart."

Kailel watched his cousin holding the smallest Shaederin for a moment, then said, "We will need to employ guards. Will you not at least stay long enough to help me with the selection? I fear I am not as wise a judge of character as you. I'm not certain whether I can tell a mercenary from an honest soldier."

"Any soldier whose services are not pledged already to a lord is a mercenary," Alere informed. "But there are some better than others. I think you will be able to tell them apart."

"I think you have too much faith in me."

"You have yet to damage my faith in you, Kailel. It would bolster, I think, if you were to develop some faith in yourself."

Kailel looked away from Alere just then, down at the deep shadows beneath them. "I have not seen as much of the world as you have, Alere. I feel naïve sometimes."

"That you can admit to that proves you are not."

Kailel met Alere's gaze. "Alere..."

Recognizing the sentimental gleam in Kailel's eyes, Alere diverted a second assault on his heart by changing the subject. "The armory appears in fair order."

Kailel confirmed the statement with a nod. "The weapons' master kept a detailed catalogue. All that was missing lay with the bodies and were recovered before burial. Apparently our thieves were more interested in elven art and gold than blades."

"A foolish lot they were," Alere replied. And then he asked, "You have claimed your father's sword?"

Kailel shook his head. "It was broken in the battle. I buried the shards with him."

Alere had not partaken of much of the task of burial once becoming enrapt in his thorough search of the grounds. He had not been informed and said appropriately, "I'm sorry, Kailel."

"My father's blade wasn't enchanted." Kailel came forward and carefully took little Edelyn from Alere. "Perhaps it's for the best. What would the others do if we both felt vengeance's call?"

"Find a weapon that you trust," Alere advised, deciding not to reproach his cousin for his careless statement. "Find one for Tahren and Ardin as well."

"They are only children," Kailel argued.

"They are each fourteen and they are each strong. They will learn fast and well."

Kailel sighed and said, neither for the first time or the last, "I wish you would stay."

"I have put this off for too long already. I will leave when the storm passes."

Kailel turned and started back up the stairs. "In that case, I hope that it rains all night and into the morning. Then you'd at least have to assist me in the selection of weapons."

◆ ◆ ◆ ◆ ◆

IN SPITE OF Kailel's wishes, the storm lasted only a few hours. The stars were visible again when Alere led Breigh, a strong ivory mare, out of the stables. He was dressed in the traditional riding whites of a Verressi hunter and again wearing his father's sword. With it, he carried a small dagger and a bow. He carried very little supplies or provisions and only a small amount of coins. He was not planning on squandering time or money at inns or other establishments.

"I wish you would stay," Kailel said, once more, as Alere performed a final check of his gear and the finely bred horse Lord Doriel had given him before he left his land. "It has been years, Alere. Who's to say that whomever was behind the attack on our family isn't dead?"

"No one is to say, save whomever was behind the attack. But you should know, Kailel, that it is not revenge that I seek. Certainly not that alone."

"Then what?"

Alere tugged on the last straps to be checked, then gathered the horse's reins and hoisted himself effortlessly into the saddle. He looked down at Kailel and said, "The demons of Dryth are restless. Someone must quiet them."

"A pity for us that it must be you," Kailel complained, then met Alere's gaze, shadowed beneath the hood of his cloak, and said gently, "Safe journey, cousin."

Alere inclined his head, then looked to the castle's main gates, and fled from his home for the second time.

SIX
Stormbright

I T HAD BEEN no easy task leaving the *Pride of Celestia* and her crew. However, there was no time for lingering. Xu Liang had emerged from his meditation several hours before coming to Nelayne and settled his fees with Yvain, both monetarily and with a translation of the returned scrolls written by Cai Shi-meng. She seemed to appreciate the shared knowledge, but was preoccupied with staring at his previously wounded shoulder, even though it had been cleaned—with water only—and covered with the mended, stained silk of his robes. She did not specify whether she was curious about the wound or the repair to his clothing—performed by Gai Ping—that not quite neatly reconnected the image of a bird's head to its body along the seam of the over robe's shoulder.

Xu Liang did not ask. He appreciated the concern that he received from those who Fu Ran had evidently developed a strong sense of kinship with. Compassion was a divine trait, after all. Still, the wound was acquired in honorable service to his empress, and would heal quicker with her blessing, as well as through the attendance of the spirits his constant meditative state invoked. Knowing that enabled him to put the lingering ache in his shoulder and the attack that inspired it behind him for now. He had taken many important steps since the start of his journey, but perhaps none so important yet as those he would take now that he had arrived on the shores of what many would consider the outermost barbarian lands.

The ship drifted at a sluggish wake in search of a proper landing. From his portside view, Xu Liang was able to draw in aspects of the settlement forthcoming. It was beyond a settlement. The western port city reminded Xu Liang of Ti Lao with its crowd and bustle, but otherwise they were not at all similar. There was a great deal more peddlers conglomerating near the docks of Nelayne, most of them selling wares rather than food. The merchants sold out of carts and baskets, and from lines connecting many of the stands, like a colorful network of webbing. Music was played from several different sources at once, mostly with western instruments, though there were a few evidently from other cultures ... none from Sheng Fan. There were dancers and magicians performing wherever they found space among the merchants. Beyond the waterfront, the city itself rose in the form of grimy white towers and proud-looking brick structures standing close together, life flowing between the narrow gaps like blood through veins.

Xu Liang had seen the city before, but only twice, and both times it seemed to have changed somehow in his absence. Inevitably it was growing, but even a growing city in Sheng Fan maintained some sameness in appearance. Western towns seemed to spread like wildflowers, in a vast array of disordered color, size, and shape.

Guang Ci and the four other bodyguards who had never left Sheng Fan before this journey stared at the upcoming barbarian land in utter amaze. They were too disoriented by the scene to show either admiration or disgust. The veterans of Xu Liang's expeditions, however, were not impressed, nor were they overly unimpressed.

"The land keeps changing," Xu Liang said to no one in particular. However, the observation did not go unnoticed.

"Lord Xu Liang," Gai Ping said, gesturing at the city with his arm. "Don't tell me you find all of this beautiful as well."

Xu Liang smiled, "In its way."

The elder laughed, receiving the answer he'd expected. It was shortly afterward that Xu Liang was distracted from the present scenery by a vision out of the past.

When Fu Ran knelt before him as was customary of a servant in Sheng Fan and not the rogue sailor he'd become, Xu Liang found himself literally without words.

The silence did not last, as the large man swallowed his pride and said, "My lord, I shall accompany you, if you will permit it."

At the request, Xu Liang thought back almost thirty years, to two people who had always been as opposite from one another as night from day. Xu Liang had been a child when Fu Ran's father fell into Xu Hong's service as a personal bodyguard. Fu Yan had given his life in service to his lord and it was not long before his quickly growing son inherited the position, only to be later charged to Xu Liang when the student was summoned to the Imperial City. They had not been raised as brothers—such was unthinkable—but perhaps a brotherly sentiment had developed between them over the many years. Surely, there was more than duty or discipline argued the day Fu Ran set out to find his place in the world, believing somehow that Sheng Fan was not it. Xu Liang recalled how stubborn they had both been, the anger Xu Liang rarely felt that had unquestionably assailed his resolve then. Fu Ran left and Xu Liang, though hurt, had long thought that he would welcome his former servant back. He realized now that he could not.

"No, Fu Ran," Xu Liang finally said. When the large man looked up, astonished by this decision, Xu Liang explained. "You left Sheng Fan seeking a freedom you did not believe could exist for you in our homeland. I'm not certain if you have found it, but certainly you have found something in your travels and aboard this ship. I will not take it from you by taking you back as you were."

Fu Ran stood slowly and stared, his mouth just gaping as he searched for an argument. He had not found one by the time the *Pride of Celestia* docked and Xu Liang left with only his eight body-guards in tow.

Once on land, their small caravan continued west. They were not headed due west—not long from the coast, they veered north, moving at a gradual angle away from the harsh shores of the country of Callipry. The immediate area beyond Nelayne was a district known as Stormbright, and the inland hamlet Xu Liang and his guards were able to observe in the near distance within a day's travel, was called Barten's Palace. Xu Liang found the name of peculiar interest as there was no palace anywhere in sight. When his party camped at night he made detailed accounts of all that he had seen and heard. Though he had not come to this place for the first time, he knew better than to think that one look—or even a thousand—would ever reveal all that there was to be seen and learned. He drew several maps during his travels and found himself constantly adding to them.

In the morning he painted the landscape. The last time he had come to this land, it was the autumn season. The trees were barren and thin at that time, skeletal and yet still beautiful. The sky had often been gray; a textured, but unbroken canopy of clouds that felt cold to look at. It was spring now, and the trees were full; a blanket of jade silk spilling down the craggy terrain that skirted the road Xu Liang's company currently followed. The sky seemed to glow overhead, even on a day when dark clouds encroached. And now Xu Liang understood the name Stormbright.

He wished he had more time. He wished that he could explore more of this realm, more of every realm in what his people simply referred to as the World and what those outside Sheng Fan had come to call Dryth. He wondered what the word meant and would like to find out, so that he might relate it to his people in a word or words they could understand. Unfortunately, the word's roots were so ancient that most of the people currently living had long forgotten its meaning. Xu Liang had discovered one similar word in one of the three other languages he had studied abroad. However, daeryd—a Calliprian word derived of the Yvarian word dirydd, pronounced 'dirith' in such a way that it almost sounded like 'drith'— meant unholy or impure, and hardly seemed something to name the cradle of life after.

Undoubtedly the unenlightened of his people could come to the conclusion that an ancestor had taken a single step across Sheng Fan's borders and been at once disgusted by the 'barbaric' outer lands and given such crude people the word with the crude sound he had made out of revulsion. They would amuse themselves with notions of the uncivilized basing an entire language upon such a noise. Xu Liang might have been disgusted with such people, except that he knew the blame lay with ignorance. If his beloved fellows could truly see the world that surrounded Sheng Fan, they would not be so quick to pass judgment.

Xu Liang had scarcely finished the thought when one of the bodyguards scrambled up to his high point overlooking the road and the land below it.

The youngish descendant of Sheng Fan dropped to one knee and pretended not to feel the crack that Xu Liang heard as he selected his ground and executed his descent carelessly, coming down upon one of the many sharp rocks that protruded from the earth. There was, however, a tension in his voice when he said, "Master Xu, barbarians have been sighted."

Xu Liang lowered his brush, once again silently marveling at the pride of his people. He asked calmly, "Where?"

"In the woods, less than a mile from the road. They are headed this way, my lord."

"What do they look like?" Xu Liang asked next, and the body-guard seemed confused by the question. As the man struggled with his answer in careful silence, Xu Liang closed his eyes and channeled his concentration.

The sounds and smells of the forest fell upon him in layers, distinct and separate details that he filtered through carefully and patiently until he found something he had not noticed before in his morning study and recreation.

He heard breathing, a heavier sound than any woodland animal made when it wasn't ill or being chased. He heard the crease of worn leather and the mild clatter of things metal as the bearers moved at an unhurried and incautious pace. He smelled lards and oils, and a metallic pungency overriding a delicate grain smell, along with the potent stench of western alcohol.

Xu Liang opened his eyes and the natural chorus of the woods resumed. He took up his brush again and said softly, "They are not to be harmed."

The guard showed surprise, but dared not question his superior. He simply nodded and returned to the nearby campsite with a slight limp.

◆ ◆ ◆ ◆ ◆

A FAINT BREEZE moved through the trees, shifting the shadows that mottled the forest floor.

Tarfan Fairwind might not have shown particular interest in the phenomenon, except that a moment ago the air had been almost utterly still. Tarfan came to an abrupt halt and looked up the hill, toward the road. His eyes narrowed suspiciously. He scratched at his thick black beard, disheveling several crumbs that had settled there since breakfast. It had been seven years since the air sighed on a still day. Seven years since the strangest bird of any in Dryth had fluttered through Stormbright with no intentions of nesting.

Could it be...?

"What's the matter?"

Tarfan glanced at the young dwarf standing too alert beside him—his niece Taya. They had only just begun the season's journey to Shillan this morning, but she hadn't been able to relax since breakfast, when she claimed to have had an ill feeling that something bad was going to happen. Taya was unnaturally assured of her ill feelings most days, and this morning was no exception. She was on the verge of drawing her short sword until Tarfan stopped her.

"No," he said. "Better not. Our overly civilized guest might take offense."

Hazel eyes that were a fair cry sharper than his old greens shot in his direction. "What?"

Tarfan started up the hill. "Come along, lass. You'll soon see."

They made their way to the road and across it, where a camp lay unsuspectingly ... or rather arrogantly, in broad daylight. If there was one thing the elf-like humans of the distant east didn't believe in, it was hiding.

Elf like?

Tarfan reconsidered. They reminded him of elves, in that they seemed a reticent people overall, and they were too damned arrogant; a juxtaposition of too few shared words and too much exuded confidence. He supposed that a lack of shared language between the east and west might have contributed to that first bit. As to appearances, these peculiar black-haired humans didn't have the ears of elves, and while they were long-lived and seemed to age slowly, they also recognized their mortality, something that most elves weren't terribly concerned with unless there was the sharp end of something poking at their vitals. So, maybe they weren't all that elf-like. They were something not ordinary. Tarfan knew that much, and he knew that he found them quite interesting. That said, he couldn't quite grasp the Fanese beliefs concerning life and honor, and the ingrained role each individual had in society—which came down to serving their 'divine' ruler—that made it functional and prosperous. No strange mage's silver tongue was going to convince him that any man was born to be a peasant and proudly accepted the fact.

Tarfan's thoughts escaped him vocally when he walked into the small camp, toward a small troop of armed men. "And what of you lads? Born with an order from your king in your hands to become soldiers?"

They didn't answer Tarfan because they didn't understand him. They were watching him though, their dark narrow eyes filled with distrust and more than likely some disgust as well. And that, he reminded himself, was why he still felt inclined to dub the Fanese and elf-like people.

Tarfan scowled at them on principle, but couldn't help admiring their armor and weapons, now that he saw them up close again. The armor made him think of dragon scales, the way it was layered and glossed, and brightly colored. Beneath the laminated tunics their clothes were as colorful, and they were close-fitting in comparison to the extravagant robes other men of their culture wore, such as the scholar they were unquestionably guarding. The soldiers also wore leather boots and elaborate, but also functional, helms that protected their necks to the shoulders as well as their heads. Monstrous golden faces adorned various places of their armor, such as at the belt and at each shoulder, giving the appearance that the armor had come to life and was in the process of devouring the arm—though Tarfan doubted that was quite what the effect was meant to be. They wore broad swords with intricately carved hilts and hand guards, and Tarfan saw long spears adorned with tassels and feathers leaning against one of the tents. Two of the men held such a weapon upright as they guarded what was evidently their master's tent. The Fanese people were a strange lot, but they seemed to have their military affairs in order. What better way to claim the advantage over an enemy than to scare the living hells out of them?

Tarfan feared for the bandits that might overlook their fierce presentation and try to take advantage of this foreign caravan. And the bodyguards weren't even the worst of it. In Sheng Fan, as in almost every other society throughout Dryth, the mages were what a body truly had to watch out for. The more harmless they seemed, the more dangerous they often were. Tarfan would have given this camp a berth ten miles wide if he didn't happen to consider this particular mage an old friend.

"What's going on? Who are these people?"

Tarfan had almost forgotten his young niece was in tow. He looked back at her to give explanation, but stopped short, verbally and physically, when someone else decided to do it for him.

"We are travelers from afar, madam, basking in the gentle hospitality this land never fails to bestow upon us."

Tarfan hadn't forgotten the man's soft, pleasant voice. He also hadn't been able to forget the way the mystic presented himself and carried himself, as elegantly as a heron, without seeming at all ridiculous or decadent.

The mystic pressed his hands together and bowed at the waist, "Master Fairwind, I am honored to be in your country and in your company again. I apologize for my lack of notice, but I departed in some haste from Sheng Fan."

"Stand up straight, lad," Tarfan barked. "You're too tall to be doing me any favors by bending in half!"

Slowly, airily, the mystic straightened. A vague smile appeared on his lips. "It is clear that you have not changed. I am glad, my friend."

"Friend?" Taya blurted, staring wide-eyed at the beautiful stranger. "Tarfan, you know this … person?"

"His name is Xu Liang," Tarfan said. "He comes from a realm not yet on any maps known to this region. Xu Liang, this is my niece, Taya Fairwind."

Xu Liang turned toward the young dwarf-woman and bowed. "I am honored."

Taya took a step back and eyed the raven-haired, opal-skinned human as if he were a troll proposing marriage. If her face showed anymore disgust, Tarfan might have been inclined to backhand it. She had the ill manners and thick skull of her father, that much was all too certain. When she glanced at her uncle and saw the disapproval glaring in his eyes, she managed to alter her features to mild petulance by the time Xu Liang stood straight again.

Tarfan sucked in a breath and held it for a moment, then said to the mystic, "So, tell me, what shot you across the Sea of Tahn and up old Wolf's Fang so fast that you couldn't send word ahead? I might have had a proper welcome prepared for you."

Xu Liang angled his head thoughtfully. "Wolf's Fang?"

"You came from Nelayne again, didn't you? You climbed a minor mountain as you strayed from the jagged coast. Wolf's Fang … because the terrain gives the impression of a wolf's jaw, full of sharp teeth."

"Is that what you call it?" Xu Liang bowed slightly this time. "You must excuse me." And then he turned and retreated back into his tent.

Tarfan started after him.

Taya caught his arm. "He's … he dresses like a woman." As she hissed the words she glanced at the guards as if they might be listening in, when they actually hadn't understood anything she or Tarfan—or even Xu Liang in that moment—had said. They were educated in war only. The only language they knew was that which they had been raised to speak in their homeland.

"Plenty of mages wear robes," Tarfan said to his overly concerned niece.

"He's eerie," Taya concluded. "That ill feeling I had before is returning. We should leave now."

Tarfan freed his arm and took hold of hers in the process. "Come along, lass. There's nothing to be afraid of here."

"Afraid?" Taya reclaimed her arm and stuck her chin out indignantly. "I am not afraid."

"Then you won't mind stepping inside and sharing a bit of wine with a polite stranger." Tarfan went into the tent with Taya reluctantly following. "You did bring that peculiar brew of yours, didn't you?"

Xu Liang glanced up from the small wooden table he was kneeling behind, then continued making confident but thoughtful strokes with a small brush on a sheet of unfurled parchment. "I assume you are referring to wine? I don't have any personally, but my men would be more than willing to share."

Yes, to share the pointy ends of their spears with an offensive little barbarian. Tarfan recalled the looks they'd given him, then just as easily forgot the alcohol when his gaze settled on the remarkably detailed map spread before his foreign friend. He caught motion in the corner of his vision and was forced to notice the simple, yet elaborate sketch that had drawn his niece away from the tent's entrance. The landscape was one of several modest, but beautiful paintings upon curling parchment, laid out along the wall of the tent.

"You're a man of many talents, Xu Liang," Tarfan said.

Xu Liang's attention stayed with the map he was altering. "It may never be as accurate as yours, I fear. There is so much yet to be seen and learned of this realm."

A cloud of dismay moved across the scholar's fair features with his last statement. Tarfan had never seen such an expression on his friend's face and asked firmly, though not without some delicacy toward the potential of unhappy subjects, "What brings you to Stormbright?"

Xu Liang closed his eyes and set down his writing brush. He said quietly, "A great evil is stirring in Sheng Fan. It threatens to destroy all that the Emperor, and now the Empress, have struggled to build and maintain."

Tarfan went to the small table and sat down opposite of the mystic. "I'm listening."

"I thought you might," Xu Liang said with a nod. "I came to Stormbright to call upon your services, Tarfan. You know this region and those neighboring it far better than I. My knowledge of the land would not be so dire an issue, as I am always willing to expand it and to take my time doing so. However, time is a thing I do not have in abundance now. As we speak, Empress Song Da-Xiao is under constant attack."

"Attack? From what?"

Xu Liang opened his eyes again, indicating how uneasy this discussion made him. It may have been some years since Tarfan had last seen the man, but they'd met twice in the time Xu Liang had spent outside of his homeland. On one occasion they'd embarked together on a lengthy journey to the cold mountains of northern Andaria in search of an ancient city. They had come to know each other well and, being that Tarfan could claim no other Sheng Fan allies, he had mastered this one's mannerisms of speech and expression, and they had not changed at all. Tarfan could tell that this was not one of those trifling matters Xu Liang had already come up with a half dozen solutions to before it had even truly become annoying. This was serious. Tarfan could tell also that the man was blaming himself for something.

"For many years there has been a state of civil unrest in my homeland," the mystic said. "As you know I have dedicated much of my life to assisting the Song family in its struggle to maintain a peaceful and unified Sheng Fan. Mostly that has been done through my scholarship. An unwise advisor cannot hope to advise wisely. Neither can an absent one, and I fear now that I have been absent too many times when my emperor has needed me. I tried not to make the same mistake after his death. I limited my travels and even formed a bond with the young empress that goes beyond my office. I did this all to be certain that there would be no challenge she would have to face alone. And yet, she faces her most dire threat … and I am not where I belong."

Tarfan gave his friend a space of silence, then said, "You've got uprisings in your empire and here you are agonizing about not being there. A fair guess would be that you're not here to draw maps and paint landscapes."

The faintest smile drew to Xu Liang's lips. "No, my friend."

In the brief silence that followed, the uncharacteristic look of chagrin overshadowed the mage's calm mien once again. "As much as I have dedicated my life to supporting the Song family, I have surrendered it to the study of artifacts. There are six in particular that I must find for the Empress, as quickly as possible. You see, it is not the uprisings that I fear, but the Dragon."

SEVEN

Anatomy of a Myth

THE STORY OF the dragon Chaos unfolded in all its culturally preserved wonder, excluding no detail, even as the storyteller was forced to take pauses when considering Calliprian words that would satisfy the Fanese legend. The language being spoken was not exclusive to Callipry, and was perhaps better known as the common tongue of men and dwarves in the region expanding farther west and into the south. It had a broad range of words to choose from, but Xu Liang hadn't quite grasped how to use all of them appropriately and as well the slower—for lack of a better word—tongue of the western world seemed to extract much of the grace from the telling of the ancient story.

Somehow Xu Liang managed to get through it and when he opened his eyes at the end of his tale, he saw that his audience sat enthralled. Either that, or they were utterly befuddled.

Tarfan's mouth hung and his brow furrowed while he pondered the legend, or the words themselves. His niece sat wide-eyed beside him, seeming uncertain whether to smile wistfully or frown skeptically. A humorous amalgamation of both expressions adorned her round face.

And then, finally, Tarfan said, "You can't be serious!"

Xu Liang gently asked, "About what?"

The dwarf seemed shocked by the return question. He looked to his niece—who shrugged—then back at Xu Liang. He shook his head tersely. "You can't sit there and tell me that you—a highly educated man—believe some prehistoric lizard is going to stir awake under the earth, tear his way out, and send us all into oblivion!"

Xu Liang raised his eyebrows in amusement, and with some relief. "I don't believe that I did."

Flustered, the dwarf folded his arms tightly across his chest. "Well, what are you saying then?" he grumbled.

"There are truths in legend, but all legend is not to be taken as truth," Xu Liang said, and he selected his next words carefully. "I know that the Celestial Blades exist, that they are magical and connected to one another, even if they were not delivered to us by the Ancient Gods."

Tarfan nodded gruffly. "All right. I follow you. You want the Swords, but what about the dragon attacking your empress? You did say dragon, if you'll recall."

Xu Liang inclined his head. "Yes. And the legend spoke of Spirit Dragons, shadowy guardians of the Infernal Regions. Perhaps what threatens Sheng Fan is an entity without physical form, an ancient spirit trapped and looking to escape after a long sleep. I know that there are living dragons in the world. I have seen one now myself, and felt its majestic presence." Xu Liang closed his eyes and held the memory for a moment when it surfaced. Then he sighed. "In Sheng Fan, I have felt another great presence, though it is of no mortal creature. Something awakens, and while I may not know precisely what it is, I know that it must be stopped and that the Swords are the key to its undoing."

The dwarves stared at him for a long, silent moment.

And then Tarfan asked, "What makes you think they're here?"

Patiently, Xu Liang said, "Lend me one of your maps and I will show you."

Tarfan reached into his haversack cooperatively and eventually fished out a rolled parchment, one of several. He leaned forward and spread it across the small table as Xu Liang slid his own map aside. As expected, it showed a detailed illustration of the western continent and a portion of a southern one as well. Xu Liang made a few precise folds on his own map, which displayed what he knew of the east. It included Neidra and the southwestern continent of Dehura, which was separated from Sheng Fan by a small sea, as well as Aer to the north and also the uppermost continent to the west of Aer called Yvaria. After making the careful folds, he slid his map over Tarfan's, bringing the known world together. The dwarvish characters beside those of the Fanese writing system presented an encouraging contrast.

"There," Xu Liang said quietly. "What do you see?"

The dwarf squinted and considered. At length he said, "I see a deformed horseshoe."

Xu Liang suppressed a laugh. He turned the map around so that it faced the dwarf right-side up, then traced the outer edges of the continents with one finger, connecting them where the oceans kept them apart, beginning with Dehura. "Look closely, my friend, and see here, the snout ... and the edge of its crest as its head is turned just so ... its neck curled with its body..." He traced the northern continents. "The back arcing here..."

"I don't see it," Tarfan grumbled.

"I do!" his niece spoke up proudly. She leaned over the map. "Here's where its leg would be tucked." She bit her lip, then stabbed southeastern Xun and southwestern Neidra respectively, connecting the two with an imaginary line. "The eyes would be here and here, and the brow would come across like this." She lifted her hand and studied the image she was creating in her mind. "But it doesn't have a tail, unless it's under the ocean."

Xu Liang lightly touched her small hand as it jabbed at the southern Sea of Kryden, and slid it to the beginnings of a land labeled Cadihn on Tarfan's map. "Or unless it begins here and curls just below the body, and we simply haven't discovered it yet."

Her cheeks flushed with embarrassment and she slipped her hand away. "Oh," she said softly and sat back, looking at the small rug beneath them and the table.

"That's as vague as the constellations," Tarfan complained.

"And yet," Xu Liang argued patiently, "the constellations hold significant meaning to almost all peoples."

"So what's your point? I thought you weren't taking that legend literally."

Xu Liang thought a moment, then said, "Remember that the dragon was referred to in the legend as Chaos. The Swords are weapons against chaos. Weapons against the dragon."

Tarfan kept his green eyes on the map, and slowly shook his head. Finally, flustered, he threw his hands out. "Confound it, mage! Are you going to explain all of this to me, or are you going to make me figure it out myself? If it's the latter, get me a large ale and I'll see you in the morning!"

Xu Liang sighed. There were times when the dwarf's patience proved as stunted as his frame. "It is my theory that the legend not only explains how such impressive items as the Celestial Swords came into being, but that it might also suggest where they can be found, using the dragon as a map and the map of Dryth as the dragon. Supporting the theory is 'Pang Xiu's Manual for Slaying a Dragon'."

Both dwarves looked at him.

"Whose manual for what?" Taya blurted.

Xu Liang waved his hand dismissively. "It's an obscure manuscript, I know, but even the strangest writings can be useful when regarded properly." He pointed to the map again. "According to the manual there are six vital points to every dragon; the heart, stomach, spine, lungs, and each of its eyes...and these points are where one must attack it."

"Hey! You said there were six swords," Taya recalled, smiling again as her enthusiasm returned.

Xu Liang nodded and continued. "As the manual reads: 'Stab through its eyes and it cannot see. Cut open its stomach and it cannot eat. Severe its spine and it cannot move. Puncture its lungs and it cannot breathe. Impale its heart and it must die.' By coincidence or intent, the Spear of Heaven and Pearl Moon were acquired, one in Xun and one in Du...which lies just to the north and east of Neidra."

"The second eye," Taya pointed out.

"Yes," Xu Liang said. "And both were brought here, to the Imperial City."

"Which is just above where the first eye would be," the young dwarf said.

Finally, Tarfan joined in. "If those are the eyes, then that would make Upper Yvaria the spine," the dwarf said, stabbing the Northern Continent with one stout finger.

Xu Liang hated to contradict him, now that he'd decided to become involved, but... "Recall that chaos has returned to the world. The Dragon is awakening. As it uncurls its body the different parts move. I know this is drastic, but I believe the spine is rather here." He touched Tarfan's illustrated line of rigid mountains curving through the lands of Lower Yvaria and Andaria.

"The Alabaster Range," Tarfan mumbled thoughtfully. "I suppose it does have a certain spinal look about it. Well...what about the organs, then? The beast's midsection seems to be submerged."

"Chaos was considered a creature of evil," Xu Liang said. "Perhaps the heart would be cold. Upper Yvaria?"

Tarfan shrugged. "What about Aer?"

Xu Liang shook his head. "I have searched Aer for many years and found nothing. I believe, if any of the other Swords had been discovered they would have been mentioned in local legend or rumors."

"And the lungs? As I hear it, dragons breathe fire. The deserts of Cadihn are about as hot as hot comes."

"Perhaps so, but the lungs and the heart are close to one another in the body. Again, I will look to the Northern Continent."

"That leaves the stomach," Tarfan said. "The stomach relates to food. I imagine a dragon would require a lot of it. Maybe a lot of mutton." He pulled at his thick whiskers for a moment, then stabbed the map.

Xu Liang, whose ideas on the location of the stomach had been faltering, looked eagerly.

The dwarf explained the large nation he'd selected. "You'll find no place that raises more sheep and sustains more pastures than Treska, the land of the ignorant, aggressive, self-deluded, common man."

Xu Liang overlooked the dwarf's less than generous appraisal of Treska's inhabitants and said, "That's far from here."

Tarfan nodded and lifted his finger. "Through the elven lands. The Shillan elves aren't so bad, but the Zaldaine are a sure pain in the backside. Elitists, the lot of them, and warlike. Worse than your people, if you'll forgive my saying so."

"Of course," Xu Liang replied absently, his concentration on the large nation of Treska and the various routes to it. Not only were there the lands of the elves to consider, there was also a great river that nearly split the Western Continent down the middle. It drew out of the Andarian mountains, seeming to almost intentionally divide the elves and humans before splitting the southern nation of Caleddon and branching off into various parts of the Sea of Orlan.

Tarfan saw what Xu Liang studied. "They call it The Strand, ironically. It's the biggest river in all Dryth. At least, the biggest I've ever come across. Big enough to serve as an effective natural border between lands better off separated. There'd be a river of blood if not water."

Xu Liang looked up, startled by this information.

"Elves and humans have despised one another since their creation," Tarfan said. "The humans of the western land can never seem to have enough power, following the will of one god, whom they believe is the wisest and most just, and who must therefore cancel all others. The elves look down on men as a lot of hideous, blasphemous brutes who defile everything they touch. There may be some truth in that, considering some men I've met, but unfortunately, ordinary men breed much faster than elves. And they have a strange knack for accomplishment. They'll have this land, someday, then maybe they'll look to Sheng Fan, where—judging by its size and what I've learned of your people—they'll be soundly thrashed."

Not if Sheng Fan destroys itself from within, Xu Liang thought miserably.

They all looked at the map for several moments, each lost in their own thoughts.

And then Tarfan said, "It's pretty far-fetched."

"I know," Xu Liang admitted. "But the Ancient Gods have some say in this as well. In the legend, it was the sun and the moon, each with two servants, that gave up their beloved weapons. The sun rises in the east—Sheng Fan, where the spear wielded by Cheng Yu was discovered. The moon was shining full the night before the sword of Mei Qiao came into my possession. This place is called Stormbright."

Tarfan considered. At length, he said, "There's no such blade in these parts. I can tell you that much certainly. Anyway Callipry doesn't seem to fit with your 'dragon anatomy' theory. Yvaria, on the other hand, does. You'll not get a worse storm than that which brews in the Flatlands just north of the Alabaster Range. Most your worst storms occur during the peak of the day. There's one of your sun god's servants … maybe."

It was Xu Liang's turn to consider. "Perhaps," he said, thankful that he might have found a destination. Wandering without aim wasted so much precious time.

The dwarf seemed to be in the midst of a brainstorm. He tapped the Northern Continent next and said seriously, "Night lasts the longest here, right where you said the creature's icy heart should be."

"It's something to start with," Xu Liang said, sitting back. "And it's more than I hoped for when I left my homeland. I thank you."

Tarfan stood, his eyes filled with adventure. "Thank me when we find those blades, mage! I'm coming with you!"

❖ ❖ ❖ ❖ ❖

"YVARIA?" TAYA WAILED. "Are you out of your mind? I can't go to Yvaria!"

"Don't be difficult," Tarfan said, carefully packing his haversack after returning home and emptying it. "We were setting off to Shillan this morning. It's no farther away. We just need a few different things to cope with the colder air." He picked up a flask and stroked it lovingly. "Something warmer to drink," he murmured before tucking the brandy away.

"I can't go to Yvaria!" Taya insisted.

"Then stay here!" Tarfan barked. He looked around his cluttered cabin set in the forest well away from the Stormbright Caverns.

He preferred life above ground, someplace easier to get to when he returned from a long trip. He was a dwarf that defied tradition, rejecting any tools that weren't helpful in climbing mountains rather than digging through them. It upset his family for a long time, but they remembered his name easily enough in a pinch, most recently when Taya's parents passed away. Tarfan was the oldest brother of twelve. It was his responsibility to take in his orphaned niece. He did and it had not been easy. Three years of adolescent mayhem! She'd been struck with wanderlust as well; the intense desire to wander as far away from authority as she could get. She would probably jump at the chance to be left alone and to fend for herself, even in this nightmare of things out of place.

The young dwarf woman stamped her foot. "You said we were going to leave Stormbright this season and go someplace exciting! What's exciting about a gigantic heap of cold rocks?"

Tarfan went back to his packing at the round table in the center of the main room. "Weren't you listening to Xu Liang, about the dragon and the magic swords?"

"The dragon isn't real, and getting eaten isn't exciting. It's disgusting. Anyway, why should we be concerned about his magic swords? I think he's crazy."

"Oh ... crazy. I see. That's why you were as enthusiastic as a knee-tall youngster in a baker's kitchen when you saw the dragon's image in those maps."

Tarfan picked up his fattest journal, bound in green leather, featureless except for a small silver stamp in the shape of a leafy tree, a shield traced around it—not as a militaristic symbol, but as a sign of guardianship. To the elves of Shillan the tree itself represented the harmonious growth of nature and knowledge, both theirs to protect. It was a Shillan scholar who'd given Tarfan the blank book, as a token of friendship. If not for their intolerant cousins to the south, the Shillan elves might just have made for good neighbors, for men as well as for dwarves.

He was reminded of his friend from the distant east and slipped the journal in his bag, along with a quill and a bottle of ink. Then he closed it up and turned to his young niece, whose face was flushed with silent embarrassment.

"I'm going with the mage," he concluded. "You can come along, or you can stay here and sort through this mess, and wait to have all your questions about Fanese myth and legend answered when I get back."

"All right," Taya gave in, as Tarfan knew she would once he piqued her curiosity. "But I still have a bad feeling about this."

"I'll document that later. Xu Liang's camp is a couple hours away and daylight's fading. I don't want him to think we changed our minds."

◆ ◆ ◆ ◆ ◆

XU LIANG HAD turned the topic of discussion as was necessary to make it acceptable to the dwarves, who he'd found to be very practical, if not very stubborn creatures. Tarfan's reaction to the possibility of a resurrected dragon god came as closed as he should have expected. Xu Liang didn't know himself whether or not he believed it himself, but the tremors beneath his homeland were real and growing in intensity. Soon it would not take one as sensitive as he had trained to be to feel them. And they were not normal quakes. Something was rising in Sheng Fan, something terrible.

Take heart, my empress. I have found an ally who will assist me in finding the others. He knows these lands well and he is worthy of your trust.

"You were hurt, my brother."

I am well. You must not trouble yourself with such concerns. It is you that the land needs most of all.

Xu Liang opened his eyes and felt a pang of remorse deep inside of him. Song Da-Xiao had called him brother since he returned to the Imperial City and learned of Song Lu's death. Seeing her sorrow and her fear at being left alone among corrupt officials, skeptical warriors, and dangerously apprehensive family members, he immediately took an oath with her, that they would be from that day forward as brother and sister. Beyond his station and obligations, he would support her always and defend her to his last, dying breath. It was a mutual pact usually made between Fanese men—soldiers most often—but it seemed appropriate under the circumstances. There was no one to adopt her, who would not try to seize power of the Empire and for the same reasons—and considering her age at the time of Song Lu's death—there was no one to marry her. She'd lost a father and brother. Xu Liang did all that he could to replace some of her loss and to inspire her strength. He feared, however, that she had come to rely on him too heavily.

Xu Liang sighed in a useless attempt to try and alleviate some of the weight he bore. Then he stood and emerged from his tent into the cooling night air. He smelled rain faintly as a storm passed to the north.

Gai Ping approached and knelt before him. "My lord, the little ones return."

Xu Liang nodded. "See that they are made comfortable for the night and treated with respect. We set out in the morning."

Gai Ping inclined his head obediently and left.

Xu Liang's gaze wandered north. The storm breeze stirred long strands of his black hair as he turned his face into it. He felt a sudden sense of foreboding as he watched the sky above the treetops flash with the reflection of distant lightning.

A blade of storm ... would they find it beyond the mountains, in the shadow of the Dragon's spine? And who would be carrying it?

EİGHT
Knight of Andaria

DARKNESS AGAIN. *Always darkness—even by day. Is there no light left in this world that will shine upon me? I have never acted with malice in my heart. I have never sought to harm. I wanted only to protect. God, why have you turned away from me?*

Tristus Edainien considered throwing his head back and screaming the question at the blackened sky, but he refrained, held by the bitter fact that he would not be answered.

"Perhaps there is no one to answer me," he mumbled to himself. "Perhaps my faith has been misplaced in nothing ... a void."

His jaw muscles began to work involuntarily.

"If only my memory would be swallowed by such darkness."

Shame and anger filled his weary body, made wearier with the white-gold partial plate armor of the Order. Specifically, it had belonged to his father, who died in service to the One God. Tristus felt like a desperate thief taking it from his parents' home after having his own armor stripped from him by the Order Masters at the Eristan Citadel. He had been cast out and retained no rights pertaining to the Order, least of all the right to don such a symbolic suit. There was no question what it represented, and he was inviting trouble by flaunting it.

But what else could he do? He needed armor and to sell his father's for the sake of purchasing other armor was unthinkable. Besides this had all come in error. He'd earned the right to wear this armor and to serve as a Holy Knight of Eris. He would plead his case in the sacred city itself, to the winged children of the One

God, who above all—even the laws and ethics of mortal men—enforced justice. They were the true swords of God and the guides of mankind. They would have the answers Tristus sought. They had to. There was no one else.

Tristus—young still, though he felt ancient—wiped his gloved hand over his face and pushed errant brown curls away from his eyes, mentally retracing the steps behind him. He started further back than he intended, recalling his childhood, how as an under-sized child it was believed that he wasn't meant for the Order. He had been taught early to accept a path less physically demanding and saw more books than practice swords. Yet he wanted more than anything to become a knight, a protector. He abandoned his books whenever his mother wasn't watching to practice with the other boys. They accepted him out of respect for his father, a hero in Andaria. He worked hard, slowly gained inches, and his thin frame began to fill out. It was eventually decided that he would follow in his father's footsteps after all. Tristus followed those steps diligently, and at some point lost his way, straying onto a path so foul and so twisted as to make him wonder if he'd left the natural world alto-gether and come upon a living hell. Perhaps, then, he could never reach Eris. Perhaps here it didn't exist.

Even if that were true, he would never abandon his search; it was all he had left.

He'd been among the Alabaster Mountains almost since leaving his hometown of Tesina more than a month ago. The region had been growing steadily less wooded, the openness exposing the pale rocky terrain that had given the vast range its name. It ran south to north, spreading wider in some regions, invading the dark pine woods of lower Yvaria to the east, and spilling onto the otherwise featureless plains known as the Flatlands on the other side. At their center the great river wound through steep cliffs and stark canyons that looked like vast cracks separating what was once united. Heavy clouds skirted the peaks, forming a pocket of tolerably chill air between the cold rock and freezing upper air. The winds were sudden and powerful, deadly to one who chanced walking too near a ledge. They were deadly to a human, anyway. The mountain goats and elk didn't seem threatened, not even by Tristus, who may have been the first human to set foot across their uninviting terrain in years, maybe longer. What had they to fear with the angels pro-tecting them?

As quickly as the thought came, it blackened. Were the angels protecting them?

Tristus despised his moodiness, his depressing angst over the life that had been taken from him and his unnatural determination to have it back. Unnatural...why that word?

Because you're not natural, he thought and scowled at the ugly memories it summoned. Eventually the scowl dulled and he was simply sad again, existing in pathetic mockery to all that his father's armor stood for.

"Idiot," he mumbled. "You don't even know where you're going. You're wandering like the homeless fool that you are. And now it's begun to snow."

The flakes began their descent without warning, drifting slowly at first, then dropping heavy and constant, obscuring his bearings. Tristus had decided to walk his horse—as if he would sense a sudden drop any quicker than the animal. He couldn't say how long he'd been on foot, but stopped abruptly when a sudden shriek penetrated the heavy air. A moment before, he'd heard only his and his horse's footsteps, along with the newly falling snow, which had begun to accumulate quickly. The shriek sounded somehow out of place through the whispering curtain of heavy flakes and cold air. It might have been a bird, but it was not one he'd ever heard the like of. It made a hideous sound, like death's cry.

"Could you possibly be more dismal?" he asked himself, tasting the bitter sarcasm as it sounded.

Tristus frowned and moved slowly forward, unsure if he was headed toward the sound or away from it. His hand dropped unconsciously onto the hilt of his sword while the other gripped the reins. His breath preceded him in small, frosty clouds. The rapidly descending flakes melted and refroze as they landed on his warm skin. He felt the cold stinging his brow and cheeks, stiffening his mouth. Absently, he drew up the hood of his cloak, then dropped his hand once again to his sword, more swiftly now, as he heard a man cry out.

More shrieks like the first followed the human sound. Tristus thought surely that they were coming from ahead of him, maybe not far. He acted on impulse, abandoning his horse and running through the curtains of snow, toward Heaven only knew what.

◆ ◆ ◆ ◆ ◆

IT SEEMED TO take an eternity to get to the source of the sounds. For a moment Tristus thought he'd strayed far away from them. And then snow suddenly burst up from the ground ahead of him, like a wave breaking on the shore. A heavy sheet of white fanned as it descended, blending once again with the rest that which blanketed the ground.

Tristus descried two forms in the near distance, two humanoid shapes in mortal struggle. The black cloak of one individual billowed behind it while the thick ivory cape worn by the other was flattened beneath the body. The man in black was hovering over his pinned opponent, clawing at him with his bare hands.

Tristus moved to stop them, calling out, but his voice was drowned by a sudden, deep ringing sound, as if someone had struck an enormous bell in the river canyon far below. A blinding flash of golden light followed and Tristus had to turn his face away. The shriek sounded again, clashing horridly with the lingering chime. When Tristus dared to look, the combatants were apart, but far from finished.

The warrior with the white cloak was on his feet, making visible the silver-gold plate armor that adorned his chest and shoulders. The rest of his attire, not including the heavy cape, appeared little more than a white belted tunic. In his hands he gripped a spear of palest gold, or of platinum. It was beautiful, accented by the stoic grace of the man wielding it. His opponent was as a shadow in comparison, featureless and dark, and carrying no weapon. It should have been no contest.

And it was with that thought that Tristus stole a second look at the feral dark man, who was no man at all, but some manner of beast. The face was twisted and grotesque, black as its naked flesh with two yellow slits glaring from it. There were sharp horns protruding from its brow. Its ears were more pointed than the purest-blooded elf and it had a tail that lashed beneath a mantle not of cloth, but of leathery skin and delicate bone. They were wings, not billowing in the wind, but stretched out behind it as it stood riled and vicious before its enemy.

"My ... God..." Tristus breathed, his previously frozen jaw suddenly feeling slack.

With the words, the winged beast turned its foul head and focused deliberately on Tristus. The look of malevolence in the thing's golden eyes was so pure it made Tristus want to wretch, but he could do nothing. Paralyzed with sudden fear, he could only stare as the demon shifted in the snow on taloned feet and came at him.

Voices assailed him moments before the beast did. "Get out of here," one shouted. "Move now!"

Another hissed, possibly only in his mind. *"Pathetic mortal! I shall peel the skin from your flesh and drink the blood until there is nothing left of you but a heap of bone and dry tissue. Even in death my image will be burned upon your eyes for all eternity. You will learn that one of your kind does not look upon mine lightly."*

Tristus stood utterly still, staring evil in the face. He now had a face to give to evil, and the demon was right; he would see it forever. He would never forget the distorted mockery of a man's face, the eyes golden slits, the brow sharp and rigid, the tongue lashing out of its thin-lipped and fanged mouth.

It was gliding toward him, wings outstretched, slim black arms reaching.

Tristus was on the ground before he knew it. The air erupted out of his lungs and he gained none of it back as long hands coiled around his neck, squeezing and scratching at once with clawed fingers. All Tristus could think was that he had been damned. His journey into Hell had been predetermined, but why? He wasn't evil. He'd never once acted with malice in his heart.

"To act as an instrument of evil, whether willingly or unwittingly, is the same as to be evil. Your remorse earns you life, Tristus Edainien, but you no longer have a place here."

The past words of the Order Master attacked him nearly as brutally as the demon. Both brought tears of pain to his eyes and drained him of all will. He would die in darkness. Such was his fate.

Mother, Father ... forgive me.

He closed his eyes and still saw the demon, grinning madly as it choked the life out of him.

◆ ◆ ◆ ◆ ◆

HE OPENED HIS eyes to darkness, cold and bleak. The Abyss?

"It is only night," someone said, as if in answer. "Do not be afraid."

Tristus sat up slowly, feeling groggy but otherwise well. He touched his neck, searching for claw marks that weren't there. He looked around at snow, sparse trees, and the incessant cloud layer that hid the mountaintops from view. "What ... what's happened?"

He slowly focused on the man sitting nearby. The sculpted face appeared improbably haggard with weariness and his white cloak hung sullied and tattered at his back. The stains appeared to be blood. Perhaps the claws had raked his back. He seemed unharmed otherwise.

In answer to Tristus' question, the man said, "You were attacked by a shade demon. Above all things, they resent humans, as to them they are shades of their past. A past so distant that it is no longer truly connected to humans. Still, they harbor a deadly grudge." He sighed and his breath seemed to shudder. "Do not worry, though. It is gone. You are safe now."

Somehow Tristus believed that.

The man smiled somewhat, as if sensing Tristus' unquestioning trust. His lips smiled, but there was pain in his eyes … eyes the color of sky and light.

That pain drew Tristus forward with concern. "What of you? Are you injured?"

The stranger surprised him by saying, "I am dying."

Tristus instantly wanted to help. He rose to his knees, not knowing what to do, but feeling that he should do something. "Where are you hurt?" Even as the question formed he recalled the demon's long nails scratching his own neck and instinctively lifted his hand to touch wounds that weren't there. He watched the man, watching him, and said, "You healed me, didn't you?"

"Yes," the man answered quietly, displaying almost no emotion and not a trace of fear, even as he seemed to be fading right in front of Tristus.

"There must be … something that can be done for you."

"There is nothing to be done for me," the man said. "Perhaps, were things as they should be, I might survive, but they are not and I will die soon … for now. I'm sorry you must witness this, but I could not bring myself to leave your side."

"What do you mean? What are you talking about?"

"The demon's touch, while harmful to you, is poison to me … in my state."

"I don't…" Tristus looked again at the man's white cloak, seeing the blood and shreds anew. He saw the feathers half fallen, sticking out at unnatural angles. Bone gleamed through in some places. Blood-sodden tufts of down scattered the snow around him.

Tears came immediately to Tristus' eyes as he realized just what he was witnessing; an angel, dying. Perhaps he'd gone farther on his quest than he believed he could. Perhaps, atop one of these enshrouded peaks lay Eris, the Kingdom of the Angels, God's winged children.

"You are not destined to darkness," the angel suddenly said, inspiring Tristus to look into his eyes that were a shade so pale as to almost have no color at all. While Tristus marveled at this, the angel added, "Your life shall last as long as your will, in whatever light you choose to follow."

The tears finally escaped and tumbled down Tristus' cold cheeks.

"I cannot grant you redemption," the angel furthered to say. "Forgiveness will redeem you, when you are ready. Though I fear that is a long way off, for it is a heavy burden that you bear upon your heart. Perhaps I can offer you this light as comfort on your shrouded journey ... Knight of Andaria." The angel picked up his spear that had been lying in the snow beside him and passed it solemnly to Tristus. "Its name is *Dawnfire*."

Slowly, reverently, Tristus pulled *Dawnfire* into his grasp. For a timeless span, he and the angel held the glorious weapon together. Tristus looked into the beauteous creature's crystalline gaze and wanted to say so many things, but exhaustion suddenly overcame him and not a word escaped as he lowered the spear into his lap and fell fast asleep where he sat.

♦ ♦ ♦ ♦ ♦

WHEN TRISTUS OPENED his eyes again, it was day. The angel was nowhere to be seen and his hands were empty. He thought at first that he'd dreamt the event still fresh in his memory. And then he spied the spear resting beside him in the snow that was already melting in the filtered morning sun. He hesitated before touching the weapon again, then slowly reached his hand toward it and stroked the cool platinum shaft before carefully curling his fingers around it. He lifted it, surprised by how light it was—from tip to butt it was easily as tall as him. He marveled at the craftsmanship and then wondered if he'd gone mad. Did an angel truly mean for him to have such a fantastic weapon? An outcast from the very order of knights devoted to the Angels of Eris? What would the Order Masters have to say now, and the priests?

They would call him a liar and a blasphemer. They would never believe he had been chosen to behold such a miracle, to be saved by one of the True God's children and then granted its heavenly blade. They would believe the account of the demon more readily, and they would blame its trickery for his delusions and then confiscate the spear as a tool of evil's will. How could the faith of such righteous men be so selective as to question a miracle and turn it to devilry so easily? Perhaps if it had happened to someone else...

But it happened to me. This weapon came to me. I will not question it.

Tristus took up the spear, then placed it neatly on the ground directly in front of him and knelt solemnly before it. He prayed, and in his prayers he vowed never to allow evil to be performed with or upon the blade entrusted to him. "I will continue to serve your will, God, beloved Father of Heaven. And I shall not forget the sacrifice made by your messenger, whose name I did not know, but whose memory I shall embrace for as long as I am upon this world and afterward, should you permit my passage. I thank you, dear God, for this gift and for your blessing and for your guidance." At the end of his prayer, he touched the tips of two fingers successively to his forehead, his lips, and his heart, where the starburst-behind-a-sword insignia of the Order happened to be engraved upon his armor.

Then he stood with renewed determination and found his horse standing patiently where he'd left it, grazing on a patch of freshly exposed grass. The short blades glistened with beads of melted snow in the hazy shafts of sunlight penetrating the cloud canopy. He spent the next several moments rigging straps to hold his new weapon in place with the rest of his gear, which wasn't much. Once that task was complete, he mounted and set off in the same direction he'd been going. Though he was no longer certain he was looking for Eris, he knew he didn't want to return home.

Perhaps it would be better if he left Andaria altogether, at least for a while. The light of *Dawnfire* may have been glorious, but it still could not burn away the awful memories or the guilt that came with recalling them.

NİNE
Whispers of Chaos

THE INN OF the Howling Wolf had a bustling, cheerful air about it, and at the same time, it invoked an underlying sense of gloom. After several days' travel from Stormbright into Lower Yvaria, the company felt not only weary, but chilled. As the air gradually cooled around them, so that even a soft spring rain felt icy soaking through their clothing, the chill swiftly began to bite down on their spirits as well as their flesh and bones. There was something profoundly disturbing about the deep forest they'd entered and something indescribably unsettling about the broad smiles and loud voices of the patrons crowding into the lodge at Nidwohlen.

Half the bodyguards came in with Xu Liang, Tarfan, and his young niece. The others stayed outside, watching over the horses and equipment along one of the town's forested paths. The manner in which Nidwohlen had been built among the woods, which lay beneath the beginnings of the Alabaster Range, added a shadowed depth that only furthered to instill the sense of isolation and discomfort.

Xu Liang's exploration into this region had never brought him to this village before. He had come to it now purely as a measure of expedience in getting into the mountains, since crossing them seemed the best way to reach the Flatlands on the other side.

"You feel it, too," Tarfan observed, several minutes after they'd seated themselves at an unoccupied table in a corner near the common room's large, blazing hearth. "There's something peculiar about this place."

"Gypsies," Taya whispered, as if in explanation, but when Xu Liang glanced at her, he saw that her eyes were elsewhere.

The mystic discreetly followed her gaze to one of the larger tables near the bar, where a crowd of at least a dozen colorfully dressed individuals carried on multiple animated conversations at once. Men and women alike were laughing and drinking, and where there weren't enough chairs for everyone two of the women sat in the laps of men, who balanced them with one hand and drank large mugs of ale with the other. Xu Liang contained the feelings of disgust rising within him at their public display. He was far from Sheng Fan now and unqualified to judge the behavior of those he would encounter.

Tarfan seemed to disagree. He quaffed from his mug, then blanched at the sight of the gypsies. "Bah! Disgusting folk! Wild ... weird. Don't trust them." He stabbed the rough wooden table with his forefinger to emphasize. "And that's a fair warning, friend!"

Xu Liang simply listened and said nothing. He watched the gypsies curiously until someone coughed beside him. He looked to the young guard as Guang Ci made a sour face and shoved the cup of western alcohol at arm's length across the table.

Tarfan laughed derisively. "What's the matter, boy? Can't handle your drink?"

Unable to understand the words, Guang Ci answered the dwarf's tone with a scowl and said to Xu Liang in Fanese, "It is swill. These barbarians poison themselves."

"There are some 'barbarians' who would say the same of us if they tasted our food and drink," Xu Liang answered. "Which, I'll add, we have brought with us in limited supply. Perhaps it will be in your interest to not taste some of what you consume on this journey."

The guard nodded regardfully, then said, "I wish that I could get by as you do, my lord, without having to taste anything but the clear water of Mount Ding Zhu."

"And when that runs out, I will taste nothing at all," Xu Liang told him seriously. "It is a great risk that I take with my body for the sake of keeping my spirit at its strongest. The Empress and I are depending on the strength of your body, Guang Ci, and at a time such as this, of your stomach."

Guang Ci grimaced and recovered his cup, looking pale when a skillet of red meat and vegetables, still boiling in grease, arrived shortly afterward, placed down by a barmaid wearing a full skirt and a puffy-sleeved, low cut shirt with multiple stains. Her yellow-brown hair was carelessly pinned up, slipping from the loose binding in tendrils that clung to her face in the overheated barroom air. She set bowls and forks out before the company of foreigners.

"Is there anything else I can get for you?" the barmaid asked in the most common Yvarian dialect, which both Xu Liang and Tarfan understood. The dwarf answered her and when she left he was the first to begin filling his bowl with the steaming western recipe. Taya followed closely. The guards took their time. It was evident in their faces that they envied their fellow guards outside, who had been charged with watch duty and would be dining on Fanese rations beneath the large dark trees of the Hollowen Forest.

The meal was taken in slowly, even by the previously eager dwarves, as the strangeness of the place—for a moment uplifted by Guang Ci's and Tarfan's outburst—began to settle again.

Xu Liang stared at the empty bowl in front of him, not seeing it as he contemplated their trek through the Yvarian mountains, recalling that the Alabaster Range was much more treacherous than the mountains of Ying, which had wider passes and less jagged ledges. Xu Liang almost consulted Tarfan about what he would consider the quickest, safest route, but he maintained his silence when he sensed someone approaching. He looked at the slim youngish man long before anyone else might have noticed him, startling him briefly.

At first the individual who'd strayed from the table of gypsies halted, a look of astonishment on his bold, dark features. Then he smiled somewhat crookedly and swaggered to the table of strangers, a half-empty mug in his hand. He was dressed modestly in comparison to some of his fellows, wearing black trousers and a full-sleeved white shirt, unlaced to his breastbone, along with a deep red vest adorned with embroidered patterns that formed no discernible images. Small golden hoops dangled from both ears, which were partly hidden by his thick crown of wild black curls. His eyes were dark and cunning.

The gypsy stopped at the end of the company's table and finished off his ale before speaking. He wiped his mouth with his sleeve and finally said, "Would those be your men outside?"

"And if they are?" Tarfan replied gruffly.

The gypsy seemed more amused by the dwarf's rough tone than offended or intimidated. He traded his empty glass for Tarfan's, throwing back the swallow that remained, then looking at the dry mug with disappointment. He said, "Best to get them inside, little man."

The dwarf began to rumble, his face reddening. "Little man! You outstretched, bauble-wearing..."

Xu Liang intervened. "May I ask what inspires such advice?"

The gypsy looked at him. His smile broadened with amusement. He set down the misappropriated mug and leaned slowly over the table, glancing over all of its occupants before settling his dark gaze once more on Xu Liang. He said, "You may, yes."

Xu Liang did not repeat himself. He met the man's gaze coolly in the silence that followed, waiting for his answer.

The opportunity for fun slowly escaped the gypsy, and a frown came to his lips just before he straightened and said seriously, if not somewhat bored, "Evil dwells in the forest of night. Best get your men in, I say."

Xu Liang inclined his head in acknowledgment and looked to Tarfan as the gypsy sauntered away. "Do you know what he speaks of?"

The dwarf shrugged. "Gypsy superstition! They make their living on startling the ignorant with their tricks and lies. Sometimes they take themselves too seriously, particularly when they're drunk." He glared at the empty mugs in front of him. "There's nothing worse than a soused gypsy!"

"Perhaps," Xu Liang said softly. Then he rose. His bodyguards did as well. "Only one of you," he said in Fanese. "The others stay with the dwarves. Protect them if the need arises, exercising only what force is necessary. It is not my desire to build a reputation for myself in this land. Guang Ci, accompany me." He switched to Tarfan's preferred tongue. "My friend, I will return shortly. I wish to see for myself if the man speaks only nonsense."

Xu Liang departed, and across the common room of the Howling Wolf, the gypsy troupe watched over the rims of tipped glasses and out of the corners of their eyes.

♦ ♦ ♦ ♦ ♦

"GYPSIES," TARFAN murmured with disgust. Then he glanced at the three guards left behind, sitting rigid and unsure in the absence of their master. It was clear that he wondered what Xu Liang had said to them before leaving.

Beside her uncle, Taya took in slow forkfuls of food, her eyes wandering the crowd. The gypsies were the most colorful of the locals, by their look, their manner, and their talk. The rest of the patrons consisted of a smattering of townsfolk, keeping loudly to themselves. In spite of the mage's obvious foreign aspect—foreign beyond what most Yvarians experienced in their simple lifetimes— not one person outside of the gypsies so much as glanced at them, and the gypsies lost interest quickly. Xu Liang and her uncle were right. The place was odd.

Taya's eyes continued to wander from table to table, eventually settling on a pair she hadn't noticed before. Though much of their features were obscured in the shadow of the distant corner they occupied, they didn't look Yvarian. Taya tried to get a better look at them, but they were wearing thick black cloaks with the hoods drawn up so that their faces were darkened from view. There was food in front of them, but they didn't seem to be eating. She stared at them in silent wonder until dinner at her own table was interrupted for the second time.

"You travel with strange folk, dwarf," a large, bearded man was saying.

Taya watched as the heavyset gypsy took Xu Liang's seat, continuing to speak to her uncle. The ill feeling she'd experienced days ago was coming back.

The red-vested youth from before smiled at his companion from the end of the table, arms folded casually across his chest. "Stranger than us? Strahm, you injure me."

Strahm chuckled, inviting others at the gypsy table to laugh as well. The bodyguards sat quietly in their places around the table, obeying whatever orders Xu Liang had given them, paying no attention to a conversation they couldn't understand.

"Strange armor," the large gypsy said when some of the laughter subsided, glancing at one of the bodyguards. "Doesn't look like anything forged in Stormbright to me."

"Neither is the dagger your friend's fingering," Tarfan growled, and Taya discreetly lowered her hand to her sword's hilt.

She sighed with relief when the red-vested man spread his hands before him as if in a display of peace, though she didn't like his crooked smile.

"Where do you suppose they come from, dressed like that?" the one called Strahm asked.

His companion shrugged. "Where does a soldier don armor adorned with demon faces? Where are the lords slight and delicate as a painted doll?"

"Evondorf," Strahm blurted. "The count and his sons, as frail as his daughters, oozing in riches, speaking with their long noses in the air."

The other held up a finger in contradiction. "But this stranger is not oozing in riches, none but the silk of his robes and his hair. And his nose is not all that long, nor is it in the air. Yet, there is an eerie confidence about him, like he knows something that we do not."

Tarfan laughed. "If it's the man's intelligence that intimidates you unsightly orphans, go back to your caravan! It's the only place you'll find people as dung-headed as yourselves!"

Surprisingly, the gypsy ignored the statement and concluded his own. "He is not from any class or part of Yvaria, my friends. He is as strange as strangers come, and..."

"And?" Strahm prompted, as if he'd rehearsed the cue.

The other gypsy's smile faded slowly. "And I think that I smell magic."

"Would you be referring to real magic over your gypsy trickery?" Tarfan barked.

The gypsies bristled now and Taya's heart leapt into her throat. She wasn't afraid, but she always felt a small rise of panic before a fight began. Her uncle seemed to stir a lot of them—particularly when he'd suffered too much to drink—and he was busily stirring at the moment.

"I advise insolent rabble such as yourselves to go back to your drinks and your women before I give you a taste of something that was forged in Stormbright!"

The larger gypsy stood, throwing back his chair in the process. Tarfan shot up as well, reaching for the war hammer at his back. He climbed up onto his chair, then stepped one foot onto the table, glaring at the gypsy. Taya hopped down from her own seat, unsheathing her short sword while the red-vested gypsy presented his dagger and his larger companion balled his enormous fists. The other gypsies were just beginning to move away from their table, either to watch or to help, when the bodyguards made their presence known.

Each of the Fanese men rose nearly unseen out of their seats, grabbed up the swords leaning beside the chairs, and tore them from their scabbards. They rushed the gypsies, knocking them back in such a fierce tide of action that Taya was sure they'd killed them on the spot. Somehow the gypsies lived through the moment and slowly picked themselves up off the floor, standing wide-eyed and unsure at the ends of the guards' bloodless swords. One of them hissed at the gypsies in Fanese, clearly giving a first and final warning as to what would happen if they tried anything else.

Tarfan watched the gypsies back away scowling and hoisted his hammer onto his shoulder. He chuckled. "I almost forgot what it was like having these lads around!" He looked to Taya, who stood dumbstruck and filled with adrenaline that had nowhere to go. Her uncle said, "Never wonder how the mage has managed to live as long as he has."

Taya just shook her head.

♦ ♦ ♦ ♦ ♦

WIND STIRRED THE tops of the trees high overhead, none of it reaching the town scattered beneath them. The pole-hung lanterns stayed motionless along the dirt paths that connected one building to the next, casting shadows upon the shadows. An owl alighted on one of the low wooden poles, then fluttered away into the depth of the night to continue its search for a meal. Horses milled about. Many of them were attached to carts, some of which were completely enclosed with doors at the rear to allow entrance. Lanterns adorned nearly every cart, and a few of them were glowing, perhaps in a vain attempt to add more light to what seemed unwilling to be lit.

The darkness hadn't quite settled this deeply when Xu Liang and the others arrived in Nidwohlen. It would not have mattered, except that this darkness had a presence to it, a will almost. The gypsy might have been correct in his claim. And now Xu Liang was faced with the decision of bringing his men indoors and entrusting the horses and much of the equipment to the respect—or lack thereof—of these strangers, or attempting to leave Nidwohlen now.

They had entered the Hollowen Forest at its southeastern edge and traveled only a few hours in. Tarfan's maps showed that the mountains were less than a day from the town. However, less than a day could be most of a night and while they had lanterns, firelight did not seem effective against such a thick cover of darkness.

"Lord Xu Liang," Guang Ci spoke. "What troubles you?"

The mystic turned to face the bodyguards, having forgotten for a moment that they were standing with him in the shadows. He looked into each of their faces, searching now for that instinct of theirs that had forewarned him of the rogues at Li Ting. He saw only the restlessness of men too far from their homeland. Perhaps he was reading too far into the darkness of the Hollowen Forest and the strangeness of Nidwohlen's residents. He started to speak to his men, but then fell silent when one of their horses suddenly jerked its head and pulled away from the pole its reins were wrapped around.

Gai Ping went to the animal to calm it, begging the assistance of his fellows as the others started to panic as well. Xu Liang looked around at the horses belonging to Yvarians and noticed that all of them acted nervously, though none quite so nervous as his own. Undoubtedly, like the villagers, these animals were more accustomed to whatever moved through the darkness here.

A nearby presence stole the mystic's attention. Xu Liang looked to one of the enclosed wagons sharing the bole of the enormous conifer the company had stopped beside earlier in the evening. He watched a thin old woman move slowly down the two steps suspended beneath the wagon's door. She leaned heavily on a plain walking stick. Once on the ground she stood in the warm glow spilling out from what may have been her home and began to speak to the still air around her. "It is chaos that makes them uneasy."

Xu Liang frowned pensively, wondering at her choice in words. Was she unconsciously referencing the Dragon, like Cai Shi-meng when he'd written about the *Spear of Heaven* as a weapon against chaos? The unlikeliness of that almost brought an amused smile to his lips as he pictured himself a paranoid doomsayer on a mad quest for weapons that would come together and do nothing more than glow a bit brighter than they might have on their own. And then he thought of what he'd felt in his homeland, and what his empress felt, and all traces of mirth drained from him in the very instant. Somehow the Dragon was real. Somehow it was waking.

"Or being awakened," the old woman suddenly said, and she looked directly at Xu Liang. She smiled a toothless smile at his silent dismay. She had read his mind.

"Yes, I can hear your thoughts, young man. Come," she beckoned. "Come closer and talk to me for a little while."

Xu Liang recovered himself and his manners, bowing respectfully at the waist. "Forgive my rudeness, madam. I was not expecting to meet one of such talent."

"Come," she said again.

Sensing nothing at all threatening about her, Xu Liang stepped closer. He bowed again. "I am honored."

Before he straightened, she took his hand, pressing her thin, old skin upon his own that was smooth from lack of toil and from the youth he managed still to hold onto while his mind seemed to age at a much more rapid pace.

"Let me see you," the elder said.

Xu Liang didn't understand, until she reached her other hand up to his face and he finally realized that her white eyes weren't looking at him. He held still while her gentle fingertips traveled over his features, stroking his brow and cheeks, and carefully tracing the soft shape of his mouth and the smooth edges of his jaw.

"You are a lovely man," she concluded. Then, almost affectionately, she touched his cheek once more with the back of her hand. She added, "And not from Yvaria."

"No," Xu Liang said truthfully. "My homeland lies far to the east."

The woman nodded. "Yes. It is there where your heart breaks."

Xu Liang did not deny her statement. "I fear my homeland will soon be in ruins." He didn't realize the woman still had his hand until she squeezed it comfortingly.

"Weep not for what you may lose," she whispered. "But for what you have already lost. A wound that is seen and recognized is one more quickly healed."

Xu Liang couldn't honestly say that he didn't understand her, and it was thinking that he might have known what she meant that prompted him to slide away from the subject. "Forgive my diversion, madam, but you mentioned that the horses fear chaos. What did you mean by that?"

She let go of his hand and touched her ear. "Listen. You hear it as well. The whispers of chaos. It comes and it has many messengers to announce its coming."

Xu Liang straightened and closed his eyes, hearing nothing but the stirring of the horses and the wind in the very tops of the trees. He realized shortly that he was hearing what the old woman meant for him to hear, for it made him feel watched and unsafe. He looked at her again and asked, "What messengers of chaos are there in Yvaria?"

"Not a dragon," she said, wrapping her knit shawl closer about her shoulders. "In Yvaria chaos has come on black wings, but not a dragon's wings." She lifted her chin and closed her cataractous eyes, seeming to absorb the impure wind. And then she said, "Yvaria has the keirveshen."

"The keirveshen?"

The woman nodded slowly, opening her unseeing eyes again. "It has always had the keirveshen, but their numbers are growing. There are not as many to hunt them as there once were."

"What are they?" Xu Liang asked.

The elder turned on him suddenly, and gripped his arm in both hands, tightly. A look of fear came to her face. "You must heed my words, wise child of the East! You will survive the darkness. That is not for you to fear, but when all around you is bright … that is when chaos will come for you! Fire will consume you, and while you escape the burning, the heat will smother you slowly!"

She left him in the next instant, heading back for her cart, climbing the steps much quicker than she'd descended them, and closing herself in.

Xu Liang stared after her, slow to absorb having had his death foretold to him by a western seer. Eventually he saw the dwarf staring back at him from the other side of the cart.

"Don't listen to her," Tarfan advised. "Never trust a gypsy! Lies and trickery." He continued mumbling as he came forward, Taya and the rest of the bodyguards behind him.

"Did something happen?" Xu Liang inquired, seeing the tension in the guards' faces and the unease in Taya's as she continually looked over her shoulder.

"We got tired of waiting for you," Tarfan said quickly, then cleared his throat a little too deliberately and stepped around Xu Liang.

Xu Liang recalled the dwarf's short temper, and didn't have to ask any more questions.

"Are we leaving here now?" Taya asked impatiently. When Xu Liang nodded, she stomped around him, grumbling. "This is not what I meant by exciting!"

Xu Liang stood alone for a moment. Slowly, his eyes sought the old woman's cart. He could hear her inside, humming to herself, sounding suddenly unafraid. Eventually he turned away and joined the others of his group, preparing to push on through the oppressive darkness.

♦ ♦ ♦ ♦ ♦

AS THEY MOVED away from Nidwohlen, the companions began to feel the wind, seeping through the edges of the Hollowen, rustling the branches and stirring the shadows as the lanterns Tarfan and four of the bodyguards held up swayed in their grasps. Most of the company walked, since four horses had been the fee for boarding the *Swimming Dragon* back in Sheng Fan. Four imperial horses may have seemed exorbitant to some, but Xu Liang insisted, after the owner of the fishing junk had agreed to perform the service to the Empress without cost, having guessed as to Xu Liang's station through his dress, manner and rumors fisherman often heard of the sorcerers in service at the Imperial City. The man stood to miss a day's fishing and since it would be burdensome to travel with eight horses aboard ships and through mountains, it seemed adequate compensation for the journey and the humbled man's silence.

Tarfan, who was used to long treks on foot, led the way with the ever-alert Guang Ci close behind him. Two more guards with lanterns walked just after them. In the middle of their small caravan, Xu Liang rode upon the one of their horses that could not have been sold, a gray steed named Blue Crane, given to him by the late Emperor shortly before his passing. Gai Ping rode beside him to his left and to Xu Liang's right, Taya sat upon what had previously been Guang Ci's mount. At the rear, one bodyguard walked the horse bearing most of their equipment, flanked by the last two men, who also carried lanterns.

Of course, the light did nothing in the way of covering their passage, but it enabled them to travel faster. The guards were trained for long marches and little sleep. A veteran like Gai Ping had endured far worse than this. As to Xu Liang, riding upon such a fine animal as Blue Crane, who walked with a smooth gait and rarely panicked—the darkness over Nidwohlen was an unusual occurrence—he was able to concentrate on his meditation. The longer the journey lasted, the more he would come to depend on it, and on Blue Crane. Once he returned to Sheng Fan, it would take considerable time and caution to resume a normal habit of living. An event such as what had taken place aboard the *Pride of Celestia* was a danger he could not afford again. He should have listened to Fu Ran and stayed well away from danger, but he could not, on good conscience, abandon the others to those who seemed determined to be his enemies.

Thinking about the Fanese giant made Xu Liang think about his younger years at the Imperial City. He recalled himself at just eighteen, arguing duty with Fu Ran, who only aggravated the situation by constantly grinning and making light of what his friend –and master, at the time—believed were exceedingly wise words. Even Xu Liang suffered a stage of youth where his ego had swollen to almost unbearable proportions, and he realized now that because of it, he may have been the primary cause for Fu Ran's flight from his homeland.

Before he'd matured enough to truly possess wisdom, and to become an advisor to the Emperor, Xu Liang had only knowledge and a blind love for the Empire and its sovereign, like so many others in his position. Fu Ran's rogue nature at the time frustrated and angered him, as no one nor anything ever did or ever could. Not even the loss of the Emperor, whom he'd grown to trust as a father, inspired anger in him. He recalled feeling only sadness then, and again with Song Lu's death. In both instances, especially Song Lu's assassination, Xu Liang had duty to overwhelm any emotions and keep them safely at bay while he focused on keeping the Song in their rightful place.

Gai Ping's voice pulled him from the memories. "My lord, the air grows colder by the moment."

Xu Liang answered the unspoken question without looking at the elder. "I'm all right, Gai Ping. I apologize for concerning you."

"You … seem distracted," the guard ventured.

Xu Liang nodded. "A little. Perhaps."

On his other side, Taya joined in, unknowingly repeating what Gai Ping had just said in Fanese. "You look bothered by something. Is it what that old gypsy woman said to you?"

"No," Xu Liang replied patiently. "I am aware of my own mortality, so it does not disturb me to have someone reveal my death to me."

"Do you believe she was telling the truth?" the young dwarf asked. "Do you think she really knows about such things?"

"I cannot say. Truthfully, it does not matter. The telling was so vague that it would be impossible to recognize the moment when it came."

Taya seemed to disagree. She said flatly, "It was fire. The old woman said you'd die in a fire."

Xu Liang glanced at her sidelong. "Did she? A fire would be bright, but what fire can consume a body without burning it? Perhaps she meant that a fire would surround me, that I would be trapped somehow and die slowly choking on the ash and smoke. Perhaps she only used the word fire and meant something else entirely, as is often the case with oracles." Xu Liang sighed. "Or perhaps she meant nothing at all and it was, as your uncle calls it, inane babble."

Taya looked at him for a long, thoughtful moment, then said, "You don't believe that."

Xu Liang shook his head. "No. I believe that it meant something, but I choose not to dwell on its meaning. There are other matters that concern me more."

"Like the Swords."

"Yes. Like the…"

Xu Liang didn't finish his statement, drawing Blue Crane to an easy halt and calling to the others to stop as well. The wind was growing steadily stronger. Soon it was blowing the lanterns almost horizontally in the bearers' grasp. Xu Liang had decided to carry *Pearl Moon* at his belt once they started into the wilderness. He watched now as it began to cast its pale blue glow with such intensity that it bled through the scabbard. "Tarfan, something's coming!"

The dwarf was already on his way back, struggling on his strong, short legs as the sudden gale tried to push him into the horses. "I sense it, too! It feels like a blasted dragon!"

"We should douse the lights!" Taya suggested, holding tight to the reins of her mount as her dark hair was blown out of its binding in the wild wind. She turned her head to protect her eyes from bits of dirt blasting her eyes at it blasted her skin.

"The moon's begun its descent! We'll be in pitch darkness," Tarfan argued.

And then the flames in the western style lanterns went out, and left them no choice. Blackness tumbled over them as if a god had thrown down a blanket over the world, granting them a heart-stopping instant of true night before *Pearl Moon's* glow came through, highlighting traces of the world around Xu Liang as the eerie lighting hovered around the boundaries of his vision.

The wind died, and all was suddenly quiet.

Xu Liang held his breath, feeling his uneasy heartbeat but not hearing it. He could not see the others, only vague outlines of what was immediately near him. He kept thinking of the gypsy seer's word for Yvaria's evil: keirveshen. Keirveshen, in the traditional Yvarian tongue—that of its oldest inhabitants—meant 'shadow folk', people of shadow.

Sound slowly returned to the forest, but it was no sound any of the companions delighted in hearing. It was the shuffle of many feet, the clacking of many thin objects upon the branches, and a chorus of sporadic flutters. Xu Liang thought of birds settling on perches, or bats...hundreds of them.

Chaos has come on black wings...

Xu Liang thought frantically, but this was no way to find him at his best. He served the Empire with study and planning. He could not fight what he could not see. Certainly, he could cast no winds without the risk of harming one or more of the others. Whatever had come had done so on its own wind besides, and would likely be unaffected by a spell that could never match the intensity of such a gale without many weeks of meditation. A spell such as that would probably have been Xu Liang's last, even preparing for it. His only recourse was his blade, but there was only one *Pearl Moon,* and maybe hundreds of the enemy. Hundreds that would overwhelm his blind companions before they even realized what had come at them. His hand rested on the hilt of the Celestial Blade, his thoughts reeling.

"*Keirveshen! Ellum lathar Aerkiren!*"

The voice rang out of the darkness, pure and confident, a resonance like nothing Xu Liang had ever heard. It carried an almost physical force, one that calmed at first and then inspired action in the next instant. The mystic drew *Pearl Moon* and held the glorious sword skyward, forming a beacon with its glow. The light filtered down the magic blade, illuminating the bearer and forming a shimmering dome around all in his company.

In the seconds that followed, the shadows stirred. Forms threw themselves at the dome and were deflected, just as *Pearl Moon* would deflect another blade in combat. Ripples of magic radiated throughout the dome where winged attackers struck, like stones dropped in water. However, this water could not be penetrated. Xu Liang and the others were safe for now in the soft, protecting glow of Mei Qiao's robes.

Outside, hoof beats pounded through the deeper darkness beyond *Pearl Moon*'s radiance. The unknown rider was illuminated in sporadic blinks of violet light as his weapon painted swaths of magic upon the shadows. Creatures shrieked and died, and fled in terror—what little they knew of it. Their child-sized humanoid shapes danced in the light of the dome and writhed in the lightning strokes of the other blade... a Celestial Sword.

They had found one, in the shadow of the dragon's spine.

TEN
The Twilight Blade

DAWN BROUGHT THEM to the edge of the Hollowen Forest, where they took rest and waited. At some point during the night, *Pearl Moon* had ceased to glow and Xu Liang knew the threat had gone, but so too had the other Celestial Blade and its bearer. They would wait for him, as long as was necessary.

• • ◆ • •

TARFAN WAS BEGINNING to worry. The mystic sat at the edge of their camp with an eerie possessedness about him as he stared back into the woods that had disgorged them in a heap of fright and confusion. All but Xu Liang. After the sword spell, he had one focus; the foul Hollowen. Not the forest itself, Tarfan knew, but the ghost that had passed through it and frightened away the devils. The mystic claimed it had been a sword, one of the Celestial Blades he'd devoted so much of his life researching. Maybe, in that respect, he ought to know, but no one else had seen anything. One instant they were in sightless blackness and the next they were trapped beneath an overturned bowl of sorcery, praying the fiends left outside wouldn't claw their way through. Under the mystic's shield, Taya had had the presence of mind to relight a few of the lanterns, and once the sword's spell lifted, they bolted.

And now, here they sat, too close to the very woods that had tried to kill them the night before.

Tarfan sighed, gnawing disinterestedly on a tear of dried venison while Taya slept and the guards organized themselves and the gear. When the oldest one walked past him, heading toward Xu Liang, Tarfan stopped him by grabbing his elbow. The man, carrying a small bowl in both hands, looked down at him without expression, managing to make Tarfan feel two feet smaller in the process. Still, with gruff confidence, he detained the man and said, "Is that some of the mage's holy water? I'll take it to him."

The guard continued to stare, silent. He frowned with disapproval when Tarfan made a careful reach for the bowl. The dwarf sighed. He hated to offend anyone, but resorted to the crudest most understandable form of communication he could think of. Indicating the bowl with one hand, he patted his chest with the other, then pointed toward Xu Liang.

The man's almond-shaped eyes narrowed. Tarfan's insides clenched and all he could think of was the swift, sudden movement that had taken the gypsies down at the Inn of the Howling Wolf.

And then the guard spoke, bending to offer the bowl. Tarfan didn't understand the words, but the man gesticulated as he spoke in such a way that he understood he was being warned not to spill the dish's precious contents. Tarfan promised with a nod and thanked him, and proceeded to take slow, cautious steps toward the mystic.

"Breakfast is served, lad. Drink up!"

Xu Liang turned at the waist, accepting the small bowl in one hand with such grace that Tarfan felt like a lame-footed muck goblin in comparison. Not so much as a drop escaped as the mystic brought the dish to his lips and drank its contents down. When he was finished, he held the dish in his lap in both hands and thanked Tarfan.

"Shouldn't you be taking this opportunity to meditate?" the dwarf asked with concern he couldn't hide.

"I acquired much rest during the early days of our journey from Stormbright. I will be fine. Thank you."

Tarfan followed the mystic's gaze into the forest and he sighed, sitting down on the ground next to him. "How do you know this stranger will come?"

"The Blades call to each other and, as a consequence, so do the bearers."

"How can you know that? You can't count your empress with her magic spear."

"No, you're right," Xu Liang said. "I cannot. Duty and my sense of kinship with the Songs have always drawn me to my empress. I learned this about the Swords last night, when *Pearl Moon* answered that blade and I responded to its bearer. It is one of the Celestial Swords, Tarfan. There is no mistake."

Tarfan drew in a long breath and held it for a moment, studying the bleak, empty conifer forest. Echoing birdcalls filtered out of the thick woods, haunting notes that seemed to mourn life rather than announce it. At length the dwarf said, "What if he got caught up in hunting down those beasts and chased them halfway back to whatever hell they fluttered out of? Maybe he's too preoccupied to..."

The words tapered into stunned silence when an ivory horse and a rider equally pale strode out of the Hollowen. The man, fair in face as well as form, was dressed entirely in white—shades of white, which included the plush pale silver of his tunic as well as all clasps and buckles required to keep the various articles in place, all of which were silver. The fabric of his heavy cloak blended almost perfectly with his ivory skin and the white-gold of his long, thick hair, which was braided back tightly, adorned with a single silver-white owl's feather, in the tradition of a certain secluded mountain people of Upper Yvaria.

The man, Tarfan realized suddenly, was no man, but an elf.

♦ ♦ ♦ ♦ ♦

THERE IS NO REASON for me to be here, Alere thought to himself.

And yet, he could not take his eyes off the bearer of the blue sword. The frail man emanated an aura like nothing he had ever seen or felt. It went beyond the strange call of their blades. This man was as a ghost, more spirit than body. It wasn't a wonder his party had attracted so many of the demons. They thrived on quenching souls. The brighter the soul, the more satisfying its death was to them. The perverse creatures must have been salivating, anticipating this kill.

Aerkiren had cut their foul, lashing tongues from their devils' maws. It had taken other parts of them as well; tails, hands, heads...there was not much left of the brood that had been skulking in the deeper night of the Hollowen. While *Aerkiren* had destroyed them, the other blade had simply stopped them, cold and fearful as Alere had never imagined the shadow folk could be. They were afraid of what drew Alere. They were afraid of the strength of this man's soul, that had radiated through his sword last night and threatened to destroy them utterly. Still, the keirveshen's fear would not last.

I should be on my way, Alere thought. *There are more demons to quell.*

Even as his mind prompted him to move on, his mouth betrayed him by speaking out to the strangers. "Who are you people?" he asked in a tone that spoke neither friend nor foe. He chose the language used by most of the dwarves and men of the south, as the human did not look Yvarian. Of course, the silk-clad stranger did not look Andarian or Calliprian either. Perhaps Treskan.

The peculiar man stood before Alere had decided on his origin. Pressing his slim hands together, he bowed to Alere. It seemed a gesture of respect, and so Alere inclined his head in return, but he said nothing more, awaiting his answer.

The man spoke in a familiar tongue but with a strange accent. "I am called Xu Liang. My companion is known as Tarfan Fairwind. We are honored in your presence."

Alere's eyes narrowed as they fell upon the dwarf. He said, as a mere statement of fact, "Dwarves have never been honored in the presence of anyone, least of all an elf of the upper lands."

The stout creature folded his arms tightly across his chest and began to grumble, confirming that the old wounds acquired between their people many years ago still had not healed. Alere smiled thinly, and was about to take his leave when the human spoke again.

"Your sword speaks to mine. Are you not at all curious about what they are saying?"

"Would you claim to understand the language of swords?" Alere asked, somewhat dubiously.

"It is the language of siblings yearning to be reunited," the delicate foreigner replied, and Alere thought fleetingly of his home in the Verres Mountains. Could these strangers somehow help him get back there faster? Were they also seeking to rid Dryth of its demons? He'd studied them long from the forest and seen that there were warriors among them. Warriors led by this sorcerer, who carried an enchanted blade similar to Alere's? Perhaps.

Alere glanced down at his own sword, drawn to it as the etchings upon the blade began to shine through its sheath. It was singing … in daylight? That had never happened before, except in the midst of combat.

Aerkiren, what is it you are saying?

And then, as if in answer, across the open ground that lay at the edge of the forest, a light began to shine. Alere looked up and saw the human holding out his blade, displaying it as the edges glowed softly blue. Slowly, Alere drew his own blade, and had to squint in the sudden brilliance of both blades shining together.

◆ ◆ ◆ ◆ ◆

XU LIANG SPOKE to the elf of the legend of the Blades, and of his homeland and the events taking place there. In return, the elf gave an account of events that had driven him from his home and his quest to end what he called chaos. Of course, it was a common term for darkness or whatever turmoil a land or people faced, but it was in the inflection of the elf's voice that Xu Liang experienced the recurring and uncanny sensation of a sameness of meaning, just as he'd felt reading Cai Shi-meng's scrolls and listening to the gypsy woman. Yes, chaos was the Dragon, affecting all parts of the world as it rose out of its ancient slumber.

"I do not think my father knew any of this," the elf, calling himself Alere Shaederin, finally said. He was seated on a rock amidst their camp, staring at the two swords lying flat on the ground between he and Xu Liang. They were glowing still, though not as brilliantly as they had upon their introduction. "He believed the blade was of elven make and I would agree, to look at it."

"It may be forged by the hand of an elf," Xu Liang offered. When Alere silently issued his calm gray gaze, he explained further. "I am not as well versed in the history of the elves as I would like to be, but I understand that your people are as ancient as mine. Great cities were constructed in Sheng Fan while the humans of many western cultures existed with whatever shelter nature provided to them. Your kin filled books with words while those same people were still struggling with the spoken word. The legend speaks of the gods casting their weapons down, but perhaps they only cast inspiration down upon our ancestors."

Alere considered. At length, he said, "You speak of a goddess who holds the moon in her robes. It is not my intent to blaspheme, nor do I intend any disrespect toward your beliefs, but is it possible that your goddess and mine are the same, viewed differently?" The elf seemed to replay his own words in his mind, struggling with the notion in spite of how easily it came to him. "The Mother of the Sky protects us beneath her veil," he started.

"Could that veil be an extension of Mei Qiao's robes?" Xu Liang said helpfully. He added simply, "Perhaps."

The elf looked again at the swords, both vastly different yet connected through an undeniable sameness. "This is strange," he whispered. "I have traveled for days and nights, wandered without aim or purpose save to demolish evil where I find it. I don't know what happened at my home those few years ago that seem so distant. I feel that there is a single source to be blamed and to be found ... to be punished, but I know not where to look. These blades coming together may be a sign to follow, but I cannot help wondering it if will lead me astray."

Xu Liang considered carefully. The truth was that he could not let the Twilight Blade—the weapon of one of Mei Qiao's two servants—leave him now that he'd found it. Somehow he had to convince the elf to part with it or to wield it at his side. Neither seemed a reasonable outcome. How could the elf give up a sacred sword that had been in his family for unspecified years, the instrument of his revenge against his parents' killers? At the same time, how could Xu Liang return to Sheng Fan to confront its direst threat with an elven warrior in tow?

There were few in Xu Liang's homeland who were aware of the elves at all, let alone any who recognized them as an accomplished and civilized, as well as reverent, race. Those who had explored outside of Sheng Fan as Xu Liang had were not often as open to what they discovered and frequently rejected it, as they rejected all else not of Fanese origin. As well, this skilled fighter, who'd cut through the shadows like a devil in his own right, made Gai Ping and the others uneasy. Tarfan and his niece did not pose a threat in their eyes, but this one's cold, colorless gaze offered no comfort, not even to the dwarves.

Xu Liang had to admit to himself, after hearing Tarfan's account of the politics between humans and elves in this region, that he was not eager to have an elf quite so near. While Alere seemed completely enrapt in his revenge against all demon kind, what might happen if ingrained prejudices surfaced at just the wrong moment, convincing him that all who were not elf were the same as demon, and just as responsible for the tragedy that had befallen his family?

"I don't know you," Alere said suddenly, and Xu Liang held his breath, his expression calmly neutral. The elf continued. "Yet somehow I believe that I can trust you. I think it is your spirit, speaking to me as the auras of these blades speak to one another."

Xu Liang frowned with wonder. "How so?"

Alere looked at him, his quiet features revealing nothing. "We elves of the north can see such things, and hear them. Your spirit is very strong, stronger than any I've ever come across. I don't know if it is just your magic, or if it is your nature, but I sense no malevolence. Your spirit speaks of loyalty, as was displayed when the magic of your sword spread to protect all who were with you, rather than just yourself."

There was no admiration in the elf's words. He didn't even sound friendly when he spoke them, but Xu Liang was moved and inclined to bow his head and thank Alere for his comments.

"Understand," the elf continued to say, "that I cannot part with my father's sword... but I will join you, Xu Liang, on this quest of yours." He stood and Xu Liang's eyes followed him. He added tonelessly, "For a time."

Xu Liang nodded once more in acceptance to the terms. He watched the elf to his white horse, which he promptly mounted. "Where are you going?"

"Since I have joined this quest, it is in my interest to clear away the litter that has been trailing at your heels." With no further explanation, Alere Shaederin turned his mount around and rode quickly back into the deep woods of the Hollowen.

Xu Liang stood slowly in his wake, and Tarfan arrived beside him.

"Is he leaving then?" the dwarf asked impatiently.

"I believe he will return," Xu Liang answered, still staring into the woods.

Tarfan muttered an oath to himself and stormed away.

"What's happening?" Taya asked, groggily, having recently awakened.

"We're keeping the damned elf!" her uncle barked.

The dwarf maiden yawned. "What elf?"

♦ ♦ ♦ ♦ ♦

ALERE RETURNED TO the forest and waited. As expected, his quarry came to him.

There were two men, one of them quite tall and strongly built. He could not hide his thick form beneath the heavy cloak he wore. The other had nothing to hide. He was neither tall nor short and possessed a lean frame. Both men were armed. Alere had spied them leaving the town of Nidwohlen during his scout of the woods surrounding it. They departed shortly after Xu Liang's caravan and kept a telltale distance, wanting to keep up and also to escape detection.

They had succeeded in neither. Alere had detected them and when the company's lanterns went out, the pair became disoriented in the dark and fell back to what they considered a safe location to wait for dawn's light. In that they must have been successful, since the shadow folk had not left them in unsightly shreds throughout the area. Unfortunate for them. Now that task would fall to another hunter.

When the two humans came into view, Alere drew *Aerkiren* and guided his strong mare Breigh onto their path. He forewent charging and calling out his war cry, decided instead to give these pitiful brigands one chance at escaping with their lives.

The cloaked strangers saw him and stopped. They said nothing and for a moment, neither did Alere. He studied them at this nearer distance, and saw nothing of particular interest. The strong man emanated resilience and stubbornness, which among humans was often interchangeable with stupidity. The other seemed simply quiet, withdrawn.

Finally, Alere said, "I know that you are following a caravan that passed through here last night. I advise you to turn back."

The strong man grew instantly rigid and took a step forward.

Alere didn't so much as twitch, eyeing him coldly, prepared to do what he must.

The other man stopped his companion. It took both hands and stepping in front of him, but the strong man eventually came to reason and drew back. The smarter one turned back to face Alere and drew down his hood, revealing a sun-browned human face with stark Yvarian features. He'd cropped his dark hair short and somehow earned a wide scar across his narrow chin.

Alere wondered if the injury had been acquired before he left his caravan, or after. Gypsies weren't known as seafarers and these men stunk of brine, something Alere had breathed in too much of

on his brief journey across Windra's Channel getting from Upper
Yvaria to Lower. He could almost see the grains of salt embedded
in the man's hardened skin. Without question these two had spent
a great deal of their lives on ships.

"We intend no harm," the former Yvarian said. "We seek only
passage through these woods."

"You're a terrible liar, for a gypsy," Alere informed him, speaking
in tones that would sound even, if not indifferent. It did not matter
to him personally, whether or not the man was lying. "It is my best
guess that you are acting as the large one's guide through territory
you recall from your childhood. Don't tell me you've forgotten what
lurks in the Hollowen Forest. You dared the wrath of the shadow
folk because you could not risk losing the caravan that left Nidwohlen ahead of you."

"And just what is it to you?" the strong man demanded, and the
other reached back his hand reflexively to stop him coming forward
again.

Alere had nothing to conceal and said truthfully, "I have pledged
myself an ally of the man you have been clumsily following. I will
let you go no further. Try, if you dare."

And that, in spite of his companion's urging, was as much as the
strong man was willing to take. He threw back his hood and reached
more swiftly than Alere would have expected for the weapon
hidden at his back. He freed the immense blade and dropped it down
in front of him, his peculiar foreign features distorted worse with
a wide, demonic grin. "I've got ten thousand hells in store for you!
Choose which one you'd like to see first!"

A small frown came to Alere's lips. And then he spurred Breigh
forward, raised his sword, and cried out. "*Ellum lathar Aerkiren!*"

The strong man seemed somewhat taken aback by the sudden,
stark words, but he showed no fear and stared eagerly at his
charging opponent. He waited until Alere was almost upon him,
then predictably lifted his huge sword to unseat him. Alere gave
Breigh the slightest command, which the well-bred mare responded
to automatically and agilely, taking him away from the strong
man's reach. He would turn her about quicker than the overgrown
human could right the awkard blade in his grip. That was Alere's
intent, but he was struck from his saddle after all, taken out of his
seat by a blade he could feel but that he could not see, and which
didn't cut him.

He had the wind knocked out of him twice—once as the invisible force struck him and again as he hit the ground on his back—but he managed to roll onto his knees to block the next attack. The blades hissed and threw sparks as they connected. And now Alere gave a little smile himself. Unbeknownst to his opponent, *Aerkiren* negated all other enchantments belonging to any weapon brought against it. The blow was still heavy, but Alere managed to push the giant back and rolled out of range. He rose to his feet, secure in knowing that there would be no invisible extension of the large sword to be concerned with for the remainder of this battle.

Alere and the giant stalked each other, gradually closing the gap between them.

"Is that all you've got?" The strong man laughed. "A few tricks and quick feet? That's no way to enforce your bold tongue!"

The giant hefted his great sword above his head and swung down.

Alere darted beneath the death arc and slashed at the giant's side as he ran past him. He felt *Aerkiren* bite, but didn't let the blade linger, moving quickly out of range of the sword that was almost as tall as him. He spun about to face the giant, who was readying his powerful weapon again, unconcerned with whatever damage had been done.

"I can do this all day!" the giant boasted.

Alere didn't doubt it, and he didn't have time for this. He glared coldly. A moment was spent in concentration, then he swung his blade out horizontally and watched an arc of twilight glow leap off the edge of the sleek blade, racing across the open space between him and the giant, who didn't rely on his disenchanted weapon to save him.

The man hurled his great body out of the magic's path, slamming into the forest floor. His cloak trailed him in two pieces. The shortened garment fell against his back, the edges still glowing hot as the severed fabric fluttered smoldering to the ground. Now a look of shock came to the giant's features. And then, slowly, he began to laugh.

Alere gave a quick glance to the man's companion, who had at some point found a tree to stand beside, and deemed him no immediate threat. He glared at the giant as the man was standing up, hefting his sword over his back as if to put it away. If they wanted to leave, Alere would let them, but he only granted mercy once to an

opponent not of demon origin. If they persisted with their tracking of Xu Liang and the others, however ineffective, he would kill them.

The giant arranged his sword in its harness, still chuckling. "Xu Liang acquires two things in this world; hell-bent enemies or avid devotees."

"You're wrong," Alere informed him, relaxing his stance, but keeping his blade out. "I am neither."

The giant shrugged. "Give it time."

"I find you strange and annoying," Alere told him. "Whatever your relation to the Fanese sorcerer, you seem to me to pose a future problem. I may have to do away with you after all."

"I don't like you either, sprite, but..."

"I am an elf. And you are doing very little to appeal to any sense of mercy I may have had toward you."

The giant's all but forgotten companion intervened, stepping away from his tree. "He's Fanese by birth and Aeran by adoption. You'll have to forgive him his lacking grasp of the languages of this region." He took another step. "I say again; we intend no harm. Xu Liang was recently aboard our ship. We have a message for him."

"Then why do you skulk behind like rats instead of presenting him with this message?"

"There hasn't been—"

Alere showed the man his sword as he came closer.

The gypsy stopped and Alere summoned Breigh to him with a click of his tongue.

He said to the strangers, "I do not trust you. However, since you are unskilled assassins whom I will have no trouble dispatching, I will allow you to make your way to Xu Liang to present this supposed message."

When the mare arrived, he sheathed *Aerkiren*, then swung himself swiftly into the saddle, looking down upon the humans with impersonal disdain. Their foolishness was a fault of birth first. "I suggest, however, that you hurry. The camp is not far from here, but I sense we will be leaving shortly."

◆ ◆ ◆ ◆ ◆

WHEN FU RAN arrived, understandably he was not in the best of moods. After Alere explained his altercation with the peculiar strangers and gave his description of the 'giant', Xu Liang decided to wait for him. It was clear when the elf and giant saw one another again that there was no favor between them whatsoever, nor was it likely that anything resembling it would develop. The forthright elf showed no signs of being truly offended or threatened by the larger human, but he watched him with distrust in his eyes. It would have been unacceptable to Xu Liang, but for the Twilight Blade and the fact that Alere had cleared their path of demons the night before.

"Why didn't you announce yourself at Nidwohlen?" Xu Liang inquired of Fu Ran, finishing up a painting of the upcoming mountains that he had begun while waiting for the elf to return.

Fu Ran paced behind him, stomping off the anger. "We wanted to keep an eye on that rabble at the inn without them knowing it. If we'd have caught up with you in the woods ... but that sudden wind. We lost you when the lanterns went out."

"And this message that you have for me?"

"Bastien and I have been tracking you from Nelayne," Fu Ran sighed. "The day after *Pride* docked we noticed the ship that pursued us from Sheng Fan coming in. It left in a few hours, but not before letting off a small troop of men, maybe a dozen. I recognized one of them ... from Ti Lao."

Xu Liang lowered his brush, frowning. "And the others?"

"There were two men evidently of some rank or station. The rest were common fighters. Bandits, I suppose. Assassins. Don't ask me how we managed to overshoot them."

Xu Liang ignored the last statement and asked quietly, "One of them was large with a proud face, wearing blue?"

"Yeah," Fu Ran answered. "Do you know who he is?"

"He is the man who ambushed us at the village on the Tunghui River. Our disagreement began there, and we discussed our differences again when those pirates boarded the *Pride of Celestia*. I would not say that we came to a comfortable resolution."

"He's the one that injured you," Fu Ran guessed. Xu Liang heard the big man's fist hitting his open palm. "Bastard!"

"Perhaps they have given up by now," Xu Liang suggested, though he recalled the determination in Xiadao Lu and doubted it. For Fu Ran's sake, he said, "I have encountered no one unexpected from Sheng Fan, other than you. Once we get into the mountains, it is unlikely that anyone will be capable of easily tracking us."

"The Dragon's spine," Fu Ran said suddenly, and somewhat wistfully.

Xu Liang glanced back to see him gazing at the Alabaster Range. The former guard looked at the brush painting next and sighed, "I guess your theory turned out to be correct."

"The elf carries the Twilight Blade," Xu Liang confirmed, feeling strangely happy and depressed at the same time. In a moment, he added, "It seems like I have already been gone for so long, Fu Ran. I have only to find three more, and then I can return, but then there will be a worse struggle as I rush to understand what I know so very little about."

Fu Ran knelt down, not to bow but to rest a hand upon Xu Liang's shoulder in friendship. He said gently, "You're doing all that you can, more than I think even Emperor Song Bao would have asked of you. I know why you've come this far, but no one, nor any blade can truly stop a god. I don't care what the legends say."

Xu Liang agreed. "History is written in eras, and this may be a dark one. The Dragon is a symbol of that darkness. I think the Swords will help to unify the people against it, as they are symbols of balance and protection. That is why I must find them, and bring them to our ... to my empress."

Fu Ran broke a smile and effectively lightened the mood by saying, "It's probably better that the elf can't speak Fanese, then."

◆ ◆ ◆ ◆ ◆

MY BELOVED EMPRESS, as my spirit reaches yours, my body enters the frigid mountains of this fascinating land. We have found the Twilight Blade, or rather, it has come to us from the colder regions even farther north along our journey. It has wandered from Upper Yvaria, where I suspect we will still find one other, the Night Blade. I believe we will discover those once wielded by Cheng Yu's servants in the plains on the other side of these mountains. Perhaps my return will be sooner than I predicted. With the Swords in Sheng Fan you will be triumphant over those forces which threaten to destroy it. You will bring peace to the land and your dynasty will be fortified upon that harmony. Hold strong, my empress.

ELEVEN
The Limits of Sorcery

THE INTERIOR PASSAGES of the Hall of Imperial Peace had been made off limits. The order had been put forth, not by the Empress, but by her unofficial guardian—the Silent Emperor, whose private ambitions may have been hidden from some, but not from others.

Han Quan stood at the end of a deceptively empty corridor, studying the random circular patterns in the stone. Han Quan pressed his hands together and closed his eyes. He spoke softly, repeating the same verse over and over, until strain textured his features and beads of perspiration formed across his brow.

"Curse you, Xu Liang," he muttered tersely at the end of his ineffective chanting.

He calmed himself, then spoke one more word of magic and spread his hands apart, turning his right over to catch the pebble he'd formed of the air. He flicked the stone into the corridor ahead of him and watched the unseen, unheard winds catch it and spiral it violently about the passage. His frown slowly lifted as he watched the pebble hit a void and fall dead to the floor.

"Ah, that is new." Han Quan chuckled to himself. "This will not last, Xu Liang. You will soon learn that a young, pampered whelp such as yourself is no match for one of my wisdom and skill. The Empress will be eating out of my hand long before you return from your hopeless quest and together we will decide your fate, and the fate of Sheng Fan."

Han Quan turned from the Wind Corridor and headed back to the outer passages and courtyards. He knew there were other ways to the central hall, other corridors that would be similarly trapped by the younger scholar-mystic, who distrusted his colleagues, even after his since-famed purging from office of all who struck him too rebellious. An upstart surely, a child without question, but even a rebellious child could hold power and Xu Liang's was not to be taken lightly. He, like all true sorcerers of Sheng Fan, had been mentored by his ancestors in this calling and by the gods themselves—in Xu Liang's case, the gods of the winds. The aeromancer's youth was no statement of his talent, but only a promise as to how much greater it would become if he were permitted to live so long.

If only you would be gracious enough to die in the barbarian lands, Han Quan thought with a small grin. *But that would hardly befit your reputation.*

There were many in the Imperial Court who took their young superior for vain and, of course, he would have to be in some measure. Xu Liang's excessive beauty was no secret—to himself least of all, as it had been the source of much unhappiness for him. This, he had confided to Han Quan, believing his older colleague to be a firm Song loyalist... and he was, he simply was not a supporter of what may soon be the Xu Dynasty, if the Empress did not obtain a new tutor and advisor. It was upon the Song Dynasty that Han Quan's would be built.

Fortunately, Xu Liang was still young enough himself—and vain enough—to be persuaded by flowery words and flattering behavior. He did not suspect his elder of any ill intentions against him and he would not, so long as he didn't return to the Imperial City.

With that thought, Han Quan closed his eyes, feeling the anger behind them burning his eyelids. *Xiadao Lu! Why do you continue to fail me? Bring me Xu Liang's head, if you value your own!*

◆ ◆ ◆ ◆ ◆

SLEEP ENDED abruptly.

Drawn to consciousness by the threat of danger, Xiadao Lu took up the weapon lying beside him and rose quickly to his feet, prepared to gut the intruder. He found no one in the tent and dove quickly into the night beyond to find it empty as well. He heard only the crackling of two torches that kept the small camp lit and the day-old mountain snow eerily aglow. Past the reach of the firelight there existed nothing but deep shadows. Against the starless sky, one could not even make out the silhouettes of the sharp mountain tops surrounding the cliffs. Far below the treacherous landscape was a river canyon with no route down to it—none that could be found, except by accident in the night. Such was the main reason they had elected to make camp shortly after the sun had set, bleeding its last red light over the freezing earth as it dropped out of view. The only way Xiadao Lu coped with the delay was in believing that Xu Liang's group would have to stop as well, else risk plummeting to their deaths in the canyon below.

Still, they had fallen more than a day behind. Ma Shou's sorcery had limits. If they lost too much ground, he might never be able to locate Xu Liang's trail again. Sadly, Ma Shou was not as devoted to his craft as his fellow. He would not give up food and drink, and real sleep for a taste of pure water every third day and a purified soul.

Ma Shou also claimed that, while such strength of spirit would likely bolster his ability to locate Xu Liang, it would undoubtedly attract Xu Liang's attention as well. The Imperial Mystic would sense the strong presence behind him, and he would look over his shoulder and ponder the matter until he understood it. A confrontation would probably result, and while Xiadao Lu would welcome one, Ma Shou reminded him that Xu Liang had not been made Imperial Tactician on a whim, or by a child. It was Emperor Song Bao himself who had recognized the man's skill at defeating an enemy long before a single soldier stepped foot onto the battlefield. He stressed that they must use the element of surprise while it was theirs.

Xiadao Lu did not agree, but he accepted the circumstances for now.

◆ ◆ ◆ ◆ ◆

ALERE WOULD NEVER have guessed to find himself in the company of others on his quest for revenge, least of all one quite so large as the motley troupe he'd been traveling with for nearly three days now. A Fanese sorcerer, a small army of Fanese warriors in demon armor, two dwarves, a wandering giant, and a gypsy sailor. It was strange, but somehow not unsettling to an elf who had fortified his strength in loneliness. The loneliness of being orphaned, of living in a stranger's home, and of the battlefield. He had been prepared to face his hunt alone for as many long years as it took and all too suddenly, he'd found a stranger whose sword spoke in familial tones that *Aerkiren* answered with equal warmth. Not only that, but there were others as well.

Alere marveled at the idea of the Swords being the product of the gods' inspiration. That those same gods might have been summoning them together, calling upon their bearers to take up this war against the evils of Dryth that had been breeding unchecked for far too long. He considered these things with a flute to his lips. The perfectly carved white wood resonated with his mood. His fingers shaped a haunting melody of the somber tone that was carried high and clear on the cold, crisp air.

"It is said that where a mountain elf plays, keirveshen wail in torment," someone said when Alere's song had ended.

Alere lowered his flute and said, "Your people nurture many foolish myths."

The once-gypsy made no sound, but Alere could feel his dark eyes on him.

In a moment Alere added, "The Fanese guardsmen are handling the watches. Shouldn't you be asleep?"

"I have trouble sleeping on land," Bastien admitted. "I have not forgotten the stories told by my people, many of which are not myth."

"Only garishly adorned reality." Alere replied. "The keirveshen need no embellishment. They are hideous enough as they are. They fear an elf's music because only an elf can make it, and they know that a hunter of their kind is near."

"Why do your people hunt them?"

"Humans fear them too greatly. They would rather hide from them and tell tales by firelight, collecting coins for retelling the horrors endured by others."

"And elves don't fear them? Not in the least?"

Alere glanced back at the dark-skinned human. "My people are a doomed race. Our numbers dwindle. Our life spans are beginning to be measured in decades rather than centuries. Long ago, many of us fled the mountains for new regions because of the shadows and those of us left are too few. The shadows are too many for us and yes, my people fear them. While they make corpses of men, they make ghosts of elves."

Bastien frowned softly. "What do you mean?"

"An elf's spirit cannot be taken by shadow. They are left behind when their bodies are destroyed. That is partly why they fear us. Whatever plague attacked Yvaria centuries ago, or longer, elves were immune. Men became twisted shadows of themselves. They became the keirveshen. Elves survived, and as much as they are resented for it, they are feared for it. The demons attack us in legions when they dare and it is a brutal slaying on both sides that takes place." Alere turned around and lifted his gaze to the blackened sky. "For many long years, because of elves like my father, the shadow folk were silent in the Verres Mountains. We had finally reclaimed our home. A bright time lay ahead of us. Our populations would replenish in the peaceful days that followed. We lived as other people and warred with other mortals only when they dared to attack our lands. And then the keirveshen returned, stronger and fouler than they were before."

"They killed your father," Bastien deduced, speaking quietly. "Didn't they?"

Alere did not answer. He lifted his flute once more and resumed his song.

◆ ◆ ◆ ◆ ◆

NO STARS AGAIN this night. Such darkness ... will it never end? Even Dawnfire *is having difficulty penetrating it.*

Tristus glanced at the platinum spear given to him by an angel of Eris. The weapon had begun to glow two days ago—not as intensely as it had against the shade demon, but it glowed nonetheless and there were times when the white-gold hue seemed to intensify. A few moments ago the spear had shone so brightly, Tristus could feel the heat from its magic, but it seemed to be fading now as he proceeded through the night, unable to sleep as he pursued his unknown quest.

Andaria was far behind him now, but the mountains stayed with him. They were colder this far north. The snow fell as stinging bits of ice and the winds raked over the skin like clawed fingers.

In truth Tristus was afraid to sleep, for fear of not waking up after the bitter cold embraced his idle body and seeped beneath his skin, freezing his blood and his heart. He was rapidly losing interest in the mountains and had begun to consider heading east or west to escape what seemed like an endless path. He'd begun to hear things as well. A strange bird that seemed to weep rather than sing. It sounded close sometimes and made him think of death, the angel's death in particular, as if its fellow winged creatures were mourning its passing.

Thinking of the angel made Tristus reconsider the demon it had slain. Could there be more of them? Would he be able to wield *Dawnfire* and save himself, or would those haunting yellow eyes burn into him again and there would be no one like the angel to stay his death?

Death? Tristus wondered, or was it everlasting torment the demon promised? He suddenly felt less concerned.

I already have everlasting torment, don't I? Perhaps there's nothing to fear of demons, after all.

Even as he formed the thought, Tristus felt the tears of despair warm his dry, frozen eyes. The memories always came swiftly, threatening to rush over him with tidal force.

"How long will this last? How long before what is left of my heart can rest?"

He heard the eerie birdsong again. The dreadfully soft melody compounded his sadness and he felt compelled to shout at it.

"Be silent! You foul, heartless creature! Can't you leave me in peace!"

In the next instant, he choked on his voice and lowered it.

"Please stop reminding me. Please…God, let me show you my remorse with my blood rather than my tears. I cannot bear this isolation, this lonely exile." He looked up at the starless sky. "Give me an enemy if you must, but I can't be alone anymore. I can't…"

His answer came with silence. Even the mourning bird had ceased to weep.

Tristus stopped and lowered to his knees, exhausted, the harsh winds of endless winter swirling about him.

◆ ◆ ◆ ◆ ◆

"WHY here?"

Silence filled the passageway within the Temple of Divine Tranquility; the Jade Hall, it was called. Jiao Ren looked from one section of carved green stone to the next, and at the flickering firelight that shone through the panels of jade tracery separating the hall from the innermost sanctum of the temple. And then he looked at the older man in rust-toned and pale blue-patterned robes and bonnet. The shade of the official's wardrobe was not truly the deep blue of Ji's banner, but it was often only the military who implemented strict adherence to the color code. Scholars, mystics, and other officials weren't often at the risk of being mistaken for an enemy by their own on the battlefield, given that they were rarely seen in battle.

"Lord Huang Shang-san," Jiao Ren prompted respectfully as the silence continued, following his question to the elder.

Huang Shang-san looked up from the polished wooden floor he'd been gazing at, as if entranced, then took up a study of the dark rafters overhead. He said thoughtfully, "Why not here? Isn't that what we should be asking, General Jiao Ren?"

Jiao Ren regarded the Minister of Ceremonies with patience. "I'm not sure that I follow you."

"The Temple of Divine Tranquility is in a more centralized location than the Palace of Imperial Peace. In the past, this is where the Seven Mystics gathered to attain the level of utmost solitude required to summon their most powerful spells. They have not done so for many years. It is as if they no longer feel at peace here, and even Xu Liang shies from its shelter, placing our empress instead within the Palace of Imperial Peace during his absence." An abbreviated laugh escaped on the official's breath as he contemplated this. "The palace is more a hall of ceremony than a temple. I do not understand it."

"He must have a good reason," Jiao Ren answered.

"Undoubtedly," Huang Shang-san agreed. "But what? He did not explain much to me before he departed for the barbarian realms. He left me with rather cryptic instructions. Following them has led me here, shortly after you told me of the tremor you felt from the wall overlooking it. I find myself as puzzled as you."

"Well, Lord Han Quan is one of the Seven Mystics and he is also a geomancer. Let us consult him on this matter."

Huang Shang-san reached out for the young general. "Let us not, Jiao Ren. Among my instructions, was the explicit command to share them with no one."

"You are sharing them with me," Jiao Ren reminded.

The minister shook his head. "I am sharing only my thoughts with you as I ponder matters you know nothing about. Han Quan will have many questions and he will leave with answers I might not even realize I have given."

Jiao Ren frowned. "I'm beginning to form questions of my own."

The elder did not seem concerned to hear this and gave his attention back to the ceiling. He said, "You will respect my silence, because you respect Lord Xu Liang, who has undoubtedly given you instructions as well."

"I am the chief lieutenant to the Empress' army," Jiao Ren said. "In matters of state and scholarship Xu Liang may supersede, but where the physical defense of the Empress and her city are concerned, I consider myself his equal. He cannot simply leave, and leave me to wonder why the Empress must sequester herself."

Huang Shang-san smiled, evidently amused by Jiao Ren's insistence in this matter. "I shall assume, then, that you were satisfied with his explanation, else you wouldn't be standing here, reminding me of your title and responsibilities."

Jiao Ren sighed, "You're right. I still hold my rank because Lord Xu Liang trusts me." In a moment, he added, "It is mutual. I would not question him—not openly or in secret—but I do feel unsure about what is going on in this city."

"It is not this city alone," Huang Shang-san corrected, "but all of Sheng Fan. The epicenter of the disturbance lies here, and it is for Empress Song Da-Xiao's protection that Xu Liang left her in the care of the ancestors."

"She is very young," Jiao Ren said, finally letting out some of his true concern. "How long will she be able to maintain the state she is in? How will we even know if she cannot? Lord Xu has stationed a guard of a dozen men at the interior, whom no one has seen since his departure. The winds surround them and the Empress, and to what purpose other than slow starvation?

"And there is Fa Leng to consider. Xun squeezes the province with its advantage of a much nearer headquarters. By the time we replenish our troops, it is nearly time to do so again. This does not seem to me like Xu Liang's typical way at handling rebellion."

"That is because it is not," Huang Shang-san answered with understanding. "Know that there are limits even to what Xu Liang can accomplish, particularly when he has divided himself between his homeland and the outside realms. We must be stronger now, general. And we must be patient."

As the Minister of Ceremonies spoke, a rumble shuddered through the previously still air. The torch flames in the chamber beyond fell flat for a moment, then rose once again to light the empty sanctum.

Jiao Ren felt suddenly queasy and overheated. Beads of perspiration formed across his brow and he noticed Huang Shang-san wiping his own face with his sleeve. "Lord Huang..."

The elder nodded. "Yes, Jiao Ren. I felt it, but I cannot tell you what it was."

Because you do not know or because you will not say? Even as the question formed in his mind, Jiao Ren bit the words back. He would know when it was time for him to know, and not before. In spite of his military rank, Huang Shang-san and others of the top ministers held more command in the Imperial City than he did. There was nothing to do but wait.

TWELVE
Cold Dawn

"**H**E'S human."

"And I'm a dwarf! Can you make any other plain-as-day observations, elf?"

"You're a dwarf without much armor," Alere replied without tone. While Tarfan blustered and fumed about the implied threat, the elf added, "This man is heavily armored in a fashion I've never quite seen the likes of among men. The metal's strangely pale. And here... what's this emblem?"

"He's a knight of Andaria," Tarfan blurted angrily. "Wouldn't expect a mountain elf to recognize one. Though, what a knight of Andaria is doing this far north..."

"Is he alive?" Xu Liang asked when it seemed that elf and dwarf were intent to leave out the only truly important detail concerning the stranger.

Alere was kneeling beside the unconscious man, but it was Tarfan who had to step forward and check his pulse as the elf made no motions to do so. The dwarf nodded once.

"What should we do?" Taya asked, mounted once again upon Guang Ci's horse, having taken well to her daily riding beside the mystic she'd grown to admire and respect. Xu Liang treated her with patience even when she complained about her ill feelings or asked too many questions. He seemed to encourage her questions while Tarfan constantly enforced his guardianship upon her, telling her to sit still and be silent.

In this instance, the mystic gave his answer to everyone. "We must stop and tend to him lest he share his horse's fate."

Taya looked upon the frozen animal with pity. Then she remembered her pouch and the herbs, roots, and petals she always carried with her own journal—that wasn't filled with Tarfan's silly history lessons or diagrams of worthless artifacts. During the years she'd been traveling with her uncle, she had taken up a study of the plant life in different lands. Through reading, interrogation of locals, and experimentation, she had learned quite a lot about the various poisons and medicines found in nature. It was her secret desire to become a healer, and so she leapt at this first real opportunity with alacrity. "I can help!"

Everyone looked at her, even the guards who couldn't possibly have understood what she said. The elf seemed disinterested, Bastien was neutrally quiet, and Fu Ran seemed mildly curious. Tarfan frowned dubiously.

Xu Liang, however, kept his eyes on the ice-rimed stranger and said—as if she were of equal status and importance to everyone else on this expedition, "Please, do so. The weather is looking disagreeable. I'd like to move away from these heavier clouds before it begins to snow again."

◆ ◆ ◆ ◆ ◆

CAMP WAS MADE again, only a few hours after they'd left the previous site. Taya went to work heating water and the herbs necessary to banish chill from the body. She added a few shreds of carrot and some honey to improve the taste and to add some nourishment. The stranger, removed from his ice cold shell of armor, lay in relatively dry shirt and trousers under a stack of blankets. He was breathing, but he'd yet to regain consciousness by the time Taya carried the herbal stew to him. She tried nudging him and speaking to him, but it was no use.

"If we can't wake him, we may lose him after all," she reported when Xu Liang entered the tent. "The chill inside will take him while he sleeps."

The mystic observed the sleeping stranger for a moment, then asked if he could try something. Taya nodded, shocked that he would ask rather than simply do whatever he had in mind. She bobbed her head again when he issued his customary half-bow and approached what he clearly viewed as her patient. He knelt down beside the man, considered briefly, then touched a spot on the knight's wrist without ceremony or ritual of any kind.

The young man groaned, his eyelids fluttered, and he stared bleary-eyed at Xu Liang. He seemed mildly startled, but otherwise reasonable, so Taya started to bring him his medicine, hoping he would be equally calm about it.

And then, as if suddenly remembering to panic, the knight's eyes shot wide, showing the world their intense blue color. He bolted upright and did something that made Taya gasp out loud: He latched onto Xu Liang's arm, twisting up the mystic's silken sleeve in his tight grasp.

The questions came almost too quickly to understand. "What's happened? Where am I? My armor! Where is it?" He looked all around him, still gripping Xu Liang's arm. "Where is *Dawnfire?*"

And then, in a tone Taya had never heard the mystic take with anyone, Xu Liang said, "Take your hand from my arm at once." He wasn't loud, simply ... commanding.

The young man obeyed, a peculiar awe capturing his features and quieting his panic. Apology followed. "Please," he started to say, but Xu Liang wouldn't let him finish.

"You are disoriented," the mystic said. "Be still and rest. Our healer will tend to your chill and when you are warmed again, you may recoup your belongings. Both they and you are safe here, so long as you do not attempt to harm any of us."

Slowly, the stranger shook his head. "No ... I wouldn't. I won't. I just..."

"Rest," Xu Liang said again, softer this time. Then he stood and left, handing the affair over to—Taya beamed proudly to herself—*their* healer.

Her smile faded a bit when she saw the knight's eyes shift from the tent entrance to her. His limp brown hair was curling as it dried, draping a face that wasn't ugly by a good shot, but it was drawn and sad. His eyes were big wet pools of sky blue beneath a soft brow. The young man's nose was straight with a decent shape to it and his lips were almost too generous. The rest of him was long—though not too long—and well arranged; a tad undernourished currently, but surely capable of bearing the weight of his armor.

He smiled half-heartedly at her. "I know I seem a wretch to look at right now, but I'll do you no harm, little one."

Taya felt her heart beat just a little faster. Give her a stout, bearded dwarf any day, but if she was going to be surrounded by young human men, thank the Heartstone of the Stormbright Caverns they were a handsome lot! Xu Liang was walking art, of course ... once one got used to his exotic style. Taya was proud to have matured enough over the course of her current travels to understand such things now. The bodyguards were bold and dignified, if not handsome in their own right, and then there was Fu Ran, who had the impressive features of a titan. Even Bastien, with his sun-chafed skin and his scar wasn't bad to look at. And the elf ... well, he was an elf.

Taya carried her bowl to the Andarian and watched him take it in both hands.

For a moment he seemed to bask in the steam rising off the liquid mixture. Then he shrugged, "It doesn't smell half bad." He drank it down, displaying his hunger. Then he offered the bowl back to Taya with thanks. "It didn't taste half bad either," he added.

Taya beamed with pride again. Tarfan always blanched at her cooking and had to be tied down and have his jaw pried open to get some of her medicinal concoctions down his gullet.

"I hope that I didn't offend that cleric," the knight suddenly said. "I..."

"Cleric?" Taya was confused until she recalled that Andaria didn't have sorcerers. Their magic-users were known as clerics. "You mean Xu Liang," she said.

The knight frowned, puzzled. "That's a curious name. I don't think that I've ever heard one quite like it."

"It's Fanese," Taya informed. "You have to be as well traveled as me and my uncle to have heard of a name like his. Or a name like Gai Ping's, or Guang Ci's, or Fu Ran's, or Deng-"

"Please," the knight interrupted, as she reveled in demonstrating the particular pronunciations of each guard. "I understand. Thank you. As I was about to say, if I've offended him, I'm sorry. I only didn't expect to wake this morning under a roof of any kind, let alone beneath a kind stranger's gaze."

"It's all right," Taya took the liberty of saying. "I don't think he holds grudges. He just has a lot on his mind right now. We weren't planning to camp this early in the day, but we couldn't just leave you up to your neck in snow."

"Thank you," the knight said, sounding weak while he appeared to think back on the severe cold outside.

Taya simply smiled, deciding she liked his gentle, polite way of speaking. Andarians were high on propriety, tradition, and ceremony. According to Tarfan the Andarians and the Fanese were the only people in the known world that could literally die of shame.

"Perhaps I'd better take a few moments rest," the young knight said, and finally laid back down. "Only a few," he murmured, pulling the blankets up to his chin and closing his big, pretty eyes. "And then I'll … be … on my…"

Taya sighed wistfully as sleep claimed him. She brushed an errant tendril of hair from his boyish face and patted him gently on the cheek. "You've been a very good patient. The first one I haven't had to chase down and hog tie."

◆ ◆ ◆ ◆ ◆

"SO, WHAT DO you think about the stranger?"

Xu Liang scarcely heard Fu Ran while he stood beside Blue Crane and watched the clouds ribbing overhead in the tumultuous mountain air. It was going to snow soon. There were already light flakes in the air and daylight left more swiftly in the mountains. If they were lucky they would have a few more hours to travel by before the darkness settled again. At this rate, it was going to take a week or longer just to get to the lower regions of the Alabaster Range. This was unacceptable. But going around the mountains would have taken longer. There was nothing they could do. Time would move as time did, without regard or remorse.

Fu Ran's words eventually filtered into Xu Liang's thoughts and he gave a belated reply. "He is … troubled."

"How do you mean?" the large man asked.

Xu Liang lifted his hand to stroke Blue Crane's soft pelt and thought of the knight's sudden grip on his wrist, so tight that he could feel the man's faint fever through his robe. He wondered now if it was arrogance or fear that made him react as he did to the man's action. While he was not accustomed to being groped, he'd been outside of Sheng Fan enough to set aside certain expectations where the behavior of others was concerned. Certainly, Fu Ran had handled him with less respect in his rough way at shielding him from harm. Perhaps it had to do with the pain the man's sudden, desperate touch had inflicted. But he could not have known how fragile

Xu Liang currently was, how the faintest physical contact could amount to a serious affliction if he wasn't mentally prepared for it.

"Xu Liang."

He thought a moment more, then answered his friend. "I sense something about him that troubles me. Perhaps that is the better way of putting it."

"What's he doing in the Yvarian mountains?" Tarfan asked from his perch on a cold boulder, where he struggled to hold a map open against the wind. "That's what I want to know. Knights of Eris aren't cause seekers."

"Eris?" Xu Liang inquired.

"Eristan," the dwarf muttered. "The Divine Citadel, a temple to the highest order of the Andarian knighthood. They're not soldiers of men or kings. They're warriors of God."

"Which one?" Fu Ran asked him.

"The One," the dwarf answered with emphasis. "The True God, the Great and Glorious Father of Heaven and of the Winged Children, the Angels of Eris, Swords of Heaven."

"Swords..." Xu Liang started.

Tarfan shook his head. "No relation to your Celestial Blades, mage. There's a reason I wouldn't let you wander civilized Andaria by yourself, didn't you know? They'd have a man like you tied to a stake and set afire for blasphemy!"

"No," Xu Liang said. "I didn't know. I thought you said the Treskans were the ones to be concerned about in that aspect."

Tarfan dropped his hands and therefore his map into his lap and sighed. "About the only thing separating Andaria from Treska is a pasture. The Andarians spread the faith that drives the Treskans. They don't suffer sorcerers. The Andarians tolerate some rituals involving magic if it pertains properly to their religion.

"Like, for example, if an officially recognized cleric prays over a dying soldier that he be saved and chants a healing spell that does, in fact, save him, its considered God's mercy, or something to that effect. Summoning the wind on a still day, using words they couldn't even repeat properly, let alone understand, is called witchcraft. That earns you a stake and a toasty fire."

Xu Liang couldn't suppress the mildly sardonic smile that came to his lips as he considered that there may indeed have been barbarians in the western world. "Well then, let us try not to impress too offensive an image upon the young man before we send him on his way. We have little to spare, but perhaps..."

At that moment, someone cried out. It came from the only tent they'd set up, leaving no question as to who it was.

Xu Liang walked away from Blue Crane to investigate. Fu Ran followed with Tarfan sliding off his boulder to do the same. Guang Ci and Deng Po were about to enter, but Xu Liang waved them away, decided against a misunderstanding leading to anyone's death or injury.

Inside, the knight was stalking around the tent, strapping on pieces of his armor as he searched for something. The look of distress on his face was almost painful to behold. He caught sight of Xu Liang and the others crowding in the entranceway and didn't wait for them to say anything, demanding, "Where is *Dawnfire*?"

Xu Liang considered that such might have been the name given to his horse and took instant pity upon him, thinking that his mental faculties had suffered to such a degree that he believed the animal might be hidden in the tent.

"The animal has perished," Xu Liang explained with the gentle patience one gave to a small child. He saw no other way to approach the man's apparent mode of behavior.

The knight stopped his search, a look of abject dismay and confusion on his youthful features. "What?" He seemed to understand in the next moment and a half smile crept into his panicked expression. "*Dawnfire's* not—it isn't a horse. It's a spear."

An inaudible gasp escaped Xu Liang's throat, and he watched with renewed interest as the man held his arms out as if to display the weapon's length.

"A great platinum staff with a marvelously crafted blade," the knight said. "What's happened to it?"

"We found no such weapon with you," Xu Liang offered, but the knight wouldn't have it.

"That's impossible!" he shouted, tears filling his eyes and quickly spilling onto his flushed cheeks. "I didn't let it go!" He brought his arms in toward his chest, as if in demonstration. "I was clutching it just before I … just when…"

Xu Liang studied him with a sensation of puzzlement and a deliberate administration of patience.

The young man dropped his arms to his sides. "I've failed," he said.

And there he stood in utter dejection and a misery so profound it angered Xu Liang as much as it inspired pity within him.

Taya moved from the place she'd been standing out of the knight's way and gingerly touched the young man's arm. He covered his face with both hands and began to weep.

Xu Liang tried to take his eyes from the spectacle of grief, but he found himself unable in his dismay at what he was seeing. He had seen such weakness and self-blame once before and it was nothing he wanted to see again. And yet, he was mesmerized, trapped in this bitter reflection of the past.

"Now what?" Tarfan said, breaking the spell. "If he's not mad…"

"I know," Xu Liang said. "We must learn more about this spear, if it actually exists."

"I'm not mad," the knight suddenly announced. "I'm not. I swear to you!" He did nothing to support his claim by saying next, "The spear was given to me by an angel, who saved my life."

◆ ◆ ◆ ◆ ◆

TRISTUS DIDN'T EVEN believe himself. When he came to consciousness in a warm place beneath the gentle gaze of the most beautiful woman he thought he'd ever seen, who changed into a man no less fair right before his eyes, he was sure he'd lost himself in a dream. And then he realized he was awake and he reached for the angel's spear, and came away with the stranger's arm…and things only went worse from there. He felt like a lame animal, the way the dwarf medic stared at him, and he'd felt like a foolish child the way the man in the strangest cleric's robes he'd ever seen scolded him. And he was withering in Xu Liang's quiet gaze now, while panic slammed in his chest and festered in his stomach. He felt ill and he must have sounded like a lunatic.

He set his teeth on edge, listening to the debating of the others; a titan of a man with peculiar tattoos on his arms, a male dwarf, and now an elf as well. The latter had appeared almost without notice. By the look of him, he was Zaldaine, one of the war-loving breed. But if that were true, what was he doing in the company of humans, and this far north?

"Could it have been stolen?" the large man asked. "He obviously fell asleep. Or maybe he was hit on the head."

"There were no tracks," the elf informed. "But, depending on how long he was unconscious, the late snow might have covered them."

"I wasn't hit on the head," Tristus told them. "There was no one around. No one!"

He backed off, thinking of how he'd prayed last night for the loneliness to end. His prayer had been answered. They weren't enemies; they were worse. They were people who couldn't help him that were trying anyway. Pity motivated them, and Tristus felt so ashamed he could scarcely contain himself.

"It was only darkness," he murmured. *It's always darkness.*

The eyes of the man Taya claimed to be Fanese flashed with interest at his last statement. Tristus caught his gaze and dared to hold it for a few seconds, reasoning why any of this should matter to a stranger. He couldn't think straight and gave up before he'd actually begun. What difference did it make? *Dawnfire* was gone. He'd failed. He'd failed the angels and lost all hope of restoring whatever honor he had left. Everything the Order Masters had said was true and he had nothing now. He wanted to die, but he didn't even deserve that mercy, and knew with a fresh wave of despair that he would be forced to live. He didn't even have the will to lift his own sword against himself. Even if he did, these people that had been sent to torment him would stop his suicide, he was certain. He would fail even in that final effort.

"What is your name?" Xu Liang suddenly, finally asked.

The question caught Tristus off guard and he hesitated before finally stumbling through his answer. "Tris-Tristus ... Edainien."

The beautiful man digested the information, nodding slightly. Then he asked, "Can you tell me what brought you here, Tristus Edainien?"

Tristus drew in a breath and nearly choked on it, but managed eventually to breathe somewhat evenly and with his eyes set on Xu Liang—seeing none of the others—he gave his account of everything that had happened to him since he'd left Tesina. Most of it had been uneventful travel alone with his depression, but rather than dwell on the obvious, he described his personal quest without giving the specific reasons behind it and, as his stomach slowly began to unknot, he spoke of his encounter with the angel and the demon. He described *Dawnfire* as he'd yet to describe the weapon even to himself in his own mind, leaving none of its glorious detail out. And when he was finished, he expected to be either ridiculed or pitied.

Surprisingly, he was neither. The space inside the tent took on a very serious air in the moments following his story, and now the worry was in his audience instead of just himself.

Xu Liang closed his eyes while the others began to murmur amongst themselves and with no one to notice, Tristus took a moment to study the first human he'd set eyes on since leaving Tesina. Strangely, he felt that the angel was a more realistic sight. Such perfect fairness as what stood before him now he had never witnessed before—in a man or a woman. Statues of marble were carved this smooth, so flawless. Every aspect spoke of unerring grace, from the eyes and ears, to the nose and chin ... and the mouth. Tristus' stomach knotted again. Warmth needled his heart and he looked away instantly, flushed with embarrassment.

"The spear you call *Dawnfire* must be found," Xu Liang finally said.

"Yes," Tristus said on an unplanned breath, keeping his eyes on the rug beneath him.

"It's begun to snow," the elf reported. "We should leave at once."

"Xu Liang," the dwarf said, "It'll be tough for anyone alone on foot to make it out of these mountains. He has his gear, but it'll be heavy. Should we spare the lad a horse?"

Tristus almost fainted in his shock. He looked up quickly, pleadingly, forgetting to be angry. "What are you saying? You can't just send me away! The spear was given to me. I'll look for it. I'll find it. I must!"

The dwarf came forward sympathetically, laying a strong hand on his shoulder—or as near to his shoulder as the stout creature could reach. "Lad, don't you think you've been through enough? Go back to your home, back to your family in Andaria."

Now the anger came. He pushed the dwarf's hand away. "I have no family in Andaria! And no home to go back to! This is all I have. This hopeless journey through barren ice and rock that you seem to think I've seen enough of.

"Trust me, old one, when I say I have seen far worse. I have seen horrors the likes of which most men cannot even imagine. Do not misinterpret the youth you see before you, for I am no boy playing at soldier and I am no fledgling knight! My fear stems of a darkness so deep ... and so terrible..."

The anger began to wane, quickly replaced with tears. Tristus stopped himself and looked around at his startled audience. He pulled in what he might have said next and drew back into his previous slump of depression and worry.

A long silence settled. And then Xu Liang said quietly, "He is right. The blade came to him. It may come to him again."

The dwarf threw his arms in the air. "It's your quest, mage!" He left in a bluster of unintelligible curses.

Others filed out shortly after him. And then Xu Liang said something in what could only have been Fanese—it sounded so exotic—and the two strangely armored men at the tent entrance, whom Tristus had overlooked somehow, performed a quick, respectful bow and left. The large tattooed man lingered a moment before deciding to exit himself, and at some point the elf had already gone. Eventually, Xu Liang lifted himself up and headed for the tent entrance.

"Wait," Tristus beckoned.

The man, whose silken mane was almost as long as his robes, stopped without turning back. He glanced over his shoulder at Tristus.

"Won't you tell me what your quest is about?" Tristus asked. "What has it to do with *Dawnfire*?"

"Perhaps nothing," Xu Liang answered mysteriously.

"I ... I don't understand."

"If you are meant to, you soon will." On those cryptic words, Xu Liang departed.

Tristus stared after him, confused and exhausted. "They think me mad."

And that was when Taya reminded him of her presence by saying, "I don't think so."

He looked glumly over his shoulder at her. "Why not, little one?"

She frowned at once and set her fists on her hips. "First off, you can stop calling me little one. My name is Taya."

"Taya," Tristus sighed apologetically. "Forgive me."

Her features softened again. She said, "This is all very serious to Xu Liang. He wouldn't humor your insanity if he believed you were insane."

Tristus looked away from her, back at the tent entrance. "Then I have misjudged him, and for that I'm..."

"Stop being sorry about everything!" Taya snapped. "You're beginning to make me sorry I put honey in your broth. It's clearly mucked up your brain!"

Tristus almost laughed, in spite of everything. When she came near enough to touch his arm, he bent over enough to take her small hand in his and lightly kissed the back of it. "You're very kind, Taya. And you have my thanks."

She smiled back warmly, then helped him to collect the rest of his armor.

THİRTEEN
A Place for Everyone

THOUGH IT HADN'T been asked of him, Alere rode ahead, acting as scout. The task came to him so naturally, and was performed with such efficiency that everyone accepted his frequent disappearances and sudden returns automatically. Xu Liang began to let go his concerns about the elf's personal mission, having now a worse threat to his party.

Unlike Alere, Tristus was unstable. Though it didn't seem that it would be intentional, he could do them tremendous harm. He had inflicted minor wounds upon the company already—Tarfan had spent several hours not speaking to anFyone after the morning's decision—but on the other hand, he may have brought them one step closer to uniting all six Swords.

Based on his description and the manner in which he claimed *Dawnfire* had glowed while he'd unknowingly crossed their path, the spear must have been the Dawn Blade. The only true question in Xu Liang's mind was whether or not this emotional warrior was intended to be its bearer. It was not his place to judge who should or should not be in possession of one of the Blades. Fate simply selected the bearers by presenting the weapon and having the unsuspecting individual take it up. It was, however, a reasonable argument that if the Dawn Blade was meant for Tristus, it would not have escaped him so easily. Perhaps he'd dropped it, as fate intended, and the true bearer had simply found it lying in the snow.

After three long hours of silence since leaving camp, the very topic of debate decided to speak. Still weak, Tristus guided Guang

Ci's mount with Taya riding happily behind him—the two seemed fast friends. He had offered to walk, but Xu Liang insisted that he ride, wary of another possible collapse if the knight pushed himself too much, too quickly. As well, he was probably more skilled at handling a horse through the rough terrain. Taya had been struggling and at times had to be led by one of the guards. It also seemed unlikely that the knight would attempt to break away from them and take up his own search for the Blade if it meant abducting Taya as well.

"Master Xu Liang," the knight said with respect he didn't seem to know anything of upon his sudden awakening that morning. "Won't you please tell me what you know of *Dawnfire*? I know nothing of it, except that it is holy and that it gave me a greater sense of peace to hold onto than I've known for some time."

"And now I know as much about it as you do," Xu Liang said truthfully. He still did not know for certain whether this '*Dawnfire*' was one of the Celestial Swords. He wouldn't until he held it next to the others.

Tristus tried a new approach. "Why is it so important to you? Will you tell me that, then?"

Xu Liang looked at him, not with disapproval, and said, "You are persistent."

"I've had to be all my life," the knight replied. "I have a feeling that now I stand in the midst of the most important occasion I will ever know for the rest of my life. I cannot back down."

Xu Liang stared a moment, intrigued in spite of events previous, and then he brought his gaze in front of him again. He said, "There is too much to say, Tristus Edainien. Do not speak to me for what remains of the day. I will answer your questions when we set camp tonight."

Tristus agreed with silence and Xu Liang closed his eyes to concentrate.

◆ ◆ ◆ ◆ ◆

TRISTUS WATCHED IN wonder as the mystic seemed to fall asleep on his horse. "What is he doing?" he whispered to Taya.

"I told you he's a mystic. They're Fanese clerics, who require lots of concentration to perform their spells."

"Maybe they are called mystics in this Sheng Fan you speak of, but in Andaria mystics are strange people who claim to see into the future and things of that nature. They are rarely heard, let alone trusted."

The young dwarf abruptly rapped his armored side. "Well I don't care," she snapped in a sharp whisper. "Don't you get any ideas about committing him to any fires!"

Tristus was horrified at the thought. He looked over his shoulder quickly and had to swallow his initial words, fearful that they might come out too loudly and disrupt the Fanese cleric. He whispered, "I would sooner impale myself upon my sword than see one of such grace destroyed."

"Why not?" Taya sighed, sufficiently canceling the effect of his words. "What's one more bodyguard when there are already so many?"

Tristus stole his gaze away from Xu Liang long enough to look upon the armored men in his company. "These men, with similar countenances, is that what they are? Bodyguards?"

"Yep," Taya answered, seeming proud to have the answers. "The big bald fellow is too, or he used to be. My uncle isn't, of course, and neither is the elf or the quiet fellow walking with Fu Ran."

"Fu Ran? The big man there?" He nodded toward the individual.

"That's him."

Tristus immediately envied the guards, that they should have such a task appointed to them as shielding a man like Xu Liang with their lives. Men and women of high rank or station in Andaria often surrounded themselves with guards and personal aides, but the devotion seemed so much less than what Tristus had witnessed here. Xu Liang's guards moved with him without creating an obstruction or having to be told. They were alert as duty commanded, but also as if they held some personal stake in what would be lost if they failed in that duty. Tristus couldn't blame them, nor Fu Ran, for returning to his past obligation. To serve a man of such elegance that was not decadent and wisdom not depraved, who showed lenience and patience while still maintaining authority ...

I've known him less than a day, Tristus thought in amaze, *and he has won me. I would gladly give my life to spare his.* He wondered suddenly if he should trust such feelings—the first other than despair that he had experienced since the angel. With the angel, there was no question. It had been purely a miracle. Xu Liang was no angel, in spite of his grace, and Tristus had heard about men charmed by unholy magic to perform some manner of evil for a sorcerer. He had heard worse things in the charges brought against him by the Order. And they were wrong in what they said. *Strike me down, God, if you must, but they were wrong.*

Tristus glanced at Xu Liang once more and somehow the memories of his dark past failed to surface. His heart seemed to split and fall into his feet, the reverence he was feeling in this man's presence threatening to overwhelm him. *Let me serve you, sorcerer of Sheng Fan. Please do not turn me away.*

"It's not polite to stare!" Taya hissed, and Tristus looked away at once, feeling his cheeks redden with embarrassment and remorse.

"I'm beginning to worry that your brain is slower to thaw than the rest of you," the young dwarf continued. "I can see us now, careening over the edge of the canyon, all because you've never met a Fanese cleric. Here comes that ill feeling again!"

Tristus reached his hand back to quiet her, his gaze at the front of the group as another member of it was approaching. "Hush, little one. Taya," he added softly, before she could rap her tiny fist against his side again. The very last thing he wanted was the dwarf maiden's bruised knuckles on his conscience as well. "The elf's back."

◆ ◆ ◆ ◆ ◆

ALERE GUIDED BREIGH alongside the caravan, moving against them until he reached the others on horseback. Then he turned the mare about, matching her gait to the slow pace carried on by the other horses. He would rather have delivered his question to the old guard to Xu Liang's left, but as Alere did not speak Fanese, he settled on the dwarf girl. "Does he meditate now?"

"He does," the knight answered, and Alere looked at him, catching the human's gaze in return. There was a look of indignation in his sky-colored eyes, as if he knew Alere intended to ignore him. Beneath that, there was a pleading. He wanted to be one of them, not a straggler half of them pitied and the other half distrusted.

What he didn't know was that Alere neither pitied nor distrusted him. He simply had no respect for a warrior who'd been so careless as to have lost his horse and his weapon—the two items he should have cherished most on his unknown journey—through a lack of preparedness or of endurance, or of common sense. Maybe all were lacking. It was a wonder his armor hadn't suffered beyond its few dings and that he still carried the sword that had obviously come with it. At best, he was disadvantaged by his youth, but as he wasn't quite so young as he looked—Alere suspected—it seemed he had worse problems. His aura was a confused cloud of unpleasant emotions, accurately reflective of the instability he'd already displayed.

In spite of this, Alere did not personally despise him and he held no grudges against a human simply for the sake of it. He said, "There are tracks ahead of us, made by two shod horses. They lead away from us, into a pass heading northwest, into the lower mountains."

"That's the way we're headed," Tristus noted. "Toward the Flatlands."

Alere nodded. "They came out of the south, paralleling our route along the river canyon. I cannot say for how long. As well there are people behind us...a day's ride, maybe less."

The knight looked over his shoulder. "It seems to be getting a bit crowded in these mountains. Before you found me, I would have welcomed a pack of hunger-crazed wolves, but now I'm beginning to miss the solitude." He looked at Alere quickly, then glanced toward Xu Liang, and finally set his gaze on the ground passing slowly beneath him. "Please don't mistake me. I'm very grateful to all of you. I will find *Dawnfire* again, and if it's what Xu Liang is looking for, I will turn it over gladly, along with my services."

"Your services as a knight who has mysteriously abandoned his Order? Who wandered the unforgiving higher regions of the Alabaster Range until he lacked food and water, pushed his horse dead, and nearly himself as well?" There was no malice in Alere's tone, but it injured the human all the same. A watery sheen came to his eyes, but Alere spared the knight no truth. "I think you misinterpret your position. You have strayed into circumstances beyond your control and it is my advice that you be prepared to pay for your misguided wandering with your life. The keirveshen may claim us all before this is finished. And there will be no 'angels' to save anyone."

Tristus refused to look at him and said nothing.

Alere glanced at Taya. "I shall give warning of the riders ahead of us to your uncle and then go to have a better look at the company in our shadow. I'm curious to know if they are following. You will share this information with the mystic when he returns?"

"Yes," Taya sighed, scolding him in tone and expression, a reproach that Alere thoroughly ignored in his leaving.

♦ ♦ ♦ ♦ ♦

TAYA LEANED AGAINST the dejected knight, feeling the frightful cold of his plate mail through his cloak. "It's all right, Tristus. He didn't mean it. Elves never mean anything, they just open their craws and let out whatever may come."

"He's right," Tristus said, almost too quietly to be heard. "Why should he take me for anything but a burden? Intentions don't matter when it comes down to it. It doesn't matter how badly I've ever wanted to protect anyone or uphold anything because I've failed ... in the worst way imaginable. My past will follow me, and it may come back to haunt all of you as well."

Taya didn't know what he meant by that, but she felt suddenly very cold and, though she would never have admitted it, very afraid.

♦ ♦ ♦ ♦ ♦

NIGHT POURED OVER the clouded peaks of the Alabaster Mountains and forced the companions to stop. There were no stars visible and the moon was in hiding. Between the darkness and the swirling mist created by the winds stirring the constant snow cover, not even lanterns were much help. They were moving away from the river canyon and therefore away from the danger of plunging into its vast depths, but there weren't enough lanterns for everyone and it would be easy for someone to take a wrong step and wind up separated from the others. In the steady wind, it would be difficult to even hear a voice cry out, let alone determine its direction.

There were three tents, provided by the Fanese. Two were small and traditionally triangular in aspect while the third was somewhat larger and held a circular shape. A rug was put down inside and two Fanese style torches were arranged to offer heat and light.

Normally, Xu Liang would have had the large tent to himself and the guards not on watch would share the smaller shelters. However, in the extreme conditions, all bedrolls were welcome to be set out wherever there was space available in the larger tent.

Tristus had watched the highly efficient bodyguards perform the task of setting the tents, tending to the horses, and arranging watch shifts among themselves. They would not allow any assistance and didn't seem to require it. The others began filing in out of the cold, and Tristus lingered near the animals, seriously contemplating taking up a position for the night away from the others.

They would probably only think that suspicious, Tristus thought glumly. *They would think I meant to sneak off and seek* Dawnfire *alone, or they would suspect something worse.*

My armor, my sword… it means nothing to them. The Fanese don't recognize the Order for what it is and while the elf and dwarves do, they have doubts about a holy knight who's wandered so far from Andaria. As well they should have.

The Knights of Eris moved in numbers. They very rarely set out to do anything alone, and nothing that would carry them so far out of their homeland without significant cause. They were defenders of the Andarian Church and patrolled the region under its protection. The clergy had long ago put an end to religious quests, claiming that one who sought 'tokens' of God demonstrated a lack of faith and respect in the True King of Men, and it would not be tolerated.

Yes, Tristus had defied the Order. Defiance was all that was left to him, his only method for finding truth and the solace that lay in knowing that truth. He looked to Eris itself first, and while he did not find the legendary city, he found the angel and *Dawnfire*, both guides toward the answers he needed as a fish required water. He was suffocating without them, dying a slow, tormenting death. The elf did not understand that. Elves understood only seclusion and vengeance against all who dared invade upon that seclusion.

Even though Andaria currently engaged in no hostilities against the elves, Tristus was the enemy of any elf just for being human. If Alere were Zaldaine, and made aware of Tristus' Treskan blood on his mother's side, he'd have likely killed him on the spot. As it was the white elf happened to be a distant cousin of the slightly darker elves of the south and all the knowledge he'd been given concerning Tristus was whatever the old dwarf blurted next concerning his knowledge of the Order and his suspicions about Tristus.

"What are you still doing out here?" Taya demanded, tugging at his arm. "Hurry up! It's freezing!"

Tristus looked at her, touched by her kindness, which may have been a kinder way at keeping an eye on him. "There are six of you already to crowd into the mystic's tent—seven if you count Fu Ran twice, as you ought to. I've been handling the outdoors this long. Perhaps I'd better…"

Taya frowned peevishly. "You've been handling it all right, with a chill that nearly killed you and a fever that surely will if you don't keep warm and dry! Anyway the more bodies in there, the more heat for all of us!"

Tristus mustered a half smile, knowing that he would give in sooner or later and that it may as well be sooner, since it did happen to be freezing. "I suppose that someone ought to be present to assist your uncle in protecting the innocence of a lady so fair and gentle as you."

"They're an elf and a bunch of humans," Taya said flatly, though even in the dark Tristus could see her cheeks blushing.

Tristus said, "Two of them are sailors."

"One of them twice your size, so keep your sweet tongue still and get your backside in that tent!"

Tristus laughed and relented, following Taya toward the canvas shelter that shuddered in the wind and glowed from the fire within. All mirth drained out of him once he reached the entrance and he almost turned back, but Taya seized him by the wrist and dragged him in. Two steps inside, he stood motionless like a lost child, his bed roll tucked under his arm. No one seemed to notice him.

The elf had yet to return from his scouting. Tarfan had curled himself in a ball of blankets and beard beneath one of the torches and was poring over a map, mumbling to himself. Fu Ran sat near the entrance, eating and talking with Bastien. Xu Liang sat cross-legged at the far side of the tent, his eyes closed. Was he meditating again?

"Taya!" Fu Ran beckoned. "Bring us more of that stew and tell us again how far you had to chase your uncle to get him to eat it!"

The dwarf maiden sighed. "The problem with sailors is that the same story keeps them amused for days," she murmured to Tristus. "Oh well... set your blanket down somewhere and I'll bring you a bowl."

She was gone before Tristus could say anything. Tristus stood still a few moments more, listening to Fu Ran's jovial roar, Bastien's amused snickering, and Taya's healthy giggle. Tarfan's murmuring had become snoring and the torches crackled invitingly. Tristus looked at Xu Liang, appearing at peace and so still that he almost didn't look alive. But he was alive. He glowed with life, with such grace that the very sight of him filled Tristus with warmth and hope. The dark memories that had chased him so deep into the mountains fell away and Tristus stepped forward, further out of their reach.

He crossed the tent and stood before the mystic of Sheng Fan. He continued to stare, and soon felt as if *Dawnfire* had returned to him and were in his grasp again, giving him light and granting him direction. He began to lower to his knees, but someone caught him by the back of his armor and dragged him away. He went down hard on his arm, numbing it from his elbow to his fingertips. Daggers of shadow stabbed his mind, keeping him down. The heavy foot crushing down on his chest persuaded him as well.

Fu Ran glared at him, his wide mouth quirked with a frightening half smile. "If I catch you that close to Master Xu Liang again, you're going to need that overgrown knife you're carrying to cut your way out of this metal shell!"

"I—wasn't going to hurt him!" Tristus gasped. "I only…"

"Fu Ran!"

At the stinging sound of the voice, the giant immediately took his foot off of Tristus and turned to face Xu Liang. He dropped down onto one knee as if it were purely and unstoppably instinct, and bowed his head.

The mystic, frowning mildly, but otherwise appearing undisturbed—he hadn't even opened his eyes—said, "Remember that you no longer serve me. I do not require your protection." He finally looked at the giant, adding, "You came here of your own volition, to provide us with an urgent message and while we are grateful, you are just as much guest along this expedition as Tristus. At the moment, I would think him less danger to be present in this tent than you."

Chastened at first, the giant remained still, frowning perhaps as he scolded himself. And then he stood, glaring at the man he'd acted in defense of seconds ago. For a moment it seemed that he was trying to think of something scathing to say, and then he laughed, an abbreviated, bitter sound that carried more effect than any words he might have come up with. He turned away and made an unconcerned path back to the opposite side of the tent. The others, who had all risen out of their previous relaxation in the moment, slowly returned to their affairs and Xu Liang closed his eyes again.

◆ ◆ ◆ ◆ ◆

HOURS PASSED AND the sounds of slumber filled the tent, offset by the crackling of the torches and the occasional crunching of the bodyguards' boots in the snow outside as they patrolled their small camp. The elf returned all but unnoticed and slept as silently, apparently having discovered no imminent dangers near their route.

Xu Liang remained awake, as did the knight, whom he'd not forgotten.

The Andarian had been sitting upon his bedroll, saying nothing and scarcely moving, as if to stay unnoticed after his humiliation at Fu Ran's hands and Xu Liang's words. Xu Liang could have allowed Tristus to finish giving his explanation, but so appalled was he by the former guard's typically thoughtless brutality, he could not contain himself. In his way, Fu Ran was just as much lost and confused as the knight, and until he resolved his own matters he had no business commenting or acting on someone else's.

Xu Liang meant what he'd said, besides. He did not require Fu Ran's protection. He had purposefully instructed Gai Ping and the others to stay out of his tent and act as guards for the whole group as a gesture of trust to the others. He needed what help he could get, and he did not need any of them believing that he thought so highly of himself—or so little of them—that he needed bodyguards near at all times. This was not Sheng Fan, and they could not afford that separation. Xu Liang would not be able to wield all of the Swords himself, even if he could wrest them from the grips of their chosen bearers.

Fate mixed with trust had delivered the Twilight Blade and now, possibly, the Dawn Blade as well. Alere seemed to be fitting comfortably into the group, but Tristus was as yet an uncertain element, just as *Dawnfire* was. Xu Liang would not risk losing either of them before he could understand them. The consequences in the event of an error would be too dire.

Finally, Xu Liang spoke to the restless body perched just a few feet away. "You should sleep."

Tristus seemed surprised. "You're awake?"

"I have not slept since I left Sheng Fan's Imperial City. When I meditate I am at rest, but I am not truly asleep."

"Oh," the knight said quietly. In a moment, he asked, "Do you hear everything that is said or goes on around you, then? Always?"

Xu Liang smiled a little in order to appear less stern, though he did not open his eyes to look at the knight. "No. When I am deep in concentration I must trust those around me. Until recently, I have trusted only my bodyguards."

"The others are your friends," Tristus said, as if to make a point. However, he added nothing more and left Xu Liang to wonder as to what that point was.

At length Xu Liang said, "Perhaps you remain awake to hear the answers I promised and have yet to give?"

"Perhaps," the knight replied strangely. "To be honest, I'm not sure anymore. In a single day I have been dealt more revelations than one man is entitled to. I think."

Xu Liang opened his eyes, sure that in another moment he would see the young man rise and take his leave, determined to seek *Dawnfire* on his own. However, Tristus did not move to leave, but only to lie back. His light eyes glistened in the torchlight as he studied the flickering shadows on the ceiling of the tent.

"Should one continue to follow the faith of a group that's cast him out?" the knight asked, seeming to ask no one in particular. "Shouldn't it stand to reason that if he was true to that faith that the group should have been true to him? Is it unreasonable to ask forgiveness of one who is all-forgiving?"

"One must follow what one believes in," Xu Liang offered. "Whether it is reasonable or not."

The knight looked at him. His smile was too pale to hide his suffering. "Like you believe in your quest?" Before Xu Liang could answer, Tristus had another question. "What are you looking for? What brings you to this land so distant from your own?"

"The desperate fear of losing all that I hold dear," Xu Liang answered honestly, surprising both of them. He added calmly, "Selfishness."

"What makes you say so?" Tristus asked.

The reply came easily. "Who are men to stand against forces far older than they, and far greater? If the time of a land has come, how can we hope to lengthen its span? If a palace must fall, what fool attempts to hold up the final pillar that supports it?"

"The fool who calls that palace home," Tristus guessed. "Unreasonable perhaps, but not selfish. If that fool succeeds, it will be the selfish ones who fled to spare their own lives scratching at the door to be let back in."

Xu Liang gazed upon him with wonder. "How is it, Tristus Edainien, that you can find justification in another man's quest, that you know so very little about, and none in your own?"

The minor mask Tristus had managed to lift over his depression shattered. He looked back at the ceiling. "I have nothing to save in my quest but myself." His voice carried softly, but it was laced with tones of disgust and self-loathing. "There is selfishness, my friend, in its purest aspect."

Xu Liang disagreed, but before he could say as much, shrieks rose above the wind and the snapping of the tent fabric. Tristus bolted upright, a look of terror in his eyes. He stood quickly and headed for the tent entrance with one hand on his sword, following Alere, who was already on his way outside.

◆ ◆ ◆ ◆ ◆

TRISTUS' REACTION TO abject fear was often to charge head-long at the source of that fear, to face it rather than be chased by it. It was no act of bravery; he often wound up standing cold with panic or fighting madly and inexpertly. He did not fear men, even if they were far more skilled or phenomenally stronger, so he'd had no trouble proving himself in the knighthood's ranks. He feared demons, though, and he knew all too quickly where he had heard this inhuman cry before and how he'd proven himself helpless against its source. His palms were sweating in his gloves and rivulets of perspiration formed across his brow, stinging as they crystallized in the freezing mountain air. His heart hammered loudly enough to have seemingly escaped his chest and been battering against the inside of his armor. Still, he drew his sword and looked into the snow-dotted blackness for the demon.

The elf watched the sky as well, his keen eyes sorting through the snow, finding a shadow amid the blackness that Tristus had overlooked. He drew his slender elven blade and answered the demon's hideous shriek with a confident phrase or oath in the language of his people. The demon dropped out of the sky—a man-sized monstrosity—claws outreached.

Tristus didn't get to see the outcome, suddenly given his own opponent. The demon landed on all fours in front of him, its black wings fanned against the night and the snow, its thin lips peeled away from its sharp teeth in a malignant grin. It knew his fear. It tasted it on the air with its foul tongue before leaping at him. Tristus did not stand paralyzed this time, but began to swing madly. The demon disarmed him almost immediately and brought him down.

With horrible visions of burning eyes returning, Tristus grabbed for the dagger sheathed at his thigh and plunged it deep into the darkness looming over him.

The demon clapped one clawed hand to the wound, then shrieked directly into Tristus' face. The horrid sound seemed to latch onto his mind physically and created a piercing ringing in his ears that blocked out all other sounds. Still, Tristus scrambled out from under his startled opponent and with his head swimming, took up a search for his thrown sword. Images of others drawn into the battle as multiple demons descended upon the camp swayed in and out of focus in his peripheral vision. He thought he saw flashes of purplish light near where he'd last seen Alere, but his concentration was on finding his sword and he didn't wonder long at the source of the glow.

"Cowardly mortal!" hissed the demon, taunting and terrifying him as effectively as the first he'd encountered. "Come back here and die the many deaths you deserve!"

Tristus fumbled through the snow, sliding his hands back and forth over the crusted powder. His fingers jammed against what could only be the hilt of his weapon and he grabbed up the blade at once, rolling over as he heard quickened footsteps behind him. A rush of darkness, a flash of steel, and a scream from both parties preceded the demon's end. It slumped over Tristus, impaled upon the end of his sword, its great leathery wings forming a morbid tent over its shocked and relieved opponent.

♦ ♦ ♦ ♦ ♦

FU RAN SAW the idiot boy fall beneath one of the ugly winged men with another one coming directly behind the first. He charged across the snow, having removed the enchanted tassel from his two-handed sword, and cut the second monster out of the air before it could attack. It landed in two loosely connected pieces close by, its dark blood melting the snow and sinking its hideous remains into a slushy pool. Fu Ran grimaced, then grabbed the first demon by the back of its neck, and ripped it off the knight's body.

The younger man seemed surprised to see who had come to help him, but not grateful. He rose instantly with his sword, a look of rash courage in his features. Like Zhen Yu, he was quick, and too close for Fu Ran to do anything but flinch aside and take a less damaging hit.

The knight's armored shoulder slammed into Fu Ran's arm, shoving him further away while he planted his feet, held his sword in front of him with both hands, and gored another demon—a demon that had intended to attack Fu Ran. The sleek black creature hissed and fell limp. Tristus kicked the corpse off the end of his weapon and stood ready for another.

"Not bad!" Fu Ran laughed to cover his amaze and gratitude—and some relief. He lifted his own sword, then added, "For an idiot!"

Tristus was too panicked and excited to respond.

◆ ◆ ◆ ◆ ◆

THE KNIGHT AND the giant stood with their backs to one another, fending off attackers as they dropped out of the blackness. Taya and Bastien fought closely as well, with Tarfan nearby, caving in demon chests and skulls with powerful swings of his war hammer. The bodyguards fought with orderly ferocity, leaving pieces of their victims heaped in the snow around them. The mystic had yet to draw his sword, but used its power, firing bolts of its pale blue magic at assailants with one hand while he held the other in front of his face, touching two fingers to his forehead as if in some manner of prayer. The softly glowing darts of energy lanced through multiple targets at once, dropping demons as effectively as the swords—and in two cases, spears—of the bodyguards.

Alere had emerged from the tent prepared to fend off nearly all of these keirveshen alone, as he had done their smaller kin in the Hollowen. He was pleasantly surprised to find himself in such capable company. He decided to trust the others to their own battles and concentrated fully on his own, hoping that none of the humans allowed themselves to be bitten.

FOURTEEN
The Dark Affliction

MORNING CAME. The demons were all destroyed or had fled. A grave silence hung in the air, disrupted only by the squawking and flapping of a flock of carrion birds investigating the night's dead. Seven bodyguards went about their duty, picking up camp, preparing to move on, waiting, as everyone else, for their leader to give the word.

Xu Liang said nothing. He knelt beside the feverish Deng Po, his dark eyes open to absorb the man's suffering, his thoughts a mystery.

"I'm beginning to worry," Taya confessed quietly to Tristus. "I told him more than an hour ago that there was nothing to be done. The elf told him last night, but still he sits there, refusing to let the poor man be put out of his misery."

The knight sat beside her, bent over one raised knee, his sympathetic eyes filling with tears Xu Liang was far too proud to shed. "Perhaps such actions are forbidden in Sheng Fan. Perhaps their religion does not allow it, or maybe just their custom. Whatever the case, it is not our place to question or interfere."

"But when he…" Taya bit her lip, struggling to form the image, let alone the words. "If Alere is right and he changes, then he'll … won't he?"

"Then," the knight sighed, "if Xu Liang does not, one of us will have to do something."

"But he looks so sad," Taya said unhappily.

"I expect he is," Tristus whispered. "I expect very much that he is."

◆ ◆ ◆ ◆ ◆

TARFAN WATCHED his niece inch closer to the human for comfort she'd have sought from her uncle only when sun shone full in the Abyss. He knew better than to think any romantic ideas could seriously form between the two, but the feelings of protection and jealousy could not be helped. She was his family, after all—and just who in hell was this knight anyway? A bleeding heart, 'woe-is-me' pup with a suit of armor he either stole or dishonored! Xu Liang had his own reasons for bringing him along, and Tarfan forgave the mystic ignoring both their misgivings where those reasons were concerned, but even Fu Ran, who had lately thrown the boy to the ground on his own suspicions seemed a little too friendly now. No, the boy would have to do more than smile and best a few demons to win Tarfan Fairwind.

I've got both eyes on you, knight!

It was with that thought that Deng Po cried out, and Tarfan looked away from Tristus, at the Fanese guard writhing on the pallet that had been kept out for him. His features were contorted with agony, his hands clutching the blankets so tightly that his knuckles turned white. He clenched his jaw, straining the tendons in his neck. A vein burst into view on his forehead. He'd been bitten by the keirveshen, poisoned with its unholy saliva that burned now through his bloodstream, rotting him from the inside out. Alere called it the 'dark affliction', and warned them in his heartless way to kill the man, lest he become one of the shadow folk.

And where was the elf now? Gone, as usual. Not a care in the world save cutting apart Yvaria's devils wherever he found them.

Xu Liang spoke to Deng Po in Fanese, his tone quiet but firm. "What's he saying?" Tarfan whispered to the giant, who was knelt down behind him and still towering over the dwarf's shoulder.

Fu Ran whispered the translation. "He asks Deng Po for his forgiveness and tells him that he dies this day with honor. He...tells the rest of us to leave."

At once the large man stood and began tapping shoulders among the attentive audience, gesturing for them to exit the tent. Everyone did, casting looks of sympathy back at Xu Liang and his dying guard. The surviving bodyguards went about their business grimly, knowing that they had lost one of their own, but knowing as well that he had given his life in fulfilling his duty to their master.

• • ◆ • •

DENG PO DID indeed die with honor that day, and he was honored in the silence that followed the caravan through the cold, desolate mountains of Lower Yvaria.

In the end, Xu Liang had taken Deng Po's life. He could not allow his suffering, nor could he risk the transformation Alere had warned about. Deng Po would have expected nothing less and would have accepted his fate proudly, if he'd been lucid at the time. Still, Xu Liang could not get past the fact that he had buried a son of Sheng Fan in a foreign land and with little ceremony, almost none. Alere advised against a pyre, uncertain yet as to whether or not the group he'd seen and then lost near the river canyon was in pursuit. The guard was buried with his spear. His sword would be brought back to Sheng Fan and given to his wife and son.

The Empress would feel this loss. Xu Liang would not be able to hide it, not completely. He would offer apology and comfort when he meditated next. For much of the day no one had spoken to him. He watched them, lost in their own thoughts, saying nothing, pressing on because they'd come too far to turn back.

I am involving too many innocent people, Xu Liang thought. *Acting for the benefit of Sheng Fan does not justify it.*

"Look," someone said, and Xu Liang focused on the path ahead of them, which had begun to spread and to flatten out. Mist drifted across the terrain below the mountains, showing patches of dry earth mottled with shrubbery and sparse, leafless trees beneath the stark yellow glow of the midday sun.

"The Flatlands, at last," Tarfan sighed. He looked up over his shoulder at Xu Liang. "Doesn't seem much of a place to find a sacred sword." He shrugged. "But I suppose neither were the mountains."

"We should cover as much ground as we can before the evening snow," Alere advised. "In this open land we will leave clear tracks. When the snowfall begins we should hold camp, then begin again in the morning and let the sun melt away any trace of our passage we might make in the night's leaving."

"The elf's right," Tarfan admitted in his gruff manner. "The weather's predictable in this region. You can tell the time of day by the amount of white on the ground."

Xu Liang nodded. "Shall we begin?"

The company proceeded, Tarfan leading the way into the mist as the sun burned it off, with Guang Ci and a fellow guard close behind. Gai Ping, Xu Liang, and Taya and Tristus rode in the middle, flanked by two bodyguards. The last two guards walked with the supply horse directly behind them while Fu Ran and Bastien took up the rear. Alere rode back into the mountains to have a last look at the path behind them.

The sun was setting before Alere returned to report nothing out of the ordinary behind them. They pressed on across the refreshingly even land for another hour before the snow began to fall, beginning as rain and quickly freezing.

Xu Liang had already done his meditating and spent a moment observing the fall of night over the vast wasteland when they stopped. He had given all that remained of his confidence and hope to the Empress. He survived now, like the others, wondering when the keirveshen would strike next. They were unpredictable, attacking swift and unseen. The only way to fight them was to wait for them and to try not to be caught off guard by their savagery.

"It is our souls that they crave," Alere said, standing next to him. "Yours especially."

Xu Liang looked at the elf.

Alere explained, "They see what I see; the brilliance of your overly purified soul. To them it is a brightness glaring in the darkest night, shining constantly in their eyes, keeping them restless. Most often they shred through the bodies to quell souls. It is as putting out a torch, so to speak, only they douse the flame in blood. Sometimes, in their frenzy, they take bites out of their victims, as they did your guard. They attack in number because, as you have seen, they are not invulnerable. The suddenness of their attack—the wind often, and the blacker night—is their only magic, a spell of fear cast down upon their victims, meant to at least make them hesitate and give the keirveshen the advantage of first strike."

"It works," Tristus said when he joined them outside the tent. "The beasts we fought last night were the same as the one I described to you when you found me. The angel I spoke of called it a shade demon. As a child, growing up in Andaria, we had stories of drey demons that I would compare them to. In an older tongue I think the word means kin … kin of demons, I suppose. The angel didn't mention their bite, but he said that to his kind their touch was poison."

"An angel!" Tarfan blurted, stepping out of the tent as well. "You hit your head, boy, and had a bad dream!"

"Think me mad if you wish, Master Fairwind," Tristus said, with alarming respect for one who had been treated as poorly as he had by the dwarf. "I know what I saw. More importantly, I know what I felt. Even if he wasn't an angel, he was real. And he entrusted his weapon to me. I'll never forgive myself for misplacing it."

"You've misplaced your senses, knight! Anyway, you said the fellow had wings. And you also said that you never saw his dead body after he claimed he was dying. How do you know he didn't just drift down, reclaim his weapon after he realized his error, and then fly away without leaving a trail for the elf to see?"

"I don't know that," Tristus replied. "But I doubt it."

"And why is that?"

"Because I was there, old one, and you were not."

"He does have a point, Tarfan," Xu Liang said, at the risk of temporarily alienating his stout friend once again.

The dwarf grumbled a bit, then sighed and went back inside.

"These lands are long," Alere said next. "It will take many days to cover before we arrive at Windra's Channel."

"From there we will be heading into Upper Yvaria," Xu Liang observed. "And if there was an opportunity to have discovered one of the Swords here, I will have missed it."

"Unless *Dawnfire* is that opportunity," Tristus said. "In which case, I will stay here and look for it until it is in my grasp again. Then I shall head north, seeking you out. I will present the weapon to you, for whatever purpose you need it."

Xu Liang looked at him, seeing only traces of his profile in the light escaping through the tent's entrance. "Why?" he asked irresistibly.

Tristus gave his answer to the snow-filled sky. "Because I feel that your cause is noble, whatever it may be. And because you and the others saved my life when you could have left me to freeze. I will assist all of you in any way I can … so long as you will have me."

Xu Liang didn't dare let the opportunity slip by him. He said quietly, "You are welcome, Tristus Edainien, and you have my thanks. However, know that I cannot return to my empress without all of the weapons I seek. You should know as well that these weapons are coming together and my actions only hasten their reunion. If you are the bearer of the Dawn Blade, our paths will not stray far, nor for long."

Tristus lowered his gaze. "Your empress ... I can only imagine." His thoughts seemed to stray for a moment, then he asked. "And what is your station, Master Xu Liang?"

"I am a scholar and an officer of the Imperial Court," he answered. "Tutor and advisor to my empress. I serve her best as Imperial Tactician, responsible for the defense of the Imperial City and its interests, which have been known on several occasions to take me away from the Imperial City itself. I am a guided aeromancer—guided by my ancestors to call upon the winds in service of my empress. I have been chosen by Mei Qiao to wield her sword, *Pearl Moon*, one of the six Celestial Swords given to man by the gods to protect this world from chaos."

Tristus looked at him. A weak smile utterly failed on his lips. "I guessed you were important, but I never would have..." He shook his head as words seemed to fail him as well. And then he said, "Things must be very different in Sheng Fan."

"They are," Xu Liang confirmed. *And I miss it very much*, he added to himself.

FİFTEEN
Fury Unleashed

THE NIGHT PASSED without event. The morning began with a strange sense of stillness.

Taya emerged from the tent early to find Tristus already up, silhouetted among the sparse trees against the rising sun as he stood alone several paces away from the camp. He was looking up at the sky and did not notice her staring at the lonely image he painted. She'd started breakfast by the time the knight wandered back and greeted her with one of his unhappy smiles, as if the light-less expression hid the sheen of tears in his blue eyes. He offered to help and she let him, happy that she didn't have to bark at him for assistance like she did the others. All except Xu Liang, who she didn't dare to ask and who'd probably never prepared a meal or even con-sidered washing a dish in his life. The bodyguards seemed to handle all of the mundane tasks for him as well as for themselves. The elf partook of the meals when he was around, but he was always too quick to get away before Taya could tell him it was his turn to give the stew pot a rinse in some melted snow. Fu Ran and Bastien were simply slobs, apparently used to someone else doing the kitchen chores aboard their ship, and Tarfan had never been a tidy dwarf. Tristus, on the other hand, being a soldier who might have had to spend weeks or months in a war campaign, had been taught to make the best of life away from the conveniences of home, and to do it in a clean and orderly fashion. Though Tristus admitted that the Knights of Eris had not recently seen much for war, the training still held, as did his manners.

"How can you sleep in all of that metal?" Taya asked him, simply to pass the time.

The knight looked at his own armor, as if he'd forgotten he was wearing the well-kept layers of chain and plate mail—only enough to cover vital areas, but it still seemed heavy and uncomfortable. Then he shrugged and proceeded to slice one of the last whole carrots from Taya's pouch into the tiny pot that barely made enough stew for those eating it to have a taste. They had plenty of jerked meats, biscuits, and even some dried fruit to live on, but in this cold region it was nice to have something warm to eat.

"You've seen how much trouble it can be for me to strap on all of this armor," Tristus said pleasantly. "I dare not ask all of you to wait for me every morning."

"I wouldn't mind," Taya offered, dropping a few dried greens into the pot.

"But as you're especially kind to me, I think I'll continue to sleep in my layers" Tristus said. "Anyway I'm sure it's my armor that's protected me from the claws of those demons and given me a fair chance to strike back. I'd hate to be unprepared should they attack again in the night."

"Isn't it heavy?"

"Very," Tristus replied. "But I've worn heavier suits, bulkier than this. In the past, particularly in full cavalry gear, I've felt like I was wearing a giant kettle. Men have nearly suffocated from the weight falling down in such a harness, but sometimes it's necessary. What you see here is much lighter than it looks and offers almost normal mobility. The responsibilities and expectations placed upon a commanding knight allow for nothing less."

"That's a grand general's suit you're wearing, pup!" Tarfan blurted while he joined them outside the tent. He snapped up Taya's spoon and prodded the stew experimentally, wrinkling his nose. "Most grand generals I've met are quite a bit older than you."

Tristus didn't look at the elder dwarf. He glared at the carrot as he sliced it. "This is my father's armor, Master Fairwind."

"Is it?" Tarfan persisted, putting his typical choke hold—born of stubbornness and meanness—onto the poor knight. "Where's yours?"

"I ... it..." Tristus' face was reddening, as were his eyes.

"Lost it? Wrecked it maybe?" Tarfan dropped the spoon in the pot and set his fists on his hips. "Or maybe you never had one!"

"I had to leave it behind!" Tristus shouted. Then he cried out again as he nicked his finger. He dropped the carrot and the knife, drawing his injured hand reflexively to his body and scowling at Tarfan. "I told you before I'm not a boy playing soldier! I am a Knight of Eris! If you must know, I held the rank of captain! I inherited this armor from my father when he died in service to the Order!" The tears were rolling down his cheeks, but he ignored them. "He died in an ambush staged against a priest he'd been accompanying on duty! He fought alone against nearly a dozen men while that fat cleric and his personal guard escaped! They abandoned him. They abandoned me as well, and I don't see how it's any of your business!"

Taya reached out a hand to him, but he shied away, standing. "And now there's blood in the soup," he choked. He spun about and left, mumbling something about how they didn't have any more carrots. Taya didn't know whether to laugh or cry, but she did have the presence of mind to snatch the spoon out of the pot and soundly knock her unfeeling uncle on the head.

"Ow!" Tarfan complained. "Is it my fault the lad's emotional?"

◆ ◆ ◆ ◆ ◆

TRISTUS WALKED AWAY without looking back. Escape was the only thing on his mind. Unfortunately, there was no place to hide in the wide open region, not unless he wanted to run about a mile to one of the long-dead trees that were somehow still standing on the broken landscape. He tried to lose himself in their small camp instead, heading for the horses, where he leaned against the nearest one, crying like a boy half his age might. It had been so long since he'd had anyone to hold onto, or to offer him the merest physical comfort that he actually felt calmed by the impassive animal. He lifted his arms around the gentle beast's neck, and buried his face in its soft pelt, letting the tears fall as they may. He didn't want to hate any member of the group, but he was beginning to strongly dislike the old dwarf.

"It's because he's right," Tristus murmured, forcing himself to draw a breath, though it rarely did any good once he'd given himself to a fit. "It's true ... I have no right to wear this armor."

He continued on for several moments, despising his weakness, despising himself. When he felt eyes on him, he stopped and peered slowly over his arm at the old Fanese guard. He coughed in his embarrassment and lack of breath, then slipped away from the horse the man was attempting to gear up for the day's journey.

"Forgive … me. I didn't realize…" He stopped himself, recalling that the man spoke only Fanese. Awkward didn't begin to describe the way he felt about the fate God had granted him.

♦ ♦ ♦ ♦ ♦

GAI PING WATCHED the young barbarian, faltering in evident apology. The boy's face was streaked with tears, defying the strength his armor suggested and the bravery he'd shown in battle against the winged devils.

"That is no way for a warrior to behave," he said, knowing that the youth didn't understand him. He hoped anyway that he would understand his firm tone and stern expression. It was in evidence that he needed a father's words at the moment and Gai Ping, already grandfather of three, felt himself suitably qualified for the task, in spite of certain language barriers.

He hefted Blue Crane's saddle up into place and began buckling it onto the calm animal, keeping his eyes on the young barbarian. "I can see that others ridicule you, take advantage of your…"

Gai Ping stopped momentarily when he heard his words echoing strangely. It was Lord Xu Liang's voice, trailing his, speaking in the barbarian tongue as he approached, so that the boy could understand.

Appreciative of his master's timing and eloquence, he continued. "They take advantage of your fear and the sadness you carry. Show them no fear and use your sadness as a strength, let it feed your resolve instead of breaking it down."

When Lord Xu Liang finished translating, the boy looked shamefaced at the ground and soon left without saying anything. Gai Ping returned to the task in front of him.

"He heard the words, Gai Ping," Lord Xu said. "I think perhaps he has gone to absorb them alone."

Gai Ping nodded, secretly wishing that he could sometimes take the same liberty with Lord Xu as he just had with the barbarian. The young lord had also been some time without paternal guidance, and while he possessed one of the strongest minds in all of Sheng Fan, he still had a boy's heart. Master Xu didn't have to show his tears for Gai Ping to know that his master had wept over Deng Po's death.

The barbarian that was pale of hide and hair arrived suddenly, reining in his white mare and speaking urgently to Lord Xu, who nodded in reply. Receiving acknowledgment, the pale one rode away slowly, toward the others in the group.

Lord Xu sighed. "It would seem that those 'simple' bandits from Li Ting have caught up with us once again." He slowly frowned, donning the resolve he wore as armor into every battle. "This time we will have to fight them with the intent to destroy their minor numbers. They have had every chance to withdraw from this endeavor and have refused. In this instance, their persistent defiance must be paid for in blood; theirs this time. We cannot fall here. The Empress needs us."

Gai Ping nodded once and went about gathering the rest of the guards.

◆ ◆ ◆ ◆ ◆

"THEY ARE COMING out of the southeast, about a mile south of where we exited the mountains," Alere informed. "It is possible that they realized they'd been spotted and sought a different route."

"You're saying they're the same group you spied behind us before?" Tristus asked, peering into the distant mist that still clung to the horizon while the sun began its work on the previous night's blanket of snow.

"They are," the elf answered, as if that were enough explanation.

The opportunity to press him further passed when Xu Liang summoned everyone's attention. The company gathered around their leader, who spoke in level tones, showing neither fear nor eagerness. He said, "Only two of them are mounted, causing them to move somewhat slower, but Alere tells me they are near and will be here shortly. More than likely, they pressed through the night, unconcerned with leaving a trail as we were. This land is very open, easy enough to traverse but with no place to hide or confuse our path. They are marching toward us openly with the intent to inevitably catch us, and we must answer their challenge now or later. I choose to do so now."

"Tell us how you want to handle it," Fu Ran said eagerly, grinding his fist into his palm, quickly recovered from the other night's argument.

Xu Liang inclined his head once, utterly composed as he revealed his plan to annihilate their pursuers, which—given the straightforward circumstances presented by the terrain—involved very little subtlety. He explained first that these were trained soldiers, not wild, unarmed creatures. At least one of them was exceedingly strong and another was a sorcerer of undetermined potential. They carried with them the determination of the Fanese people, which was no small thing, and a troop of no less than eighteen men. A few more, Xu Liang noted, than Fu Ran had counted in Nelayne. Undoubtedly some of them were 'borrowed' pirates from Zhen Yu's crew.

It would be Guang Ci and Tristus' duty to rush at them on horseback and confuse their charge. Both were excellent riders and, unlike Alere—who may have been the most skilled on horseback—they were each heavily armored and least likely to be killed by an unseating blow. Their aim was to be the men on foot. They were to avoid the two riders unless it proved absolutely impossible. It was Xu Liang's plan to lure the enemy commanders past Guang Ci and Tristus by riding part way out with Alere. Once the two leaders were engaged with the bearers of *Pearl Moon* and *Aerkiren*, Tarfan, Taya, Bastien, and all the remaining guards but Gai Ping were to run toward the foot soldiers and assist Guang Ci and Tristus. Gai Ping, an excellent bowman, had the task of attempting to shoot the enemy riders off their mounts from further back, while Fu Ran protected him from any attacks—either stray or deliberate—that may put down the elder.

"So this is how the Fanese do battle," Tristus commented after mounting the horse he'd been assigned to, taking one of the guards' tasseled spears when Xu Liang handed it up to him. He gripped the weapon unfamiliarly at first—it was nothing like a lance and much lighter than a halberd—but shifted and rotated the shaft until he got it comfortably balanced.

"This is how the Fanese do battle away from Sheng Fan," the mystic replied. "I suppose the Andarians would stand in rows and wait until the enemy was visible through the mist, at that point charging headlong into a troop they mistook for little more than scurrilous rabble, who would turn and run at the first opportunity made available to them."

Tristus smiled with grim sarcasm at the mystic's accurate accounting of the elitist Order Knights. "It's a wonder any of us are still alive."

Behind Xu Liang, Guang Ci swung himself into the saddle of his own horse and said something to Tristus, who naturally looked to Xu Liang for help. "He says to sweep the weapon in long arcs."

Guang Ci said something else and Tristus looked at the guard, receiving a visual demonstration of how to swing the spear back and forth high over the horse's neck, striking low in such a way as to knock the enemy down rather than risk losing the weapon by stabbing and getting it lodged in a falling body.

Tristus nodded. "I understand." He looked down at Xu Liang again, reminded of something. "I'd like to offer my thanks to the elder gentleman who spoke to me this morning. He's right. I shouldn't let Master Fairwind's brusque nature get to me."

"He was speaking of more than Tarfan's brusque nature, but I will give him your thanks, Tristus Edainien. I wish you good fortune in the forthcoming battle." After saying that and presumably repeating it in Fanese to the mounted guardsman, Xu Liang gave a departing bow, then joined those preparing to follow Tristus and Guang Ci's lead.

◆ ◆ ◆ ◆ ◆

"YOU HAVE A LOT of faith in that boy, for having just met him," Tarfan grumbled as Xu Liang approached.

Xu Liang did not smile when he said, "There is something about him that troubles me, but it is nothing I feel to be a deliberate threat. I believe he is in earnest when he offers his allegiance ... to all of us."

"Do you honestly believe that teary-eyed pup is meant to wield one of the Swords?"

"Time will tell. And in the meantime, the knight has proven to be a capable rider."

"Are you so sure he's actually a knight?" Tarfan persisted, proving unusually petulant in this matter.

With patience, Xu Liang said, "He is comfortable with a weapon and not afraid to fight, though fighting scares him—as it should all men, regardless of strength or ability. I believe these qualities are a result of training."

"You've got ten of us going against eighteen," the dwarf mentioned next. "Maybe more, if the elf didn't spy them all."

"I am trusting that by the time you and the others get to them, Guang Ci and Tristus will have evened things a bit with their advance strike. I know that you are not a trained soldier, my friend, but I also know that you are both strong and skilled. And I have faith in you and the others."

Tarfan grumbled something incoherent and stepped away with his war hammer clutched tightly in both hands.

Alere rode up to them. "They'll be upon us in moments."

"Any sign of an attack from the rear?" Xu Liang asked.

The elf shook his head. "None that I have seen. Still, you should let the giant protect your guard as planned. The mist is heavy. If we're as distracted as you claim we'll be by the commanders, it would not be difficult for one or more men to pass us."

Xu Liang nodded, then went to Blue Crane and mounted with ease that seemed to surprise almost all of his companions. He drew *Pearl Moon*, quickly glanced over the others taking up their positions, then nodded again to Alere, who whistled into the air, his birdcall giving Guang Ci and Tristus the signal to advance the enemy.

♦ ♦ ♦ ♦ ♦

THE MIST USED to cover their advance was just beginning to clear, all too quickly revealing what Ma Shou had feared. "They were prepared," he said to Xiadao Lu.

The large man saw. His eyes narrowed, and he sneered with defiance. "Xu Liang, you fool! You dare to insult us by sending only two men?"

"Is he trying to cover his escape?" Ma Shou wondered, doubting the scenario even as he spoke it.

"Ah, there he is," Xiadao Lu said with satisfaction. "He comes himself! Attack!"

"Such a fool," Ma Shou muttered while his companion rode away.

♦ ♦ ♦ ♦ ♦

ONLY ONE RIDER came. Watching him come, it seemed like it would be no trouble to bring him from his horse, but Tristus recalled that he had been given orders. He dared not be the one to ruin Xu Liang's plan before it'd even been given a chance to work. He waited until the last moment, seeing the strange halberd carried by the enemy rider as he extended it to drag Tristus off his mount, then steered wide away and let the man charge between him and Guang Ci, who had moved accordingly. With Alere and Xu Liang coming, the first rider didn't bother with circling back. Tristus lowered his grip on the Fanese spear and started swinging a second before he reached the mob of armed foot soldiers. None were dressed in much armor, and several darted out of the way just to avoid the horses, let alone the dual spears diving in and out of their small force.

Tristus felt a man crumple under the horse's hooves, blocked from running by his fellows. A moment afterward Tristus felt his shoulder hitch unpleasantly as he toppled another man with the spear. The second man might not have been dead but he was on the ground. Once he cleared the group, Tristus circled back, crossing paths with Guang Ci while the guard performed a mirroring pattern of maneuvers.

He didn't notice the second rider at first. It was some time before he spied the individual sitting idle away from the trampled, confused soldiers, seeming to pray as Tristus had seen Xu Liang do in battle against the demons—just before firing daggers of magic through their unholy bodies. Tristus didn't wonder whether or not this Fanese cleric was casting a spell, noting that his target appeared to be the oncoming guards, along with the dwarves and Bastien. Behind them, Alere and Xu Liang both confronted the first rider. All three men were still mounted, the horses charging in brief spurts to avoid or deliver a blow. Fu Ran and Gai Ping were just visible in the lingering mist nearer to their campsite. Tristus rode toward the magic-user, knowing he wouldn't make it in time.

♦ ♦ ♦ ♦ ♦

THERE WERE TIMES when Tarfan yearned for the long legs of a man or elf, and this was one of them. There were battles ahead of him and behind him, and he simply couldn't move fast enough. The guards were several strides ahead of him and Taya, with Bastien jogging between, keeping his shifty gypsy eyes on everyone. Up ahead, Guang Ci plowed through the ranks, leaving Tarfan to wonder where in the Abyss the supposed knight had gone to.

Tarfan heard thunder in that moment, sounding loud and low enough to be in the sparse cloud that lingered over the morning's battlefield. He saw the lightning afterward, only it wasn't lightning. It was a great rolling ball of fire! And it was a half a heartbeat away from hitting Taya square and burning her to cinders. Tarfan cried out to his niece, reaching out for her as she stood suddenly stunned in the path of certain annihilation, like a startled doe. He dove, and tackled her, prepared to take the brunt of the fire himself, praying that she would be spared.

Thunder sounded again—the thunder of impact—and a tremendous heat rushed over the fallen dwarves, slamming into the hard ground behind them. Tarfan smelled scorched flesh, wondering for just a second if it was his own. When he realized both he and Taya were alive, he shot upright to have a look around, finding a dead horse in front of him and behind him, the smoldering body of a man.

"Tristus!" Taya wailed, bolting for him as he struggled upright, his white-gold armor smudged black all along the breastplate.

Tarfan turned to glare at the mage responsible, leaping aside just as the Fanese man rushed by on a white horse, his blond braid trailing him like a serpent's tail. He was going after the knight.

Tristus saw him coming and hurried to his feet, knocking Taya aside to protect her. He'd lost his spear, but found his sword, and avoided having his head sheared clean off by lifting it to deflect the rider's shorter blade.

"Go help the others!" Tristus shouted back at them. "I'll deal with this one!"

Tarfan wanted to argue, but he knew what Tristus wouldn't say. The dwarves were simply too short to be of much help against a man on horseback. "Come on," he urged Taya, dragging her by the arm until she came on her own.

◆ ◆ ◆ ◆ ◆

XIADAO LU SHOULD have known better than to trust that coward Ma Shou to ride with him. While he was likely standing safely behind the men, casting flame spells, Xiadao Lu had two enchanted blades to deal with. He suspected they weren't simply enchanted, but actually forged in magic. He knew that Xu Liang carried *Pearl Moon* and could only assume he was seeing it for the second time as the pale blue light traced its sleek edges. The pale barbarian's blade must have been one of the other Celestial Swords, since it glowed with a similar power. If so, Xu Liang had been more successful than Lord Han Quan expected.

No matter. Xu Liang would never return to Sheng Fan alive, let alone to the Imperial City. Whatever Swords he had discovered would be taken when this battle was won and brought back to Lord Han. Xiadao Lu and Ma Shou would only have to head back for the coast and be at the rendezvous to meet Zhen Yu within the allotted time.

Xiadao Lu, with the luck of a dragon and a geomancer's enchantment, tasted victory. He knew how easily Xu Liang would go down if struck and this puny, pale specimen in league with him would pose little trouble once isolated. He swiped away Xu Liang's next attack and swung to his other side to knock back the other's blade, waiting for the moment when their timing would be just off, and someone's neck or chest would be exposed. If Xu Liang went down first, he would have to die, else there would still be his wind attacks to be concerned with. The pale one, so far as Xiadao Lu could tell, was no sorcerer. He moved like a warrior and with a confidence that spoke of winning against terrible odds. It would be easiest to swat Xu Liang away with a lethal blow and move onto the entertainment of facing a better challenge in his pale, devil-eared companion.

An arrow flitted past Xiadao Lu's ear, having come from the thinning mist further ahead. Xiadao Lu ignored it and kept fighting, though he thought about breaking out of their mounted dance long enough to charge at the archer—or archers—responsible. However, the mystic and the barbarian kept him too busy. A second arrow grazed his neck. He growled, striking harder at his opponents. The third struck his chest and fell away as the enchantment on his armor forbade harm to the wearer. It was effective against only one source at a time, unfortunately. Otherwise it would have been no trouble to cut through any number of barbarians Xu Liang wanted to send at him.

"You will fall!" Xiadao Lu promised the Imperial Mystic, just before a fourth arrow grazed his horse and reeled the animal into panic, dumping him from the saddle. The incident proved more convenient than his attackers intended, as Xiadao Lu was then able to rise to his feet and charge past the other two horses, planting himself as soon as he caught sight of the bowman. There were two enchantments cast upon his armor, the second a reserve spell cast by the geomancer, that could only be used once. He was certain he had come to the ideal moment to use it. He lifted his right foot, spoke a quick activation phrase, and stomped down on the cold, hard earth. His boot instantly became cast in a faint green glimmer. The light quickly drew toward the ground, starting an unnatural tremor. A wave of energy rushed forth, directly at the archer, and sent him flying.

The sound of hoof beats postponed any gloating. Xiadao Lu turned to see the pale barbarian coming. He readied his weapon and dared him on. A glint came to the white devil's eyes and he smiled, lured Xiadao Lu's weapon up, and then cut down.

"Fool!" Xiadao Lu laughed, following through with his own swing, feeling the shaft strike lower than he intended when he inexplicably lost his balance and fell onto his side, his body suddenly racked with pain. He lay on the ground and felt his life draining rapidly out of him, blood soaking his chest. Somehow the devil's blade had penetrated his enchantment … and his armor. "Im-possible … !" he coughed as he tasted warm bitterness at the back of his throat.

He lay on the ground, unable to form another word, or soon even another breath.

◆ ◆ ◆ ◆ ◆

XIADAO LU'S FINAL word went almost unheard as Xu Liang rushed to Alere. The elf slowed his mare and half climbed, half fell out of her saddle before she'd even come to a full stop. The crack of the warrior's weapon across his back was enough to make Xu Liang believe the elf's spine had been shattered, but he seemed to have full movement, even if it was uncoordinated at the moment. And in the distance, there was Gai Ping, victim of what was obviously a geomancer's spell. Xu Liang knew the sorcerer with Xiadao Lu was a pyromancer and wondered if he'd grossly underestimated the larger of the two rogues, if he too had studied the mystic arts. He wondered also how Alere had managed to harm the very man who'd previously survived at least two wind attacks that should have killed if not severely injured him.

"His armor," Alere said through his teeth, struggling to return to the battle he may not have realized was finished, even as Xu Liang helped him to stand. "The spell … is in his armor. *Aerkiren…*"

The elf collapsed into Xu Liang's arms, collapsing Xu Liang as well. Xu Liang lowered to his knees, supporting his ally with what little strength *Pearl Moon* had left lingering in him. The loss of consciousness finally forced Alere to drop his sword and he lay still and silent, his back stained red across the shoulders.

"Fu Ran!" Xu Liang called into the clearing mist. He lowered his voice when the large man came. "Fu Ran, tell me how Gai Ping is."

"He lives," Fu Ran answered. "What..."

Xu Liang didn't let him finish. "Take Alere from me. I must assist the others. This is not their fight."

"I'll go," Fu Ran offered, but as soon as he crouched down, Xu Liang carefully shoved the elf at him and returned to Blue Crane. "Stay with them," he instructed the larger man, who nodded resignedly.

♦ ♦ ♦ ♦ ♦

AS SOON AS the barbarian knocked him out of his saddle, Ma Shou cast a quick flame spell into the air, signaling the handful of bowmen he'd left behind as support to begin firing. The arrows flew out of the nearby mist, and the tide of a losing battle turned. Almost at once, two of Xu Liang's bodyguards went down, and it was shortly after that when the half-sized woman cried out.

Ma Shou had almost been enjoying batting away the overzealous attacks of the armored barbarian with his twin blades, until that tiny cry lit a fire in his opponent's eyes. Three wild, powerful swings drove Ma Shou back and ultimately threw him to the ground. He was spared only by his hurried blocking and finally, a wall of fire that took the last of his energy from him. Still, he thought the crazed barbarian might have rushed through the fire and tried to do away with him anyway, but he was distracted by the melee nearby, and charged into it like a madman.

When an arm flew into the dissipating flame wall free of its body, Ma Shou decided the fight had gotten ugly enough. He found his horse and quickly rode off into the thicker mists, back toward the mountains. There were devils in the mountains, but they burned easily. He would wait for Xiadao Lu and any other survivors.

♦ ♦ ♦ ♦ ♦

XU LIANG WAS horrified at the sight he came upon. No one was left standing.

How could that be? How could everyone be dead?

He sighed relief when someone stirred, and did so again when he saw that it was Tarfan. "How badly are you injured, my friend?" he asked while dismounting, wondering why the dwarf was waving his hand at him as if it had caught fire.

"I'm not hurt!" the dwarf barked. "But Taya is! I've got to protect her! Now get on your horse and get away from here!"

"I will do no such thing." He crouched beside the dwarf. "Where are the others?"

"On the ground, keeping low and out of the way of that madman!"

Xu Liang heard something in the near distance, like a person cry out in pain, and looked around, finally seeing the arrows stuck in the ground and in the body of a guard nearby. He couldn't tell if he was dead. He looked unconscious. "Where is Tristus and the sorcerer who rode with Xiadao Lu?"

"The fire-spitter's gone!" Tarfan hissed. "Ran away more scared than the rest of us! Tristus went to take down the archers that the elf forgot to count! The rest is a long story, now get the hell out of here!"

"Tarfan," Xu Liang started in disapproval and with a little uncertainty. His next words failed to sound when he heard footsteps coming. The individual was running.

Though the mist was thinning, the increasing sunlight glared off the moist air, creating a blinding effect. Xu Liang couldn't see who was coming and so rose with a spell in mind, prepared to buffet the individual away with the winds. In truth, he didn't have the energy for another physical confrontation.

The silhouette of an armed man formed in the shining mist. He was strangely quiet, except for the sound of his footsteps. Whether or not he saw Xu Liang, he kept coming, his sword raised. Xu Liang uttered the necessary chant, one hand extended in front of him, and summoned the wind.

Out of the mist, the knight came. Xu Liang started to relax, seeing that it was an ally, hoping that the burst of wind wouldn't do him too much harm.

The spell struck Tristus. He staggered back a half step, his sword arm pulling slightly back, then coming forward again as the knight continued his charge ... deliberately.

Xu Liang found himself momentarily confused, facing an unexpected betrayer, or someone Tarfan had rightly suspected a madman. The knight's features were a mockery of his once sympathetic fairness, twisted and contorted with a rage unlike any Xu Liang had witnessed before.

"He's a berserker now!" Tarfan hollered from his position on the ground, hovering over his niece. "He doesn't recognize you! He's gone mad! Leave!"

In spite of the dwarf's urging, Xu Liang called to the winds again. Tristus was coming too fast and he had no intention of leaving the others, besides. Whatever had come over him, the knight had to be stopped.

A wall of air struck Tristus, this one stronger than the first and reinforced with Xu Liang's continued prayer. The blast halted the crazed warrior in his tracks for an instant, but he remained on his feet, leaning into the wind, shouldering against what would have leveled another man with the first strike, including the mighty Xiadao Lu. The knight's state enabled him to endure, his strength enhanced through madness. Xu Liang maintained the wind, hoping the break in the slaughter that must have perpetuated Tristus' unexpected condition would calm him enough to be put down. Though it was not his desire, Xu Liang would kill the knight if he had to, before he would let him finish off the others.

"A dark fury's got hold of him!" Tarfan shouted. "He'll kill you! He can't stop himself!"

Then I must stop him, Xu Liang thought, giving still more effort to the spell.

For a moment, Tristus began to lose his footing and slid backwards, but his eyes were lit with unnatural determination, and he pressed on, snarling with the strain. He inched forward, his sword held to strike when the distance between them was finally covered.

Xu Liang thrust both hands out in front of him, closed his eyes, and factored out everything but the wind. *Ancestors... hear me!*

◆ ◆ ◆ ◆ ◆

TAYA WOKE UP to a storm. She looked around groggily, her neck and shoulder throbbing fiercely, making her head and stomach hurt as well. It wasn't raining. There was no lightning. Only the sound of the fierce winds. Why couldn't she feel them? Her uncle was her only shelter, not nearly enough to block what sounded like a hurricane.

And then she realized it was no storm, but a spell. She could see Xu Liang, strain attacking his calm features as he worked his magic against ... Tristus! Taya sat up, choking on her own voice as her head spun and her stomach surged upward.

Tarfan steadied her.

"Stop," she murmured. "Stop them!"

"There's nothing we can do," Tarfan snapped, his voice breaking slightly under the stress of watching two who were supposed to be allies pitted against each other.

She wondered if he'd finally discovered some respect for Tristus, who had used his own life to shield Taya's. She felt like her uncle had, like the moment had granted power to his swing as a new sense of camaraderie formed. Taya had been handling herself just as her uncle had taught her to. The guards were as formidable as ever and just when the enemies' numbers began to deplete, more suddenly arrived. Arrows had fired out of the mist. Guang Ci and another guard dropped like overripe apples from an overladen branch. And then something sliced Taya, and she cried out, overcome by a form of pain she'd never felt before. Tarfan finished off his own opponent and moved to assist, halted almost literally dead in his tracks when Tristus charged onto the scene.

The knight had swung his sword in a great arc, and sliced the man who'd attacked Taya almost clean through from shoulder to waist. When the bandit failed to drop at once, Tristus let him have it again, slicing off his sword arm and finally his head before he moved onto the next victim. Taya didn't remember much beyond that. She'd never been witness to anything like that, or like this.

"Stop them!" Taya insisted.

"I can't! If I attack the knight, we both go tumbling into the next countryside. Or else I get shot to the horizon and he still goes at the mage. If I interrupt Xu Liang, we all get cleaved like dead meat on the butcher's block!"

"What's he doing?" Taya cried. "Tristus, are you crazy? Stop it!"

Tarfan put his arms around her while they watched the knight gaining ground. "Close your eyes, girl."

"Tristus, please stop," Taya sobbed. "Please!"

The rage wouldn't die. The knight pressed onward, eyes on his target. He brought his sword in front of him, as if deciding it would be good enough simply to impale the mage standing in his way. The gap between Xu Liang and death grew ever smaller.

"In Heaven's name," Tarfan said, holding Taya as tightly as he could without crushing her.

Tristus was shoving his blade forward, finding more ease in the task as the mage's wind finally began to weaken. The point edged past Xu Liang's hands, up toward his chest. Taya closed her eyes.

◆ ◆ ◆ ◆ ◆

THE WIND DIED. It had left Xu Liang. He had no more strength. He could feel the heat of the life slain upon Tristus' blade, the blade that would shortly claim him and in the process all of his dreams of a peaceful, unified Sheng Fan.

My empress...

The clatter of steel interrupted his final message to his oath sister.

Xu Liang opened his eyes, just as the knight—having let go his sword—dropped to his hands and knees before him, shaking in the aftermath of his unnatural rage. Tristus gasped for air until he finally had enough to keep and then he sat still, holding that breath until his weary body shuddered once more and sobs escaped.

Xu Liang was drained, dangerously near to fainting, and left with only one choice. That was to kneel in front of the very man who'd nearly killed him and perhaps in that event, everything he'd lived for as well. Xu Liang sank before the weeping knight, unable to feel anything while he concentrated on regaining his strength. Behind him, the dwarves seemed too afraid to move, and so the four of them huddled among the dead or dying, silent except for Tristus, who sobbed brokenly over his gore-stained sword.

SİXTEEN
Truth Revealed

TWO MORE GUARDS had been lost of the seven that remained before the day's battle. Their wounds were simply too much for the combined knowledge and skills of the group, which included no healing spells. They were wounds that could have been inflicted by the enemy, or they could have been inflicted by Tristus, who in his berserker rage, had declared everyone his enemy. No one knew. No one had seen, except the dead guards, Hu Zhong and Yuan Lan. Tristus couldn't remember himself and no one dared to press him at the moment, uncertain as to whether or not the 'dark fury'—as Tarfan had called it—had actually left him. He'd been left alone outside the tent, lying still—the last anyone dared to look—right where Fu Ran had left him after dragging him back from the battlefield. The knight had been barely conscious in his state of exhaustion.

Tarfan had fared the best of all of them; he was angrier than he was hurt. He'd acquired a few bruises and scrapes altogether. Xu Liang was physically uninjured, but he felt as if his mind were about to collapse in on itself, and he'd barely managed to carry himself back to the camp. He sat among the others now, unable to concentrate in the way that he needed to while they bickered and fumed.

Guang Ci, who had taken an arrow to the shoulder and been easily patched up, sat in front of Xu Liang, reaching for his sword every time a frustrated voice or arm raised too loudly or too near his master. In the young guard's eyes, Xu Liang could do no wrong and his battle plan had been perfect, thwarted by the ineptitude of the others, including their scout, who lay unconscious on the other side of the tent.

Alere had been struck hard enough by Xiadao Lu to have the wind knocked out of him, for his skin to break, and possibly for his left shoulder blade to have cracked. It was difficult for Taya to tell beneath all the swelling and bruising. Taya herself had been sliced deep across the shoulder and required stitches. Gai Ping suffered from a dislocated shoulder, which fortunately Fu Ran was able to assist in putting back into place. Oddly enough, it was the giant who'd done the damage to the elder guard pulling him out of the way of Xiadao Lu's magic assault. Fu Ran himself caught the edge of the spell and twisted his knee trying to escape it. The last three guards had been grazed by arrows, sliced by sword, and bruised by whatever else had been raised against them.

Bastien was simply missing. Whether he'd crawled into the mist with his wounds and died, or been burnt to ash by the pyromancer, or—though no one wanted to consider it—hacked beyond recognition by a certain berserker, no one could say at the moment. Daylight was fading and everyone was too confused or aching to search for the man. If he was alive and well enough, he would likely find his way back to camp. If not, his body would be easier to find during the day.

"This isn't what I meant by excitement," Taya sniffled, checking on Alere's bandages, resisting the urge to go to Tristus, who she was evidently ashamed to admit scared her more than a little after his secret unleashed itself on everyone.

"So now it's out," Tarfan blurted for at least the tenth time. "The boy's a berserker! That's why he was booted out of the Order. He probably had a similar fit in the middle of a previous battle and started striking down his own comrades! He might have considered sharing something like that with the rest of us before he—"

"Would you?" Taya demanded, wiping at her eyes, as if the incessant tears were beginning to annoy her. "Would you want anyone to know something like that? And how exactly would you drop it into a conversation. 'Oh, by the way, I killed the last company I was with in a horrible demonic rage, but don't worry I think it's passed!'? Of course he wouldn't tell us!" She turned back to Alere. "Anyway he saved my life, and probably the rest of our lives as well. That sorcerer had us. He had us right where he wanted us! We almost burned!"

"A pity the lunatic boy tried to kill the wrong mage!" Tarfan yelled. "The fire-spitter got away!"

"But none of his men did," Fu Ran pointed out.

"None so far as we know," Tarfan grumbled. "You couldn't even count them coming off their ship, and not even the elf discovered the extra archers."

"I doubt that the pirate they were dealing with gave them that many of his own crew," Fu Ran argued without raising his voice. "Anyway they left, and after seeing the knight's tactics, I doubt they'll be coming back. We took most of them down and forced the others to retreat. In Sheng Fan that's counted as a victory."

Tarfan jabbed his finger into the much larger man's gut. "Well here, in the middle of forsaken wastelands that's called a damned close call!"

Fu Ran walked away from the dwarf, resuming his pacing in what space the injured left him, and in spite of his damaged knee. "You'd rather be chased across the wastelands until those bastards finally caught up with us. They weren't going to give up and now the confrontation's over with. A close call, but it's done!"

"Done is it?" Tarfan's face was red with frustration, his dark beard bristling. "Done? You great, bone-headed lummox! How can it be done while we're toting around an armored box of disaster! In fact, what's to stop him charging in here at any minute and making cutlets of all of us?"

"He didn't attack us before," Fu Ran reminded. "It was the heat of the battle. It had to be. He just panicked, that's all."

"Panicked? You didn't see his face—whiter than the mountain sprite over there—when you pulled him out from under that demon the other night?" Tarfan indicated Alere with one flung arm. "If he was going to lose it, that was where he should have lost it!"

"The knight is not responsible for this. It is I who have brought all of you here and it is I who will accept the blame for what has befallen you."

Tarfan and Fu Ran both stopped to look at Xu Liang, having perhaps forgotten that he was even present during their argument.

Quietly, Xu Liang continued. "Fu Ran is correct. Overall, we claimed victory this day. Still, my plan was imperfect, as it involved people who were not mine to command. My bodyguards did what duty required of them, even in death. The Empress herself appointed them to this task, but the rest of you came as friends and allies. I understand now what Tristus was saying, and I have disgraced myself with my inadequate decisions and my betrayal of your trust. I cannot ask for your forgiveness, but I will offer you my sincerest apologies and condolences for any losses suffered."

Xu Liang stood, bowing to his stunned audience. When he straightened again, he said, "Alere is called to this journey by forces higher than myself. I believe he knows that and will continue on, in spite of what has happened today. But you... Tarfan, Fu Ran, and Taya... do not have to be here. I will understand if you decide to turn back and offer whatever I have to spare that will aid you on your journey home."

"Where are you going?" Tarfan asked Xu Liang when he walked to the tent's entrance.

"I must speak with the knight." Xu Liang held out a hand to stop Fu Ran and Guang Ci as they came forward simultaneously. He said in Fanese, "I must speak with him alone."

The guard and former guard halted and grudgingly remained behind while Xu Liang exited the tent and approached the slumping form silhouetted against the sunset. At the very least, Tristus hadn't fled. Whatever he was thinking and feeling, whatever he had heard the others saying about him, he didn't have the strength or else the desire to flee the unpleasant circumstances.

Looking at the depressed knight, Xu Liang didn't know what to feel. Inside of this young man was an enemy, one to be greatly feared, but it was not an enemy that sat before him now. It should have been easy to separate the emotions, but Xu Liang was having difficulty. Fear and hatred clashed against compassion and the trust he'd felt just hours ago, before a terrible evil emerged from behind a mask of virtue. Now the torment behind the man's soft eyes was clear, but at what cost? Had he been the death of Hu Zhong, Yuan Lan, and Bastien? Or had his rage been more focused than even he knew?

"They call them soul burners," Tristus said miserably and, seeing that he was conscious again, Xu Liang stopped more than an arm's length away from him.

The knight continued. "In Caleddon, where weirdness and witchcraft flourish, where the children tell tales of demons to their parents, and where men drink the blood of other men, they are given that title. Such things are rejected in Treska, automatically. It is a reflex, like breathing, to denounce the possibility of magic as anything more than foolish superstition and common trickery used to scare or entertain peasants. In Andaria, such things are considered, but only as a menacing darkness that must be burned, like unwanted growth, lest it take over the green and gold fields of our sacred lands." He sounded bitter, perhaps even mocking in that statement.

Xu Liang offered silence.

Tristus accepted it for a time. Eventually, he said, "It was an old man from Caleddon, who told me about them."

"Them?" Xu Liang inquired delicately. "The soul burners?"

Tristus nodded sullenly. "They are wraiths, spirits that take up residence in an unsuspecting body and attack the soul, toying with it, driving the person mad."

Xu Liang selected his words with care. "Is that what you think is inside of you?"

"I don't know what's inside of me," the knight admitted, sounding confused and detached. "I was just thinking about that old man. He'd been caught practicing his strange craft in a village not far from the Citadel one day, and was brought before the High Order Master, whom he accused of harboring a soul burner. I was guarding the old man's cell when he told me about them. The High Order Master had the poor fool burned the next morning for his blasphemy."

The knight laughed suddenly. It was a strangled and alarming sound in his state. "Do you know he's afraid of me? The High Order Master?" Tristus nodded when Xu Liang said nothing, adding, "He is. He would have had me killed, but he feared that whatever is inside of me would awaken and go after him, as it went after the others. Instead he had me banished. He held a trial and everything, not one to make me seem guilty of anything so much as it was meant to make me realize myself a danger to others and unfit for the Order because of the ease with which evil could use me. My intentions didn't matter, he said. My faith wasn't strong enough."

Tears crowded his last statement. He gained control of them and continued, "The Order Master stripped me of my rank and my command, and once I'd safely gone he told everyone of my curse and my deed, that I'd given up my honor and my faith, and turned against God. People I'd grown up with shunned me, speaking openly and behind my back of how I shamed my father's legacy. My mother died of shame and grief. There was nothing I could do but leave."

A long silence followed Tristus' words.

Believing the knight to be relatively under control, Xu Liang chanced a step toward him.

Tristus took notice of the movement suddenly, and convulsed away from him. He was quickly on his feet, backing away. "Don't! Please don't. Just stay back."

Xu Liang stopped, and watched the knight wheel away from him. Tristus took several steps into the near darkness before he dropped to his knees in defeat. Xu Liang thought about seeking Gai Ping for assistance, but he quickly reminded himself that it was his duty to bring the Swords and their bearers together, since he'd opted not to wait for fate to do so on its own. He realized, since taking the bearers into serious account, that he would have to earn their trust and give them his in return, unconditionally. Those in discord among themselves could not hope to stand against chaos, in any form it chose to take.

Xu Liang started forward again, surprised when Tristus didn't leave or urge him back.

"The Order Masters are right," the knight mumbled. "My faith isn't strong enough. No matter what or who I try to follow, I only ruin things. I destroy them utterly. Whatever is inside of me, I cannot banish it on my own, and I cannot control it."

"On your own, perhaps not," Xu Liang said, sitting down as he began to feel tired. It would take many hours to recover from the day's exertion. "Perhaps with someone to help you..."

"There is no one to help me," Tristus decided. "*Dawnfire* was my salvation ... and I lost it."

"It is not conviction I hear in your voice when you say such things, but desperation," Xu Liang told him. "You want something to save you from this fate. You want to believe that something can, so that you do not feel as much blame when the fury escapes."

He was simply guessing and wondered if he should worry about the knight's sudden silence following his words. He wouldn't have the strength to fend him off if he attacked again.

◆ ◆ ◆ ◆ ◆

IT WAS NOT HARD to read the reservation in the mystic. Tristus didn't attack, and he wouldn't. He was far too aware at the moment, and he was sure that he had never hated anyone more in his entire life than he hated himself presently. He'd just viciously slaughtered at least a dozen men, turned against Tarfan and Taya, and the others assigned to that battle with him. He could only think of how ashamed and terrified he was to have attacked Xu Liang, whom he was only a few solemn words away from being oath bound to serve and protect with his life. In his mind the vow had already been made. It would only be another test of his honor failed.

He had no memory of any of the battlefield's final moments. He recalled only feeling an intense, burning anger, all thought gone save one: He must kill. Something stopped him. He awakened from his killing trance with the tip of his sword just inches away from the mystic's heart. He'd have murdered him in another second. He'd have murdered the others as well, and honor didn't have anything to do with it. It was his humanity that was in question now. He was no better than a demon.

The thought paralyzed him. The tears stopped and he stared at the shadowing ground, forgetting for a moment even to breathe.

God, I'm not even human!

He thought of Taya's fear while Tarfan led her away from the field of corpses and the individual responsible for leaving them there—in pieces! —and shuddered.

I'm a monster!

And yet, the others let me live. They could have killed me in my exhaustion and instead they brought me back. Why? How can they ... how can Xu Liang treat me so fairly after what I did, what I might have done?

What I didn't do, Tristus amended.

He sat up slowly, wiped his eyes, and drew in a long breath. He let the air out carefully, then raked a hand through his limp hair and vowed to himself, *I'm never going to cry like this again. And whatever you are, trapped inside of me, foul murdering thing ... I'll never let you out again.*

In a moment, he looked at Xu Liang. The mystic's eyes were closed. Tristus didn't know if he was meditating, but he approached him slowly, crawling so as not to alarm him. He couldn't say where his sword was at the moment—he'd barely been conscious when Fu Ran half dragged him back to the camp site—but he imagined that the others, recalling his berserker state, would fear him whether armed or not. He recalled the look on poor little Taya's face clearly enough. It would haunt him for some time. The thought almost stopped his approach toward Xu Liang, but there was something stronger than his consciousness when it came to the mystic, that drew him as surely as the rage took him over. But the sway of whatever held him when he looked upon Xu Liang was not a danger.

Tristus arrived at the mystic and was maneuvering onto one knee when Xu Liang opened his eyes, and froze him with the action. Too stunned to be nervous or embarrassed, Tristus stared for several moments into those dark, mysterious eyes, having a thousand questions generated in his mind with every beat of his heart. All the while Xu Liang said nothing, his gaze unwavering.

A display of trust, Tristus realized slowly, and he wondered what to say now that the very thing he'd meant to solemnly ask for had been granted. He hovered before the mystic, looking at him as he'd only dared to once before. Weariness did not degrade the details Tristus had captured in his memory from the first time he gazed upon such grace. Every feature, every line, remained perfect, drawing a stunning portrait of patience and intelligence, and even of kindness. That last trait was something every figure of authority Tristus had ever known—including his own father—had been direly lacking. The mystic's eyes were depthless, pools of wonder that had unquestionably seen things Tristus could only dream of. Tristus wanted to see those things. He wanted to see the land and the people that had enabled such a person as Xu Liang to exist. He wanted to see the empress that had inspired him to journey so far from his homeland, and … he wanted …

"The wise employ caution." Xu Liang spoke suddenly, drawing Tristus out of his second trance for the day.

Tristus quickly dropped his gaze to the ground, feeling twice as embarrassed as he did the first time he'd stared so deeply at the mystic, as this time he had a witness; the very subject of his admiration.

However, it didn't seem that Xu Liang meant to scold him when he rose to his feet and said, "With the sorcerer having survived and the shadow folk abounding we cannot allow our guard to fall. There is still a long journey ahead, for those of us continuing on."

Still looking at the dark, cold earth, Tristus said, "I will come, if you and the others will have me. I know this may be difficult to accept, but I meant none of you any harm today and I would not seek to harm any of you in the future. I intend to take Master Gai Ping's advice and make my weaknesses strengths. I include whatever lurks within me when I say that."

"Gai Ping will be pleased to know that at least one of us is wise enough to regard his wisdom seriously," Xu Liang replied. "And now

I advise you to rest, Tristus Edainien. There are not many of us left who will be able to defend this camp tonight should the need arise."

Before the mystic could leave, Tristus quickly stood and beckoned after him. "I can help," he said when Xu Liang stopped. He glanced at the tent entrance, and felt a nervous spasm inside as he considered the others' reactions to him. He recalled his vow but moments ago and said again, with renewed determination, "I can help."

◆ ◆ ◆ ◆ ◆

"UNBELIEVABLE," TARFAN mumbled. He looked over his shoulder at Fu Ran, held a hand out to indicate the subject of everyone's interest, and said, "I don't believe it!"

No one paid attention to the dwarf, their eyes fixed on the young knight, kneeling beside Alere with his head bowed and one hand hovering just above the elf's ruined back. A faint white light glowed under his palm. His other hand just touched the insignia on his breastplate and his lips moved in quiet prayer. The words were ancient, and even elegant. They sounded important, and they must have been, since the elf's broken skin was slowly beginning to mend itself.

"Incredible," Tarfan breathed in wonder. "A cleric? Him?"

Tristus finished his prayer with a traditional Andarian gesture, then withdrew his healing hand, and looked at his astonished audience. He smiled what might have been considered the first real smile since the company had met him and said, "I was schooled for the clergy before training to become a knight." He glanced up at Xu Liang, his expression altering to one of apology. "I might have said something sooner, but there still would have been nothing I could do for Deng Po. God's mercy where demons are concerned is often to grant the poor soul a quicker release from its tormented body. I'm sorry about the others as well. If I'd not been so irrational and exhausted after … after what happened, I might have gotten to them in time."

"You are doing all that you can," Xu Liang said appreciatively.

"A real cleric," Tarfan marveled, stepping closer to the rapidly healing elf.

Fu Ran grabbed his shoulder. "Get in line, dwarf. My knee is aching like you would not believe."

Xu Liang intervened before Tarfan could do more than bristle. "I know some of you have a long walk ahead of you," the mystic said, "but perhaps we ought to be careful about tiring Tristus too much."

"It's all right," Tristus said at once. "It's the very least that I can do." He turned to face Taya, who stood at the foot of the elf's pallet. "I can heal your wound too," he offered, seeming to know as he spoke the words that no amount of prayer was going to mend what actually hurt the girl. Tristus watched her hesitate, then extended his hand to the dwarf maiden and said, "I meant what I said before, Taya. I'll do you no harm. You needn't be afraid."

She almost looked sad at first, perhaps even shy in the face of what she remembered from the battlefield. And then she lifted her chin indignantly and said, "I am not afraid. I've seen plenty of foul tempers in my time among men! Throw another fit like that, sir, and you'll be making breakfast for the lot of us for the next week!"

"I won't," Tristus said, immediately relieved. He laughed as she marched toward him, then scooped up her small hand and looked seriously into her hazel eyes that glimmered with unshed tears. "I promise," he whispered, then slowly stroked a lock of dark hair out of her eyes and pulled the lady dwarf into his arms, where she began to weep. "I'm so sorry, Taya. I'll never give you cause to be afraid again."

"You'd better not!" Taya snapped through her tears. "I'll have your head myself before I'll let you lose it like that again!"

◆ ◆ ◆ ◆ ◆

THE NIGHT BROUGHT snow and healing, and rest. Their company of fifteen was down to eleven. Bastien still had not returned and, though Fu Ran would display no sadness, Xu Liang knew his former guard did not look forward to the dawn's search for his shipmate's body.

It seemed that Tristus had been forgiven his deadly rage, as he had not—to anyone's knowledge—actually harmed any of them and had certainly proved indispensable in restoring their health. All but Xu Liang's. Time would recover him, as it had before. He did not dare to meditate too deeply, but was resting his mind and gradually restoring his spirit when the elf awoke with a start.

Alere found his shirt and dressed himself mechanically, ignoring or possibly forgetting the wound that had left him unconscious for much of the day, and that remained with him in the form of a fading bruise. He didn't bother with his tunic or cloak. With his lithe torso loosely veiled, he took up *Aerkiren* and headed for the tent's entrance.

The elf's rush of movement, though silent, stirred Tristus, who had climbed out of his smudged and bent armor to allow Taya to care for his minor wounds. Unfortunately, an Andarian cleric couldn't use his healing art on his own body and—as Taya sternly informed him—even a minor wound could become serious if allowed to fester. The knight had been sleeping on his back, his shirt open, to allow the undressed burn upon his chest to begin healing beneath a layer of disinfecting salve that, according to Taya, worked quickest when exposed to air. In Alere's wake he rose and emerged into the freezing night air as heedless of his lack of protection against its bite. He brought his sword, the once gleaming blade blackened in some places after his battle with a Fanese pyromancer.

Xu Liang rose shortly afterward and joined the two, who were already in conversation.

"I feel it as well," Tristus was saying. "You're right. Something's amiss. But if not the keirveshen, then what?"

"There are stories of these lands, told often by gypsies, of things that dwell beneath the snow at night. I myself have heard tales of warriors slain in this region, their corpses cursed by the spell of a necromancer, doomed to awaken and fight once more when blood touches their bones again." The elf sighed, his frosty breath accurately reflecting his attitude toward gypsy myth. "Superstition, I'm sure, but I have often found that even the most absurd superstition can be based upon elements of truth. And I don't like this feeling that's descending upon me."

Xu Liang closed his eyes and let his spirit reach outward, across the featureless dark terrain. The cold embraced him at once, reaching within as he extended his senses without. He smelled the death from the day's battlefield and heard the quiet rush of many heavy snowflakes thickening the blanket that already covered the land. He heard nothing of natural life, not a single wolf or a bird...nothing. He began to wonder about things unnatural that may have been lurking in the icy stillness.

Gradually, Xu Liang pulled his senses back in, past the creaking, clanking armor and weapons of the two bodyguards on watch, past the scent of salves and cooling sweat that lingered about the elf and human in front of him. He opened his eyes and said quietly, "There is something out there."

Tristus looked back at him, but Alere kept his eyes on the darkness beyond camp.

The knight said, "Do you know what it is?"

Xu Liang shook his head slightly, his eyes straying to Alere as he wondered if the elf did know and wouldn't say. He had done well keeping the power of his blade a secret. Xu Liang was still guessing when he assumed it was *Aerkiren's* magic that shattered the enchantment on Xiadao Lu's armor. He'd not found the time to ask the elf about it.

"What goes on out here?" Tarfan asked. He held a blanket around him and blinked sleep from his eyes. Then he gasped and uttered an oath of alarm.

Xu Liang saw what alarmed him in the same moment. Multiple figures, all of them as pale as the snow and looking as if that snow had given them life, stalked across the darkness, headed directly for their camp. Xu Liang thought of Alere's story and the drastic amount of blood that had been spilled upon the Flatlands that day.

The elf seemed to recall his own words at the same time, and repeated them softly. "Slain warriors, doomed to awaken when blood touches their bones once more."

"Some of us certainly gave a fair contribution today, didn't we?" Tarfan grumbled.

"How could I have known?" Tristus said as he caught the dwarf's eyes glaring at him.

"You couldn't," Fu Ran replied, coming out of the tent with various articles of clothing draped over one big arm. He handed Tristus his shirt of chain mail. "None of us could, so let's not face whatever those things are half dressed and half asleep."

The knight stabbed his sword into the snow, quickly buttoning his shirt and taking the linked tunic from Fu Ran. "There's no time for strapping on all of my armor. I'll still be half dressed."

Alere accepted the rest of his layers of white and Tarfan exchanged the blanket about his shoulders for his thick leather jacket. "Here we're at it again!" the dwarf said. "More danger than I'm used to on an expedition, but it serves me right for traveling with a troupe of rebellious children!"

"Perhaps, when this battle is finished you and Gai Ping can seek solace in each other's conservative maturity," Xu Liang replied. "For now we must focus on the matter at hand."

"You're right," Tristus agreed. "But how do we slay ghosts?"

"If they are ghosts," Alere said.

"Unless you see any relatives in that lot, I vote they *are* ghosts!" Tarfan spat.

Alere ignored him, speaking to Xu Liang. "That would explain why we haven't been attacked by the keirveshen. They fear a spirit that roams without its body because that often means the spirit cannot be quelled."

"I rephrase my question," the knight said, reclaiming his sword now that the shirt of closely linked steel covered him. "How do we slay ghosts that can't be slain?"

"Maybe we should ask them," Fu Ran suggested, pointing to a pair of riders charging toward the oncoming force. Their mounts were almost too dark to be seen, as were the riders themselves, covered head to toe in armor the color of night. Were it not for the gleaming weapon of one and the wisps of orange-blue flame that trailed the swing of the other one's sword, they might have gone into battle completely unnoticed. The warriors issued no battle cries and made little sound cutting through immaterial flesh. Even their armor and the animals they rode put forth very little sound.

Everyone watched in amaze. The snowfall had almost stopped for the night, but now it had begun to rise from the earth as the great horses kicked up a veritable storm of their own across the icy carpet.

"It's *them*," Alere said mysteriously. In a moment, he glanced back at the others and offered explanation. "The people who've been ahead of us since we left the river canyon. Two riders."

"Who are they?" Tristus wondered aloud.

"They are elves," Alere said with no pride nor any perceivable sense of kinship. He almost seemed disgusted, but then he'd yet to generate any warmth at all toward anyone since he'd joined the group.

"Warrior elves? Zaldaine?"

Alere answered the knight in definitive tones of animosity, presumably toward the newcomers, displaying emotion other than eagerness in battle for the first time. "They are landless elves. Nomads once. They used to travel in small numbers and call themselves Seekers of the Flame."

"What flame?" Tristus asked, again, given in to his stubborn curiosity.

"The flame of the sacred bird they worship, who supposedly restored their slaughtered people from the ashy remains left behind by the armies that destroyed them and their land near a millennium ago."

"The Phoenix," Xu Liang whispered, familiar with the creature of legend.

"Yes," Alere said. He scowled suddenly. "They have been leading us, and I did not see it."

He stepped away from the others and called for Breigh. The mare came at once, and though Tristus tried to stop him, the white elf mounted and charged off across the snow, toward the elves who were battling ghosts.

"I'm going after him!" Tristus announced, jogging toward their remaining three horses.

"You must take Blue Crane," Xu Liang said, and ignored Tarfan's shocked and protesting sound. "He is faster and will not panic, even in circumstances so strange as these. Go quickly, Tristus!"

The knight obeyed and Tarfan appeared as if he would collapse in his disbelief. He threw his arms up in the air as if to draw up the blood that had drained down into his feet. "Have you lost it, mage? The boy's killed two horses already and you know damned well you're in no condition to walk to the end of this journey!"

Xu Liang watched as Tristus bolted away from the camp atop the magnificent gray. He said softly, "Blue Crane will return to me. He was a last gift of friendship, meant to carry me safely on my travels. He does not take his duty lightly, as it was given to him by none other than Emperor Song Bao, whose presence during Blue Crane's birth served as a blessing upon the animal. In all of Sheng Fan, no horse is Blue Crane's equal."

Tarfan was not easily convinced. "And in all this blasted world no menace is equal to Tristus Edainien! I'll guarantee you that!" When he saw that Xu Liang would not change his mind, the dwarf stomped off to join Taya, who was just emerging from the tent. "But it's your horse," he grumbled. "Do as you like!"

"Now what's happening?" Taya wanted to know.

"Nothing unusual," her uncle answered with gruff sarcasm. "We've only attracted more danger!"

• • • • •

TRISTUS EXPECTED at least a mild fuss from a horse about to
be mounted by a stranger, but, as if he'd heard his master's orders
himself, Blue Crane allowed Tristus onto his back without so much
as a snort in protest. The steed took commands as easily, and when
he ran, Tristus became filled with a sudden, intense admiration for
this spectacular steed. Quick as the wind, light as the air, and with
a presence as powerful as the surge of a coming storm. It was only
natural that the beast belonged to Xu Liang. Blue Crane could find
no more suitable master than an aeromancer. Tristus felt the bond
between the two immediately and knew better than to hope he
would have any opportunity other than this to ride so fantastic an
animal. Even the fair, agile Breigh had difficulty keeping ahead of
Blue Crane. The distance between them closed swiftly.

Tristus hollered out when the animals drew near enough for him
to be heard. "Alere, you must stop! We don't want a fight with them
if it isn't necessary!"

The white elf ignored him and pressed ahead, bent on this task
as he was on destroying the keirveshen.

Tristus kept after him, but quickly resigned himself to the inevitable. Alere had rode out here to start a fight and he was going to
get one, if not from the Phoenix Warriors, then from the undead
soldiers, who were just beginning to take notice of two more play-
mates. One would never guess he'd been so badly wounded just
hours ago. But then, Tristus knew the elf hadn't been lying about on
that pallet all day and most of the night nursing his wounds alone.
He'd been nursing his wounded pride.

Tristus had caught the elf's gray eyes open, staring at the magic
sword lying beside him, replaying the day's battle and what he
considered his loss. The thoughts had been clear in his expression,
and they were clearer now. Not only had he been struck down by
a human, he'd been helped by one as well, reliant on that aid in the
moment it had been provided. Drawn as he may have been to the
quest, he was afraid of being drawn that deeply into the company.
He led an independent life and thrived on that independence, that
separation from others. He sought to reestablish the division by
facing these enemies alone. Even knowing that he was not welcome,

Tristus followed, fearful that the elf would suffer more than a bruised ego if he persisted.

The undead, dressed in layers of transparent clothing and flesh that showed the reanimated bones that carried them, crumpled easily beneath the blows of the two rogue elves. However, as quickly as the reborn warriors fell, their blood-stained skeletons rose again. Where the corpses had been lying, Tristus could not say. Perhaps they'd been buried beneath the frozen earth. Wherever they'd risen from, they had risen with their old weapons in hand, blades of solid, immortal steel. They moved slowly in their strange state, but were certainly no less deadly for their sluggishness. Tristus noticed the dark-clad elves avoiding their attacks and delivering their own with caution, though it seemed pointless.

And then he saw the gleaming spear. He thought instantly of *Dawnfire* and almost went for the wielder himself, sure he was in the presence of a thief, but then he realized the shaft was black, not platinum; a deep obsidian lacquer that clashed brilliantly with the blazing silver of the serrated blade mounted to the pole. As the blade danced amongst the dead, streams of silver bleeding after it, the ghosts became ice, and bodies that had once been simply knocked down by the other elf's sword were shattered with a second strike. Flaming crystals scattered into the night and became fizzling embers upon the snow.

As he arrived at the battle, Alere gave his Verresi war cry and handled the undead in his own fashion. The sword *Aerkiren* painted swaths of its twilight glow upon the darkness, streamers of eerily luminous liquid trailing each strike, spilling from the lethal wounds Alere delivered. The risen warriors fell in quickly fading pools of their own ghostly blood, their bones disintegrating into the snow.

Though he felt a rise of panic every time one of the undead drew near him, Tristus satisfied himself with knocking down any of the cold wraiths that attacked him, waiting for the moment the elves would run out of victims and seek to fight amongst themselves.

SEVENTEEN
Firestorm

ALERE DID NOT take kindly to being toyed with. These two were no random wanderers. There was purpose in their movement, the way they'd avoided being seen, but still managed to leave a trail. Alere would end this foolish game with their burning blood smoldering on the edge of his blade.

As for the knight; he'd grown to respect Tristus since witnessing his skill and did not wish to hurt him, but he would not allow him to get in the way. He'd also heard what the others had said about him and understood now the confusion he'd sensed before while in the knight's presence. It must have been difficult for a man to harbor such a destructive force, and at the same time to possess one so gentle as that which had mended everyone's wounds.

And a destructive force it was indeed, to have withstood the magic Tarfan described in his argument with Fu Ran. Without question, the knight was a slave to Ilnon, the God of Vengeance. It wasn't often that the god's rage captured a human soul and kept it. They often didn't survive the encounter. Yet somehow Ilnon had found a reliable host in this one, however unwilling Tristus seemed to be. Alere couldn't help but to wonder if he pushed Tristus out of this fight whether Ilnon would return the blow.

The thought was put aside by the sudden depletion of wraiths to be dealt with. It appeared that the time to contend with the rogue elves had come.

• • • • •

EACH OF THE elves cut down their final spectral opponents and then faced one another in a triangle of contempt and arrogance the likes of which Tristus had never seen in this world. He'd witnessed the natural hostility between men and elves, and thought he'd felt a bit of it himself when he'd first met Alere, but the potential for hatred between elves was something he'd never considered. It was a thousand fold worse than the vie for power amongst the most conceited priests—the murderous gazes Tristus looked upon now.

Golden eyes narrowed within the sleek black helms as it was evident the newcomers were sizing up the lone mountain elf. No doubt, in their arrogance, they saw an easy kill. And it was not a wonder either, that they had completely factored out the human in his company. But if they'd really been aware of the companions for days, what made now the time to kill them, as opposed to any number of times previously?

Alere said they were leading them. *Leading us to where?* Tristus wondered to himself.

And then one of the Phoenix warriors spoke. "So now you have seen us." The voice was a man's, fitting with the lean, powerful frame the armor scarcely made secret. "Was it really any wonder to you, hunter?"

Alere seemed to take offense with every aspect of the voice, perhaps worst of all that it formed words in no elvish tongue, but rather a dialect common among men, whose roots lay far away, in Treska. Alere had been using it frequently to communicate with the dwarves as well as with Tristus. In fact, all of the companions, except for Xu Liang's guards, had simply slipped into using the language most of the time. However, this was no politic way of communicating. This was a deliberate means to insult Alere, who didn't have to look down his slender nose at everyone for his station in elvish society to be clear. He was no commoner, and clearly did not take well to being treated as such.

The white elf held *Aerkiren* toward the ground, but it could scarcely be considered a relaxed position. He said, "You can die anonymously, or with your identities given. It makes no difference to me, but you have mere moments to decide."

Sweet Light of Eris, that was subtle! Why don't you just spit at them the next time?

Tristus' hands began to sweat in his gloves while he considered what to do. This was like watching dogs raising their hackles and bearing fangs just before flinging themselves at one another in a ferocious struggle for dominance. Very soon the elves were going to be at each other. Tristus felt very assured of that.

"*Ellum sekve, nothdon,*" the other Phoenix Elf said. It was a woman, her voice smooth and even, confident as one who is accustomed to being obeyed.

These words, though spoken in elvish, seemed only to incense Alere and he snarled his own response. "*Evtol kiel arimve, aven!*"

"*Tolve kiel?*" the male murmured and made a dramatic display of showing Alere his keenly crafted elven blade, fire seeming to trace its razor thin edge.

For some reason this made Alere smile, though it was not an expression that made Tristus feel especially warm or that gave him any hope for the outcome of this meeting.

◆ ◆ ◆ ◆ ◆

"WHAT IN THE infernal regions is going on out there?" Fu Ran wanted to know.

Xu Liang held his hand up to silence the former guard, then said, "'You will come with us, child of death.'. Orphan, I think the term means. 'You do not command me, girl.': These are Alere's diplomatic words. The response is, 'We do not?'."

"You can hear them?" Taya asked wonderingly. "How?"

"I don't hear anything," Tarfan grumbled. "Must be more magic."

"It seems Alere was right," Xu Liang said next. "They want us to go with them somewhere. Since the male Phoenix Elf is waving his sword about in the negotiating, I do not suspect that their motives are entirely peaceful."

"You mean this isn't just a friendly greeting with an invitation to the nearest ale house," Tarfan blurted flatly. "What should we do?"

Fu Ran was wrapping his enchanted tassel around the hilt of his two-handed sword. He hadn't tried the enchantment since the elf negated its effect with his own magic blade, but he didn't believe the damage to be permanent. The Aeran wizard who'd put the enchantment in place may have been a bit of an eccentric, but he knew his craft better than most. He conjured enchantments to last. Besides, the elf had taken the enchantment away from the sword, not the tassel itself. Fu Ran hoped his logic would hold later.

"This will not make Alere happy," Xu Liang said. "But we must surrender, for now."

"What?" Fu Ran was shocked by this unheard of decision from the mystic. "Why?"

Xu Liang lifted the scabbard tucked into his belt, and just slipped *Pearl Moon* from its encasement. With his eyes lingering on the soft glow Mei Qiao's sword emitted, he said, "Because the female carries a Celestial Blade."

◆ ◆ ◆ ◆ ◆

THIS IS MADNESS, Tristus thought. *It's going to take a miracle to keep these elves from killing each other.*

And it was just at that moment that a miracle was delivered. Nothing from God above, but something just as breathtaking. As if the moon had come out of hiding, full and lustrous, a silvery blue light was cast over the open land from a source not in the sky, but behind Tristus and Alere. It had come from the beautiful sword worn by Xu Liang. The mystic held it up as a torch, speaking to the elves without words.

Two of the elves answered, though not necessarily willingly. Alere's slim blade began faintly to hum, the elvish characters emblazoned upon the metal gleaming brightly enough to illuminate both him and Breigh in the darkness. Opposite the white elf on his white horse, the elf woman, clad all in black, mounted upon a horse as dark, lifted her spear in amaze. Her companion looked on with equal wonder as the bright blade radiated with crackling beams of silver light.

"It's never done this before," the woman said.

"And it isn't likely to again!" Alere growled and—well before anyone could consider stopping him—he charged the other elf.

The female raised her spear to defend herself. The blades struck, and there came a sudden boom, like Heaven splitting. Alere and the woman were thrown from their mounts, without their blades. A great wave of energy that even began to unnerve Blue Crane undulated outward from the weapons that were stuck fast. The blades defied the pull of the earth, locked in a strange and terrible struggle.

The air itself seemed to wail in the stress generated by the swords.

Tristus, scarcely able to hear his own thoughts, was about to head for Alere, who still lay on the ground in his shock, when a voice suddenly rang above the drone of magic.

They cannot leave us! Not now!

Tristus found himself looking at the blades again, squinting against the tremendous light. Somehow it looked as if the weapons were rising, being drawn higher into the sky. He had no idea what to make of that and even less idea of what to do about it, but his body seemed to require no instruction from his mind. He angled Blue Crane in the direction of the hovering blades and rode toward the wall of magic.

◆ ◆ ◆ ◆ ◆

AS FAST AS he was flung, the fervor drained out of Alere. He rose to his feet, cradling his hand—every nerve in it seemed dead—and watched with alarm as the blades sang an unearthly dirge, rising slowly back to the heavens from whence they'd come. What had he done? He'd acted out of foolish pride and anger, and had the sword of his ancestors revoked. Before his eyes *Aerkiren* was dying, joining with the sky of its creation.

And there was the knight. Foolish human. *How can you hope to defy the will of the gods? Let the blades alone. It is no longer in our hands.*

Of course, Tristus did not hear his thoughts and, out of some elusive concept of bravery that Alere often took for stupidity, the knight summoned the determination that would ultimately awaken the fury within him. Only a god could contend with gods, and Ilnon shied from no challenge. The presence of rage and vengeance would be Tristus' only defense against powers that would otherwise destroy him and that may destroy him still.

Alere's shame came suddenly, and crushed him inside. He ran to Breigh and, disregarding his numbed hand, he swung into her saddle and commanded her toward the fierce power that could well be the end of them both.

◆ ◆ ◆ ◆ ◆

XU LIANG SEEMED to be handling their apparent crisis a little too calmly for Tarfan's comfort. The dwarf watched the man in prayer and understood the motions, but somehow he didn't think any amount of begging was going to make whatever powers were involved listen. The elf had ruined everything, brought the Celestial Swords—godly weapons of order—against each other. This was the beginning of the end. If chaos was rising in Dryth, with the power of the gods broken, what would defend them?

"What's he doing?" Taya suddenly squealed, pointing across the open landscape at the knight riding to his doom. "Tristus! He's going to get killed!"

"Foolish pup," Tarfan mumbled, and didn't feel it in him to argue with her, knowing that she was probably right.

♦ ♦ ♦ ♦ ♦

TRISTUS WAS DEAFENED by the horrid sound of the wall of magic. He felt sick with the immense power it generated, but somehow he was not afraid. His eyes were on the blades, never leaving them, even though the tremendous light burned his vision. He began to feel weaker, the nearer he arrived to the blades, feeling the awesome strength of angry forces. Those same forces were speaking to him, telling him he could not have the blades and to stay back lest he be killed. Somehow, knowing only that he could not let them go, he defied those voices and their power. He felt no fear, only anger, frustration that mounted rapidly, driving his determination to have what was not meant to be his. He would have them, and he would destroy anyone and anything that tried to stop him!

It was that one burning thought that made Tristus aware of what was happening. He was aware, but he was also helpless, as he always had been. In a moment, he would be blind, lost deep within himself, and he would wake in a sea of blood. The blood of enemies, the blood of friends... the blood of anything that had blood to be spilled. A fierce dread filled his heart and pumped his own blood faster, giving power to the engine of destruction that came to life within him.

No! I promised...

But he had to have those blades!

Blue Crane brought him to the wailing wall and Tristus let go the reins, reaching up, stretching for the blades. He knew what would happen once he had them. The darkness of his past rolled up to meet the dark moments ahead of him. One hand closed on the hilt of *Aerkiren*. The other wrapped about the shaft of the second blade. *God, forgive me.*

His arms up to his elbows were needled with hundreds of tiny unseen agonies, but he did not withdraw. He began to pull against the forces gripping the blades and soon felt nothing, save for his rage. Darkness assailed him. Savage images of death danced obscenely before his mind's eye. He pulled the blades faster, determined to have their power and with them, reenact the violent imagery and to be alone again, at last free from the inevitable treachery that awaited him, to finally have revenge against the wrongs already done to him. There would be no escape this time. Not for any of them!

He gave one last, powerful tug, using all the strength available to him and finally, the opposing forces relinquished their hold. Tristus tore the blades apart from each other, shredding the wall of light, casting the remains to the opposite ends of the world as he spread his arms apart. The magic dissipated on its way to the horizons, leaving Tristus with two glowing weapons and a desperate need to still the bodies around him, all of them moving against him. *Betrayers! Murderers! He would kill them first. All of them!*

The horse beneath him reared suddenly, toppling him into the snow, deciding for him that it would be first to die. He landed heavy on the cold earth, his breath gone and forgotten. He had to get up. He had to kill!

Tristus began to rise, alarmed and angry that someone dared stop him—that they could stop him—by placing their hands on his shoulders and pushing him back. He glared up at a ghost, seeing the night sky through its transparent, luminous structure ... and immediately argued that he could be pinned beneath such an insubstantial form by again trying to rise. He failed once more, and started to writhe, sure somehow that the specter's cold touch was beginning to burn him.

"No," the spirit said softly, in the gentle tones of the more cunning betrayer. "You will not rise, Fury. I will not let you."

Do not call me by that name! Get off of me! Spare yourself one final breath, for that is as long as it will take me to rise and to cut you into—

"No. I shall not rise and neither shall you. I shall hold you here, eternally, if I must. The world will see its end and fall around us before you will rise to do harm again."

You are no match for me, spirit! You cannot last that long and I am eternal!

"We will see how long I can last. Release him and I will consider leaving."

You are in no position to bargain! He will have his revenge!

"It is not his revenge, but yours. Release him, else I will take you with me, into a vessel that would shatter as you tried to claim your first victim with it."

Be careful what you offer! I would take it and give it strength, no matter how weak.

"You would have nothing to build on. A fortress without a foundation is doomed to crumble. Leave him."

If I leave him, I will take another! My vengeance will be sated!

"I fear it will never be sated, and I hope you never find another vessel for your madness, though I know you will search. I advise you to search far from here, else we will find ourselves in this predicament again."

Tristus wanted to laugh. He felt as if someone had just said something utterly absurd to him, but he couldn't remember what, and when he opened his eyes, he wasn't laughing at all, but staring silently at Alere. The elf hovered over him, looking uncharacteristically concerned... and unbelievably alive.

Tristus frowned, unable to feel anything but confusion. "What's happened? What's the matter? You look as if you've seen a ghost. More of them, I should say."

"Never mind what I saw," the elf snapped. "You defied the gods."

In the next moment, Alere's stern features let in a hint of something softer, appreciation perhaps. Relief? He said more, gently, "And you have saved my father's sword from certain destruction. I am greatly indebted to you, Tristus Edainien."

"As am I," someone new said.

Tristus turned his head to look upon the slender armored form of the female Phoenix warrior. She'd removed her helm, revealing the vibrant red of her bound hair and the stunning yellow-fair of her complexion. Scarlet lips smiled and she said, "I am called Shirisae. The weapon you saved is *Firestorm*, the blade once wielded by the Priestess of the Flame herself, living incarnation of Ahjenta the Phoenix, and also my mother. Let us guide you personally through this forbidding landscape, to the New Home of our people, Vilciel."

EIGHTEEN
The Dawn Blade

MORNING BROUGHT more mist, along with escorted passage north.

What Xu Liang had intended to be a temporary surrender, turned out more as a temporary alliance. However, he knew that the shock of the night's events was to blame for the sudden calm that had come over everyone and that once it subsided, circumstances would be likely to change. He was hoping this opportunity would enable him to build a more lasting allegiance, one that involved *Firestorm* returning with him to Sheng Fan. With the religious attachment the fire elves had to the Blade, it seemed that a difficult task lay ahead of him. Hours of meditation had not brought him any nearer to resolving the matter, but had only informed him, through the Empress, that the Dragon continued its ascent to the surface of Sheng Fan. He assured her of his progress and that he and the Blades would soon be with her.

"Skytown," Tarfan grumbled. "A lost city of unspeakable wealth! A fairy tale! It doesn't exist!"

"Perhaps these elves only named their city after the legend," Xu Liang suggested, glancing over the rest of the company from his place atop Blue Crane.

Taya rode with the supplies for now, resting not uncomfortably in front of the meticulously arranged equipment. She was led by the bodyguard Wan Yun. Cai Zheng Rui, another of the surviving guards, walked behind them while a conscience-stricken Alere rode upon Breigh even farther back. Tarfan walked close to Xu Liang, as did Gai Ping. Fu Ran walked ahead with Guang Ci and a fellow guard Shi Dian while the two Phoenix Elves—calling themselves Shirisae and D'mitri—led the way on their ebon horses. Tristus, exhausted after his feat, rode atop Guang Ci's horse, slumped forward in slumber.

Xu Liang let his gaze linger on the knight, recalling how Tristus insisted that he would walk with the others, just before fainting. He could not remember exactly what he'd done, but after feeling the rage within him and seeing that no one had died, he seemed a little afraid to close his eyes, as if he feared that the fury hadn't actually gone away and would strike at his allies while he slept.

You have nothing to be afraid of for now, Xu Liang thought. And then he shifted his focus ahead of the caravan, and wondered when this dismal, featureless landscape would end.

By nightfall he was still left to wonder. Camp was set again in the harsh winter landscape of Lower Yvaria. Though there was more room now in the guards' two tents after the loss of three of their fellows, Xu Liang's shelter away from civilization was still cramped. The segregation the guards felt and enacted due to their station and their limited ability to communicate with the others continued. Fortunately, Xu Liang did not need space to lie down, only to sit. He would find his place when he was done strengthening the bond between himself and the animal that he would have been unable to make this journey without.

Xu Liang stroked Blue Crane's plush pelt and let the sleek beast nuzzle his shoulder, glancing to Alere when the white elf arrived after a late scout. Though it was evident that he felt remorse for his attack on Shirisae, the feeling seemed only due to the near loss of *Aerkiren*. Alere didn't trust the Phoenix Elves and had made his feelings no secret, least of all to the Phoenix Elves.

Xu Liang, though furious after the near loss of the Storm and Twilight Blades, had been careful not to scold the elf. He calmly explained to him that the Celestial Swords must never be brought against each other. Alere had replied too simply, claiming to understand. Xu Liang feared with each hour that Alere would lose faith in this quest and leave to satisfy his vengeance some other way.

The elf watched Xu Liang, even as he slid out of Breigh's saddle, seeming to know Xu Liang's thoughts. He said telepathically, "Even if we lose all respect for one another, know that I wish to see the Swords united. I consider myself an enemy of chaos, and all who would allow it to pervade the lands and lives of innocents."

Xu Liang decided to speak as honestly as the elf was. "I have not lost any respect for you, Alere. I am only concerned with your judgment."

Alere stroked Breigh's muzzle and then let her wander away. Even though he looked directly at Xu Liang, it seemed as if he was ignoring him. "My father took up *Aerkiren* to vanquish the shadows that choked and smothered our people. It was a losing battle and so is mine, but I will not abandon it, just as he did not abandon his fight. However, I will choose who I will fight beside … and who I will not."

"What is it that makes you despise the Phoenix Elves so terribly?" Xu Liang finally asked.

Alere's features held disturbingly placid. He said, "There is not an elf you could bring before me whom I would not despise if his blood was not Verressi."

That was not what Xu Liang expected to hear, but somehow he was not surprised.

"They abandoned us," Alere explained, though no explanation was asked of him. "Hundreds of years ago, we turned to our cousins for help while we drowned in the shadows and choked on our own blood, and wept as no elf has ever done, ridding our own homes of the ghosts the keirveshen left us."

Xu Liang might have spoken just then, but Alere was not finished. Traces of anger were beginning to surface, just as they had the night before, nearly costing the loss of two Swords.

"Understand," Alere said, "that the spirit of an elf slain by darkness can be just as dangerous as the darkness itself. It was fortunate for what remains of my family that our own murdered kin elected not to linger in our absence. Though I returned prepared to perform the task, I'm not so sure now that I would have been able to slay my father's spirit. I did not have to test the powerful magic that would have been required, or my resolve. It is fortunate for these new allies of yours that I did not."

"You feel betrayed by your own people," Xu Liang summarized. "You may find this difficult to believe, but I understand. It is not abandonment that the Fanese people commit against one another, however. It is aggression." As it dawned on him, Xu Liang added, "We, as bearers of the Celestial Swords, must avoid both."

It amazed him at moments like this how very little he knew about the legend he had put so much of his life into understanding. He had done so at Emperor Song Bao's behest … because the Emperor had foreseen the rise of Chaos? Xu Liang wished that he knew.

Alere shook his head stiffly. "You will have to satisfy yourself with my allegiance to you. You cannot ask me to ally myself with those who have indirectly murdered my people."

Still petting Blue Crane, Xu Liang bowed slightly, accepting the elf's terms for now. There was not much else that he could do.

"There is one more thing I would say to you," Alere announced before leaving. Xu Liang waited and the elf said, "I saw what you did for the knight."

"Did you?" Xu Liang replied, holding the elf's gaze in wonder at what he might say next.

"I saw you challenge Ilnon, and defeat him."

Xu Liang thought back uneasily on the thing his spirit had faced in Tristus Edainien. He could still feel the painful intensity of its anger as he reached out of himself to calm it. At length he said, "It was no defeat, but a negotiation. I cannot even be certain if it succeeded beyond the moment."

Alere stepped closer. "You did not negotiate for Tristus, though. You did it because you had to, after inciting the rage within him."

Xu Liang frowned and Alere continued.

"Tristus was not the only one who heard your spirit calling out in desperation when the Blades locked," he said. "I heard your panic as well, and it occurred to me also, though not immediately, that only one possessed by the spirit of a god could challenge the gods and survive the encounter. You and I both knew that, through sheer force of will—the unmatched determination of blind rage—the Blades would be recovered."

Xu Liang said nothing, still meeting the elf's cold gaze. The son of Sheng Fan, servant of the Empress and counsel to the wise, was insulted beyond measure by this 'barbarian' creature's undertones. However, the scholar and explorer, who had recently become leader to a strange but endearing band of allies, absorbed the elf's concerns with understanding.

Unaware of this internal debate, Alere continued. "You did it for the Swords, not for the bearers, of whom Tristus may yet be one."

Xu Liang showed the elf nothing of the sting he'd just delivered. He said quietly, "Now I understand your opening comment. It is you who has lost respect for me."

Alere stood silent in the following moments, revealing nothing. At some length, he said, "It was my action that forced yours, Xu Liang. And it is always consideration for others that inspires Tristus. Even in what seems like self-pity, I have come to realize that his regret is more for those he has been told he cannot protect than for himself, even though he was rejected by those same people. I believe," the elf concluded, "that I have lost respect for us both."

Having said that, Alere left and Xu Liang let him. There was nothing more to discuss. An argument would satisfy only pride, pride that was damaged further when Fu Ran finally showed himself.

In the shadows cast by the torches posted among the tents, even one of Fu Ran's incredible size could conceal himself. It angered Xu Liang at first to think that such had been the former guard's intention. However, he quickly realized that any stealth on the giant's part was not to eavesdrop, but to have the advantage over Alere if he'd been forced to confront the elf physically. Xu Liang sighed almost inaudibly and took a moment to regain control of his emotions. He didn't realize how much he would miss actual sleep until he'd gone this long without it.

"He's wrong," Fu Ran said, and Xu Liang questioned him silently. The former guard explained himself. "Whatever you did—just as everything you do—it was for the Empire." Before Xu Liang could decide how to take his disapproving tone, the larger man added, "You're killing yourself for Sheng Fan and what has it done for you?"

"It has given me life, Fu Ran," Xu Liang answered without hesitation.

"Xu Hong and Xu Mi gave you life," Fu Ran contradicted, and it was clear in his expression that he had no idea what to make of the sudden, caustic expression that came to his former master's face.

"Xu Hong gave me the ambition to serve at the Imperial City," Xu Liang told him. It was a rare instance of escape from the respect and decency that was not only expected in Sheng Fan, but that was also one's moral obligation to uphold in matters of family. The mystic, who would have been severely reprimanded if Emperor Song Bao had been alive to hear such words, caught himself on the brink of sharing the Xu family's most guarded secret, and fell instantly silent. Remorse filled him, followed by shame as he realized that none of it was for Xu Hong.

Fu Ran placed a hand lightly on Xu Liang's shoulder, and it was all the mystic could do to refrain from shrugging away from him. Fu Ran said, "You told me you didn't want me back as I was, and the more I think about it, the more I remember why I can never serve you again." He lifted his hand, perhaps unaware of the needling pain even that cautious weight had inspired, and folded his tattooed arms across his broad chest. He remembered not to smile when he added, "I didn't come here to be one of your drones, Xu Liang. I came here as your friend."

The gesture did not go entirely unappreciated, but Xu Liang needed to meditate. He had expended far too much energy without putting enough effort into recovery.

He gave up Blue Crane when Gai Ping came for him, and also took the opportunity to leave. Bowing politely before the former guard, he said, "Forgive me, Fu Ran, but I must rest."

◆ ◆ ◆ ◆ ◆

"WHY WERE YOU following, or rather leading us along, for so many days?"

"A prophet among our people spoke of a Great Awakening," Shirisae said to Tristus and the others who had gathered to hear his question answered, which thus far only included Tarfan and Taya. "I and my brother D'mitri were sent out to understand this awakening, to learn as much as we could about it, as it reflects the resurrection of our own people, hundreds of years ago. However, whether this is a good reflection or a sinister mockery, we are as yet uncertain. Thus we look upon all strangers to this region with interest. It just so happens that we were on our return to Vilciel when we came upon your company, and so we observed and guided you until it finally became necessary to show ourselves." She paused, glancing about the Fanese tent with interest. "You are an odd assortment of people. We weren't sure how to take you, whether as friend or foe."

"We still would not be certain," D'mitri said, "but that *Firestorm* has never been touched by an enemy it hasn't slain."

Tristus looked to the taller of the pair, whose hair was just as red as his sibling's. While Shirisae wore her raveled locks about her head like a fiery crown, D'mitri wore his own braid bunched at his neck. Not a trace of it had shown while the pair wore their helms, which were detailed with sleek, aquiline features—much like the regal faces the helms hid. They cast an unexpected chill, for fire elves, Tristus thought in secret.

"Our people would have been lost without *Firestorm*," Shirisae said, drawing Tristus' attention back to her. "It is the instrument through which our most revered god speaks to us. It has been passed from mother to daughter for centuries. It glows with white fire, the truest fire, when those worthy of trust are near." She seemed to hesitate, then added, "It has never shone so brightly as it did when we encountered you."

"With the ice elf in your company, you can imagine our alarm," D'mitri added, his tone sounding more of disgust than alarm.

It was, of course, just then that Alere entered the tent. The argentine eyes of one elf met the golden gaze of the other, and Tristus felt the hairs on the back of his neck rise. He was going to blurt a question to avert the pending fight, but Xu Liang's entrance stole his attention—and fortunately everyone else's as well.

While Alere stalked off, Xu Liang greeted everyone with a slight bow.

Tristus inclined his head respectfully and watched the mystic retreat to his side of the tent. His gaze lingered on Xu Liang, until D'mitri distracted him.

"*Deshra en totharen, shenra en nodara,*" brother muttered to sister.

"What does that mean?" Tristus asked pleasantly, though he didn't like D'mitri's tone.

Shirisae said, either honestly or convincingly, "My brother says that your priest has the body of a young man and the mind of an old one. He means no disrespect. It is simply an observation. Among our people the very young may be gifted with superior intelligence, but not often wisdom to rival the elders among us." She looked over her shoulder at Xu Liang. "We have been watching that one. He bears the burdens of many great minds before him."

"He did say that he was guided by his ancestors," Tristus remembered, looking at the mystic again. Xu Liang sat still and silent, his eyes once again closed to the world immediately around him. "He isn't really a priest, though. I think he prefers to be called a mystic."

A brief silence followed.

"It is late," Shirisae finally said, standing. She smiled at Tristus, who returned the gesture, then added, "You and your companions must rest."

D'mitri rose as well, but his expression remained disdainful. "By tomorrow night you will be in Vilciel, enjoying the hospitality of friends."

"Friends, are they?" Tarfan muttered after the fire elves had taken their leave. "It seems to me they fancied us their prisoners before Alere brought the wrath of the gods down on everyone."

Tristus opted not to remind the old dwarf that there was only one God that had anything to do with what went on the night before.

He understood that many people were slow to accept the truth of things when those things pertained to religion. In Tristus' mind it was best said: 'To all realms, a king.'. In other words, even if there were other powers in Heaven, they must all answer to a single ruler, the Father of Heaven, King to all, including other gods. The theory had been put forth by a highly respected priest of the First Order as a diplomatic way at spreading Andaria's faith. Some outside of Andaria saw it as arrogance. Some within Andaria viewed it as foolish and absurd, believing that truth need not be explained or justified. Tristus never questioned his faith in that truth, but there were times—all of them recent—when he wondered about the different faiths of others.

There were at least three, if not four, different religions among the companions he'd joined, and yet they all followed one cause. Tristus only wished he knew precisely what that cause was. He had a peculiar feeling he would have to hold *Dawnfire* in his hands again to completely understand. Not that it mattered. Even if he never saw the angel's glorious spear again, he would go with the others, to Hell if that was their destination. The Order may have cast him out, but he knew now that God had not. He had been summoned to this journey, wherever it may take him and in his short time with them, he'd come to respect, and even to care, about each of these people, including the surly dwarf. They had become the family the Order should have been to him. He would serve them until death prevented him doing so.

◆ ◆ ◆ ◆ ◆

SITTING BESIDE the knight, Taya felt invisible. Something had come over him, something worse than the daze and confusion he'd been in when they discovered him half-buried in the snow back in the mountains. It started after his first berserker rage—which was bad enough in itself—and had only become more apparent after his second attack of utter madness, that fortunately resulted in no one getting killed. Suddenly her forlorn, charmingly—if not somewhat confusedly—virtuous, breathtakingly handsome knight, had gone strangely quiet. He hadn't shed a tear since the night after he'd single-handedly taken down almost all of the Fanese bandits, and while that should have seemed a good thing, Taya didn't like it. Though his tearless blue eyes were still deep pools of emotion,

that emotion seemed to have direction now. Taya believed she preferred his emotions spilling out of him every which way, especially
now that there was a beautiful, taller woman around for his newly
acquired focus to home in on. If Taya had to prepare breakfast by
herself one more time, it wasn't Tarfan who was going to get hit
with the soup spoon.

◆ ◆ ◆ ◆ ◆

AFTER A LONG NIGHT watching the others sleep, guarding the
tent from within while Gai Ping and the others did so from without,
Xu Liang rose and emerged into the coldest morning yet. It was
cold, but the sky was changed, clear while the rising sun failed to
penetrate the freeze of the northernmost edge of Lower Yvaria and
therefore failed to create a mist of the melting snow. The snow that
had fallen in the night, and in the nights previous to their arrival,
remained and beneath dawn's glow, it shimmered with a pink hue,
like the blushed petals of a plum blossom. It made Xu Liang think
of the lower regions of Ying, and an intense yearning for home
tugged at his heart. His eyes felt suddenly warm against the chill air.

"Where are the fire sprites?" Fu Ran asked as he came outside.

Xu Liang could almost hear the man's big muscles yawning with
him as he stretched his massive frame. Undoubtedly, he longed
for more demanding exercise than simply plodding through the
snow. Xu Liang hoped he would not transform his restlessness into
recklessness.

"They made their own camp just south of our own," Xu Liang
finally answered.

Fu Ran looked in the mentioned direction, then laughed. "Herding
the oxen to slaughter!"

"I do not believe so, Fu Ran," Xu Liang said, more sharply than
he might have weeks ago. He was rapidly growing weary with this
small-scale turmoil. Give him rebellious kingdoms and their vast
armies to deal with. He had taken about all he could of bandits
and shadows, and individuals assaulting one another. These people
knew nothing of war. They knew nothing of its art or its etiquette.

Just before Xu Liang resorted to measuring these realms and their
people in varying degrees of savagery and ignorance, the knight
who'd personally paid tribute to barbarism in its purest example not
so long ago, stumbled sleepily out of the tent. He slipped in the deep

snow, but kept his balance and looked at the sea of blushed white shimmering beneath the morning sky as it spanned in all directions, as far as the eye could see.

The knight actually gasped, and said softly, "It's beautiful."

With those two words, Xu Liang looked again at the Flatlands of Lower Yvaria, and wondered how long he'd been blind to so simple a fact. He'd been affected by the difficulty of this journey far worse than he'd let himself believe. And now his hand ached for a brush. However, as he looked closer at the featureless beauty of the landscape, he realized that even with a brush in his hand and a tablet before him there might be no way to recapture such a scene. Of course, the grace of his painting was in fewer brushstrokes, but there would be so very few to make in this instance. He decided to commit this sight to memory and to leave it at that.

To the man who had reopened his eyes, he said, "Yes, it is."

◆ ◆ ◆ ◆ ◆

THE SUN CONTINUED its rise, the warmthless light intensifying as it shone unobstructed downward, making the surface of the snow seem as a great mirror, reflecting the brilliant light back at the sky and virtually blinding the companions. In such intense whiteness all eyes tended to divert from both Alere and Tristus— one dressed all in white and the other in highly reflective layers of metal—who only worsened the glaring effect. It was easiest simply to keep one's sights set on the black-clad elves at the front of the caravan. However, that also became annoying as Shirisae's spear— clearly the Storm Blade—continued to glow brightly in the company of its sibling Swords.

Even with his eyes closed, the sun's glow invaded Xu Liang's vision, hampering his concentration. He meditated as long and soundly as he could, then suffered with the others, glad to see the small ridge of hills suddenly along their path with dark rocks and what appeared to be gnarled tree limbs peeking through the snow. They must finally have been reaching the northernmost end of the Alabaster Range. The last of the mountains stretched sparsely out from the greater mass that dominated much of the realm, like fingers reaching for the cold, distant sea that separated Upper Yvaria from Lower. The path would not ascend quite so high as it did before, but there was meaning in the name Skytown.

In a time too ancient to be considered anything more than myth, Vilciel was said to be the City of Dragons. Unlike the dragons of Sheng Fan, these beasts were more lizard than serpent, with great wings and also great egos to match their tremendous intellects. Such creatures held themselves above mortals, but also among them as they lived in a society rather than as a mystery. They built cities, like Vilciel, perhaps with assistance from enslaved or befriended creatures who could be considered abler craftsmen than them. They also collected wealth, reared families, and waged war with anyone who threatened their way of living, or simply strayed too near. The dragons of the western world were not gods and they were alarmingly civilized, according to legend.

All this, Xu Liang learned from Tarfan and from Tristus, one who spoke of bedtime stories told to young dwarves to make them behave—lest they be captured by the dragons and forced to build them castles—and the other who told of long dead adventurers who sought the riches of the dragons of Vilciel and were never seen again. Naturally, there were conflicts of opinion.

"Have you cracked?" Tarfan blurted. "You scatter-brained pup! You can sit in the broad light of day, telling us about angels with magic cattle prods and—"

"*Dawnfire*...isn't a cattle prod." While the knight clearly wanted to maintain a proud, scandalized expression, laughter tried to break through.

The dwarf continued as if Tristus had said nothing, wagging a finger at the mounted knight while he walked below, his cheeks red from more than just the cold. "And utterly fail to acknowledge the possibility that some of those scaly slave-drivers might still be lingering about that city!"

"You don't know they were slave-drivers," Tristus said.

"And you don't know they weren't!" the old dwarf barked.

"Aren't," Xu Liang corrected. "I believe that was the focus of your argument. Whether or not they still exist?"

Tarfan turned his head sharply to glare at the rider on the other side of him. "Don't you get started, too! You weren't in on this argument from the start, so you can't get involved now, mage!"

"He's the one who asked about the dragons in the first place," Tristus reminded.

"And he'd have a straight answer if you'd keep your mouth shut!"

Taya, sitting behind Tristus, giggled, understanding—undoubtedly better than any of them—that her uncle would never give in.

The knight groaned. "For the love of..." His voice trailed when he glanced away from Tarfan, and caught sight of something that interested him far more than the dwarf's argument.

♦ ♦ ♦ ♦ ♦

IN THE NEAR HILLS Tristus saw something glittering. He leaned forward in the saddle, knowing somehow and almost at once that it was not merely something, but the very thing that had drawn him into this quest. It was *Dawnfire!*

Tristus took off without even thinking, headed for the hill where the dearly missed spear hung, caught in a tangle of dead wood. Perhaps it had been taken by a winged creature, as Tarfan had suggested, but not the angel. Maybe a demon had tried to claim it and dropped it after the burden of its Heavenly light became too much for it. However, it had come to be here, Tristus knew only that he must have it back and offer it formally to Xu Liang's cause, with him as its bearer ... as God intended.

"Hold on, little one!" he called back to Taya, recalling she was with him when her short arms suddenly clamped about his middle.

♦ ♦ ♦ ♦ ♦

"WELL, HERE GOES another horse," Tarfan grumbled. "He'll get the poor thing tripped up on a tangle of wood and break its leg, or worse. They'll be the next creatures of myth at the rate he loses them! And this time he's got my niece!"

"She would not have it any other way, Tarfan," Xu Liang said calmly. "And I think I see what he is riding toward with such haste."

"It's *Dawnfire*," Alere said, riding up to join the mystic and dwarf when they stopped. He didn't sound pleased, and the reason became apparent in his next words. "The thief is near."

Xu Liang looked at him, reading nothing in the elf's gray eyes. He knew better than to question the elf's awareness of such things, but he wished Alere would provide more details with his announcements.

"Why are we stopped?" D'mitri wanted to know, riding back with Shirisae close behind. Even in haste, his golden eyes still managed to find and isolate Alere with a menacing glare.

The white elf scowled in turn, but said to Xu Liang, "We must assist the knight and leave quickly." And then he moved to act on his words, leaving Xu Liang to explain things to the Phoenix Elves.

◆ ◆ ◆ ◆ ◆

TRISTUS REACHED the base of the hills and glanced back, unaware until that moment of just how far away they'd been from the caravan. He put the matter aside and contemplated the climb ahead of him. The hill was steeper than it looked from a distance, pocked with dives and obstructions that would make it almost impossible to safely take a horse up. It looked soft as well, like there was mud beneath the snow. Roots and dead branches reached out at odd angles. They would make good hand and footholds, Tristus told himself, dismounting.

He eyed the platinum spear, carelessly mounted in a nest of lifeless wood several feet overhead and then looked at Taya. "Wait here," he said to the flushed lady dwarf, who nodded cooperatively.

After briefly plotting a course, Tristus started up. He trudged through snow that was almost up to his knees and found it no shallower on the hill. That only made it more difficult to plant his feet, which kept sliding in the disheveled layers of powdery ice. He grabbed hold of a promising looking root and began to pull himself up almost on arm strength alone.

Dawnfire, glorious in the afternoon sun, was almost within his reach when he felt the first tremor. His hold slipped and he dropped back a few feet before he was able to catch himself. He looked down at Taya, seeing now just how high he'd actually climbed.

Thank God the snow is soft, he thought to himself, then proceeded to climb.

He came to the spear once more, and reached out for it, closing his hand around the shaft, just past the blade, which was aimed toward the ground. His heart all but stopped at the feel of the cool platinum through his gloves and at the sight of its warm glow that seemed to intensify with his touch. "You missed me too, did you? Well, no worries, *Dawnfire*. I'll never let this happen to you again. I..."

When Tristus pulled the weapon, he found it stuck, the end of the shaft opposite the blade was wound tight in a tangle of frozen vines. He gave *Dawnfire* another useless tug, then began to consider his dagger, though he was reluctant to release the spear now that he had it again.

"Tristus!" Alere called up to him. "Quickly!"

"Just ... coming," Tristus replied, repositioning himself on his root so that he could reach the vines that ensnared *Dawnfire*. He drew his dagger and began to cut. The vines gave up their hold slowly. A second tremor almost jarred his dagger from his grasp. He paused a moment, glancing at the distant caravan waiting calmly for his return. He wondered if they were feeling the minor quakes, then decided they were probably harmless, and resumed his cutting.

"Tristus!" the stark elf below called again.

"Yes, I know! I'm ... there!" With one more cut, *Dawnfire* slipped. Tristus sheathed his dagger and took the spear in his hand again. He pulled. The earth shook violently and both the weapon and Tristus dropped.

Tristus was not having near so much trouble with the concept of falling as he was with the concept of the hill rising away from him.

NİNETEEN
The Ice Giant

TRISTUS WOULD NEVER again refer to Fu Ran as a giant, for surely the Fanese warrior—along with everyone else in the company—were mere rodents in size, in comparison to what rose up out of the ice.

On his descent earthward, Tristus held fast to *Dawnfire* with one hand and somehow managed to catch hold of a protruding branch with the other. He came to an abrupt halt and almost lost his grip as his shoulder pulled exquisitely. He set his teeth together, biting back the pain and panic while he glanced down at the suddenly smaller shapes of his companions directly below. He'd ceased to fall and was now rising with the giant.

Below, Alere clearly instructed Taya to leave, slapping her horse on the rump as she turned it about to speed the process along. Tristus watched her speed toward the others, until the great awkward movements of the enormous individual he'd awakened commanded his attention. He swayed precariously, but refused to let go of *Dawnfire*. He would plummet to his death before he would risk losing the spear again. There was no time to consider how irrational that was. His one-handed grip didn't last long, slipping more with each tremendous surge of motion enacted by the rising giant, and finally failing altogether as the colossus stood fully upright and shed its blanket of snow, casting it in hurtling sheets down upon him.

Tristus was torn from his grasp by the unexpected force of the minor avalanche, and fell the rest of the way to the ground.

• ◆ ◆ • •

ALERE DREW BREIGH back, away from the cascade of snow. Glimpses of color let him know when the knight passed, as did the sudden eruption of snow where the man hit, pounded into the otherwise soft blanket by the weight of his armor and of the icefall. Tristus was sufficiently buried and the giant was gradually drawing more alert to its surroundings. Alere gave the matter brief thought, then acted with haste. He'd seen the large men of the Northern Flatlands in Upper Yvaria—standing several feet taller than even Fu Ran—and considered them giants. He never would have guessed that the talked about giants of the Flatlands also included such titans as this in their line of kin. It amazed him that such large creatures could dwell in the realm's seclusion, and it thrilled him to be chased by one. Leaning low over Breigh's neck, he gently commanded the mare to soar as she had never done before.

◆ ◆ ◆ ◆ •

XU LIANG DIDN'T wonder what the white elf was doing when he suddenly fled from the giant. Alere raced across the as yet undisturbed snow, away from Tristus and the others. He was attempting to draw the giant, luring him with his raised sword, leaving a faint trail of its twilight glow in his wake. The colossus, dressed in a patchwork of things collected from the small world it lived in, seemed to consider, though its great black eyes made note of the other minute creatures suddenly in its bed of snow as well.

It was then that Shirisae spurred her black mount toward the giant. She angled toward Alere, raising her spear, showing the frost-rimed giant *Firestorm's* radiant glow. D'mitri, held for only a moment by what he witnessed, chased after his sibling. The giant, seeing the lady elf's bright spear, suddenly checked its belt of woven roots and vines—the small trees and other growths they'd come from dangling like charms in some instances—and seemed to realize that the shining item it had recently acquired was missing. It bent to lift something out of the snow—a yellowing ivory club—and stalked after the elves, the ground shuddering in its wake.

Xu Liang wasted no time. With the giant's interest locked on the elves, he commanded Blue Crane toward the minor mountain of snow that would be Tristus' tomb if he wasn't quickly uncovered.

Fu Ran commandeered Taya's mount as the dwarf maiden arrived, but he had no hope of catching up with Blue Crane. The gray steed brought Xu Liang to his destination in a matter of seconds.

Xu Liang dismounted at once and began digging the knight out. His hands began to ache immediately with the extreme cold and effort, but he did not stop. For the first time that he could recall, he acted with no plan of action. His only thought was to save a companion from one peril, knowing full well that they would only emerge to face another, one possibly worse than slow suffocation beneath several feet of snow. Even as he concentrated on pulling armfuls of snow away from the pile that buried the knight, the giant's earth-moving footsteps reminded him of its nearness.

Xu Liang's hair spilled over his shoulders as he worked, stacking like an unrolled bolt of black silk upon the starkly contrasting ground. Snow melted and refroze around his arms, making the sleeves of his robes stiff and uncomfortable against his skin. The discomfort evolved to pain, but he plunged his arms deeper in his search, grasping handfuls of ice, continuing in breathless agony as his body protested this sudden, unshielded effort.

Pearl Moon did not guide him in this action, nor did any other magic. It was purely, foolishly physical. He might have thought of his empress and of Sheng Fan, if he'd thought at all, but instinct required no thought, and it scarcely occurred to him that he could die for this one instant of reckless abandon.

He persisted. His hands, burning with the cold, continued to dig and to search until at last his numbing fingers came against something solid. The metal he'd come to stung and only slipped away from him when he tried grasping it firmly with his frozen hands and pulling. He traced what could only be the shaft of the spear *Dawnfire* to the hand that still clutched it. He found the knight's arm, and pulled with one hand, digging away snow with the other.

Tristus wasn't helping. He must have been unconscious. Xu Liang didn't have the strength for this. He wouldn't be able to save the knight, no matter how much he wanted to.

Fu Ran arrived, rushing in to pull away more snow. "Do you have him?"

"Yes," Xu Liang gasped.

"Don't let go," Fu Ran instructed. "I'll dig him out. Just hold on!"

Xu Liang relaxed, but did not let go of Tristus. He almost cried out when the knight's ice-crusted glove suddenly clamped about his wrist. Then he held tighter and tried pulling again. "He's still alive! Fu Ran, hurry!"

Fu Ran dug down, thrusting his arms suddenly into the snow, where he found a grip on the knight and, with a great effort, hauled him out of the packed slush.

◆ ◆ ◆ ◆ ◆

TRISTUS GASPED for air as he tasted it, choking on flecks of ice that drew into his throat. He shook his head and brushed snow away from his face. Sunlight blinded him as it glared off the snow caught in his eyelashes. His chest and back ached, but he would live. He thought for a moment that he still clutched *Dawnfire*, but realized his error quickly and hastened to release the individual's arm he was holding onto instead of the weapon. Blinking the melting ice out of his eyes, he was astonished to see just whose arm he'd been clutching in place of the spear.

Tristus didn't know whether to thank the mystic or apologize to him when his vision finally cleared enough for him to see that Xu Liang had exhausted himself with the effort. Exhausted… or was he hurt? He didn't look well at all, but there was no time for debating the matter. The giant was coming back.

Tristus plunged his hands into the snow and fished *Dawnfire* out, then went to assist the mystic, who was huddled beneath Fu Ran's supporting and sheltering arm, putting a maximum effort into regulating his breathing. With a few more seconds he might have seen success, but a few seconds were all they had before the colossus would be on them.

"We have to leave," Tristus urged.

Fu Ran looked over his shoulder at the coming force of nature and agreed with a taut nod of his head. "I'll carry him to Blue Crane. You ride with him. You're lighter."

"In my armor? I'm not so sure."

Fu Ran helped the mystic to his feet. "You've got a better idea? Besides you can't ride and carry a dwarf under each arm."

"What about the guardsmen?"

"They're quick on their feet. We'll tell them to scatter. The giant can't chase all of us. Let's go!"

"Where are the elves?" Tristus wondered aloud, trying not to stare directly at the towering wild man that charged ponderously in their direction while Fu Ran carefully, but quickly, assisted Xu Liang up into Blue Crane's saddle.

"Worry about us!" Fu Ran barked, half shoving Tristus up after he'd safely situated the mystic, who was pliable in his state of utmost concentration. His lips were moving, else Tristus would have believed him unconscious.

"Go!" Fu Ran shouted, hurrying to the other horse, getting it moving before he leapt up onto its back. "I'll scoop up the dwarves! You shout at the guards!"

"Right!" Tristus answered, reaching around the slight form slumped in front of him for the reins. Xu Liang was not all that much shorter than Tristus—he looked taller than many the way he usually carried himself—but in his current state he seemed like a child. After days of admiring him nearly to the point of worship, Tristus suddenly felt protective. It was different than his previous ideas of shielding this graceful and important foreigner, whose quest he'd been swept into. It wasn't inspired by awe and not so much by Xu Liang's weakness at the moment as it was suddenly realizing that the mystic happened to be human. Tristus dearly hoped that wouldn't be his last revelation.

Blue Crane darted across the snow almost without command. Tristus held the reins in one fist while his other hand clutched *Dawnfire*, the spear and his arm braced in front of Xu Liang, holding the mystic upright. When the bodyguards saw that their master was relatively safe, they took heed of the colossus and scattered. There was not much place to hide along the open terrain, but a creature of such enormity as this must surely tire at some point. The elves must have sapped some of its energy, if not its will to pursue. What could be more frustrating than to chase such madly determined creatures as elves across the snow while one's body was still stiff from a long slumber? It must have been a long slumber. The snow cover was smooth before the companions tromped across it. The giant could have gone to sleep there, not long after plucking up the spear in the mountains, and been there for days—and thank God that was the only thing it plucked up that night. Perhaps the darkness he'd grown so weary of was to thank for his being alive now … about to be killed.

This was purely nightmare. If he'd had any idea ...

Tristus amended the thought before it finished forming. Giant or no, he'd have gone after *Dawnfire*. He only wished he hadn't lost the spear in the first place.

The ice giant was surprisingly relentless. Now that it'd seen the weapon it had originally stolen, it was freshly determined to have it back.

Fu Ran had scooped up the dwarves, as he said he would, though they were not one under each arm. Tarfan was under one arm, kicking fiercely while Taya sat on the horse's rump, facing backwards, clinging to the animal for her life. The former guard veered out of the giant's path, and Tristus thought to do the same. Unfortunately, he didn't want to lead the colossus to Fu Ran and the dwarves—or the bodyguards, for that matter, who had less of a chance at escaping while on foot. Yet if he stayed on a straight course, Blue Crane would be overtaken by the giant's immensely long strides.

Tristus acted on impulse. Trusting Blue Crane implicitly, he slowed the horse enough to guide him fully around. Swallowing his heart as it climbed his throat, he charged the giant.

The colossus slowed, bracing the great flesh and bone pillars that were its legs as if to bend forward and catch the horse coming at it. Tristus cursed himself a fool. Then he uttered a quick prayer, watching the giant heft its weapon high over its head. Slow-witted, the colossus watched them almost clear beneath the steeple of its legs before it swung down with its massive club that looked to be the bone of a large creature. It was even slower turning around than it was thinking, and that gave Blue Crane a long lead away from it.

The giant rumbled, making the snow tremble and the air shudder. And then it decided to run. It had only a brief spurt of speed to its massive size, but it was enough, and it was all Blue Crane could do to keep from breaking his fragile neck when the giant's great weapon suddenly dropped to the ground in front of the animal. Tristus drew the steed back, too quickly and, as the steed was already rearing back to avoid the collision, both he and Xu Liang spilled out of the saddle.

Tristus landed on his back, buoying up to discover Xu Liang already rising to his knees on the other side of Blue Crane. Eerily calm, the mystic drew his sword—as if that would help against an opponent this size—and before Tristus could do anything, the giant dealt them the crushing blow.

Only they weren't crushed. A luminous dome of energy had formed over the three of them—Xu Liang, Tristus, and Blue Crane—generated from the mystic's sword.

The giant seemed utterly astonished to have its weapon blocked. Utterly astonished, and wholly enraged. Scowling, it lifted the bone club back up and dropped it again.

Tristus covered his ears as the dome rang, rippling with power while it defied the immense weight and strength of the giant's attack. The colossus growled and tried again. When nothing came of the attack, it bent over to poke the dome with its finger, receiving a burn or a shock, or something unpleasant that inspired it to withdraw at once. And then it was angry all over again. It stepped back, then put its foot—booted in vegetation and packed earth—onto the dome and leaned all of its tremendous weight into the effort to crush the source of its aggravation.

The power of the dome held. For several moments while the giant grunted and strained, the energy only shimmered. And then, suddenly, it bowed outward.

Xu Liang gasped and lifted his other hand to support his grip on *Pearl Moon*, his soft features tense and straining.

The giant wouldn't give up.

Tristus wanted to help, but he didn't know what to do. He didn't know *Dawnfire's* power, just that it was magic. He started to rise, his thoughts and his blood rushing. There had to be something he could do!

Suddenly, the giant lifted its foot. It bellowed something incoherent. Tristus only knew that it was loud, thunder magnified a hundred times. The giant struck the dome once more with its bone club, forcing a strangled noise from the mystic's throat.

The dome shuddered, but it remained, and finally, grudgingly, the giant turned away and stomped toward the mountains south, resigned to loss and boredom.

Tristus hovered in mid-motion, unable to breathe at first as the terrible thrill of the moment passed. When he did manage to move, his gaze was drawn to the others, who were running toward the dome as it dissipated. Relieved, Tristus waved to let them know they were still alive, then turned to Xu Liang to congratulate an astounding effort.

He found the mystic on the ground, motionless.

Terror gripped him. Already on his knees, Tristus crawled to Xu Liang's side and laid his hand on his back. When the mystic failed to respond, he edged closer and carefully turned him over, dreading what he might find out. "Please, no. Please ... God..."

Tristus looked at the mystic with tears filling his eyes, spilling onto his cheeks before he realized he'd broken his vow never to cry again. His hand shook as he touched Xu Liang's face, stroking blood away from the man's mouth. And it was then that the awful reality struck him a blow harsher than any the giant could have delivered. He immediately took the mystic into his arms and held him close, shuddering with fear and denial as Xu Liang remained limp ... lifeless.

• • ♦ • •

PAIN WRACKED HER body for an instant almost too short to be felt. The hurt didn't really exist in her body, it was deeper, separate but still connected. It was as if a piece of her soul had split apart from the rest, leaving a great, gaping void that slowly closed in on itself, making the world suddenly seem small and lonely, and dangerous.

She tried to hold her concentration, remembering everything he'd taught her and all that he had said concerning her importance not only to the Imperial City, but to all of Sheng Fan. She tried, but it did no good. Her eyes flitted open, a sharp breath caught in her throat, and suddenly, Song Da-Xiao began to weep.

• • ♦ • •

"HEAL HIM!" FU RAN demanded. He was stomping and throwing his arms about, doing anything he could to keep from hurting someone and to keep attention away from the tears streaking his features. "Dammit! Don't just sit there! Heal him!"

"I can't!" Tristus shouted back. His arms were still locked around the mystic. No one dared unlock them, for fear that the fragile man they embraced was still alive and that the sudden movement would only hasten the fate they were hoping had not already befallen him. It hadn't. Xu Liang's shallow breath fluttered against Tristus' neck, the life drawing out of the mystic one sigh at a time.

Taya was on her knees nearby, sobbing fearfully while Tarfan stood alone in the near distance. The guards sat still and somber around Tristus and Xu Liang, though one had shouted Fanese words at the sky when he arrived and realized his failure.

It wasn't his failure. It wasn't anyone's failure, but still they each looked like they only waited for confirmation of the mystic's last breath, which would then free them to commit ritual suicide at the scene of their master's death. The elves had yet to return and were, for the moment, written off as being either dead themselves or too wrapped up in trying to kill each other to be of any use to anyone.

Tristus' arms were beginning to ache, but he wouldn't let go of Xu Liang. It would take an act of God.

"Why won't you heal him?" Fu Ran growled, sounding more dangerous by the second.

"I would, but I can't!" Tristus answered tearfully. "I don't know how!" He allowed one gloved hand to stray from Xu Liang just long enough to show Fu Ran the blood he'd wiped from the mystic's lips. "The wound is inside! I don't know where! I can't mend a wound like that!"

"That's absurd! How can the wound be inside of him! How can he be wounded at all? He wasn't even struck!"

Tristus blurted the first possibility that came to mind. "Pressure! It was the awful pressure the giant was putting on that dome. It had to be! You saw how weak he was. He tried too hard to hold the magic ... and the pressure ... that has to be it!" It didn't have to be it, but it was all Tristus could think of.

Fu Ran dropped to his knees wearily, brokenly. Tristus took genuine pity on the large man when his shoulders slumped, and he began to weep.

Look at us, Tristus thought. *We are all lost without you, Xu Liang. Where will we go from here if you leave us?*

The reality of that thought, that the mystic would indeed die here, inspired fresh tears. In the glaring daylight they burned and blurred his vision. Tristus squeezed his eyes closed and buried his face in the mystic's soft hair. In the darkness Xu Liang's closeness wrapped around him. He became acutely aware of each fragile breath. He could hear them as well as feel them. He could hear the fading heartbeat also, and he knew that when he opened his eyes the mystic would not simply be gone as the angel was. A body would remain in his arms, cold and dead, its resplendence lost forever.

Tristus buried his face deeper, wishing that he could fall into the mystic and die with him. There'd been so little time, and now there was none. He'd spent all of that time in awe, too fascinated to speak, too afraid to even think what his heart was feeling. He didn't realize where his thoughts were carrying him as they bled out of his aching soul, until his lips touched Xu Liang's neck. The warmth that still existed beneath the soft skin stirred his blood, and broke his heart. How could such grace be allowed to pass from this world? Why did Heaven bestow such grace upon mortals, only to take it away?

Forgetting himself, knowing only the will of his soaring, shattering heart, Tristus kissed the warm skin again, deliberately, and whispered words none of the others could have heard. He scarcely heard them himself. They were for Xu Liang and for no one else.

Tristus had just begun to cry again, softly, when a hand touched his shoulder. He lifted his face to look at Shirisae, whose features painted a portrait of serene compassion. Tristus resented that expression at first, ready to reject her suggestion that he let go, that Xu Liang had passed or that he should be allowed to do so.

However, the flame-haired lady elf said something else entirely, something that filled Tristus with hope. She said, "You must bring him to Vilciel."

TWENTY

The Road to Skytown

THE LANDSCAPE WAS rising as the sun set. A pall of red light fell over the Flatlands, casting long shadows. Alere could almost hear them creeping over the snow in the dreary silence. The company moved like a procession for the dead, and perhaps they were. The mystic had less color to him than before, and he had been pale to start, a tone that Alere had not come to identify with one of health among humans. He'd coughed just once when Fu Ran lifted him up to Tristus, who once again sat in Blue Crane's saddle. The sound startled everyone into thinking that he was coming around, but he remained unconscious, and the blood on the knight's arm told the tale all too well to any who wanted to hear it. Of course they wouldn't listen. Humans were creatures of control and denial, denying what they could not control. Dwarves had always been far too stubborn. It made Alere despise the Phoenix Elves worse that they would charm these people with hope only to lead them to belated mourning for what was already lost.

Xu Liang could not be saved. Not only was he physically depleted and getting worse by the hour, his spirit, too, was fading. He'd expended himself to the very last of his strength in any form and there was no foundation for recovery. His heart would beat until it was finished—if it wasn't already done—and that would be the end of it.

That wasn't what Alere wanted. He would beg Ysis for a chance to take back the harsh words he'd delivered the night before, if he thought it would be granted to him. He knew better, though. He knew far better than to expect anything from the gods. They had reasons for everything they did and rarely found it necessary to explain their reasoning to mortals, if ever.

For just a moment, when he'd heard the retelling of the events following the giant's failed interest in three mounted elves riding faster than it cared to chase—considering none of them had the spear it truly wanted—Alere almost believed the mystic had again gone out of his way only to recover one of the weapons he sought for his cause. When he listened again, and saw what Tristus believed and the moving devotion in the knight's eyes, he realized the error of his thinking. Xu Liang was the same selfless man he'd come upon in the Hollowen Forest. Alere's own shortcomings had gradually rejected his original perception of the mystic, his elven heritage refusing to accept that a human could possess such qualities. He wanted to believe he was following *Aerkiren's* will. From the start he'd been following Xu Liang, a gifted human indeed, to have won an elf lord's trust and respect so quickly.

I would count you a friend, Xu Liang, Alere thought. *And I would take back my words that were spoken in haste and perhaps with some jealousy. I will play for you tonight, mystic of Sheng Fan, when your heart has drummed its last.*

◆ ◆ ◆ ◆ ◆

FU RAN HAD never known a brother besides Xu Liang. He'd been raised with the person he would one day be expected to protect with his own life. Unlike his father, who'd managed to always separate duty from family, Fu Ran developed a close bond with the pampered student. So close that when the class separation started becoming more apparent between scholar and bodyguard—master and servant—he became angry and hurt.

The Emperor and prince both considered Fu Ran insolent, and even rebellious, and Xu Liang constantly sided with them. Of course, what else could a fledgling official have done? Fu Ran eventually swallowed his pride—that Xu Liang had actually told him was misplaced in one well-remembered instance—and accepted his humiliating lot for the sake of his friend. He would have taken almost any abuse, except Song Lu. The overbearing prince had taken to calling Xu Liang his friend as well, but unlike Fu Ran, who had no other choice, Song Lu was not willing to share. He made life miserable for Fu Ran, and Xu Liang—blinded by his budding career and 'the glory of Sheng Fan'—did little to amend the rapidly devolving situation. Fu Ran left and, as fate continually brought them together, he knew, in spite of Xu Liang's evolved wisdom and maturity, that the mystic had never forgiven him. To explore outside of Sheng Fan was one thing. To leave it altogether was unthinkable.

"Lord Xu Liang is like a son to me," Gai Ping said to Guang Ci. Both men walked close to Fu Ran, speaking softly in the only tongue they knew. "If he dies, I will carry his body to the Empress myself."

"I will accompany you," Guang Ci promised. "I would sooner die myself than to see his body left here among these detestable barbarians and their strange, filthy lands!"

"You would disgrace his memory with such words!" the elder scolded. "At the late Emperor's command, he explored the outer realms and came to cherish them."

"Careful," Fu Ran said. "He's not finished yet."

After he issued the words, Fu Ran looked to the one person among them who genuinely believed that; Tristus Edainien.

Excluding the fire elves, the knight was the stranger among them. Yet somehow he'd managed to win everyone over. Fu Ran couldn't say if it was pity come to affection or just phenomenal tolerance among the group, but even after his berserker side showed itself, the knight managed to fit himself in. And now, with *Dawnfire* in his possession, glowing against the eventide along with its sibling Blades, it was indisputable. He *was* one of them.

The thought carried Fu Ran's gaze to Xu Liang, unconscious, getting some well-deserved sleep after his victory. If only he were asleep … if only he were aware of just how close he'd come to bringing all of the Swords together. With four of them present and the *Spear of Heaven* safely with the Empress, he had only to find one more. And then he could have returned to Sheng Fan.

"He's going to make it, Fu Ran," Tristus said softly.

Fu Ran looked up to see the knight staring directly ahead, a peculiar surety having banished his tears. It was as if he knew something that no one else did. Fu Ran couldn't say if he felt comforted by that, or more depressed. At the moment he felt numb, as devoid of thought or expression as Xu Liang. If the mystic did somehow make it, he was not going to be happy.

◆ ◆ ◆ ◆ ◆

THE LAND LIFTED around them, gaining dimension and texture. No more was the terrain flat and cast with an endless sheet of snow. Steep, slender shadows loomed all around the travelers. They moved through the mountain pass feeling as if they were being passed along by many dark hands. They were in the clutches and the care of the Phoenix Elves.

Shirisae lit their way with *Firestorm*. At the wide base of one of the sheer, ominous rock formations, the lady elf stopped them. She bade them wait while she and her brother rode ahead into the darkness. *Firestorm* illuminated a third rider when the siblings drew to a halt several yards away.

The companions huddled in the soft, golden glow of *Dawnfire*, watching ... and waiting.

Tristus had not relinquished his hold on either the spear or Xu Liang for the duration of their journey into this last stand of mountains. He held *Dawnfire* in one hand, Blue Crane's reins in the other, with Xu Liang slumped over his arm. In the stillness of the wait, he gently and almost unconsciously drew the mystic closer. He felt ten years younger, verging upon discovery, one of the first of many discoveries that would dictate the course of his entire life. In his twenty-six years, he'd only gravitated toward two people this strongly. One had pushed him away, the other had been dead for two years now. While still with the Order, he'd given himself to duty and then, recently, to despair and to desperately trying to recover some sense of purpose after his banishment. He'd forgotten what it was like to be out of all possibility of mortal danger and to still be afraid.

"I'm leaving," Alere announced, and in the suddenness of his words, Tristus looked at him quickly, drawing the white elf's gaze. He didn't have to ask why. The elf saw the question in Tristus' eyes, and answered. "I will go no further. These elves are neither my kin nor my allies."

That wasn't good enough for Tristus. "Alere, you can't." He kept his voice low, but his words were urgent, pleading. "What about the quest? What about the Swords? Though I didn't understand it at first, I know now that the Blades are drawn together for some purpose. We must stay together."

Alere simply looked at him, waiting for him to finish. And then, unexpectedly, he smiled. He shook his head gently. "No. I will not stay here among my enemies. However, do not despair, Tristus Edainien. We will meet again. The mystic believes in fate, that to all things, regarding all ends, there is a purpose. *Pearl Moon* will not cease to shine this night, though the light of its bearer should wane and be gone from this world. The Swords will find each other again. And so I bid you farewell, Knight of Andaria. For now."

Tristus watched the elf, knowing that no force in this realm was going to stop him, since he'd made up his mind. He searched for words anyway and as the white elf turned Breigh around and departed, Tristus said only, "Alere..."

"There's the loyalty of an elf for you," Tarfan grumbled. "Takes the frying pan himself and dumps us into the fire."

"I don't think he would have left if he believed we were in any danger, Tarfan," Tristus said quietly, still watching Alere's departing form.

"So what now?" Fu Ran asked, and it was several moments before Tristus realized the large man was asking him. Perhaps it was only because he sat so near their fallen leader.

With his attention once again fully on the matter at hand, Tristus answered in as calm a voice as he could muster. "We go with the fire elves. We've come this far, and if there's any chance at all that they can aid Xu Liang, we must take it."

Fu Ran nodded, then began speaking to the bodyguards in Fanese, presumably explaining things to them. All five of the brilliantly armored warriors looked at Tristus when the large man was finished, their expressions unreadable.

Shirisae and D'mitri returned within the following moments. "Our passage has been granted. Be warned that the way to Vilciel from here is long and treacherous. Do not stray from the path. I will be your guide and my brother shall follow to be certain no one is lost."

"It looks as if we've lost one already," D'mitri commented, his tone sounding satisfied as well as derisive.

Tristus ignored the chill that climbed up his back, and said to Shirisae, "How long is this path? I fear our friend is quickly fading."

Shirisae regarded Xu Liang with a brief glance. Her golden eyes looked long at Tristus. "For him the journey will be easy. For the rest of you, it will be a test of your worth before our god."

"What in the blasted hells is that supposed to mean?" Tarfan demanded.

"I can give you only this information; The Phoenix is not a force for preservation, but of renewal. Use the knowledge I have given you wisely."

Shirisae started off, and the companions lingered under the cold, burning gaze of her sibling.

"Does anyone else have a bad feeling about this?" Taya asked nervously.

"I'll bet Alere didn't know about this little lump of gold," Tarfan grumbled.

Tristus drew in a long breath and held it briefly. Then, as no one else seemed inclined to do so, he moved forward, following Shirisae. Whether they were following him or Xu Liang, he did not know, but he was glad when he heard their gradual footsteps behind him.

The black-clad, flame-haired lady elf brought them to an open gateway at the base of a sleek, dark mountain. There had been no sources of light to illuminate the ancient characters etched upon the dark gray stone of the archway before the Blades drew near. Wide stairs, seemingly carved of the mountain itself, ascended from the gate, leading directly into the mountain.

"It must be treacherous," Tarfan muttered to Tristus. "If there are no doors or guards to stand against intruders."

"Someone else was here," Fu Ran reminded. "Though I don't see that other rider now."

"We'll have to be careful." That was all Tristus could think to say as his throat constricted, feeling raw and dry. And then he looked suddenly for Taya, almost forgetting that she had ridden on the only horse left to them other than Blue Crane. In the confusion of the ice giant's attack, the supply horse had panicked and fled beyond recovery. No one thought to look for the animal immediately after Xu Liang had fallen. The last thing Tristus wanted to do was insult the dwarf maiden, but he didn't want to lose anyone else, and so he spoke what was on his mind. "Fu Ran, will one of you ride with Taya? The way looks steep."

Following the words, he glanced at Taya, expecting a look of resent or indignation. He was glad when he saw the relief on her round face clearly. She did not complain when the older bodyguard Gai Ping climbed into the saddle behind her and took up the reins.

The companions, now ten and possibly soon to be only nine, entered the world of the Phoenix Elves. And a strange, dark world it was; a network of enclosed corridors without torches or windows. In many places the shadows were too deep to allow any sense of dimension. Each wall, as well as the ceiling and much of the floor, were hidden from view. The companions saw only the wide stairs immediately underfoot, each step echoing off the darkness, penetrating a silence that not even the mountain wind was bold enough to invade. No one spoke.

To Tristus' left, *Dawnfire* glowed, tracing streams of gold in Xu Liang's flowing hair, which sufficiently hid his face from view. Tristus thought that he still felt him breathing. That was the only way he knew the mystic was alive. That he had lasted this long was a miracle in itself. If he made it to any form of healing at all, surely he would pull through. If he'd lost his will, he'd have gone long ago. Tristus kept telling himself that. He made himself believe it.

"One must follow what one believes in," Xu Liang had said. *"Whether it is reasonable or not."*

Tristus heard the mystic's voice in his head and blocked out all others, including those that might have warned him of the many eyes watching from the shadows.

◆ ◆ ◆ ◆ ◆

FROM A LOW lying ridge over the mountain pass, Bastien could just see the caravan come to a stop. He'd watched them linger for a bit before they started moving again, led by the strangers in black. Phoenix Elves. The former gypsy had heard plenty of tales about the flame-haired mountain folk. They were dangerous, but they seemed to have some use for the humans currently in their company. The worst assault they'd delivered so far was a fiery glare.

Something was amiss, though. Bastien would have thought matters could get no worse after the berserker—though that did prove a convenient distraction, better even than simply disappearing in the confusion of battle—but then came the undead, the fire elves, and finally the ice giant. Even after activating the invisibility enchantment placed upon his cloak, Bastien had been just as much at risk of getting crushed as everyone else. It was that knight's doing. The mystic should have let Fu Ran deal with him when he had a mind to. Now the berserker seemed to be leading the group while Xu Liang did a fine job imitating a corpse.

What next? Bastien wondered.

In a heartbeat, he had his answer. Something stabbed deep into his leg. He yelped and reflexively twisted to end the affliction, making it unintentionally easier for his attacker to get a firm grip on his cloak and to lift him upright so that his throat just touched the edge of a blade. Sudden light flared in his eyes, but he couldn't close them as he stared in utter amaze at the elf glaring steadily back at him.

"You..." Bastien's voice lumped in his throat. He swallowed and tried again. "You saw through my spell."

"I smelled you," Alere growled with disgust. "Blame *Aerkiren* for the shattering of your disguise. I meant to kill you, but since my random stab left you still alive let us not waste your final breaths. I want to know who you really are!"

"My ... name is Bastien Crowe. I'm a sailor aboard the *Pride of Celestia*, friend to Fu Ran and any who are his allies. After the battle with the Fanese bandits, I was wounded and staggered off to escape the berserker as well as to patch my injuries. I must have lost consciousness. When I came around everyone had already gone. I followed and decided to keep a distance after I saw the other elves ... to watch them."

Alere's eyes narrowed, as if in consideration. And then he said, "I told you once before; you're a terrible liar."

Bastien smirked at the elf and his unflagging arrogance. "All right, I wanted to watch all of you. What are you going to do? Kill me over distrust? That seems to be a prominent art form with you, and you're not even selective." The blade slipped against Bastien's throat, and he panicked. "Wait! Wait ... just..."

The elf drew back slightly, and Bastien sighed. He started thinking, wondering how long Alere had been on to him. He didn't dare tell him everything, but he had to tell him something. It had to be something he would believe.

"Xu Liang isn't the only one looking for those Swords," he hissed, more from pain than out of anger. His leg throbbed terribly, and the blood was soaking his pant leg, making him shiver. "There are other scholars, other factions, seeking them ... seeking to understand them!"

"The term gypsy scholar is an absurd contradiction in words," Alere told him icily. "Whatever made you think I would believe..."

"It's true!" Bastien cried out, feeling the cold bite of the elf's magic blade. "I'm no scholar. You're right about that, but many of my superiors are very learned men and women." Because Alere failed to kill him just then, Bastien continued. "Chaos is rising in the world. Those Phoenix Elves feel it, Xu Liang knows it ... and you feel it yourself. Something must be done, but not just anything. I am member of a brotherhood that is committed to ensuring that Dryth maintains a balance. The forces of darkness are cleverer than you know. Sometimes what seems a good or just solution is actually the worst possible answer. Such matters have to be researched. We cannot have deluded and desperate people running about waking up ancient powers before anyone even truly knows which end of the spectrum they serve."

Alere regarded him with little expression beyond disgust. He said, "*Aerkiren* slays the shadows. That is all I need to know to be convinced as to its function in this world."

"And so you use the blade to slay evil, thus far without conse-quence." Bastien spoke quickly, feeling the elf's patience slipping away, like grains of sand in an hour glass. "But what of the others? What do you know about those weapons? Or the people who wield them, for that matter?"

"I know more of them than I care to know of you. This conver-sation is at an end, Bastien Crowe." The elf moved quicker than thought. The blade slid away from the gypsy's neck less than a second before the pommel struck the side of his head. A blackness deeper than the fear-spell of the keirveshen fell over him.

◆ ◆ ◆ ◆ ◆

THE STAIRS CAME to a flat span. The companions followed without straying from the general path created by Shirisae's lead, uncertain as to whether or not they were in a great hall or on a bridge not much wider than the reach of their limited light. It didn't help that Tarfan grumbled about tumbling or being thrown into the Abyss every time he thought he heard something he didn't like.

"There it is again!" Tarfan hissed. "Do you hear that?"

"All I hear is you," Fu Ran answered.

"You great lummox! Shut up and listen! It's a skittering, scurrying noise, like rain or..."

"Rain?" Fu Ran laughed. It was a tense sound. "I don't hear any-thing. I don't feel anything either."

"Now, look here, you..."

"Does it matter, Tarfan?" Tristus intervened, his voice hinting impatience though he tried to maintain a calm, even tone. "Let me know if you see something. Otherwise put up with the noises, and let's try to keep up with Shirisae. This isn't the kind of place I want to be lost in."

"I don't trust D'mitri either," Fu Ran whispered, after Tristus unintentionally failed to mention the elf behind them.

He'd actually forgotten about him. Now he wanted to look back to see if Shirisae's brother was still there, but he refrained. They could have killed them at any time. What reason would they have for not doing so earlier, if that was their intention? The thought didn't comfort him anymore than it would have comforted his friends. Following blindly didn't feel quite so foolish when he'd been following Xu Liang. They were lacking leadership now. Not someone to physically lead them along, but someone to keep them calm and even uplifted, as Xu Liang had. The mystic had rallied them to his cause, made them all determined to stay with it.

I fear I'm a poor substitute for an imperial tactician, Tristus thought to himself. The thoughts that followed were interrupted by the sight of a great doorway—it was clearly several stories high—glowing a fiery orange. Tristus wanted to stop and gawk, but he kept onward, following Shirisae into the light that somehow failed to illuminate the space around them. As soon as he entered the doorway the cold of the mountains abandoned him, and he felt as if he'd entered a furnace. A quick look around let him know that he had.

"By the blasted hells," Tarfan murmured in awe.

"By them?" Fu Ran said. "We're in them!"

It certainly seemed that way. All around them, the smoothly sculpted walls were aglow with the constant light from a great pit of flame, its depth unfathomable. It seemed to span more than a mile ahead of them and untold miles in either direction, through two archways of equal grandeur to the first, though the latter seemed inaccessible by foot. Their purpose would likely remain a mystery. Beneath the first arch, the companions stood upon a wide ledge that narrowed into a bridge of stone spanning across the flaming chasm. The heat was incredible, but somehow no one complained of burning or sickness.

"You are safe from the shadows now," Shirisae told them, turning to face the companions before proceeding onto the bridge.

"The shadows?" Taya asked, looking back to where D'mitri was just coming through the doorway.

"They followed us this far, but they will not enter here," Shirisae continued, speaking over Tarfan's 'I told you so' to Fu Ran. "Our armor blinds them to our souls, but none of you are so protected."

She looked at Tristus. "It was the light of the blade you call *Dawnfire* that held them at bay. They fear it, just as they fear this fire."

Tristus glanced at the platinum spear still glowing in his grasp. "The demon I first encountered didn't seem so wary of it, and the bearer at the time was surely far more skilled than I can hope to be."

"Nevertheless, here the shadows fear fire. The lower passages are infested with them, and it would have been almost impossible to lead you by this route if not for *Dawnfire*. We would have been forced to climb the exterior mountain paths. The time saved should benefit your friend."

Before Tristus could respond, Shirisae turned back toward the bridge. "Know that the path is still dangerous and that we still have far to go before we reach the city of Vilciel, New Home to my people."

"Why aren't we melted to the bone yet?" Fu Ran asked. "I'm hardly sweating."

"Dwarven architecture, my friend," Tarfan said, proudly but also irritably. "You'll find none better. Even the dragons knew that. The great lizards didn't take well to cold, but it was about the only place in Dryth they could exist in relative peace, and so they constructed furnaces to keep their cold blood pumping. Since the arrogant reptiles didn't want their slaves roasted—and the slaves didn't want to roast—a ventilation system was devised to draw the heat where they needed it, and away from those they needed working."

"Ventilation?" Tristus said. "This can't be attributed simply to tunnels and shafts. It seems as if you could touch the flames themselves and still not get burned."

"Yes, well don't," Tarfan advised. "Dragons have been known to lay down an enchantment here and there, but I guarantee that a lot of the coolness has to do with the structure of this chamber and the ones surrounding it."

"Doesn't anyone else wonder why the pit is still on fire if the dragons occupied this place hundreds of years ago?" Taya asked.

"Let's not worry about that just at the moment," Tristus said, before Tarfan could blurt one of the alarmist ideas undoubtedly crossing his mind. "Our priority is getting to Vilciel, quickly, before we lose Xu Liang."

With that enforced, Tristus started after Shirisae.

The others followed in somber silence.

◆ ◆ ◆ ◆ ◆

TAYA FROWNED UNSEEN, disliking these fire elves more by the second. If Tristus wasn't blinded by friendship and his knightly duty to save an ally, maybe he wouldn't have been so quick to trot after the proud, strong, elegant—and taller than a dwarf—Shirisae.

"The way she looks at him is really beginning to burn me," Taya complained to Gai Ping, who naturally said nothing, since he wasn't linguistically equipped to carry on a conversation that wasn't in Fanese. "I thought elves were supposed to be attracted to other elves! Not that I'm interested. Of course, I'm not. He's a human, after all, and much too stretched out for one of my perfect stature, but someone's got to look out for him and it may as well be me! You know I'm right, Gai Ping, so just sit there and be quiet."

The bodyguard glanced down at her upon hearing his name, but said nothing.

"I'm getting a really bad feeling about this place," Taya concluded, gazing warily into the sea of fire they were crossing.

◆ ◆ ◆ ◆ ◆

THE END OF the bridge proved only a brief reprieve. Another ocean of flame followed with another bridge to cross, just as narrow as the first. Tristus was beginning to have serious misgivings about this place, but there was nowhere else to go. Perhaps, if he'd been in Andaria, there might have been a master cleric to take Xu Liang to, one who knew something of more than surface wounds, who knew which prayers were most appropriate and how to speak them properly. Tristus' training and skill lacked considerably since he'd abandoned his mother's plans for the clergy in favor of knighthood. He hadn't asked Taya, and because she hadn't volunteered information that would contradict him, he doubted any herb was going to repair whatever damage had been done to Xu Liang as a result of his extreme exertion.

"Do not be troubled, knight," Shirisae said, looking back at him, slowing her mount to let Blue Crane catch up. "You are proving yourself worthy of our god's attention. You passed through shadows and left them cowering in your wake. You cross fire and do not panic."

"I didn't know the shadows were there." Tristus said. "Not demons, at any rate. And I've a little too much on my mind for panicking."

"These flames have been known to drive humans mad," Shirisae informed. "Many have thrown themselves in, simply because they could not take waiting to fall."

"Waiting can be difficult," Tristus answered, glancing nervously at the erratic dance of the great fire. He thought of treasure seekers finding the endless gold of these flames and being driven to hysterics just from the disappointment. Tristus could not have imagined going through all that he'd gone through just for riches. To a greedy person, finding that those riches were non-existent must have been the felling blow. He shifted his focus momentarily to Xu Liang and considered that he might have a worse disappointment ahead of him.

"He will be restored," Shirisae promised and he looked at her, wondering if restored was the proper word. Before he could say anything, the lady elf resumed her place at the front of the line.

♦ ♦ ♦ ♦ ♦

THEY HAD ONE more bridge to cross before they arrived at another staircase. It curved gradually, and after more than an hour's travel, they emerged into the freezing night air. A second gateway stood at the edge of a wide, shallow ledge near the top of the mountain they'd been climbing on the inside. A wide, ice-covered bridge with a solid stone balustrade spanned to the next mountain, northward, where another gate awaited, along with a road of steps leading to a walled conglomeration of grand, frost-rimed buildings at the top.

Tristus' mouth literally fell open at the sight of Vilciel. Every structure, every detail was beyond natural scale. Icicles as long as trees were tall adorned immaculate colonnades. Smooth stone edifices were supported by fantastic columns big enough to mount the entire Eristan Citadel on the top of just one. Torches seemed as small suns hovering about the mountaintop. Windows were wide enough to line armies across. It was without question the most awesome setting Tristus had ever looked upon. He didn't even consider that he would see its equal, not anywhere in Dryth.

"Dragons lived here," Tarfan said, sounding breathless himself.

Tristus tried to picture it, but in the moment he required all of his imagination just to take in the city itself. Its former inhabitants would have to be envisioned later. "It must have been glorious," he managed to say.

No one answered. His companions were all speechless.

"Come," Shirisae instructed, and led them across the wide, mountain-spanning bridge.

A depthless drop into cloudy blackness lay to either side. Flecks of ice swirled about in the air, a permanent dusting of snow fanning across the bridge, accumulating along the balustrades. The chill wind lifted strands of Xu Liang's extremely long hair, brushing them across Tristus' face. Balancing *Dawnfire* across his lap, he smoothed the dark locks back down and held them in place with the weight of his freed hand so that he could see. It occurred to him in passing that the mystic must have been quite proud of his mane to have grown it so long and kept it at such a length. The ends of Tristus' hair just reached his jaw bone and he'd been thinking a trim was in order.

Behind him, Taya suddenly squealed. "What is that?"

Tristus looked up from Xu Liang's silken mantel at something else as black as night; the pelt and feathers of a griffin.

TWENTY-ONE
The Fire of Ahjenta

"VILCIEL SPANS SEVERAL mountaintops," Shirisae explained, stroking the great raptor head of the griffin as it lowered before her.

The rider atop the fantastic beast regarded the lady elf as reverently, having come down from a watch tower to greet her.

"As well," Shirisae continued, "the greater walls and towers are difficult to climb quickly. The griffins are an indispensable asset to us."

None of the companions were bold enough to approach the amalgamation of lion and bird of prey, but—after Taya had stopped screaming—they all looked upon it with respect.

"Tristus Edainien," Shirisae beckoned. "Bring your friend here."

Fu Ran grabbed his arm, unsure.

Tristus did his best to reassure with a calm, determined voice. "It will be all right," he said, and when the large man relinquished his hold, Tristus guided Blue Crane forward, regarding the griffin with caution now, more out of respect for its sharp talons and beak than its majesty in the moment.

"It will be quickest to bring Xu Liang to the Temple of Healing by griffin's back. It rests high above us. Preparations can begin while I guide the rest of your party to a place where you can rest and be replenished."

"I want to be there," Tristus said at once. "I want to witness the healing."

"Is it that you do not trust us?" Shirisae asked, neither surprised nor upset.

Tristus looked at the griffin and its armored rider, then at Shirisae, whose golden eyes seemed to secretly smile at him. He was slow accepting her reassurance, but finally shook his head. "No. It isn't that, lady. It is only that..." He thought fast and said convincingly. "... I am a Knight of Andaria, who has pledged his services to this man, to guide and protect him on his travels. I must stay at his side until I have fulfilled my duty, or until he commands otherwise."

"He can scarcely do so while unconscious," Shirisae said. "However, it is not customary..."

He didn't let her finish. "I must!" She looked at him sharply just then and though he inclined his head as a gesture of apology for raising his voice, he maintained his stern tone. "I am honor bound, my lady. By the Holy City of Eris and my God, I cannot leave his side. It is not an issue of trust."

Shirisae watched him silently for several moments, long enough that D'mitri came forward to see what the matter was. The siblings exchanged words briefly. Shirisae's eyes never left Tristus.

Finally, she nodded once and said, "Very well, Knight of Andaria. You may accompany him, but no others. This is a delicate ritual and must not be corrupted by the presence of too many outsiders, lest the subject be lost to us."

Tristus almost regretted his insistence, fearing that he would somehow ruin a sacred healing ceremony, but he couldn't let Xu Liang disappear into the hands of strangers while they all sat in wonder. At least, he hoped, the others could be provided with some comfort knowing that the mystic was not alone. He looked back at Fu Ran, telling him silently to explain matters to Xu Liang's remaining bodyguards so they wouldn't try to kill anyone in their confusion and concern over their master's departure.

Fu Ran nodded, almost imperceptibly, and turned to face the others.

In front of Tristus, the griffin rider waited. D'mitri dismounted from his horse and Tristus allowed the elf to assist in the moving of Xu Liang from the back of one graceful creature to that of another.

"You will not require your weapons," Shirisae told him when he climbed down from Blue Crane. "Perhaps you'd like to leave them with one of your companions."

Pearl Moon was already in the custody of Gai Ping. When Tarfan came to take Blue Crane's bridle, Tristus handed him *Dawnfire* as well, along with his father's sword. "Please, will you guard these for me, Master Fairwind?"

While at first the dwarf looked awkward holding such a long spear, he mustered a proud expression, then consoled Tristus with a warm smile. "Don't you worry, lad. There's no one better to entrust a weapon with than a dwarf. This war hammer has been in my family for more than two hundred years. Not a scratch on it."

While that wasn't entirely true—the weapon was heavily battle worn—Tristus trusted the old dwarf, who stated with his eyes on Xu Liang and his smile slowly fading that he was placing a heavy trust in Tristus as well. Tristus briefly clasped Tarfan's shoulder to offer reassurance, then climbed onto the griffin. The creature abandoned the bridge almost immediately, sending a current of terror coursing through Tristus, who'd never flown on the back of anything. He'd actually never even dreamed of it.

◆ ◆ ◆ ◆ ◆

SHORTLY AFTER THE first griffin made off with Tristus and Xu Liang, Shirisae summoned her own griffin, and was gone faster than Taya could glare. She took her precious spear with her and in her absence, D'mitri turned to the others, looking as if he were trying to decide which one of them to hurl off the bridge first. He must have decided Fu Ran would be too much trouble.

In a moment, without anyone going over the edge, he said tersely, "Come with me."

They went … across the bridge and into the city, through streets wide enough to sustain great rivers and into buildings that could house thousands and still have room for more. Surprisingly, the fire elves managed to make an otherwise uninhabitable city look inhabited. While the streets weren't terribly full in the cold—and possibly due to the hour—indoors they had converted large halls meant for dragons to comfortably occupy into enormous residences and marketplaces. Elves in armor walked alongside elves wearing the fine clothes of the gentry or the more common—although still well-kept—attire of the workers among them; the artisans, merchants, and even entertainers. Children ran through the inner streets, playing with wolf pups and sometimes young griffins. It was a city, just as anyplace else, and at the same time like no place else in Dryth.

Food and supplies came from sections of the city designated to handling such affairs. According to D'mitri, on a mountaintop housing what he called the Crystal Dome, plants and vegetables were grown. In the lower regions of the city where the furnaces didn't dominate, the elves cultivated spider farms, spinning the silk from a rare breed of rodent-sized arachnids. Also in the caves beneath the city, mushrooms grew in abundance and were harvested for food as well as for medicinal purposes, as were certain other fungi. Vast mineral ores, some of which possessed very unique properties, were found in the underground caverns. While in the past they'd been mined by dwarves, the elves brought them to life once again, and by doing so were able to craft swords and armor, among other useful things.

The elves of a ruined land had found a 'New Home' in the ruins of this land. They kept very much to themselves and flourished, their only true enemy being the living shadows that infested the inner parts of the mountains. They found ways to deal with them.

"The hunter elf would like to believe that his people are the only ones who suffered at the hands of the keirveshen," D'mitri was saying while he led the companions up a staircase several yards wide. "While it was true, the Verres Mountains were attacked by unusually large groups, they were not attacked exclusively. We live with demons in our cellars and do not blame or seek help from other elves. We didn't, when an army of men invaded our homeland. We accepted our fate and the gods admired our courage in the face of circumstances we could not alter. Our ancestors were resurrected and given the chance to begin anew in a different land. By the time we settled in this land, the time of the Verresi was already at an end. Many of their own had already left them."

Fu Ran smiled as Taya marched behind the conceited elf, miming his mannerisms while he harangued on about the differences between his people and Alere's. The flame-haired, yellow-skinned elf had an opinion of himself that was actually quite comical, even considering his strong, athletic frame and regal features. He simply took himself too seriously, and expected everyone else to as well. Fu Ran had spent much of the incidental tour sizing him up, plotting the different ways he would put him down if it proved necessary, or if it seemed like something fun to do that he could get away with. He didn't want to get the others into trouble, but what he wouldn't give for just a few minutes alone with this elf. And all this time he'd been thinking Alere was an imperial pain. At least Fu Ran and the white elf had been properly introduced.

When it became clear that D'mitri was ignoring the dwarves because they were dwarves and the bodyguards because they clearly didn't understand a word he said, and that he was actually speaking almost directly to Fu Ran, he decided to nod a few times and make sounds of acknowledgment while his eyes took in the scenery. Occasionally he grinned at the curious youngsters, scaring the life out of them after they thumbed their perfect little noses at him when the adults weren't watching.

At some length he decided to ask their host a question, and in so doing interrupted part of a speech on why D'mitri's role as brother of the next Priestess of the Flame was so important. He asked seriously, "Do all Phoenix Elves have red hair?"

D'mitri, who'd been gesticulating while he lectured, slowly lowered his hand and scowled with such genuine, highbred umbrage it was almost obscene. It was Song Lu all over again, only more fun because he didn't have to tread carefully around him—at least, not too carefully.

"What if the dragons come back?" Tarfan asked, reminding the elf of his presence.

D'mitri finished glaring at Fu Ran, then said, almost as an after-thought, "We are not concerned with dragons."

"Maybe you will be, if they come home and find out there's been an infestation," the dwarf grumbled.

"Why *are* the furnaces burning, by the way?" Taya finally asked.

"They are eternal flames," the elf sighed, as if more bored now than bothered by his sister's guests. "Cast by dragon magi. They can never go out, and anyway they help to heat the city. In case you'd forgotten, we are in a cold mountain region."

The lady dwarf mimed his last statement behind his back, then showed him her tongue, which he utterly failed to notice.

◆ ◆ ◆ ◆ ◆

THE TEMPLE OF Healing was an enormous structure consisting of one main level with an intermediate second story forming a balcony around it. There were at least a dozen support pillars running the length of the hall, slender columns of smooth stone.

Tristus stood beside one of them, looking down at the center of the great room, which lay several feet below, open and unobstructed with the exception of a solitary stone altar. The room was entirely constructed of gray stone with a polished, marble sheen. Orb-shaped lanterns of stained glass hung on brackets on the pillars, casting a green hue over much of the hall.

The second story mezzanine was as far as Tristus had been allowed to go. The griffin had landed on the edge of a great archway, leading into the building on the second level and shortly thereafter, Xu Liang had been whisked away by flame-haired elves in black robes, as if they'd been expecting him. Shirisae arrived just in time to convince Tristus to proceed to the mezzanine and watch from there. It had been several minutes since she left to be part of the healing ceremony. So far, the hall remained empty except for Tristus, who was beginning to worry, in spite of Shirisae's reassurances. They didn't really know the fire elves. But then, he had to remind himself, Xu Liang and the others hadn't known him either.

Tristus stood close to the second floor's railing, almost in the shadow of one of the pillars. He felt like a child who'd crept into the temple at Eristan to watch a knight receive his rank in full, religious ceremony. Though there was feasting and celebration afterward, the ritual itself was actually very lonely, consisting of the one to be knighted, no more than three clerics—two attending the one who would perform the ceremony—and long hours of silent prayer.

It was said that a Knight of Andaria never communed more closely with God than during his entrance into knighthood. Tristus could testify to that. After the donning of various symbolic robes throughout the cleric's part in the ceremony, then being left alone to fast and to pray for a full day before receiving the sword and armor that, in his case, would one day be taken from him, he experienced two visions and heard a voice he had not before—and never again—heard the like of. A knight did not speak of his communion, and so he would never say openly that it was God's voice, but to this day he believed within himself that it could have been none other. He had been humbled then in the sacred silence. He found the silence in this temple unnerving.

Worry was set aside for curiosity when a line of black-robed figures entered the chamber below, their crowns of flame hair hidden almost entirely by deep hoods. They approached from the south end, breaking into two rows as they reached the altar. Tristus watched almost a dozen pass before he saw the pair with the litter between them, which bore Xu Liang. The mystic's colorful silk robes had been replaced with a long black garment similar to those worn by the elves, making him look paler as he lay unconscious with his hands folded upon his chest.

He looked dead. Was this a healing ceremony or a funeral?

Tristus gripped the balcony railing tighter, then slid away from the pillar for a better view as the two figures bearing Xu Liang walked the litter to the altar and transferred the mystic onto the stone bed, almost without disturbing a hair, so smooth were their actions. When they were finished, they lined up with the others, adding one to each row flanking the altar. They stood in silence, their hooded heads bowed. Were they praying?

Nothing's happening. Tristus bit his cheek to keep from hollering down at them and demanding to know what they were doing, or why they weren't doing anything.

And then, two more figures entered the room from the north end. Both wore robes without hoods. Their long, flowing red hair gleamed with a curious hue in the greenish lighting. Both were women, one wearing a black feathered mask that concealed all of her face but her chin and her bright red lips. The other was Shirisae, carrying *Firestorm*. Tristus presumed that the masked elf was the clan's priestess; Shirisae's mother, Ahjenta. The manner in which they stopped at the head of the altar seemed to confirm it.

Shirisae knelt down, pivoting to face the priestess as she glided to a halt beside her. She bowed her head and presented *Firestorm*. The priestess took it and held it upright, tapping the butt upon the stone floor once. A small crack of thunder filled the chamber, drawing Tristus' gaze irresistibly toward the ceiling and walls as the sound resonated deeply. When he looked down at the altar again, Shirisae had carried herself to the foot of it, and was standing with her head bowed like the others.

Another long silence filled the chamber.

And then the priestess stepped closer to the altar. Holding her slender hand above Xu Liang's head, she spoke in a tongue Tristus had no hope of understanding. Her voice carried strong and crisp, though it did not lack the softness of her feminine grace. Recognizing prayer, even though he did not recognize the words, Tristus was inspired to bow his head. Closing his eyes, he reflexively recited his own prayer in his mind. And then, in the same tranced manner, he performed the solemn gesture of respect to God and the Angels, his hand lingering over the insignia on his breastplate as he opened his eyes again and saw the priestess stepping back from Xu Liang.

Tristus watched in awe and suspense when the priestess lifted *Firestorm* in both hands, holding the great spear above her head as if in supplication to her own god. She began speaking abbreviated phrases that were answered in humming monotone by her disciples. As she spoke, *Firestorm* began to glow. Not as it had before, but strangely different.

The bright blade did not crackle with a luminous silver light, but seemed to catch fire. Emerald flames licked the still air and spread along the weapon's shaft, over the priestess's unprotected hands and down her arms. The fire stopped at her elbows, looking like gauntlets of green flame.

The priestess continued her chant, oblivious to the magic blaze, her disciples answering. The rhythm of the ritual intensified, as did the green flame encompassing *Firestorm*.

A sensation of horror filled Tristus when the flames leapt down onto the priestess, engulfing her fully, then rising back up into the air, as if fueled by the body it was burning. But it wasn't burning her. Tristus could scarcely breathe, watching her stand motionless and now quiet in the jade inferno, that was rising upward and ... was it taking shape?

With a suddenness that made Tristus crouch down to avoid being blasted, the green flames shot outward in three directions. Two bands of fire spread across the chamber like great wings, and a third column lifted toward the high ceiling, curving and somehow gaining dimension as it plunged into shadows, dashing them away with its eerie radiance. The whole chamber glowed as the beaked face formed of jade flame glared down at the figures beneath it. No, it was of silver fire. The lighting in the room had cast jade upon it.

For a heart-stopping instant the Phoenix hovered in the air, still connected to the priestess who had summoned it. And then, like a hawk sighting its prey, it dove for the altar.

Tristus was too terrified to do anything but stare as the flaming bird threw itself at Xu Liang, narrowing in its rapid descent until it appeared more a shaft of fire than a bird. It shot into the mystic like a bolt of unholy lightning, seeming to drive itself directly into his heart.

It was over in an instant.

The fire died upon impact, or pulled itself entirely into the mystic's body. The chamber darkened, and a terrible silence settled.

Unable to breathe, Tristus raised himself slowly, peaking over the banister at the altar below, expecting to see ashes where Xu

Liang once had been, to find that the healing ceremony had actually been a glorified cremation. He watched the priestess lower *Firestorm* slowly, her golden eyes fixed on the motionless form still lying on the altar.

Tristus wondered now if the ceremony had been a genuine attempt to heal, but failed.

And then, slowly, the mystic's pale hands moved. They only just lifted and fell back down upon his chest, but it seemed enough for the priestess. She spoke a single word and stepped back from the altar, then turned and left. The others fell into motion after she'd gone, including Shirisae, who presided over the careful handling of Xu Liang as he was placed back on the litter and borne away.

"What's happening?" Tristus asked, when he finally gained the voice and courage to speak.

Shirisae looked up at him, her golden eyes seeming to smile again. She said proudly, "Ahjenta has restored him. He must sleep now, while the sacred flame runs its course."

Tristus wasn't aware of the tears in his eyes, until they spilled onto his cheeks. "Thank you, Shirisae."

The Phoenix Elf smiled with her lips this time and said, "You must go to your companions and relay this news. I am sure they are eager to hear it." Then, before he could ask it, she answered his question. "I will bring you to him after the sun has risen and you have rested some yourself. Go for now, Knight of Andaria, and know that Ahjenta has bestowed upon your friend her most sacred gift."

♦ ♦ ♦ ♦ ♦

FU RAN STOOD on a balcony overlooking a busy section of Vilciel's indoor city. Behind him, the rest of the group wandered about a posh suite of rooms, finding various places to sit for only a moment at a time while they waited for Tristus. Food and drink had been brought to them, but no one could eat. The knight had been gone for hours. The sun must have been almost up outside, but the district they'd been brought too was too far in to tell. Great braziers hung from decorous outcroppings, illuminating a dragon-sized palace that was beginning to feel more like a cave, or a crypt.

A sudden stir of voice and movement rose suddenly from within the room, and Fu Ran wheeled away from the balcony, striding just into the suite before coming to an uncertain halt as he looked upon Tristus' tired and tear-streaked features.

The knight stood with his back to the door, his moist eyes taking in everyone, breaking everyone's heart, just before he said, "He's ... alive."

For an instant everyone was too stunned by this news to react. And then, as if suddenly realizing what he'd just said, the knight brought one hand to his face and began to weep with relief.

Taya went to him and Fu Ran filled with such elation he couldn't contain himself. Grinning and laughing, he scooped up the nearest body to him in a great bear hug meant for Xu Liang. Tarfan protested at once, kicking his feet and grumbling oaths through his own tears of joy.

The guards, who didn't understand what Tristus had said before breaking into tears, but feared the worst, understood now. Smiles shattered their stone countenances, expressions that were also softened by relief.

◆ ◆ ◆ ◆ ◆

THE SLIGHT FORM beneath the black silk shroud of the canopied bed writhed and twisted, trapped in nightmare. The mystic's hair clung to his pale, sweating face and neck while he tossed his head upon the pillow, grasping it with slender, trembling fingers, twisting the sham as his other hand twisted the sheets that were quickly tangling about his body. He gasped and moaned as if afraid or in pain, desperate to escape what could not be escaped. It was the price of resurrection, one that humans often paid with interest accumulated through their ignorance of the Flame.

"We should have left him as he was," Ahjenta said, standing in stern silence beside her daughter. Though the two elves were separated in years—more than two hundred—they were not separated in grace.

They were both as otherworldly in their grace as the rare fire rose, whose petals flushed a burning red-orange upon a vine with sleek black thorns. The younger of them only seemed a less mature flower. Unquestionably, it was her lack of maturity that possessed her to bringing this frail human specimen to their city.

"He may die a worse death now, if he rejects the Flame," Ahjenta told her daughter.

"I know," Shirisae said softly, but still with the confidence that had persuaded her mother to perform the dangerous ritual in the first place.

Ahjenta had felt that confidence days before her daughter's return, and knew hours before the peculiar humans arrived that there would be little time for debate.

Timing between death and resurrection was always sensitive. Action had to be taken while the spirit remained trapped in its vessel. This one's spirit was so faded, Ahjenta almost believed her daughter had brought a lifeless husk before her, expecting a miracle that even the Phoenix could not grant. And why? Because *Firestorm* had spoken to her? The blade had spoken before, yes, but perhaps never so brightly. It was what Shirisae believed the sacred weapon was saying that unsettled Ahjenta.

"He is human, my daughter," Ahjenta finally said, unable to take her child's confident silence any longer. It was not curiosity, or mere concern, that anchored the younger elf to this room, to this bed of unearthly suffering. It was something far deeper and, to Ahjenta, something far more disconcerting.

"I know, Mother," Shirisae said again. She added, "But he will live. Though his body is weak, his mind is very strong."

"It is not of this frail mortal whom I speak," Ahjenta snapped, drawing her daughter's gaze. "Do not think that I am unaware of your motives, child. I know why you want this one to survive … and it shames me."

Shirisae frowned and looked away from the man suffering before them. "How can you be ashamed of what the Phoenix itself has decreed?"

"How can you be so sure anything was decreed at all? Recall that our minds are joined, Shirisae. As my heiress, and heiress to the power I hold, it can be no other way between you and I. And I know, daughter, that there were others present."

"One other," Shirisae replied, frowning. "A northern elf, which to me is far more detestable to consider than a human."

"Except that you do not find this detestable at all!"

Shirisae started closer to the bed.

Ahjenta grabbed her arm only to have her daughter tear away from her grasp. They faced each other in cold, burning silence. At length, and in as dignified a tone as she could muster, Ahjenta said, "You're in love with him."

Shirisae lifted her face proudly, defiantly. "I am. But it doesn't matter. The Phoenix has chosen. It is out of our hands. Tristus Edainien will sire the child who will become my heiress after I am Priestess of the Flame!"

Ahjenta's golden eyes glared at her child, struggling to contain herself. She said coldly, "Know that if I believed that was the only reason for this one's resurrection, I would kill him now, with the very fire that may yet save him. However, you are not the only one with a seeing sense, daughter. I know that there is more to this frail creature than even you have considered, and for that reason I will pray that the Phoenix carries him through this night." And now Ahjenta lifted her chin with disdain. "Certainly our god would not answer your prayers alone; the Phoenix is not motivated by foolishness and selfishness."

"It is your selfishness that would label my faith foolishness," Shirisae countered. "*Firestorm* is more mine now than it is yours, and I believe what it says to me."

"Your beliefs are too often the fragile whims of youth. Be thankful, my daughter, that you shared my womb with a brother rather than a sister." On those words, Ahjenta left, and left her daughter to look upon the tortured mystic and to consider just what it was she had done and intended to do.

TWENTY-TWO ☉
Resurrection

XU LIANG FELT like a child; lost and afraid. For a timeless span he had been cringing in the darkness, seeing nothing, hearing only disembodied voices. He didn't know what to do, if there was anything at all to be done, and that was bad enough in itself. The situation only worsened as he gradually began to feel more blinded, more detached from everything and anything, until he became certain that he would simply cease to exist. He wasn't prepared for the fire. Having light cast suddenly into his dark world was more frightening than being lost. He had options now, and none of them were welcoming.

The fire had been a wall at first, spreading like a serpent uncoiling over dark water. It didn't burn, it simply was. The jade flames danced for an eternity, and then they were gone, having collapsed into the floor. The remnant smoke rose like a vaporous green mist toward the ceiling. Between the glowing planes of floor and ceiling, the darkness remained, but it was changed. He could not describe how, not even as it swelled to envelop him.

He lurched away from it, out of the shadows as they suddenly came to life, reaching out for him with slender, clawed hands. He found himself suddenly standing in the light, a green light that reminded him too much of the Jade Hall in the Temple of Divine Tranquility, where he'd first felt the Dragon stirring out of slumber. He felt nothing now, and the stillness disturbed him far worse than if the floor had been violently quaking.

The passage formed by the fire was featureless and without dimension, a band of pale green floor and ceiling spanning infinitely between walls of living shadow. Xu Liang stayed away from the walls, walking forward until he saw a shape ahead of him. It was the robust figure of a man, running.

Xu Liang recognized the mounted axe at once and began chanting a spell to defend himself. However, his call to the winds went unanswered.

Xiadao Lu struck him across the face with the shaft of his weapon, knocking him flat.

Xu Liang sat up slowly, surprised to still be alive, touching his fingers to his remarkably undamaged cheek.

"Do you think I did not hear what you said?" Xiadao Lu bellowed. Only it wasn't Xiadao Lu. It was Xu Hong.

Xu Liang stared at the man's transformed features, wondering if they'd really transformed at all, or if there was actually some resemblance between the fierce warrior and his adoptive father.

Regardless, the man's deep, angry tone sounded like Xu Hong. "Disrespectful whelp! Who is it that trained you, sponsored you in your studies … sheltered you when I should have delivered your strangled infant corpse to Xiang Wu? I should have had your mother executed! And you, her worthless, weakling spawn…"

"Father," Xu Liang said at once, with the reflexive respect he'd learned early during his childhood beneath Xu Hong's roof. He maneuvered quickly onto his knees, bowing before his recognized father. "Please, forgive me. I spoke in haste. I am indebted to you."

Xu Hong said nothing more.

A gentle hand slid beneath Xu Liang's chin, and lifted his face. "Don't be ridiculous. It is I who am indebted to you."

Xu Liang looked up at a handsome young man, who smiled in a proud careless manner. It was the same smile that had graced the noble youth just before his final departure from the Imperial City. "Song Lu?"

"You act as if you don't recognize me." Song Bao's son spoke in light, but bold tones, enunciating his confidence in himself, his father, and the Empire. He had always lived without fear, without hesitation.

Xu Liang had always admired him for that, and he'd feared him for the same reason. It was not a mortal fear. It was something deeper than life, and Xu Liang felt it again now. He began to tremble and was unable to hold his prince's gaze.

"Forgive me," Xu Liang begged, looking at the green floor.

"Where is it?" Song Lu suddenly asked. "The amulet I gave you. Why aren't you wearing it?"

Xu Liang's hand went instinctively to his chest, reaching for a beaded necklace that was not there. It hadn't been there for years. "I…I left it in your…"

In your tomb, he almost said, but narrowly stopped himself, seeing that his prince was living.

Xu Liang struggled with this image. "I…wanted to protect you."

"Xu Liang," Song Lu said, assisting him to his feet. "I meant for it to protect you." The prince wrapped his arms around him in a gesture of brotherhood. "Oh well, my friend. It doesn't matter now. It is good to see you again."

Xu Liang stood tense and fearful in Song Lu's embrace, recalling too much too quickly. Song Lu was dead. The ease of serving two strong, confident leaders had ended long ago. The Empress… She was alone!

Song Lu lowered his head onto Xu Liang's shoulder, holding him closer. The tuft of his small beard tickled against Xu Liang's neck. And then the prince stroked his hand through Xu Liang's hair, and pressed his lips lightly upon his skin.

Xu Liang's pulse flared, though he felt cold. His hands trembled, carefully touching the body pressed against his own. He couldn't decide whether to push him away or draw him closer, and wound up simply clutching the prince's silken tunic as Song Lu began kissing him.

He tasted the prince's affection on his lips only briefly, before he found the sense to pull away. "We cannot do this."

Song Lu kept his hands on Xu Liang's shoulders, his smile replaced with a frown. "We cannot love each other?"

Xu Liang steeled himself, and said calmly, "You have the honor of your family to consider and—"

Song Lu's strong hands squeezed silence from him. "There are times when I hate your wisdom! This isn't about politics, or the Empire! This is about my feelings for you. I love you, Xu Liang!" His hold slackened and his hands finally slipped away. "I suppose this is where you'll tell me that I must love the Empire first. You know that I do. I revere my father and plan to succeed him with equal strength and passion toward the protection of Sheng Fan. I will marry a woman I don't love, and can never love, and acquire heirs. I am devoted to the Empire!"

Xu Liang winced internally at the nature of the passion his prince was exhibiting, not toward the Empire's interests, but in defense of his own.

Song Lu lifted his hand to gently, briefly touch Xu Liang's face. "But my heart will never change toward you. And I know that you love me, though you dare not admit it, even while we're alone."

Xu Liang said nothing, stiffened and speechless in his struggle to maintain his resolve.

Song Lu's features suddenly hardened. "I look at your silence as a betrayal! It is the same as lying to me—you, who are supposed to be my most trusted counsel and friend!"

Xu Liang looked at the prince without seeing him. "Please, Song Lu ... you cannot understand."

"What is there to understand?" someone new asked.

Focusing, Xu Liang saw that Song Lu was no longer there, that he'd been replaced by a hauntingly familiar man dressed in the violet and gold robes of a lord of Ying.

"You are beautiful," the newcomer continued. "He cannot help himself."

Xu Liang stared at the older reflection of himself, noticing the traces of silver at the man's temples and in his thin mustache. Xiang Wu's hair extended past his shoulders, but it was nowhere near as long as Xu Liang's. The angles of his face were sharper, his eyes slightly narrower, giving him a stern aspect.

Reverence filled Xu Liang, but he held back, knowing that the dignity of two houses rested upon his discretion.

"Fools!" Xiang Wu said suddenly. "Is it a wonder Sheng Fan has fallen to the state it is in? Can they honestly be so blind as to not recognize a son of Ying? Or is it that they fear that pompous bag of wind who has the gall to claim you as his son?"

Xu Liang frowned. "You know?"

"Look at yourself," Xiang Wu replied, walking toward Xu Liang, his hands folded behind his back. "How could I not know? For me it is as looking into a mirror that displays my youth. Although, you do strongly resemble your mother as well. Perhaps Xu Mi is what everyone sees when they look at you. That might explain their ignorance a little better. However, that does not explain yours."

"What do you mean?" Xu Liang asked quietly while the elder turned partly away from him.

Xiang Wu scolded him fiercely with a simple sideways glance. Then he looked away again. "Where shall I begin? For a man who is reputed to be of fantastic intelligence, you have certainly made some foolish decisions. How can you have weakened yourself so terribly, knowing your importance to the Empress and to the Empire? You would argue that you did it for those things, and that you greatly strengthened your spirit in the process, but now you see how unreliable the spirit is. It tires quickly, more quickly than the body, as it is taxed by far worse strains than any physical hardships that may arise."

"Emotions," Xu Liang realized, speaking quietly still.

"Yes, emotions," Xiang Wu answered firmly. "The emotions you feel for these *allies* of yours. In your condition they are also your enemies—worse than your enemies, because they are closer and they attack you while you are defenseless, trusting. You should have put more consideration into the bearers of these Swords, instead of only the Swords themselves."

"How can you know about them? I did not tell you."

"You told me!"

Yet another voice.

Xu Liang looked away from his father, and at Jiao Ren. The young general stopped several feet away. He dropped a sword onto the green floor and kicked it toward Xu Liang. "Take it. I don't want to be guilty of attacking you while you are defenseless."

"Why would you want to attack me at all?" Xu Liang wondered, refusing to claim the weapon as it spun to a halt at his feet.

"You killed her," Jiao Ren snarled. "And now I will kill you, armed or not. Make your choice, Xu Liang!"

Xu Liang's confusion troubled him worse than Jiao Ren's anger.

"I loved her!" the young general shouted. "Not only as the Empress, but as a woman! She saw only you, Xu Liang." His voice lowered, sounding of a man possessed. "And you killed her!"

Xu Liang was too startled by the accusation to react. He would never harm the Empress. His life, the meaning of his life, was to defend her. To ...

"Your love is for the Empire," Jiao Ren hissed. "You care nothing for Song Da-Xiao. Any Song will do upon the throne, so long as they worship you. How convenient for you that the Emperor and his son—and even his daughter—should all look to you with such devotion and trust! I used to wonder what others meant when they referred to you as the Silent Emperor. Now I understand! Fight me, or simply die, Xu Liang! It makes no difference to me!"

Xu Liang saw the young man coming, but his mind remained stuck on the words. Jiao Ren was a man of honor and dignity. He would never have spoken the Empress' name so intimately, nor made such threats to another of the Imperial City. Xu Liang considered him as much friend as ally. No blade could open such painful wounds as Jiao Ren's accusations. None of this made any sense.

"Jiao—"

The words were halted by pain, as the young general's blade plunged into Xu Liang's body. He tasted blood. Salt joined the coppery taste while he looked with both shock and grief into Jiao Ren's satisfied glare. He couldn't breathe. As he gasped vainly for air, the young man's face transformed. It thinned and gathered fine lines. The eyebrows turned white and a thin white beard grew from the narrow chin. The hard mouth smiled without showing teeth. Eyes that seemed somehow darker gleamed with savage triumph.

Xu Liang didn't know why he should be so terrified—death was imminent—but this final act of betrayal was too much. Breathless and in horror, he could only gasp the elder's name. "Lord...Han Quan..."

The elder's smile broadened, as if he was pleased to be recognized. "And to think, you might have become a true mystic. The order of the Seven Mystics is older than the Empire! You thought yourself worthy to stand among our ranks? An overrated child? Yes, the ancestors speak to you. You have charmed them, as you have everyone else. However, it will not last. Fate is against you!" His features slowly tensed. "You will die, and the Empire will be mine. Now, witness true power, boy!"

With his last statement, the elder twisted his hand, which had somehow come to be inside of Xu Liang in place of Jiao Ren's sword. Intense agony swelled throughout Xu Liang's suspended body, but he did not scream. He couldn't, even as Han Quan pulled back his hand, clutching Xu Liang's beating heart.

The elder laughed wickedly while Xu Liang collapsed to the floor, then began to chant, his voice booming in the infinite space. Somehow still alive, Xu Liang watched as the organ plucked from his body became stone in the elder's grasp.

"Your time is over," Han Quan decreed, holding the stone heart above his head. "Now die!"

The elder hurled the stone upon the green floor, where it shattered instantly, fanning outward in a mix of dust and jagged shards.

◆ ◆ ◆ ◆ ◆

"YOU MUST wake!"

Tristus opened his eyes slowly, sensing that someone was over him, but he was unable to descry who through the grayness in the room. He had no recollection as to where he was. He only knew that he was exhausted, more tired after a few hours of real sleep than he'd been before attempting the nap.

Someone shook him. "No! You must rise! Come with me!"

Tristus thought that he recognized the voice, though not its urgency. He opened his eyes again as his eyelids drooped, commanding focus. He saw the red hair first. "Shirisae?"

Everything came back at once. He sat up and almost knocked their heads together in the process. The lady elf dodged the blow, gripping Tristus' arm while he gripped hers in turn. "What's the matter?" he asked. "What's happened?"

He'd never seen an elf look so alarmed as she did currently. There might have even been tears in her golden eyes. Before she answered him, Tristus began organizing himself, searching for his shirt and his boots.

In the relief after seeing Xu Liang survive the Phoenix Elves' healing ceremony, he'd felt comfortable enough to trust their situation, and to sleep out of armor. He'd given up his shirt to allow Taya to check on the lingering burn he'd acquired facing the Fanese fire mage and felt safe enough to sleep without it, relaxing with the cool black silk of the bed sheets against his skin. He didn't anticipate a sudden awakening in the solitude of the mountain city, but perhaps he should have known better.

"Did you wake the others?" Tristus asked, pulling on his boots.

Shirisae shook her head, her intensely red hair glinting in the light that filtered through the draped windows. "Their presence is not required at the moment. You must hurry."

Tristus didn't argue. He rose from the bed, stepping the rest of the way into his second boot. He buttoned his shirt as they walked. "Shirisae, please tell me what this is about. Is Xu Liang all right?"

The fire elf pulled him by the arm, as if too afraid to answer, which made him too afraid to ask any more questions. He followed her out of the guest suite, treading quietly past the sleeping bodyguards, who insisted on setting their bedrolls out in the main room.

Once in the hall, Shirisae moved with haste, practically running. Tristus jogged after her with little choice in the matter, as she kept a firm grip on his arm. They moved through the indoor city with little notice paid to them. There weren't even guards posted, so secure were these elves in their stronghold on top of the very world.

Shirisae guided him through enough streets, and corridors and up enough staircases that Tristus was thoroughly, hopelessly lost by the time she stopped in front of a great glass window stained with images of dragons. There were three separate images, each displaying a different colored dragon. It almost seemed that the beasts had struck a pose for their portraits, but Tristus didn't have time to study the massive work of art as Shirisae turned back on him, clutching both of his arms now, looking almost terrified.

"Whatever you see, Tristus Edainien, know that all was done that could be done, and for good cause. Know also that there is still hope. That is why I have brought you with such haste."

Tristus was beginning to understand and he was beginning to feel cold with fear, but somehow he managed to stay calm. He pulled out of Shirisae's urgent grasp and gently took her hands in both his. "My lady, you offered hope that we could not have asked for. We can expect nothing more."

Shirisae seemed to absorb his words and calmed considerably. She stepped back, keeping one of his hands in her own while she led them up another staircase, and finally into an enormous chamber that appeared not to have been modified to suit the elves. It seemed that way, but then Tristus began taking notice of the furniture, all normal sized and making the vast room seem more like an enormous audience chamber rather than a space of unfathomable purpose for dragons. Soon the strangest part of it became the emptiness. The decorative chairs, tables, rugs, and even tapestries existed without the grace of life, giving the room the chill of a tomb. The warmth he felt in spite of that must have come from the furnaces, as Tarfan has explained, since there were no fires in the room beyond the standing candelabras placed by the elves, apparently to light a wide path through the gloom.

Tristus shuddered inwardly and then came to a sudden stop, hearing a voice in the open air. It was as a gasp, a panicked draw of air mingled with a pained moan.

Shirisae squeezed his hand, pulling him onward. "Be strong," she warned.

The bed came into view slowly, looking like a tent of shadow, with the black silk cascaded over the tall, slender iron posts, almost completely enclosing the mattress within. There was a gap where the canopy had been pulled apart, like drapes.

Tristus saw movement within and picked up his own pace, quickly overtaking Shirisae. And then he saw Xu Liang, tossing fitfully in his sleep, muttering words in Fanese, a look of anguish on his face so terrible as to send cold fear lancing through Tristus' soul.

He twisted out of Shirisae's grasp and rushed to the mystic's side. He reached for Xu Liang's hand and regretted it when the mystic seized his arm at once, digging his fingers into his skin, almost drawing blood through his sleeve.

"What's wrong with him?" Tristus demanded. "How long has he been like this?"

"It is the Flame," Shirisae informed from a distance. "His body is rejecting it, seeking to embrace death while his mind keeps him alive. It is as I suspected. He has the will to live, but as my mother feared, he may be too weak physically to endure. He will not wake."

"You mean he'll die after all," Tristus translated, angry, though not at Shirisae.

"He will remain trapped in his nightmares until his will finally breaks and submits to the peace his weary body longs for."

"Then wake him!" Tristus shouted, pleading.

Shirisae shook her head, remorse capturing her features. "We tried. He will not wake."

Tristus pulled away from Xu Liang's grip as he began to lose feeling in his arm. The mystic's pale, sweating hand found the sheets again and resumed twisting them. His lips moved, uttering Fanese syllables. When his body fell into brief respite, Tristus carefully reached out and stroked the mystic's hair away from his face.

Xu Liang's delicate brow creased, and he spoke several phrases in his native tongue, his chest rising and falling rapidly as he gasped for air between the indecipherable words. He sounded afraid and angry, and sad all at once. Tristus wished he knew what to do, but there wasn't time to think. All too quickly, Xu Liang was turning again, grabbing at the sheets and the pillows, seeming on the verge of screaming.

In a moment of blind desperation, Tristus grabbed hold of the mystic's bare shoulders and tried forcing him still. He was strong enough to stop the slight man's turning from side to side, but Xu

Liang's hands still clawed and his legs slowly tread the silk pooled around his body. "Xu Liang, listen to me! You have to wake up! You'll die if you don't!"

The mystic didn't hear him. He must have felt Tristus' hold, however, as he began writhing as if to escape it. Tristus grasped at this possible response, climbing onto the mattress to pin the mystic's body with his own, praying that he wouldn't hurt him. "I won't let you leave! Do you hear me, Xu Liang? I won't let you!"

Xu Liang seemed to unconsciously take him for a threat, either that or he mistook him for an opponent out of his nightmare. He brought his hand deliberately against Tristus' chest and began uttering what sounded like a spell. Recalling the daggers of light that Xu Liang had used against the keirveshen, Tristus called for Shirisae to get down and forcibly redirected the mystic's aim. A pale glimmer of blue light formed in Xu Liang's palm, and then a sudden surge of air exploded into the room, shooting across the chamber and bringing down every article of furniture in its path.

"Sweet Light," Tristus gasped. "Shirisae!"

The lady elf drew herself up from the floor where she'd dove to escape the spell. She pushed red locks out of her face and viewed the destruction, speaking softly as her heart possibly began to beat again. "I'm not hurt."

Tristus gave his attention back to Xu Liang, who had slackened suddenly, as if weakened by his spell. Tristus tried speaking to him again, begging him to wake, keeping him pinned against hurting himself or others, as it seemed now that the mystic was quite capable of doing so.

"I didn't hurt her," the mystic whispered, finally forming words Tristus could understand.

Tristus began to relax, thinking that Xu Liang might be coming out of it. "No, you didn't. Shirisae's..."

"I only wanted to protect her," Xu Liang continued, heedless of Tristus, evidently still dreaming. "My empress..."

Empress?

Tristus leaned over Xu Liang, laying relatively still as compared to before, and said gently, "The Empress is fine. She is well. You're dreaming, Xu Liang. The Empress is still in Sheng Fan, waiting for you. You must wake, so that you can go to her. Remember why you left her. Remember your quest."

"The Swords," Xu Liang murmured.

"Yes, the Swords," Tristus echoed. He smiled as relief began to settle, but it did not last.

Xu Liang suddenly became tense again. "*Pearl Moon!* The dome ... the..."

"It held," Tristus said quickly. "Xu Liang, it worked. You saved us. None of us are hurt." He thought of the dreadful moments that followed the giant's attack and his own reactions to such tragedy. His hand strayed to the mystic's straining neck, then, as if the memories played in reverse, he lifted his hand and slid his fingers gently over Xu Liang's chin and across his lips, wiping away the blood that wasn't there, feeling the warm skin as he hadn't that day, with his gloves on. He added softly, "But we will all be sorely grieved if you leave us now."

The mystic relaxed and fell still.

Tristus felt an instant's rise of panic before he realized Xu Liang was still breathing. The mystic seemed no longer to be trapped in his nightmares, but he wasn't awake. Tristus looked to Shirisae for answers, but found the elf no longer present. He didn't worry about where she'd gone, or why, as he came to realize how very awkward this must have looked.

Reddening, in spite of his lack of audience, Tristus lifted himself off of Xu Liang's still form and simply stationed himself at the edge of the wide mattress. He only briefly wondered if he'd offended or embarrassed the lady elf with his efforts that might have seemed a little too intimate in the end, before he began to wonder why he should be embarrassed himself. It was not cause for embarrassment or shame to love someone, even if that love was not viewed as traditional or even acceptable. The views of others didn't negate that love. It still existed, it would only hurt more trying to deny it for propriety's sake.

"Isn't it obvious anyway?" Tristus asked the slumbering source of his confusion. "I've done nothing but stare at you since we met. Yes, at first even I mistook it for little more than awe and respect while I struggled to find some light left in this world to follow. I've not had much ease in relationships, of any kind. I'll admit that it's easier to worship than to love." He sighed. "Of course I've no idea how you could possibly feel, or whether or not you'll even live past the hour, so I don't see why..."

Tristus stopped himself, his throat swelling with tears he didn't even realize he was holding back. He stared long at the pale slender form caught up in a tangle of black silk that failed to conceal Xu Liang as well as the silk of his own robes had. He did not necessarily look smaller or weaker while exposed, though it was clear he was much thinner than Tristus. Instead he looked more vulnerable … touchable rather than off limits on pain of holy retribution.

Tristus' hand slid across the mattress, came upon Xu Liang's fingers that were still warm in his fevered state, and overlapped them. If he'd meant the touch to be experimental, he'd discovered what he wanted to know. Upon this first deliberate contact he felt his heart prickled by the warmth of desire. He wanted to lay down beside the mystic, wrap his arms around him, and hold him forever or longer.

The needling warmth entered Tristus' blood and became a stabbing heat at every pulse point. Tristus withdrew, breathless. Now he knew for certain.

Before panicking while Xu Liang lay dying in the giant's wake, Tristus would never have dared to reach out to him, and had twice felt remiss for having laid a hand on him before, even though it was by accident. Now a recurring revelation struck him once again, reminding him that Xu Liang was human … mortal, and bound to the same mortal needs and wants, and feelings as anyone else.

"Bound perhaps," Tristus murmured, feeling depressed even as his heart raced with hope. "To someone else? Your empress, perhaps?"

And then, as if hearing the magic word of awakening, Xu Liang opened his eyes. He scarcely glanced at Tristus, at once curious about his surroundings. He took them in slowly, closing his eyes frequently against the sudden light, dim as it may have been.

"Where is this place?" Xu Liang's voice carried barely above a whisper, but it was just as calm as ever.

"This is Vilciel," Tristus answered as softly. "The dragons' city in the sky."

"Dragons?" Xu Liang seemed momentarily confused. In a moment, he seemed to recall, and said, "Skytown. The elves?"

Tristus nodded. "They led us here. They healed you with their magic."

Xu Liang closed his eyes again. "It is done," he whispered.

"What is?" Tristus asked him.

"My concentration and my health are both shattered. I will be of little use to anyone, least of all my empress. How could I have been so … careless?"

"Careless?" Tristus was shocked, but tried to keep his tone soothing, understanding that the mystic was disoriented at the very least. "What you did was—"

"Reckless," Xu Liang finished, deciding in the next moment that it was time to sit up.

Tristus tried to stop him, but the mystic simply held out his hand with renewed aplomb, and Tristus recoiled automatically.

Xu Liang completed his ascent, but leaned heavily on one arm and brought the hand that had stopped Tristus to his head as if to steady it. "How long have I been here?"

"Not more than a day," Tristus answered. "We brought you here right after..."

"Where are the others?"

Wounded by the edge Xu Liang's quiet voice had taken, Tristus had to swallow his words once, before getting them out free of tears. "They're here, waiting. Except for Alere. He..."

This time it was not Xu Liang's words that stopped him, but the mystic's frown as he lifted his face away from his hand. The dissatisfaction in that expression was enough to make Tristus shudder for the second time since waking up that morning.

In Tristus' silence, Xu Liang said, "He took the Twilight Blade."

It was no question, but a statement, and it was delivered with a tone that suggested no surprise, as if Alere had somehow satisfied suspicions of betrayal. Tristus could only nod in the face of this changed person, whom he had moments ago confirmed that he loved deeply. Xu Liang's unexpected anger did not change his feelings, but it made Tristus more certain that his affections would go unanswered if he dared reveal them openly.

Xu Liang dropped his face into his hand again. "Where is Gai Ping? We must leave here. At once."

"He's with the others," Tristus informed. "And you're in no condition for travel. Not yet."

"That is not for you to decide, Tristus Edainien," Xu Liang snapped. "My guards and I shall leave immediately."

"Your guards and—what are you saying? What about the rest of us? We're..."

Xu Liang lifted his gaze once more, showing patience but no concern. "There is no quest, if that is what you intend to argue about. It is done. I must return to Sheng Fan and report my failure to the Empress."

Tristus frowned remonstratively. "Your failure? How can you say that? You're alive. You can—"

"I would not expect you to understand," Xu Liang said dismissively, causing Tristus to flinch as if he'd been struck a physical blow. "Now I must ask that you leave me alone."

Tristus hesitated, wanting to argue, wanting to express his feelings, wanting to say anything that would keep him beside the mystic, knowing that if he left he would lose forever what he'd never even had. He sat staring, searching for words, ready to begin stammering anything that came to mind.

And then, Xu Liang whispered, "Forgive me." He spoke into his hand, muffling what sounded like...tears? "Deng Po...Hu Zhong, Yuan Lan...your deaths are my blame. And now I would abandon what you died for."

Tristus remained, assuming because Xu Liang spoke a language other than Fanese, that he wanted to be heard.

"The Dragon rises," he continued, staring at the bed through watering eyes. "The Swords must be brought to Sheng Fan, but the Empress...she is alone. She has been taken from my protection...completely from my reach. If she dies, there is no one else. The Empire will fall."

Tristus watched the mystic holding back his emotions, still too proud to show them, even as they were escaping him. Tristus took a chance. "You seem to love your empress a great deal. And yet you have so very little faith in her."

Xu Liang's brow creased, but he did not look at the individual he had dismissed moments ago. "She is..." The mystic stopped himself, considering, maybe arguing with himself. After several moments, his thoughts failed to bear words.

Tristus leaned toward him, careful not to touch. "Xu Liang, I have *Dawnfire*. I know it is one of the Blades you seek. It glows in the company of the others. You are not so far off as you think from accomplishing what you set out to do. How many are you looking for?"

The mystic slowly lowered his hand. His long hair, freed from the combs that had previously held it, draped his face and even as he refused to look at Tristus it was evident that he was still frowning. It was evident in his voice, as he was not above speaking to Tristus now. "No one has told you anything?"

"I ... didn't ask. We were preoccupied just with getting here."

"Is this your idea of faith, Tristus Edainien? To follow blindly, a person or a purpose you know so very little about?"

Tristus answered the mystic's question with one of his own. It seemed a better option than professing his love. "How am I to learn, if I do not follow?"

Xu Liang lifted his face, but did not look at Tristus. His lips formed a vague, humorless smile, and he was not speaking lightly when he said, "Your persistence may be the death of us both. But if what you say is true, it would appear that you are the bearer of the Dawn Blade." His already lightless expression darkened considerably, making Tristus grieve for the resplendence that the giant may have killed, even if the mystic himself survived. "Forgive me for saying that it seems a small gain against all that has been lost."

Tristus failed to take offense, seeing how much Xu Liang cared for his empress and his homeland, enough that the tears still glistened in his brown eyes. He knew that the mystic needed time alone, and as much as he couldn't bear to leave him, in spite of everything, he sat back and stood.

"Six," Xu Liang said suddenly, still quietly.

Tristus wasn't sure that he'd heard him at first, but before he could beg pardon and ask the mystic to repeat himself, more words were offered.

"There are six Celestial Swords, Tristus Edainien, and six bearers. I ... we have discovered three to unite with the two that were recently brought to light in Sheng Fan. In Alere's absence, we have lost one ... and in the company of these elves, I am not certain whether we have gained anything more than a glimpse of another. Taking all into consideration, it would seem that my journey into this realm has amounted to a single Blade and its bearer."

The mystic sighed, and it seemed that he might subtract that last accomplishment as well, but Tristus wouldn't allow it. He said firmly, "A victory, Master Xu Liang, even in the smallest virtue, is still a victory."

Then he stepped away from the bed and took his leave, stopping several paces away when he heard a muffled sob behind him. He frowned with concern and sympathy, but he did not look back, and eventually left the chamber, guided by candlelight on one side and toppled furniture and spilled, smoldering wax on the other.

TWENTY-THREE

Separation

"**A**RE YOU crazy?"

Tristus sighed and shook his head, refusing to answer the lady dwarf this time; she had already questioned his sanity three times since he'd returned to the guest suite. He proceeded to strap on his armor, ignoring the questioning and contemplative gazes of the others while he thought back on Shirisae's awkward silence leading him back from the dragon-sized bed chamber. After he'd left Xu Liang—in tears, as he dared to recall—the Phoenix Elf had been waiting for him in the hall. She said nothing, and she didn't have to. Her suspicions were clear. Thank God, Xu Liang was too dejected and disoriented to share in her suspicions. It was obvious, anyway, where the mystic's interests lay; a world away from a heartsick knight with amorous leanings toward his own gender.

Tristus couldn't help it. He got along with women beautifully, most of the time, he'd just never fallen in love with one. Perhaps he could blame a certain handsome cleric, who'd been even more confused than Tristus, swaying toward and away from his friend and beneath the austere gazes of his superiors until he finally couldn't take it. He stopped speaking to Tristus altogether, determined to remain celibate and therefore pure in the eyes of everyone, including God, for the rest of his days. Tristus almost went that route himself, convinced that there was something horribly wrong with him, until he met a gentle older knight, who somehow made everything clear. Unfortunately, their time together was all too brief, and could be counted among the innumerable tragedies that constituted Tristus' life thus far.

You're not going to be one of them, Xu Liang.

"Tristus," Tarfan started thoughtfully, if not a bit condescendingly. "Lad … if the mage is as upset as you say, fretting about apparent losses, what makes you think running off on your own just now is going to prove beneficial to this faltering quest?"

"That's just it, Tarfan," Tristus replied, with as much patience as he had left. "This quest *is* faltering. Xu Liang is a heartbeat away from dropping everything and rushing back to his homeland, certain that it's going to crumble or disappear now that he's lost his connection to his empress. We've got to get Alere back, and we have to find that last Blade." Tristus sat down to get his greaves on. "We have to do it while Xu Liang is too weak to leave here."

"And how are you going to find the white elf?" Tarfan asked. "Determined as he was to put space between him and his fiery cousins, I suppose he could be back in Upper Yvaria by now."

"Somehow I doubt that," Tristus mumbled, irritated by this lack of support. "Anyway, the Blades glow when they're near one another. *Dawnfire* was almost literally on fire the night before I met the rest of you. I'll find him."

"And what if he doesn't want to come back?"

"I think he will, once I explain things to him."

"And if he doesn't?" the dwarf persisted.

"Then, damn it, I'll think of something!" Tristus stood, feeling red with anger and with instant remorse for having lost his temper. He lowered his voice again. "I'm going after Alere. Am I going alone?"

"I'll come," Taya volunteered.

"No," Tristus said, and when she began to protest he dropped down to her height and took her firmly by the shoulders. "I can't let you come with me this time, Taya. I have to ride hard and … Xu Liang may need your help here." Tristus grasped at the excuse as it formed. "He's still very weak and I don't think he can take any more of the elves' fire healing. He's exhausted and undernourished, and…"

"All right," Taya snapped. She tucked her arms tight in front of her chest and added angrily, "I'll stay."

Tristus smiled and kissed her on the cheek. "Thank you, my darling." He stood and left her in red-faced silence, looking to the others. "Maybe it's best if I go alone. You should probably stay with your niece, Tarfan, and Fu Ran, you might be the only one capable of reasoning with Xu Liang."

"What in the ten thousand hells gave you that impression?" the giant wanted to know, speaking for the first time since Tristus returned to the suite.

Tristus shrugged. "I don't know. You just seem like old friends."

Fu Ran's lips curled into a smile that no one found particularly comforting. And then he nodded. "You're right. My place is here. But I don't see us letting a man as prone to danger as you setting foot outside of this city by himself."

"What do you mean?" Tristus asked, genuinely confused by the large man's statement. "I'm at no greater risk than ... what? Tarfan, what are you shaking your head over?"

The old dwarf tossed his hands up in the air and stalked off.

Tristus watched him, perplexed, until one of the bodyguards came forward, speaking in Fanese. Tristus looked at the man, who was looking at him, until he was finished talking. Then he glanced at Fu Ran. "What was that? What did he say?"

Grinning as if amused and possibly impressed, the former guard said, "Guang Ci has just volunteered to ride with you."

Tristus was torn between appreciation and confusion. "How ... does he know where I'm going?"

"He doesn't," Fu Ran answered. "He read into our tones and probably heard Xu Liang's name a few times too many, and got the general idea."

Tristus thanked the bodyguard in the only way he knew how; by bowing Fanese-style. The gesture was returned rigidly.

"Don't be too hasty," Fu Ran warned, still smirking. "It's probably only his way at making sure you return with the Dawn Blade."

"He needn't worry about that," Tristus assured. "I'll be back with not only the Dawn Blade, but Alere as well and, if there is any luck left with us at all, the last of the Celestial Swords."

◆ ◆ ◆ ◆ ◆

SHIRISAE WAS WAITING for them at the bridge leading back into the mountain. She was dressed in full armor again, carrying *Firestorm*. It had been unexpected, since her brother had been the one to gladly show Tristus and Guang Ci to the only two horses they had claim to—which included Blue Crane and a terrible sensation of guilt for Tristus, who felt as if he were practically stealing the animal. Tristus would never have guessed Shirisae would leave Vilciel without D'mitri, or that D'mitri would allow it, for that matter. They seemed a close pair of siblings, and with the brother's sensational distrust, it simply caught Tristus off guard. There might have been another underlying reason for his dismay at seeing the lady elf, but he was inclined to ignore it and to concentrate solely on finding Alere.

"I will accompany you," Shirisae said, and in such a way as to let them know it wasn't up for debate.

Tristus only nodded in his surprise, not opposed to having another good fighter at his side, which she had already proven to be. As well *Firestorm* might be helpful in locating *Aerkiren* and its endearingly obdurate bearer.

They were halfway across the bridge before Tristus decided to ask any questions. "Why are you so willing to assist us? Please, don't mistake me. I am grateful, of course, but everything you've done... it..."

"My people may live in seclusion, but we are not as xenophobic as certain others of our kind. We will assist and ally with all who are found to be worthy by our god."

"What... makes us worthy?"

Shirisae's golden eyes viewed him from within her black helm. She looked away before saying, "*Firestorm*, the blade given us by the Phoenix, has chosen you, Tristus Edainien. As well, your sorcerer believes that your blade and mine are drawn to one another—as soul mates, I am inclined to believe. That the Phoenix might have forged two blades in its sacred flame and allowed them to find one another is a sign, as far as I am concerned." She drew a long pause, then added, "Your allies are now my allies, knight, and your cause has become mine as well."

"Shirisae," Tristus said, shocked at this level of devotion. "I am in your debt, my lady."

The Phoenix Elf practically glared at him, and said sharply, "You owe me nothing. We are... united in this, and as equals."

In his confusion, Tristus could only stare. Shirisae suddenly rode ahead, undoubtedly to escape his gaze. He reminded himself to apologize later for his lacking manners.

◆ ◆ ◆ ◆ ◆

XU LIANG DIDN'T have the strength to do anything more than lie back and stare into the lush folds of black that constituted the canopy high overhead. He'd spent himself by sitting up before, insisting that he was still in control, knowing now that he was utterly out of it. The strength of his purified soul had left him, used to the last strand of its heightened essence just to keep him alive after he'd lost consciousness. It was that level of consciousness that gave him control. So long as he remained in a quasi-meditative state, his magic, his awareness—his inner strength—all were at their peak ... and he could communicate with the Empress. The long hours of blackness, devoid of the smallest thought, had returned him fully to his body, which was not in its best condition, especially after he'd abused it in the struggle against the giant. He hadn't slept for long weeks, nor had he eaten. He wouldn't be able to do either normally for some time. He didn't want to sleep, after the horrifying dreams brought on by his near-death state and there would be nothing he could eat that he wouldn't reject first, until his stomach was conditioned again to accepting it.

He felt useless and helpless, and farther away from Sheng Fan than ever before. He didn't dare return without the Swords, not unless he planned to simply die by the Empress' side. They needed the Swords to fight Chaos, which could only grow stronger before it finally rose in whatever form it planned to take. Was the Empress still protected from the malevolence that had made her ill and given her nightmares before his departure? Had she used all of his training and kept her concentration whole? Or had his failure put her in the same weakened state, vulnerable to attack from whatever, or whomever cared to deliver it?

And what of his own nightmares? Could he believe anything he'd experienced? Half of it was memory—Song Lu, for example, his spirit coming down from its constant perch upon Xu Liang's shoulder to make his haunting more apparent—but some of it seemed as messages, warnings ... if he dared to believe them.

Jiao Ren turned against him? And Han Quan as well? Why? *Do they truly believe I am no better than those I expelled from the Imperial Court, that I would seek to rule beneath the Empress, with her no more than my shadow puppet? And now it seems I have other problems as well. Alere has disappeared, perhaps believing me dead, and Tristus ... his concerns are obvious and now I am faced with Song Lu all over again.*

Xu Liang's shoulder began to throb. He closed his eyes with no hope of getting any sleep, and begged his dead prince for forgiveness as his thoughts fell still and became as wordless silence in the dark.

It was a darkness that did not last. It seemed as if barely an instant had passed when light pressed through Xu Liang's eyelids, commanding him to wake. He opened his eyes slowly, shielding them from the yellow glow with his hand, peering away from the bed at … himself? A mirror? He hadn't recalled any present near the bed before.

The individual lying down on a bed draped in precisely the same folds of black looked stark white against the pitch dark of the bedding and his own long hair, which would not have been discernible from the sheets, if not for the way the light shone almost blue upon the silky strands. The man, all but lost in the layers of black, was too thin. He'd always lacked muscle, but now he also lacked vigor. There were dark circles under his eyes, which showed redness from stress, weariness, and even crying. Upon waking from one nightmare into another, the shock, frustration, and shame had been too much. Those things still haunted the face looking back at him, the mouth drawn into a depressed frown, adding a layer of grim to the overall haggard appearance.

"Damned unsightly!" someone confirmed.

The gruff voice painted an instant image upon Xu Liang's mind, and spared him the effort of looking for the speaker. He wondered, though, at the scraping sound that accompanied it, like metal against stone.

"I'd cringe away myself, waking up to a face like that!" the dwarf continued. "But, seeing as how you haven't had much for beauty sleep, we'll forgive you looking like a mountain goblin!"

"Tarfan Fairwind," Xu Liang sighed, unable to absorb the cheer his friend offered, in his uniquely abrasive way. "What in the name of the Jade Emperor are you doing?"

"Well," the dwarf huffed, as if straining over something. "In case you haven't noticed, this room was constructed for dragons. The windows are about two hundred feet away—or thereabouts—and I've never met a wilting flower that hasn't picked up just a little with some good old fashioned sunlight on its petals. I simply borrowed a few mirrors and channeled the golden glow of a fine, crisp mountain afternoon right to the bedside. You should be warming up in no time."

"The room feels warm enough already," Xu Liang said tiredly, and in spite of the chill he felt seeping beneath his skin, seeming to make his bones ache.

"It's not a natural heat," Tarfan grumbled. "And it does nothing to penetrate the gloom in this glorified cave. Now, just lie there and soak up the light, mage! My niece is preparing you a fine broth to start negotiating proper eating habits with your sensitive stomach."

Xu Liang grimaced at the thought of swallowing anything. "Please, Tarfan. I'm not hungry."

"Well, I appreciate your opinion, but it'll be going down just the same. No one's asking you to enjoy it."

Xu Liang peered over his hand, but he only caught a glimpse of the dwarf while Tarfan moved from one standing mirror to the next, positioning and repositioning so that the reflected light shone evenly around the bed. A disturbing image of being force fed by dwarves made him sink his head back down into the pillow with an inaudible sigh. "How could I have been so careless?" he asked softly of himself.

The dwarf happened to overhear. "I think it was care, actually, that got you where you are now."

Xu Liang closed his eyes, not wanting to hear the forthcoming lecture.

Tarfan provided it nonetheless. "You could have been more cautious. You could have taken off with the elves when that over-grown troll stirred out of its nap, but we'd have lost the boy for sure, probably Fu Ran as well, and maybe the rest of us, if we'd been gathered around to help dig Tristus out of the snow when the giant came back."

"You didn't expect me to leave the Dawn Blade buried, did you?" Xu Liang said quietly, detached as his thoughts drifted back to the accusations made against him in his dreams and those delivered by Alere while awake.

"As I recall," Tarfan said, speaking in slow, measured tones. "You were hopelessly unconscious long before the knight's spear began its telltale glow. In fact, I've a suspicion you didn't believe that weapon was the Dawn Blade at first, because it wasn't glowing straight away."

"But it does now," Xu Liang said, seeking confirmation of Tristus' claim.

"Yes," the dwarf replied. "Lit our path through the shadows like … never mind that! My point is that you did what you did the other day to save a life! So don't be putting on any acts about being too high and mighty to care about…"

"Have I, Tarfan?" Xu Liang suddenly asked, the words catching unexpectedly in his exhausted and overly emotional state. "Have I treated all of you so poorly? Alere spoke the bare truth, as he always does. My concern has been only for the Swords."

"That elf—"

"He speaks what he sees," Xu Liang interrupted. "My empress must come first. I would not change that, but I must treat allies and friends with respect and dignity, else I've no one to blame but myself for their leaving."

A brief silence filled the enormous chamber.

"It's not quite the same with individuals as it is with provinces or cities, or whatever you deal with in Sheng Fan, is it?" The dwarf sighed. "Still, I think you're gaining a decent grasp of it. We're all still here. We're still with you, Xu Liang."

"For now, perhaps," Xu Liang said softly. "I must speak with Tristus. I fear, in my unpleasant awakening, that I treated him very poorly and wish to make amends."

"Yes," Tarfan said, in a stalling voice. "About the knight…"

TWENTY-FOUR
The Deepwood

THE SPAN OF water that was named after the northern goddess Windra, turned out to be gray and cold, shrouded constantly beneath a turbid layer of clouds. For an Andarian Knight, a Phoenix Elf, and a Fanese guardsmen, gaining passage aboard a vessel had been no easy task. They managed by handing over a pouch of rare elven coins Shirisae had carried with her from Vilciel, to a gypsy collector of foreign coins, who happened also to be owner of a small ferry that usually catered only to fellow gypsies needing to move their troupes from one part of Yvaria to the other. The three passengers stuck close to one another and kept a watchful eye on their possessions as well as themselves and, none too soon, found themselves safely on the shores of Upper Yvaria.

That had been three days ago, and so far neither *Firestorm* nor *Dawnfire* saw it fit to produce their magnificent light any brighter than they had since leaving Vilciel in each other's company.

Tristus sighed, forcing himself to study the map Tarfan had given him. He visually traced paths to the Verres Mountains, wishing he had the merest idea of how to think like Alere. The elf couldn't be too far ahead of them; they hadn't been separated for much more than a day—though Breigh was fast and would likely be familiar with the route her master had chosen. Still...

Tristus groaned and rolled onto his back, away from the warm light of their campfire. He rubbed his weary eyes and tried not to listen to his mind's misgivings. In his heart, he knew that what he was doing was right. Xu Liang was in no condition to seek Alere or the last Blade and, after Tarfan and Fu Ran had finally given him the details of the situation, Tristus fully understood the severity of the mystic's quest. An evil was rising in Sheng Fan, radiating outward to every part of the world, stirring chaos... stirring the shadows.

"You should sleep."

At the sound of the voice, which was simultaneously strong and gentle, Tristus turned his face back toward the fire, catching a glimpse of two flames. The Phoenix Elf was seated beside his bedroll, braiding her long red-orange hair after having let it down. Her fingers worked meticulously, restoring order to what she'd convinced herself had fallen wildly out of place during their days of travel. It amazed Tristus how beautiful she was, as exotic in her own fashion as Xu Liang, with her yellow-fair complexion and dark red lips. Tristus may not have had the same feelings as other men when in the company of such a woman, but he appreciated grace all the same.

He caught himself reconsidering the thought as his memories drifted back to when he had first met Xu Liang. He'd awakened convinced that the fair creature hovering over him was a woman, and his reaction had been instant, helpless. If he'd not settled into full consciousness within the following moments, and realized that the mystic was actually an extremely handsome man, he believed that he still would be in the same blissful state of agony. He'd fallen in love on sight, and continued to fall, deeper than he'd ever fallen before. It wouldn't matter to him if Xu Liang's stunning grace had been nothing more than an illusion and a shriveled old man—or even a pit gnome—waited now in Vilciel. He was infatuated with the mystic's presence, his intoxicating aura. It only made matters worse that Xu Liang happened to be beautiful as well.

"I recognize that smile," Shirisae suddenly said, and Tristus erased the wistful expression he didn't know he was wearing. "It's a smile of hope and longing, of wondering whether or not your heart's pleas will be answered, or whether your heart will simply burst before it's finished filling with the sweetest joy you've ever known."

Tristus smiled again, helplessly. "Yes, I do like being in love. It's been so long, I'd forgotten how good it feels, even if it's a hopeless love."

"Hopeless?" Shirisae echoed. "How do you know that it is?"

Tristus looked at her, his expression fading again. He propped himself on his elbow. "Shall we be open, Shirisae? Must I speak with cryptic words and a guarded tone, or can we both admit that you know whom I love?"

Shirisae stared at him for such a long time, and with such a peculiar gleam in her golden eyes, that Tristus began to worry she might actually have been innocent of where his affections lay and that his words might have sounded more directed at her as the object of those affections. That, in turn, made him feel conceited—to believe that such a highbred lady, who was also an elf, would even consider the possibility ...

"I know who holds your heart," Shirisae finally said, looking at the ground as she tied off her braid. For a moment, it looked as if she might begin to cry, but then she lifted her chin indignantly and said, "I believe that a person such as that is the bearer of many hearts, all collected with the vanity and arrogance of a king who accepts donations into his treasury from starving peasants, all neglected as they lay sealed in a vault from which there is no escape, until they grow dark and cold ... and lifeless."

Tristus gaped in his surprise at hearing such an accounting of the person he respected as much as he adored. "Shirisae ... my lady, you're wrong. Please, do not say such a thing again."

"Am I wrong?" she replied, looking at him now, chilling him with her conviction in this matter. And then, her eyes softened with tears. She looked away, as if to keep Tristus from seeing them. "Forgive me. I know that I am wrong, that there is some hope in your heart's quest. That only makes my own more difficult."

Tristus was beside himself, and about to ask her how she could possibly know such a thing, or what made her at least suspect that Xu Liang could possibly know a love beyond his empress and his homeland when the lady elf's ending words struck him. They struck him speechless.

Shirisae did not wait for him to recover himself. She stood and said simply, "I shall relieve Guang Ci and assume watch for the next few hours."

Tristus could only nod in response.

◆ ◆ ◆ ◆ ◆

THE NIGHT WENT sleepless. Tristus packed his gear and ate his meager breakfast mechanically. Several hours into their journey across boring plains carpeted with mist and gray grass, the silence became unbearable. The sporadic caws of ravens as they alighted upon the tendrils of dry wood sticking haphazardly out of the land's shrubbery was beginning to sound like lively conversation against the grave lack of words exchanged among the three companions.

Tristus guided Blue Crane alongside Shirisae's black charger—she had been riding several paces ahead—and looked back at Guang Ci, whose attention was everywhere but on them. He recalled the language barrier after the fact.

"Shirisae," he finally said to the lady elf. "About our conversation during the night ... I..."

"There is nothing that you need to say," Shirisae told him in her calm, proud fashion. "*Firestorm* led me to you, just as it led my mother to her life mate. The Phoenix has spoken, and though the words may seem a riddle, there is nothing to debate. It is difficult sometimes for even me to accept this."

Tristus didn't know what to say. He didn't know how to sound any of the words that came to mind. The last thing he wanted was to offend her. She'd saved Xu Liang's life. Tristus would gladly give her his own life in return, but not in that way. Not as her lover or husband, or whatever she was implying.

"The difficulty is not in knowing how your heart goes," the lady elf continued without looking at him. "It is in waiting for it to come to me. I know that the Phoenix does not lie, but I did not expect these circumstances. They assail my faith and if I seem cold at times, please do not take it personally. It is only that I must be stronger now."

"Please," Tristus said, almost before Shirisae had finished. "My lady, please, you must stop saying such things. It is hard enough, bearing the weight of my own heart. I cannot bear yours as well. Whatever your god has spoken to you, however you wish to interpret those words, you must believe me when I say that I cannot love you as you would have me. You have my heart in friendship, Shirisae, though I know it is scarcely enough to repay you for what you have done."

"Fate binds us," the lady elf told him with numbing certitude. "You will come to me in time." She was not wearing her helm this morning and so her smile dealt him the killing blow. Her next words ensured her victory. "You cannot tell me you have absolutely no faith in the Phoenix. It is the Flame of my god that kept your hope alive." And then she trotted ahead, unaware of or unconcerned with the tears she'd brought to her companion's eyes.

Tristus tried to remind himself of what Taya said about elves having a tendency to speak their minds openly and without truly intending malice, but the hurt was great. Xu Liang would have died without the intervention of both Shirisae and her god; that much was true. Tristus' hope would have died that day in the snow, just as he realized the nature of that hope. He would have regretted not recognizing his feelings for the mystic for many long years afterward. Even a love that could not be answered was a love worth knowing. The world was cold and bitter enough. Finding Xu Liang had been as miraculous as receiving *Dawnfire* and meeting the angel. It had had the same effect on Tristus, casting light upon him and filling him with warmth to keep the memories of the darker world behind him at bay. Even if he were to never see Xu Liang again, he felt blessed just knowing that the man existed, that somewhere in the world his light was shining. He loved him enough to let him go, and at the same time he loved him far too much to ever love another, even though, under these circumstances, that other had enabled his love to be fully realized.

The obligation and guilt Shirisae was either knowingly or inadvertently placing upon him was devastating, enough to make the black memories of his recent past surface. Tristus feared what might come of that and had no choice but to shut his feelings away. *All that matters right now, is finding Alere*, Tristus told himself.

♦ ♦ ♦ ♦ ♦

"STOP! PLEASE, I can't take anymore. I can't feel my feet. My fingers are numb. I know you can hear me! I know you're listening. This is inhumane!"

Alere drew Breigh to a halt, his hand tightening about her bridle. He set his teeth together, needled by the human's incessant whining. He might have been able to go on ignoring Bastien Crowe, except that something he said finally struck true.

"You're right," Alere said. "This is inhumane. Breigh has no more love for you than I."

He walked back to the gypsy, whose hands were bound behind his back and whose ankles were connected by a span of rope stretched beneath the mare. He cut the bindings with his dagger and hauled his prisoner out of the saddle, dropping him unceremoniously onto the snow-covered forest floor.

Bastien sprawled on the ground, righting himself slowly. Too slowly.

When he suddenly lunged at Alere, Alere struck him back to the ground.

The man was stiff and weak from his method of travel, and from his frustration. The injury *Aerkiren* had dealt him, which was now crudely, but efficiently dressed was not helping his state.

Bastien maneuvered onto his hands and knees, breathing hard, spitting blood onto the snow. "Damn you, elf! Get it over with! I know you're going to kill me!"

"Perhaps, when it becomes necessary," Alere replied calmly. "For now, I am in need of someone to confirm this location."

Bastien glared at him, then gave a quick glance about the woods surrounding them. The trees were darkwoods, their bark almost black. The deep green needles were sharp, more like barbs, capable of not only scratching the unwary traveler, but poisoning as well, it was said. The trees were so thick in number that the only safe way to traverse the forest was to walk.

Bastien's lips curled upward as he finally seemed to recognize his surroundings. "This is the Deepwood. An elf of the Verres Mountains needed a gypsy to tell him that? I find that hard to believe."

"I would too, if that were the case," Alere said. "I know these woods, human, but I do not recall any clear routes through them, and this map is difficult to follow."

He reached for a rolled parchment tucked into his belt and tossed it onto the ground in front of the gypsy.

Bastien clearly recognized it, but he did not reach for it. Instead, he grinned insolently at his captor. "A thief as well? Riffled through my pockets while I was out, did you? Anything else I should know about?"

Alere ignored his comments. "Who is Malek Vorhaven?"

Bastien lifted his hand to his jaw, slowly wiping away the blood. "Why should I tell you a damned thing?"

"You will speak, gypsy, because you believe words will spare your life. You are a fanatic, Brother of the Balance, but you are far from noble enough to die for your cause, if you don't have to." Alere drew

Aerkiren and extended the blade, point first, toward Bastien. "You don't have to die, but I will kill you if I must."

Bastien stared at him, as if contemplating just how serious Alere might have been. In a moment, he'd come to his decision and lowered his hand. He said begrudgingly, "Malek Vorhaven is one of the scholars I spoke to you about. His residence is marked on the map, but it's not so easy to find as it looks. There's a spell of confusion on the map. That you followed it this far speaks well for your resolve."

"You are not a sorcerer," Alere guessed easily.

Bastien shook his head. "Vorhaven laid the enchantment. I discovered that weeks ago, but I held onto it anyway, hoping that what sense I could make of it, coupled with my memory, might lead me back to his mansion. He's a very clever man. Offering the map was just a gesture, a trick to lull us into a false sense of security after we entrusted him with..."

The gypsy stopped, deliberately.

Alere's eyes narrowed. "Am I to take it that Vorhaven betrayed the Brotherhood?"

The gypsy nodded slowly. "That was originally why I came back to Yvaria. It took me damned near a year to convince my captain to make the journey. Fu Ran's sorcerer friend and his quest was an uncanny coincidence. I decided to investigate while on my way to Upper Yvaria."

"It was your idea to warn Xu Liang of the bandits from his homeland?"

"No," Bastien admitted. "But it proved an extraordinarily convenient suggestion on Fu Ran's part. My captain agreed, almost too easily, and even asked me if I would accompany Fu Ran, since Yvaria happens to be my homeland. Neither of them knew I'd been plotting how I might be able to go ashore for an extended period without actually resigning."

"Your order doesn't arrange these matters for you?" Alere asked him, lowering *Aerkiren*.

"The Brotherhood gives us a mission. From then we're on our own for a specified period of time. If we don't report back, someone else investigates."

Alere didn't take his eyes off the gypsy for a moment, even though the man was unarmed. He continued his interrogation. "And your task is to assassinate this Vorhaven?"

"My aim is the same as yours, elf," Bastien replied, glaring. "To recover the Night Blade at all costs."

Alere stepped forward once more, this time he stabbed *Aerkiren* into the ground—through the map—and leaned forward, extending his hand to the gypsy. "I suggest that we find the Sword together. We can settle the cost for 'recovering' it when the time comes."

◆ ◆ ◆ ◆ ◆

A LIGHT SNOW crept down through the thick forest canopy. Within only a few moments, it grew heavier, enough that Tristus began to feel like he could sweep the falling curtain aside like drapery and walk through it. The snow had piled up past his ankles when he called the others to a stop.

"Do you think we should rest the horses?" he asked Shirisae when she looked back at him. He looked around them as his voice resonated strangely in the natural enclosure of wood and weather. The forest had come upon them a little too suddenly for his liking.

Guang Ci had looked back upon hearing Tristus' voice. Their gazes met. They spoke to one another in silence, something they'd learned to do quite well in the past days since leaving Vilciel. The bodyguard nodded once, and then took up what he may have considered a relaxed position beside his horse.

They'd been walking the animals since the forest started closing in around them. It seemed an easy place to be thrown from the saddle or to break a horse's leg. The terrain was uneven, made more treacherous beneath the fast accumulating snow.

"Do you know these woods?" Tristus asked Shirisae hopefully.

"It is called the Deepwood," the lady elf answered. "Though I've never come this far north myself, I have heard stories of it from others who have."

"What kind of stories? Not pleasant, I suspect."

Shirisae shook her head gently. "As a child I was told that a woman entered these woods and became instantly lost, trapped in a labyrinth of dark trees, forced to wander until she was driven mad. Her lover, who came looking for her, rode into the trees carelessly and was scratched by a single pine needle. He fell into a deep, eternal slumber. It is said that the woman still walks these woods, weeping and crying out for him as he lays always within reach, but out of sight beneath the bracken, deaf to her calls in his state."

"Well, I'm sure we'll all sleep a lot better now," Tristus replied in mild sarcasm. "Thank you, my lady."

Shirisae smiled briefly. The expression faded while she looked about the woods. "We were headed north and may have veered slightly west," she informed. "The nearest town should be Stachendorf, to the east."

Tristus nodded in acknowledgment. "Sounds human. I doubt Alere went there, since the Verres Mountains lay to the northwest."

"Elves don't often take shelter in human cities," Shirisae confirmed. "Least of all Verressi hunters. Still, he may have ridden through a town if he was in need of any supplies. Desfelden lies along the path to the mountains. We may be able to confirm his passage, if he was sighted by someone inclined to share such information with us."

"How many days?" Tristus sighed, beginning to regret his haste in this matter.

Shirisae considered, patting her black battle horse on the neck. "Three. Maybe four, considering our pace."

"And I'll bet the Verres Mountains aren't just lying in the backdrop," Tristus sighed, again. "And I'll wager as readily that our friend Alere Shaederin doesn't keep his residence at the base of them."

"The Mountain Elves of the north may live well out of doors, but they were a sophisticated and cautious people. They built their cities deep within the mountains, connecting them with vast networks of tunnel. They constructed great strongholds out of the rock face, their cities fanning beneath them on the shelf-like outcroppings of the unique mountains, connected by plank bridges. Families of high standing occupied the strongholds, guarding them and serving the cities for generations.

"The house Shaederin was second only to that of the king of the Mountain Elves. Though the royal family did not survive the Shadow Wars, a new king was never named. The houses fell into discord and eventually detachment. Though they fought on together in spirit—the keirveshen would always be the bane of their kind—they scarcely had any real contact with one another. For more than a hundred years since the Shadow Wars—documented to have ended at the time of their loss—they have existed in the shelter of their mountains and their silence ... hidden, forgotten. We elves of the Phoenix were not certain there were any left, but a rogue here and there, eking out what life was left to him. My brother and

I almost took Alere for such a rogue, possibly the last, but then it became clear in his eyes."

Tristus, who had never read anything in the white elf's guarded gaze, asked, "What did?"

Shirisae looked at him, and she did not smile nor did she show the merest trace of disrespect toward the white elf. She said softly, "He is protecting someone. He is young, even by elf standards, therefore I believe Morgen Shaederin has left this world and passed his duties to his son. Most likely, he acts to shield the remains of his house, all of whom must be ill or younger than him if he acts alone, as he clearly is. And so far from his home ... he must believe that he can keep the keirveshen away by destroying them in the outlying regions, before they reach the mountains again."

Tristus frowned with concern, feeling somehow closer to Alere while he learned more about him. "What if the demons return while he's away?"

"He would not have left his family totally unguarded," Shirisae answered. "But he also would not have left the region without performing a thorough hunt. It would not be difficult. They seem to be massing in Lower Yvaria currently."

"I imagine he'll be home soon anyway," Tristus said, shrugging. "I don't know where else he might have gone or ... why."

Tristus' last word scarcely sounded as his attention became ensnared in the sudden, brilliant glow radiating from the spear strapped to Blue Crane with the rest of his gear. He reached his hand toward *Dawnfire*, feeling its splendid heat through his glove, then looked to Shirisae, who lifted *Firestorm* as it transformed into a veritable beacon of silver, crackling light. Before either of them could say anything, the light began to swell ... not evenly, but somehow pressing east, filtering through the trees as if to show a path.

Shirisae peered through the dark woods that were suddenly lit. In a moment, she said, "I see a trail."

"How?" Tristus wondered. "All evidence of anyone or anything passing should be buried beneath the snow."

"I see it," Shirisae insisted, and did not explain herself.

In a moment, the light from the Blades faded to the minimal glow they had been emitting just from being in each other's company.

The lady elf kept her gaze on the woods and said quietly, "Do we trust it?"

Tristus had an eerie feeling about these woods, but he found reassurance touching *Dawnfire*. He said, "Could we ask for a clearer sign? Alere must have gone that way, chasing shadows maybe. He may need our help."

"I'll lead," Shirisae volunteered, although it sounded more like a command.

Recognizing her strength, as well as her leadership, Tristus agreed. "Guang Ci," he said to the guard, gesturing for him to join them. The guard came, and the three of them started deeper into the Deepwood.

◆ ◆ ◆ ◆ ◆

VILCIEL. A CITY built for dragons, occupied by people who worshipped a bird of flame, a god capable of granting new life ... and old pain.

Xu Liang looked out over the city surrounded by clouds and near mountain peaks, and wondered when he had ever seen a sight so beautiful and yet so terrible to behold. To him, it was as a prison mounted on top of the very world. Even if he escaped it physically, he would remember it always, and he would forever feel trapped by it. Even as he felt the chill of the mountain air biting into his flesh, his soul was on fire and his heart burned from within while the fire resurrected a thousand memories of heaven that served as gateways into hell.

"What have you done to me?"

Upon being addressed, the priestess stopped her silent advance. "Your health recovers," she said tonelessly. "And with it, your power renews."

"It may never be as focused as it was, but it has never left me," Xu Liang replied. "A path chosen by the ancestors is not easily abandoned or strayed from."

"We believe our ancestors choose our paths for us as well," Ahjenta said.

"A path of fire," Xu Liang murmured, tucking his hands into the sleeves of his own silk robes, that had been returned to him days ago. He'd only recently recovered the strength to carry himself from the bed of nightmares, as he'd come to refer to it. He hadn't expected the nightmares to follow him across the vast chamber. He asked again, "What have you done to me?"

Ahjenta waited before giving her answer. "I called upon the Phoenix to restore you, against my better judgment, but at the pleading of my daughter and of my own heart as I witnessed the desperation of your companions."

Xu Liang wouldn't hear the latter half of her statement. A frown formed on his lips, and he said, "I made my choice. My time had come. What you have done has prevented nothing, but only prolonged my suffering and delayed the inevitable. I will not last."

"Your constitution is not strong," Ahjenta admitted.

"It has not been, from the day of my birth. Magic cannot improve my state, but only lend me strength enough to make my journeys. Your Flame will enable me to finish this one, but I may never make another."

"You will return to your homeland," the priestess offered. "Is that not what you wanted? It must be, for the Phoenix cannot restore one who is not willing to be restored."

Xu Liang thought of his empress, recalling her suddenly as a small child in the arms of her brother, who had worshipped her without ever dreaming that she would become the ruler of Sheng Fan. The burning inside of him flared, raising too many emotions. Hot tears welled in his eyes, stinging his vision. *Have my efforts truly been for Sheng Fan? Or have I labored all this time for you, Song Lu ... my prince?*

The idea was unbearable. To act in selfishness could only result in ruin, and perhaps here was the evidence that he had been acting for himself rather than for the benefit of the land. He had lost contact with the Empress, the Swords had strayed apart once again, and in spite of any magic he may never see his homeland again.

"Your time has not come," Ahjenta finally said, almost gently. "You may not last to see your beauty spoiled, but there are still many days ahead of you. Many long days, trying days, of course ... but some pleasant days as well."

"You are an oracle as well?" Xu Liang asked dryly, refusing to be moved in his current state of angst.

"I have lived for many hundreds of years, *shandon*, mystic of the East. I know dejection from dying, and I know how easily many mortals—even the wisest of them—succumb to it. I offer you this advice; do not fear the memories that haunt you now, for they are things you have already seen and events you have already overcome. The future lies ahead of you, and you are one who can greatly affect it."

Xu Liang turned to look at her, amazed by the elf's concern.

The priestess showed no warmth openly, other than the color of her hair, but there seemed some compassion in her golden eyes. "In the war against the shadows, most are taken by darkness, one way or another. Those who shine above it act as beacons to those still fighting, a guide and a source of hope in these chaotic times. The knowledge you have brought to us seems to have solved the mystery of the Great Awakening, prophesied long ago. We know now that it is a thing to be feared, not revered. But we will not fear it, knowing that there are others in this war with us, one such as yourself, prepared to combat the source of the shadows that have been invading our lands for centuries, when it finally rises."

"You... believe in the Dragon?" Xu Liang asked, wondering who had related the story to her. He decided quickly that it was probably Tarfan.

"I believe that all forces in this world have a master and that—like the Phoenix, who commands the Flame of Resurrection—perhaps this dragon rules the Shadows of Confusion. The shadows rose first, to scatter and divide us, to break our will, so that when their master rises, it will only require a single, killing blow."

Xu Liang was fascinated by this theory, and he listened to the priestess with renewed interest. "Morale is often the deciding factor in a battle," he agreed. "And perhaps that is what the Swords represent; unification against our foe. Madam," he started to say, but Ahjenta did not let him finish.

"My daughter, as the future leader of our people, will make the right decision," she said and added softly, "In all things. I must believe that."

"And it would seem, then, that I must rely on it," Xu Liang replied. "I will pray for her safe return." He put his hands together and bowed to the priestess. "And I would thank you, Madame Ahjenta, for your wise words."

"I've been told it was prayer that put you into this state. Continue resting and recover your strength. The Phoenix will guide my daughter and your friends." On those words, the priestess left him, greeting Fu Ran politely as the large man made his way across the chamber.

"Taya said for you to stay in bed," the former guard reminded, but Xu Liang was far from hearing him, his gaze once again on the view of Vilciel from a dragon-sized window ledge.

"It would seem that we have gained the trust and support of these people," Xu Liang said. "When Shirisae returns, I will convince her to accompany me back to Sheng Fan."

"Tarfan gave Tristus explicit instructions not to take longer than two weeks," Fu Ran informed. "He and Taya figured that would be about as long as you would allow yourself to be stuck in bed."

"The knight has as long as he is inclined to take," Xu Liang replied, his eyes narrowing involuntarily.

"What do you mean?"

"By stealing Blue Crane, and taking the Dawn Blade, which I know he will surrender if I ask it of him, he has effectively chained me to this mountain," Xu Liang explained, maintaining a neutral voice, though it aggravated him to consider the knight's snake-like tactics. "I would trust no other animal to carry me on my journey and, knowing that the Dawn Blade is within my grasp, I will not leave it behind."

"He needed *Dawnfire* to help him search for Alere," Fu Ran said, a little too defensively for Xu Liang's appreciation.

"*Dawnfire* is not like the other Blades," Xu Liang said. "It does not always glow simply because it is in the company of the others, and *Firestorm* alone would have sufficed for their search."

Typically, Fu Ran argued. "What are you saying, then? You were willing to leave *Firestorm* behind? And what about *Aerkiren*, and the Night Blade?"

Calmly, Xu Liang said, "It was my plan to take a northern route to the coast of Upper Yvaria, to the Sea of Ice, which connects with Aer. It is possible that we would have been able to contribute to the search en route to Sheng Fan, where the Empress herself may be very ill. Now, because Tristus Edainien has taken matters into his own hands and corrupted Guang Ci into his irrational way of thinking, we can do nothing but wait."

"Corrupted?" Fu Ran stomped to the edge of the enormous archway and then turned back, forcing himself into Xu Liang's view. "Guang Ci made the decision himself. It wasn't asked of him, certainly not by Tristus. The boy was going to go alone. He didn't even know Shirisae planned to join him. None of us did until..."

"The knight is not a child, Fu Ran," Xu Liang pointed out. "It does not assist him or his position in any way for you and Tarfan to continually plead his youth and therefore his innocence. It is not innocence that enables him. He is motivated by..."

Xu Liang stopped himself short of revealing his suspicions about Tristus.

Fu Ran didn't give him a chance to change the subject.

"By what?" the former guard pressed. However, he didn't wait for an answer, incensed by the same past tension that was also surfacing anew within Xu Liang as well. "Tristus has his problems, but so does everyone. He's been nothing but faithful to us since we found him half buried in the snow and, if you'll recall, it wasn't him that abandoned us, but that shifty white elf. Alere left while the rest of us waited anxiously to celebrate your survival, or mourn your death! In fact, all of us were convinced that you were dead, except for Tristus! He was the only one of us who had even a shred of hope left when we got here—and that includes your damned bodyguards!"

Xu Liang did his best to ignore the larger man's rising voice and scathing words. He said simply, "I am not inclined to discuss this with you any further. You may leave."

"May I?" The giant grinned obscenely and performed a mocking bow, which made Xu Liang frown irritably. Fu Ran straightened, glowering. "Oh, I remember now. I don't serve you anymore, so I guess you can't dismiss me. I guess you'll have to hear an opinion, other than your own for a change!"

Xu Liang closed his eyes and drew in a breath, determined to ignore him. He would not be drawn into a shouting match with the former guard.

Fu Ran, however, would not be ignored. "You're more uptight than you'll let onto others. You're patient, by Sheng Fan standards, but I've been away from Sheng Fan for a long time and I see things a little differently now."

Xu Liang couldn't help the smirk that came to his lips. "Do you?" He opened his eyes to see the other man's anger, which was successfully provoking him. "Did you see things so differently when you asked me to take you back?"

Fu Ran tensed visibly, but continued with his statement, as if Xu Liang hadn't interrupted. "You should know that you were a spoiled brat as a boy, and as a man you're an imperial pain in the ass!"

Fu Ran may have had more to say, but Xu Liang would let him take this no further. "Since you seem to know so much about me, then you must also know that even I have limits as to what I am willing to endure for the sake of diplomacy." Though he was frowning, he maintained a low voice. When Fu Ran smiled in his typically insolent fashion, it was all Xu Liang could do to keep from yelling at the former guard. "I will not lose the Empress because Alere cannot contain his hatred. Or because Tristus cannot control his emotions. Sheng Fan will not fall into the hands of dishonorable men for the petty prejudices between elves, or the recklessness of a troubled young man. The Swords will come together if I have to take them from their bearers myself and find new bearers!"

When he heard himself, Xu Liang knew at once that he had spoken rashly and wrongly. He was behaving like a child, and how could he help it, the way Fu Ran needled him with his impudence and his ignorance? He turned away from the former guard just before he screamed at him and realized in the very instant that he had allowed things to go too far.

He drew in a long breath and held it. Upon the release, he said wearily. "Leave me, Fu Ran. I must rest."

The large man sighed, almost with remorse. "Xu Liang..."

Xu Liang would not listen. "Fu Ran, if you do not leave, I will say something that both of us will regret for many years to come."

Fu Ran hesitated. Eventually, he left, saying nothing more and Xu Liang stood in the relative quiet left behind, hearing only the wind through the mountains.

At length, he looked over his shoulder at the skyline to the north, an impenetrable wall of mountains and clouds. "Damn you," he said, maybe to no one in particular.

TWENTY-FIVE

Keeper of Shadows

"UGH! WHAT IN HELL'S name is that stench?"

"Be silent!" Alere hissed. He'd been smelling what the gypsy only now complained about for more than a day. It was a stomach-churning pungency that wafted through the dark air here, but there were fouler things in this darkness than the odor. Alere could sense the presence of the keirveshen. He kept his hand on the hilt of his sword as they progressed nearer to the place on Bastien's map that was marked 'Vorhaven's Manor'.

"There's a bog near," Alere finally said.

Bastien went for his map. "There's not a bog anywhere near this area. There wasn't one when—"

"There is one," Alere told the gypsy, concluding the matter.

"All right, there is one," Bastien murmured. "And since you haven't taken your hand off your sword for at least the last hour, do you think I might be able to have my own weapons back now?"

Alere ignored his request, pressing on through the grayness, wondering at the hazy glow that seeped through the dark trees ahead. "Tell me what you know of this Vorhaven."

"Where do I begin?" the gypsy sighed. "He used to be a scholar under the employ of the Brotherhood."

"Not a member?"

Bastien shook his head. "No. He refused to join, but he was very much interested in our objective, and we were very much interested in his knowledge. The Night Blade was discovered about forty years ago, in these very woods. It was asked of Vorhaven to study it before the Brotherhood realized exactly what it was. Those who'd happened upon the weapon knew only that it was magic, and not forged in this world."

"What would make them believe that?" Alere asked, slowing his pace, noticing that each step sank a little lower into the spongy ground beneath the half-melted snow.

The gypsy seemed to share Alere's concern about the sinking earth, but continued his explanation without comment about it. "The blade itself was black as pitch—black as night—and emanated a peculiar dark light."

Alere stopped at that point, and looked at the man. The gypsy's chafed features were bland, almost disinterested, just as they'd been when Alere met him in another dark forest. For some reason Alere had been willing to ignore this detail before. It was bothering him now. He knew that the gypsy was hiding something—and far more than what Alere suspected already.

Alere asked, "What do you mean by a dark light?"

Bastien shrugged. "I'm not quite sure how to describe it. I've only seen it once myself." He took a moment to consider, then said, "It's like a shadow that seems to glow, but there's no true light about it." He indicated *Aerkiren* with a glance. "Perhaps similar to the violet glow that emanates from your own blade, but much darker ... deeper. If it helps, the sword was named *Behel*."

Alere frowned, recognizing the Yvarian word, derived from the tongue of his own people. "No light."

The gypsy nodded and added the meaning the gypsies had given it. "True darkness." In the following moment, he said, "The Brotherhood thinks that Vorhaven simply deceived us, wanting to keep the Night Blade for himself, but it is my belief that the weapon drove him mad."

"What makes you believe so?" Alere asked.

Bastien folded his arms across his chest and looked at the thinning woods ahead of them, toward what Alere had already determined to be the bog. He said, "I was the envoy sent to request that the Blade be returned. I'd been in contact with Vorhaven before, through letters, and he'd always struck me as being quite sane ... a calm and patient man. When I met with him in these woods for the first time, I saw a mad haste in his eyes, though he still moved and spoke in a steady manner."

The gypsy looked at Alere now, continuing his account. "Vorhaven had grown somehow attached to the Blade and become eager for its power, hungry for its secrets. Secrets that would unlock that power and enable him to become its master. When I told him that I'd come for *Behel*, he stalled for time, insisting that there was still much to be learned from the Sword. I stayed for more than a month in his manor; a place that was filled with servants who were all too quiet.

"Finally, I could wait no longer. I demanded that the Blade be handed over. Vorhaven promised to deliver it the next morning— the morning of my departure. I don't know exactly what happened next, but I awoke aboard a ship bound for Aer, seven days later. I eventually learned that Vorhaven had been in correspondence with my superiors and somehow regained their trust, and tempted their curiosity with the promise of finding *Behel*'s sibling Blades. I was given a new assignment; to seek and study any lore concerning what the Brotherhood then called the Swords of the Sky."

"You decided on your own to retrieve the Night Blade," Alere surmised.

The gypsy's dark eyes narrowed. "Vorhaven has betrayed us. And he is dangerous."

A bird suddenly fluttered from its perch nearby, calling into the night as it glided to a new branch. Breigh stirred uneasily. Alere offered the mare a soothing pat on the neck, then proceeded into the bog, where he discovered that the hazy glow was the result of many torches standing in the soft, ranking earth. They emitted a low-lying cloud of smoke and light that skewed the dimensions of the earth, as well as the nature of its covering.

"Just so that you know," Bastien said. "This wasn't here when last I visited."

"And the shadows?" Alere inquired, sliding *Aerkiren* free of its sheath when the patterns the torches created on the surface of the bog began to stir.

"It's not the keirveshen," the gypsy informed. "They'd have come out by now and cast their darkness upon us. There's something under the bog. Look at the way the surface undulates."

Alere took a step back and looked quickly over the sea of murky water marked with a forest of torches. He spied a solid shape spanning across the darkness several yards away. "A bridge," he announced.

Bastien followed Alere toward it without hesitation. "Good idea. Perhaps an even better idea would be granting me a weapon."

"In time," Alere replied. "I will wait to be certain first that you are too preoccupied with slaying an assailant than me."

"I find that amusing," the gypsy said dryly. "That you believe I'd fancy killing you and wandering into Vorhaven's manor alone."

"You're not afraid," Alere stated.

"No, but I'm not stupid either."

Alere stopped, halting Bastien as well. Before the gypsy could ask, he pointed to the upcoming bridge, where two winged figures perched upon the railing, looking like statues, except to the eyes of an elf. Alere could see them breathing. He could see the torchlight glistening on their sleek, ebon skin. They were at rest, but they would stir easily.

"They guard him," Alere whispered. "Else he is dead."

"If they are guarding Vorhaven," Bastien said, speaking softly as well. "Then he's further gone than I believed."

Alere sheathed *Aerkiren* and sought his bow. He quickly strung the weapon, then handed the gypsy a pair of throwing blades he'd previously confiscated from him. "It is unlikely that I will be able to put down both of them before one can rise and call out to others. They must be silenced."

Bastien nodded. "Right. Which one?"

"The nearest," Alere answered. "I would trust your human vision no farther in this hazy light."

The gypsy didn't argue and Alere nocked an arrow into place, taking aim, waiting as he noticed the man beside him taking up a throwing stance. In a moment, Bastien announced that he was ready with a nod. Alere focused on his victim again, then gave a silent command to fire. The projectiles penetrated the orange mist and hit their marks, one immediately after the other. Both demons dropped into the bog to either side of the bridge. Alere waited for a response to the splash each body made, walking toward the bridge again when none came.

They moved slowly and quietly, halting momentarily on the islet of firm ground that came at the end of the first bridge, which led to a second, this one angling through the bog to their right. The second bridge led to a third, and so on, until a total of seven stone bridges had been traversed and Alere and the gypsy came to a simple row of wooden planks spanning the final stretch of moat. A large house of gray brick awaited on the opposite side, illuminated eerily by the fire-lit swamp that fronted it. Images of dragons were carved in relief over the wide front doors—inanimate yet still menacing-looking guards.

"The symbol of the Vorhaven family," Bastien explained. "Malek Vorhaven's great grandfather was known as the Dragon Count of Eishencroe. He ruled the city with a tyrant's fist from a grand castle overlooking it. People once claimed they could see dragons flying to and from the place in the night. Rumor is that the castle is abandoned now. Not even the current governing family, for all its famed arrogance, will dare to occupy a place of such malevolence."

Alere thought irresistibly of Xu Liang's story about the Celestial Swords and the symbolism the mystic would have found in Bastien's words. Thinking about the mystic made him wonder if he'd taken up Xu Liang's quest, and why. It seemed without question that Xu Liang had passed away. No 'fire magic' of the Phoenix Elves could heal the damage done to his body and his soul. Alere also had no reason to believe he would truly ever see the knight again, and he had no intention of ever seeking out Shirisae. What was his purpose in acquiring the Night Blade, then?

Before Alere could answer himself, Bastien was standing beneath the stone dragons of Vorhaven's mansion, trying the double doors. They moaned open, like the yawning maw of some beast and the gypsy looked back. "I wonder what this means?"

Alere gave a last look at the bog behind them, then joined the careless gypsy. "It will mean your death if you're not more cautious."

"Shall we close them again and knock?" the gypsy asked sardonically.

Alere ignored him, proceeding into a long front hall, lit with a row of chandeliers hanging high overhead. The polished floor held an uninterrupted diamond-shaped pattern, alternating in black and ivory. The only furniture was up against the wall; a bench with velvet cushions, a console table, and other small, decorative articles. Oil paintings adorned white plaster walls. Three exits from the hall were visible from the front door. Two were archways leading into shadow. The third was a squared pair of doors.

"Where are we likely to find the Sword?" Alere asked.

The gypsy's answer came too easily. "In Vorhaven's hand. He loves the weapon. He strokes the Blade and I think he takes it for affection when it cuts him. I can only assume his madness has worsened since my visit."

Alere took Bastien's words into account, then rephrased his question. "Where are we likely to find Vorhaven?"

"He's always been somewhat of a recluse, even before going mad. He'll be in here somewhere, I'm just not sure I can say where exactly. He has multiple studies in the place. More than one library as well. He didn't like to leave."

Alere started toward the nearest entryway. "He would send others to search for the sibling Blades, then?"

"Yes," Bastien answered with no special interest.

"Then it is all clear," Alere said.

"What is?"

Alere stopped and looked back at the dark man. "The shadows do his bidding. They have been seeking the other Swords."

Bastien caught on quickly enough. "That would explain the knight's story, about the demon attacking the angel who supposedly gave him that spear—the Dawn Blade. And when the keirveshen attacked Xu Liang and the others in the Hollowen."

"They were attracted to the mystic's power," Alere said. "Wanting to silence it. They, like you, followed the Sword he carried after discovering it. The keirveshen dominate the Yvarian regions because their master keeps them close, and because his search for the other Blades has taken him no further. Even before the mystic's arrival, the Phoenix Elves brought *Firestorm* with them, and I felt the presence of the shadow folk near Vilciel. I can only assume now that they are lying in wait for the opportunity, or the command, to seize the weapon."

Alere unsheathed *Aerkiren* and watched the etchings upon the blade begin to glow. "This has been in my family for generations. Ironic that it should draw the enemies it was intended to quell. That is why they attacked my home."

"And killed your father," Bastien added needlessly, and not without some trace of sympathy.

Alere rejected it with his response. "They murdered nearly my entire family. Now I understand why I was drawn to the mystic's quest and why I would seek to complete it after his passing. Here is the source of blame I was after, the target of my revenge."

While he spoke the bloodlust was rising, the eagerness to drive *Aerkiren* into the heart of the enemy he'd never known before this moment, but whom he'd been hunting for years. Nothing would sate his sudden appetite for slaying except the blood of this stranger.

"Malek Vorhaven dies tonight," Alere decided, and he stalked further into the shadows of the house, determined to kill anyone or anything that tried to interfere.

◆ ◆ ◆ ◆ ◆

THE TRACKS WERE fresh... which was impossible.

"He should have been miles ahead of us," Tristus said, stepping back from the hoof prints in the wet snow. "Days ahead, if he didn't stop to rest, as we did. Why would Alere linger in a place such as this?"

"Perhaps the more appropriate question would be whom was he lingering with?"

Tristus looked to the ground again when Shirisae pointed at it. He studied the footprints beside the path made by a horse, possibly Breigh—possibly some unknown traveler, though *Firestorm* and *Dawnfire* seemed to disagree.

Finally, he shook his head. "I don't understand. I see only one set of footprints."

"Look at their placement," Shirisae said. "Farther away from Breigh than Alere would have been walking. And recall that elves, especially hunting elves, can tread any land without leaving a trail if they choose to."

"Recall it?" Tristus said in amazement. "I didn't know it to begin with." He sighed, pushing his hair out of his face with one hand. "Still, that doesn't answer what Alere might be doing here. I don't see any demon corpses lying about, but God that smell is awful enough to be the reek of devils. Do you suppose he's hunting?"

"He never stops," Shirisae replied, gazing into the woods. "He won't, until his vengeance has been sated, and then he still may not."

"Sounds rather bleak," Tristus murmured, visually following the tracks toward what looked like a fire in the forest. However, it didn't sound or smell like a natural blaze. It was eerie, like an orange fog had settled, though what would cause such a phenomenon completely eluded Tristus at the moment.

Eventually, he sighed. "Well, if we're assuming that these tracks are indeed evidence of Alere's passing, then I suppose we may as well push on and see what we can find. My feeling of guilt for having left the others compounds with each hour."

They moved on, quickly discovering the swamp that was to blame for the foul odor in the woods, as well as a series of bridges that traversed the stinking marsh. They also took note of the many torches that provided the hazy orange glow, wondering who had placed them and who kept them lit. It seemed, in the deathly stillness, that they might not receive their answer. The place was clearly deserted. Only the torches remained, like candles kept lit in a mausoleum.

"Look there."

Tristus recognized the white mare just as soon as Shirisae pointed her out, and so, apparently, did Blue Crane. The steed drifted ahead of Tristus, almost pulling him in its eager stride, before finally coming to a halt close to Breigh in the open doorway of a house that must have been grand at one time. The animals greeted each other with gentle contact and Tristus let them be, straying into the house's dismal interior.

"Who lives here?" Tristus wondered aloud. "No fond acquaintance of Alere's, I'm sure."

Shirisae arrived beside him, her golden gaze moving slowly over the front hall. "Something resides here. I sense a dark presence."

Tristus looked at her. "How dark? Demons?"

"Perhaps some," Shirisae answered thoughtfully. "But there's something else…"

Before she finished, Tristus walked back to Blue Crane and freed *Dawnfire* from the rest of his gear. "Guang Ci," he said to the bodyguard, who still lingered in the doorway.

When the Fanese man looked, Tristus indicated the horses with a nod, then gestured toward the floor with his hand, hoping to convey instructions for the guard to remain and watch over their belongings.

Guang Ci inclined his head once, seeming to understand. Tristus returned to Shirisae, who held *Firestorm* upright while she continued to observe their surroundings. Her skin appeared to glow with an almost metallic sheen in the spear's platinum light. With her black armor and in her stoic pose, she looked like a statue.

"Where do we begin?" Tristus finally asked.

Shirisae shook her head slightly, seeming distracted. "I do not know. *Firestorm* does not say."

Tristus noticed the spear's lack of eager shine, like a candle flame guttering, then saw that *Dawnfire* had gone quiet as well. "I guess we follow our instincts," he said and started down the corridor.

He didn't know if Shirisae was coming, until he caught a glimpse of the lady elf's red hair in the corner of his vision. Relief swept over him in the same moments a sudden fear began to fill his thoughts. There was something oppressive about the air in this place, something menacing. Whatever had drawn Alere here, Tristus would be thankful to find the elf and leave as quickly as possible.

◆ ◆ ◆ ◆ ◆

ALERE'S THOUGHTS WERE on the darkness that had swallowed him as he fled from his home years ago, a blackness so true as to negate all possibility of light, even that which sang from an enchanted blade. Once again *Aerkiren* was silent, stilled by the settling of 'true night' while Alere's wandering evidently led him nearer to the sword called *Behel*. He wondered now if this weapon had been present during the attack on his home, if Malek Vorhaven had led the strike himself, and if the Night Blade possessed a power more terrible than any Alere had previously imagined; the power to quell its sibling Swords.

To betray them, Alere considered. Xu Liang admitted himself that he did not know everything about the Celestial Blades. Just because they could not be brought openly against each other did not mean that they could not find other methods of combating. Perhaps Vorhaven had mastered his Sword and discovered this method.

Could any of the Swords truly be mastered? Alere wondered next. And if so, could an individual such as Malek Vorhaven, keeper of the Shadow Folk, be the intended bearer of the Night Blade? How could the Swords fight against chaos with agents of chaos possessing them? Or had Vorhaven not been the chosen bearer and been killed long ago, having attracted the keirveshen in overwhelming numbers? Perhaps he had not been controlling them at all.

Alere didn't have any answers, but he was beginning to feel a familiar fear rising in his heart, reaching outward, gripping at his lungs and making it difficult to breathe.

From one fancifully decorated, yet dismal room to the next ... out of one abandoned palatial environment into another, Alere moved through the manor. Everything was in order, clean as if tended to on a regular basis, yet it seemed not lived in. It was as if the master of the house had passed on years ago and the servants still carried out their duties as if in a trance, oblivious to their abandonment. It seemed that way, however Alere had yet to see a single servant. He was beginning to wonder just how long ago the gypsy had last visited this place.

In a bedroom with plush red carpet and a large bed with tall, spiral-carved posts, Alere decided to sit for a moment, and gain control of his thoughts. They, like him, had been wandering aimlessly, escaping the consuming fear by ignoring it. This feeling was a trick of the keirveshen. He'd felt it enough times before to know. It had nothing to do with Vorhaven, or the Night Blade.

"You've wasted your time. This place is abandoned except for a few lingering shadows. Dispose of them and be on your way."

Seconds after speaking the words to himself, someone entered the room, as if in direct contradiction.

Alere stood at once when the woman walked in. He gripped *Aerkiren* with the intention of slaying the intruder, and was scarcely inclined to change his mind upon seeing that the individual was a simple chamber maid. He knew better than to be deceived by appearances and there was something unsettling about this woman's aura, besides. It didn't help that she utterly failed to acknowledge him. She carried folded linen in her arms and came toward the bed, as if accustomed to attending to unexpected visitors and otherwise minding her own affairs.

Alere took a step toward her. "I have business with your lord. Tell me where I can find him."

She didn't even look at him. She continued forward and Alere put his hand out to stop her colliding into him. A dreadful sensation of cold racked his body, making him shudder when the woman passed through him. Claws of ice scored his soul, and he almost dropped his sword. He managed to clutch the hilt while he stumbled away, confusion attacking his senses.

Stabbing *Aerkiren* into the carpet, he dropped onto one knee and leaned against the sword, placing his hand over his heart as it throbbed violently in its cage. He'd been in the presence of more than one spirit, but he'd never had one pass through him before. It was a frightening experience, and almost a paralyzing one. The dread and confusion that resulted of direct contact between life and death threatened to take him over.

Alere fought for control, and regained it just in time to be aware of the voice that entered the room. It was a man, laughing. Alere looked for another dead servant, wanting to be out of its path if it should come through the door. He would wait for it to walk by him, then extinguish both spirits with *Aerkiren's* help, just as he had the wraiths he and the others encountered on the Flatlands. However, no other ghosts came. The voice continued, bodiless.

"This is amusing," the unseen man said. "I should like to watch you wander about for many more days in your vain search—perhaps years—but I am currently not feeling so patient. I have been expecting you, little elf. Come, entertain me with your plans of revenge. I should very much like to hear them as I watch you expire."

Alere glared at no one. "Are you Malek Vorhaven?" He scarcely waited for a reply. "Answer me!"

Again, the laughter. "You would make demands? An infant cut prematurely from the womb, starving for lack of a mother's milk, hoping to fill the deep emptiness in your stomach with whatever sustenance comes to you. Darkness brushes your lips and you draw it in, like a suckling foal, always hungry, always eager. Eager for revenge!"

"I will not be moved by your taunts," Alere informed the bodiless stranger. "You *are* Vorhaven. You are in league with the shadows!"

"In league with them?" the voice echoed. "My dear young hunter, I command them, as it is I who created them. The gypsy did not tell you everything, but come. Come to me, elf, and I shall reveal all to you!"

"Where?" Alere demanded.

No one answered.

Alere rose and stalked into the hallway, at once forgetting the ghost behind him. His determination was renewed. He would kill Malek Vorhaven. It didn't occur to him immediately that the man would have to be several centuries old to have been in any way responsible for the foul plague that had been turning men into demons well before his grandfather was born. Such a man would have to be either a very powerful sorcerer, who had used magic to lengthen his life, or no man at all. Thoughts of revenge—of finally ensuring the safety of what remained of his family and his people—blinded Alere to those considerations, as well as to the fact that *Aerkiren* had begun to sing once again.

Alere moved through the passages of the manor, accompanied by the glow of his Sword, like one bewitched ... and perhaps he had been. Somehow, he knew where to go. Somehow, he knew which turns and which doorways would take him to the architect of his nightmares. He was halfway across a carpeted bridge that spanned a grand ballroom, when an unexpected voice called up to him.

"Alere Shaederin! God in Heaven, I've been looking everywhere for you! I feel like I've been roaming through this forsaken house for days! What are you doing here?"

Alere glanced at the human beneath him, but his gaze quickly returned to his destination; a door on the other side of the bridge. He knew it would lead him to Vorhaven, to revenge against his father's killer. He had no time for the knight. Without so much as a word to Tristus, whose presence he scarcely wondered at in his trance, Alere pressed on.

◆ ◆ ◆ ◆ ◆

"WHERE IS HE going?" Tristus asked, looking for a way up to the bridge and quickly forgetting the matter when his search led him to discover that the ballroom he and Shirisae had entered only moments ago suddenly had no exit. He knew there was something horribly foul about this place—he'd felt the malevolence growing heavier with every step through the garishly lavish rooms that seemed to serve no one—but he was just beginning to feel real terror plying at his nerves now. "Shirisae, tell me you see a way out of here."

Again, he was ignored by an elf. Not only was he ignored, but both Alere and Shirisae had abandoned him as well. Neither of them were anywhere in sight. He stood alone on a sea of black and white tiles, dreading what this emptiness was leading to.

He knew better than to hope for loneliness. He had been alone already, and survived it. Loneliness was too pedestrian an assault now. The enemy in his mind—for surely he was dreaming now—would not rest until he was destroyed utterly, torn apart by anger and despair; the combined elements that awakened the darkness within him. He could feel it rising when the first of the armored figures found their way into a room that had no doors.

They simply appeared, rising through the floor, bleeding through the walls, taking up their assigned positions in the reenactment of a dark dream. It was a reality that had become dream, a haunting memory that could never be forgotten and, as Tristus had feared, it could never be escaped.

Helplessly, Tristus watched his fellow knights come, and felt the familiar sting of tears in his vision. "Please, God ... I can't do it again." He closed his eyes ... and heard the battle begin.

Begin? It continued, as it had continued for days. Warriors belonging to a pagan cult had been gathering near the Citadel, planning a strike against the Order, to be rid of it and its arrogance, as they deemed it. They brought strange weapons, as well as strange craft, weaving spells with their twisted staves that enabled them to move the trees and to take the forms of animals. They ambushed the knights that had gone into the forest to clear them out. Their numbers were greater than the Order anticipated. Reinforcements were slow coming. Knights were falling everywhere. Tristus' men were in a state of chaos, ignoring orders, panicking while men with the heads of wild boars came at them. The Order would later call it simple trickery, the result of illusions created by poisoned air. Illusions ... of men tearing out the throats of other men with the jaws of wolves?

It was no illusion to Tristus. The acrid stench of blood and fear was no hallucination, nor was the beating he took from the wild swings of a giant man with a bear's head. He felt each blow through his armor, as if it had cut through, but the pain was nothing compared to the terrible fear that assailed him when one of his own men knocked him back and confronted the beastly attacker in his place. The older man, without rank due to a lack of sponsorship—who was a greater knight than any in Andaria who could claim wealth or high family—managed to disarm the cultist. However, he learned quickly that his savage opponent needed no weapon in order to kill.

Tristus recalled himself trying to move and getting nowhere, as if the air had become mud. He could only watch while the beast's jaws clamped onto the other knight's neck, breaking it with a fierce crunch. Gerrick, his dear friend, was dead before he hit the ground.

Tristus dropped to his knees, reliving it. Pain quickly evolved to anger. *Curse you! Curse you, whatever you are! What right have you to attack us!*

'Us' became 'me'. The anger bored inward, running his blood hot, turning his thoughts red.

Murderers, all of you!

He found his sword. He would stop them. He would kill all of them, before they could kill him.

◆ ◆ ◆ ◆ ◆

TAYA HISSED AND pulled her hand away from Xu Liang's skin. She'd barely been able to get her palm on his forehead while he turned his head back and forth on the pillow. His body writhed beneath the bedding as he struggled, caught once again in a web of nightmare.

"He's at it again," Tarfan reported needlessly, standing behind Taya, who had to climb up onto the mattress to reach the mystic. "I thought Tristus said this part of his ordeal was over."

"He didn't say the nightmares were over," Taya replied, wringing her hand as if to be rid of the lingering heat. It felt as if Xu Liang's fever had leapt out of him and infected her as well. "Tristus said the worst of his ordeal appeared to be over. You weren't listening. Anyway, it doesn't matter now. He won't wake up. I'm worried."

"Let him be."

Both dwarves looked behind them, at the flame-haired priestess who had joined them in the vast chamber.

"Help him!" they both demanded at the same time.

Ahjenta shook her head. "I cannot. This is what happens when humans are exposed to the Flame. They do not trust it. They are afraid to embrace it. It is only because he wishes to live that he survives, but it may be some time before he is at peace again. It will always be worst when he sleeps, when his spirit wanders into the deepest chambers of his mind and heart, to the long passages of his memories and his dreams. The Flame accompanies him. It would guide him, if he would let it."

"Maybe you'd better explain this to him the next time he's awake," Tarfan growled.

"He would not understand," the priestess replied gently. "Besides, the dreams are not entirely his own."

"What do you mean?" Tarfan demanded.

"His spirit has wandered on its own, away from his body. It has reached others, and it reaches for them still while it searches vainly for some escape from what it perceives as madness and a threat to its existence. What your friend does not know is that this tunneling through the walls of his dreams leads him to no escape, but only to more dream."

"Is there some unwritten law you elves have against giving a straight answer?" Tarfan griped, and he may have had more to say, but Taya didn't listen, drawn suddenly to Xu Liang when he began to speak.

"Stop them," he murmured weakly. "They're ... killing every—no, don't! Not that way. Why are you here? Why ... are you still here?"

Taya stared at him with pity, wishing she had some way to help, but she was far from even seeing the horrors Xu Liang saw, let alone doing anything to quiet such visions.

◆ ◆ ◆ ◆ ◆

XU LIANG'S SPIRIT moved ever away from his body, through the half-darkened passages of his nightmare, and somehow out of them. He emerged in a large rectangular chamber. The walls still looked shadowed in his eyes and the jade fire remained overhead, but it was higher now, and beneath him was a floor of black and white. The killing was over. Where he had once seen grass and trees, and men in armor falling beneath the fangs and claws of wild beasts, he now saw an empty room. The battle that had summoned him toward this place was done.

No, it was not done. A body slumped before Xu Liang, trembling as it reached for the weapon beside it. The knight was slowly rising off his knees, shuddering as the battle waged on inside of him, delighting the fiend that still resided within him, goading him to fight and to keep on fighting until nothing remained but a sea of blood, lapping at his feet.

How did I get here? Xu Liang wondered belatedly. *How could my spirit project itself to this place? Why? Is it because of you?*

Xu Liang looked at Tristus, who had begun stepping away from him, and saw someone else, the figure of a man who looked more elven than human, and more demon than elven. His hands clutched the spear, dousing its fire with his own flame. It was one of cruelty and rage in its purest form.

Xu Liang remembered, and he reached out, grasping the knight by the shoulder. "No, I will not allow this."

The demonic figure screamed at the mystic's touch, pulling forward almost with desperation while Tristus stepped away from it, and immediately collapsed to his knees. He dropped *Dawnfire* and began to weep.

The dark figure wheeled around, howling in rage. It escaped Xu Liang's grasp. "You cannot take him from me! He is mine!" And then it turned and threw itself forward, diving slowly back into the knight.

◆ ◆ ◆ ◆ ◆

TRISTUS WAS weeping.

Shirisae had strayed several paces ahead of him and turned to see him on his hands and knees, *Dawnfire* lying on the floor just within reach. He might have had a chance if the shadows came, if he could compose himself in time to fend them off.

Shirisae, unsure what the matter was, set aside sympathy for safety. She said sternly, "Stop that and get up. We have delivered ourselves to an enemy and must remain alert."

Tristus didn't stop. His body shuddered as the sobs escaped.

She had never known a man who could shed his emotions so freely. It touched her, even as it angered her. She took a step toward him and repeated her instructions, more gently this time.

"Just leave me alone," the knight said miserably. "Leave me alone. You'll never understand. You'll never know how I feel."

She was inflicted with the desire to go to him, as she had been numerous times before, and—as before—she resisted. Her care for this gentle human would not let her coddle to him. Something ill was afoot in this house and if they let their guard down they would both die. "Pick up your spear and get on your feet," she insisted.

He only lifted his hand to his face and continued to weep.

Shirisae's frustration mounted. She began to wonder at the reality of what she believed she was witnessing.

And that was when the mystic arrived—out of nowhere—and knelt beside Tristus. He put his hands on the knight's shoulders and frowned with disapproval at Shirisae. "Let him be. He is right. You'll never understand. You scarcely understand your own feelings."

Shirisae lifted her chin indignantly, not as awed in this man's presence as others seemed to be. "How dare you? You, who'd be lost if not for me."

"I am lost *because* of you," Xu Liang returned, speaking in quiet, overly patient tones, as if he were regarding a child. "I gave my life to save his, and you brought me back to serve your own selfish desires. Your attraction to him is a passing whim, and I am made to suffer for it. Leave him alone. It is the very least you can do at this point."

Shirisae scowled at him. "Don't glorify your deed, mystic! You saved him to spare your conscience. I've seen the way you behave toward him. You don't love him!"

The mystic's delicate brow creased. "Don't presume to speak my love to me. It runs far deeper than the girlish emotions, which currently guide you on a fool's path. My love is for an empire, for the land that gave it and the people a foundation. I live for the safety and prosperity of that land and its people ... and yet I threw my life away for one person." His gaze lowered to the floor and he drew the knight almost unconsciously toward him, absently cradling Tristus' head while the young man leaned into him, weeping softly. "I must now reflect on the deed, and suffer its consequences for your petty interest in a reckless and troublesome young man."

Shame filled her too quickly. "I brought you back because I couldn't bear to see him suffer ... not to ingratiate myself with him." The words sounded like a lie. She looked to *Firestorm* for support, but its light was dim and cold. "How can this be? You have chosen him. You brought us together."

"Yes, the Blades brought us together," Xu Liang said. "All of us. We, as the bearers of these weapons are inclined to follow their calling, but the emotions are our own. For some of us they may be difficult to understand. For others of us they are all too clear. They exist. That is all that matters, and we cannot let them divide us."

Shirisae looked at the mystic with tears glistening in her golden eyes. "Us ... or the Swords?"

"Us," Xu Liang answered emphatically. "The Swords on their own are little more than artifacts. The bearers distinguish them and activate their powers. We must understand those unique powers and use them together, harmoniously. As day balances night and contrariwise; we must achieve that same balance amongst ourselves. If we do not, this chaos will continue to grow, until it swallows everything. The heart of it beats beneath Sheng Fan. There, we must put it to rest. Then your people will be given a new beginning, a life free of the demons that plague them now."

"No," Shirisae argued. "The keirveshen are not merely spirits. They will continue to exist, whether or not your problems in your homeland are resolved. You would use us for your own purposes."

The mystic frowned. "I set out to use the Swords. I realize now that I must unite with their bearers. Yes, it is true that the keirveshen will always exist, but they flourish in the madness which radiates from my homeland. They become stronger with its awakening, taking advantage of the fear already in all of our hearts. They are being helped by one of our own. As the Moon Blade calms and protects, the Night Blade enshrouds and attacks. It attacks the mind and stirs our darkest thoughts. It is a terrible power, but one that can be governed. A malicious will governs it now and would lure all of you to destruction, if you let it."

Shirisae watched the exotically fair man, holding the knight, whom she had inexplicably fallen in love with upon the moment she and D'mitri spied him with the others. She believed that *Firestorm* had explained everything to her when it glowed so brilliantly in his presence. Now she was uncertain as to any explanation for it, but her love remained just the same. She would not let him be taken here. She would protect him, somehow, but...

"How can you know these things?" she asked the mystic. "Has your spirit left your body again? Would you risk such a feat, knowing it would undo what the Phoenix has done, what it was barely capable of doing and could never do again?"

As Shirisae watched, the Fanese man changed. He seemed to grow smaller and somehow fairer. His blue and violet robes paled, becoming faint, almost pearlescent with shimmering silver threads forming wondrous images that glittered like the stars. The color of the robes reminded Shirisae of the glow given off by the mystic's slender blade. The pleasingly round face that stared out of that radiance was not Xu Liang's. It was the face of a young woman, her black hair bound up with many strands of shimmering beads.

"There is so much pain," the woman said, her voice soft and melodic. "I wish that I could shelter you all from it, always, but that is not possible. It is in your nature to face this pain, whether you can defeat it or not."

"Who... are you?" Shirisae asked, mystified by the presence of such a radiant being as this. She could not have been real. "Where is Xu Liang?"

The pale woman did not answer. She slipped carefully away from Tristus, who slumped in miserable silence, then rose gracefully to her feet. She took three tiny steps, then knelt beside *Dawnfire*. Pressing her delicate hands together, she closed her eyes and seemed to utter a prayer. The spear answered at once, glowing so intensely that Shirisae had to close her eyes.

When she opened them again, the young woman was on her feet once more. A man with long platinum-blond hair, wearing golden robes that seemed to blush with an iridescent red hue, was kneeling before her, his head bowed.

"Your brother needs you," the woman said to him politely. "You must try harder."

"Yes," the man replied obediently. "I will do all within my power to meet your expectations."

The radiant woman looked at Shirisae next and smiled sweetly when she said, "You must let him go. I understand that it is difficult, sister, but your duty must come first."

Shirisae was struck speechless by these words.

The woman suddenly beside her, however—a slim figure with braided black hair, wearing a long silver tunic with big sleeves, loose-fitting black pants, and tiny black shoes—had much to say. "If we can find a way to be together, why won't you allow it? We have been apart so long, I cannot bear to see him this close and not be permitted to reach out for him."

"I understand," the more delicate of the two women replied peacefully. "I too have been reunited with my love, and unable to reach him. It is a price we must pay to fulfill our obligation to the Master. As well we must remember that these lives are ours only to guide, not to control. Their hearts must be allowed to move freely, wherever they should like them to go."

The woman in silver and black was silent for a moment, seeming almost resentful. At length she put her hands together and bowed at the waist. "Forgive me. I shall continue to serve loyally."

The other inclined her head in reply. The man in bright robes, who had been silent and motionless through their discussion, lifted his head and cast a quick, longing glance at the woman beside Shirisae. Then he emanated a familiar golden glow and vanished, presumably back into the spear that seemed to be keeping his spirit. In the next second, the woman beside Shirisae had gone as well and she was left facing the radiant being that could only have transcended from the beautiful blade carried by Xu Liang.

That being bowed to Shirisae. "Forgive me for having interrupted you. I will leave you now."

Shirisae blinked, and the woman was gone, as was Tristus. She quickly looked about and found that the knight was not actually gone, but that he had gotten to his feet at some point and wandered to the wall to her left, where he leaned against the bottom corner of an enormous tapestry, looking weak and exhausted. Shirisae felt as if she had awakened from a dream and couldn't remember half of what went on in that dream, but she did recall something about the Night Blade being in the wrong hands.

"Shirisae," Tristus gasped, clutching *Dawnfire* like a frightened child clung to a parent. "We have to get out of here. I can't control what may happen if we don't."

Shirisae recalled the power the knight had unleashed in order to rescue *Firestorm* and *Aerkiren*. She had seen the mystic use his spiritual powers to calm Tristus afterward. He had stilled the rage, but apparently he had not banished it. Whatever dark thoughts attacked Tristus' mind now, if they reached the darker force within him, Shirisae would not be able to fend him off without killing him. Knowing that she might fail in that task, she agreed that it was best to get out from under whatever influence was trying to pin them down.

TWENTY-SİX

The Night Blade

ALERE WENT THROUGH the door at the end of the bridge and emerged from the house, onto a large balcony overlooking a thick mist. He could not see the ground from his position, and knew by the feel of the stone ledge, as well as the look of it—it was wide enough for fifty elves to stand across it—that such an addition was not connected to the original house. This was a castle. As he determined that, it began to snow. He stepped away from the door and turned slowly to find it gone. A deep hall faced him, filled with shadows and grand marble pillars. The house of Vorhaven seemed to shift perception of all things, even of time and of physical space.

"Where are you?" Alere growled into the emptiness. "Show yourself!"

"Come," the voice insisted. "I am not far. I have never been far from you, elf. I have shadowed your steps from the moment you took up your father's sword."

Someone touched Alere's shoulder. "Don't. Don't go any further. This is what he wants. He's in your mind, Alere. He's worse than I remembered him. Much worse."

Alere's eyes narrowed, and he turned his head slowly to face Bastien Crowe. A vicious scowl formed on his lips. "Take your hand off me."

The gypsy's hold tightened. "Listen! He will do to you what he did to me. He will take your precious sword and cast you into oblivion! I spent seven months of my life wandering without direction or purpose. I scarcely recalled my own name at times! How are you going to avenge your parents with all focus and will diminished? Or maybe he'll just kill you. Would that comfort you, Alere, to know in your final moments that you'd failed, and that one of your young cousins inherited your quest for revenge?"

"Why do you care?" Alere snarled. "If this is in my mind, how did you get here? Why should I trust my eyes where you are concerned and not this place?"

"Damn it! You're not listening! This place is real, but he—Vorhaven is in your mind, luring you, positioning you where he needs you to be, so that he can—"

"No!" Alere shirked Bastien's hand away. "I would more readily believe that you are trying to delay me! I will tell you only once, gypsy. Do not interfere!"

"You fool!" Bastien put himself directly into Alere's path. "This is not the way! I know what he did to your family, but you can't let those memories control you now!"

Alere was prepared to move the gypsy from his path, by whatever means necessary. However, something else cleared the way for him.

There was no time to react as the shadows came forth and dug their claws into Bastien, not shredding, but grasping and hooking. They dragged the gypsy away unable to scream while their black, skeletal hands covered his face, leaving only his horrified eyes to be seen as he was borne away, into the hall and up toward the ceiling.

"His services are no longer required," said the bodiless voice of the shadows' master.

"Services?" Alere echoed, scanning the darkness carefully. It proved futile. He saw nothing.

"He believed that the Brotherhood reassigned him after his disappearance," Vorhaven explained. "Searching for information concerning the other Swords was my idea. I was deeper into his thoughts than even he knew. Disappointing, that he could not lure all of the bearers to me, but I understand there were certain… complications."

Alere scowled with disgust. "Show yourself!"

"Come, elf," Vorhaven persisted. "Come willingly or be carried, like the gypsy. Of course, how thoughtless of me. You prefer a fight, don't you? Very well, then, Alere Shaederin. Cut your way to me. I shall be waiting, as I always have been… at the end of your nightmares."

A thousand yellow eyes lit in the darkness, all of them looking at Alere, who suddenly heard the fearful weeping of his young cousins as he ushered them through the blackness years ago, his hand gripping a weapon he scarcely knew how to use. A cold wind sent the snow swirling about him. His cloak flapped like a banner stuck in the battlefield; tattered, dusty, and blood-stained.

Would this war never end? Could the end be lying at the other side of this hall?

Alere firmed his grip on the hilt of Morgen Shaederin's sword. "*Lothve*, Aerkiren," he begged softly, then went forward, into the awaiting shadows.

◆ ◆ ◆ ◆ ◆

"MADNESS," TRISTUS PANTED, putting an exhaustive mental effort into each step while his control teetered dangerously on the edge. He commanded his body at the moment, but he felt the rage that was always inside of him, tracing his spine with the cutting edge of its undying anger. "This place ... is a labyrinth."

"Come," Shirisae said gently. "We are at the bridge Alere crossed."

The Phoenix Elf reached out as if to pull Tristus along, and he withdrew from contact quickly.

He put out one hand to ward her back. "No. Don't touch me." Though the look on her face was calm and patient, he felt as if he'd startled and offended her. He withdrew his hand to massage his tensed features, pushing back his hair afterward. "I know you mean well, Shirisae. I would accept your help, my lady, but ... but the one inside me, whoever it is—whatever it is—would take you as a threat. Please, try to understand."

Shirisae remained collected, and said, "You do not fight this force alone. He is helping you."

Tristus looked at her. He knew better than to think that she was referring to God, but who ... who had he been leaning against in his dream of the past? He remembered he was on the verge of reenacting the slaughter. Someone stopped him. And then Shirisae told him to get up. Someone knelt beside him afterward, consoled him with a gentle touch. He didn't look to see who, and he hadn't recognized the voice. All he could hear was the rage beneath his despair, still trying to take him over.

"Come," Shirisae beckoned gently, and she started across the carpeted bridge.

Tristus followed, not too quickly. Halfway across the bridge he felt a moment's peace, and the sensation that someone was behind him. He looked and saw no one, but for an instant he was sure that he descried voices in the silence, whispers of a conversation taking place in another world, creeping into this one as a draft slides through a closed window on a winter night. It did not seem a friendly conversation. It would not have surprised Tristus to learn that ghosts roamed the passages of this house.

The thought chilled him, and he moved on across the bridge, seeking support from the railing when the dark weight of the madness inside of him came down once again.

No one's trying to hurt you, he said to himself. *Look at Shirisae. She is safe. She will not turn against you. It's this house, making you feel unsafe, but it cannot hurt you. Houses don't attack people. It's all in your mind.*

He tightened his grip on *Dawnfire*, felt its magical warmth through his glove, and pressed on. He didn't know what would happen if they were attacked, but he wouldn't leave Shirisae alone, and he was sure that he had gone too deep into the house to find his way back, besides.

We have to find Alere. Once we find Alere we can leave.

◆ ◆ ◆ ◆ ◆

BODIES LITTERED THE floor. The dark blood of the keirveshen coated the marble pillars with a wet, slimy sheen. Somehow, the elf remained white against the sea of blackness, alive against the mounds of death. His blade glowed violet in the dark, untainted. The Blade, like the elf, knew little of fear and nothing of boundaries. There was a way to succeed against all odds, no matter how terrible they seemed. Once again, *Aerkiren* and its bearer had demonstrated that.

Vorhaven was impressed. He sat back upon his throne in the great hall within the palace of his forefathers, smiling as his thumb glided over the pommel of a long, broad blade, whose tip rested against the floor at his feet. The metal appeared black, obsidian, almost as if it had been forged of stone instead of metal. An energy radiated from it, like tendrils of black mist, forming intangible fists that squeezed and choked the light around it.

"He has come to take you from me, *Behel*," Vorhaven murmured. "I will not allow it. The elf will not have you and take from me my solace; my world that you have helped me to reshape. How many centuries have I existed in night without understanding it? How long have I hidden myself in the shadows, sheltered beneath my children ... lost in my study? I was a negligent parent. My children ran wild and without purpose, without direction. You have changed me, *Behel*. You have made me understand. I know what must be done ... and no elf will stop me. Though they have tried for centuries, they have always and will always end in failure. Just like the Brotherhood."

Focusing on the elf now, he projected his voice. "The Brotherhood believes only in silencing. Others have discovered *Behel's* power and it almost killed them. They were unfit. I am able to fully understand *Behel* ... to bond with it, one might say. I can use it to restore order to this land."

"By creating demons?" the elf answered in disgust, finally coming forward, out of the black death behind him.

"The keirveshen were not intentional," Vorhaven answered, regarding the pale creature before him with as much admiration as hate. "As you may know, all plagues require carriers. I happen to be such a carrier, an individual who twists and ruins all that he touches, but who remains perpetually unaffected."

He stood calmly, dressed in the fine clothes he was entitled to wear as a member of the Vorhaven family, head of a broken, scattered household. Beneath the dark velvet and white lace was an ancient man of diseased beauty, held forever in the soft skin of his youth while his mind and spirit decayed. He'd watched his world become shadow.

One by one, his family, his friends, his lovers ... all who did not flee his curse were inflicted by it, transformed into hideous variations of the monster Malek Vorhaven saw each time he dared to look into a mirror. He could not honestly remember when or why this curse had befallen him, but he did know one thing with maddening certainty. "Elves are not susceptible, of course."

As he spoke the words, a piece of his memory flashed at the front of his mind, like a shard of broken glass turned into the light.

Elves ... long had they been the source of his envy and his hatred. Yes, he remembered now. It was her. He could still see the elf maid in the forest, looking like a ghost against the snow, white from head to toe... perfect. Her beauty was crisp and clear, as a field of freshly fallen snow, untrod upon, unsoiled. Her purpose so near to Eishencroe was a mystery to Malek, but the sensation he felt in his heart was not. He'd fallen in love with her, instantly. He would make her his, somehow... but the look of scorn in her luminous gray eyes when she looked at him!

Malek knew he was not ugly—far from it—but she made him feel like a wretched, vile creature, crawled up out of some stinking bog to attack her. There were no words to describe his fury. It overwhelmed him, and ultimately he did attack her. Sadly, his skill as a swordsman was no match for her inhuman quickness. She slashed him across the face with her slender, elven blade, and justified her disgust by making him ugly. Malek returned home in a darker, quieter rage, determined to have his revenge.

Against his father's wishes—for he was not old enough nor skilled enough—he sought the power of his house, the secret spells of his family that enabled them to rule the region. The people were too afraid to stand against them. The elves would be afraid now as well, and he would have the woman who dared to cut him.

The wound burned as perspiration entered it. He touched his cheek absently while he continued to consume the powers of the ancient tome locked in his father's private library. He had entered without permission and read fast to avoid being caught, knowing that he would be no match for his father in a test of sorcery. He was looking for a spell to satisfy his hatred. He left the library angrier than before, certain that he had failed. While he'd taken in the magic, he'd cast no spell, finding nothing that suited his plans for revenge. His thoughts only grew darker in the time that followed.

It was during the Autumn Feast, when all the members of his house gathered to celebrate the harvest and the turning of the seasons, that his cousin of sixteen—blossoming as all young Vorhavens did, with beauty and arrogance—looked upon Malek and made mention of his scar.

He glared viciously at the girl, reminded at once of the appalled look on the elf woman's face. He could no longer remember what he said to his cousin, only how he felt, the anger that became a twisted satisfaction as the girl's fair image putrefied before his eyes. Shadow consumed her. It poisoned her flesh and ravaged her soul, leaving a demon in its wake. A foul creature that leapt over the dinner table to make a feast of the horrified observer seated across from it.

Vorhaven smiled at the elf responsible for reminding him of that. "You are as handsome as she was beautiful, hunter. You remind me of her, your gray eyes looking at me with a similar disgust. Do not worry. You shall not be forced to look upon me long. Death will blind you."

The elf did not seem threatened, but he also did not attack. "You know the Blade I hold," Alere Shaederin said. "Do you also know what will happen if it crosses with yours?"

"*Aerkiren*," Vorhaven purred. "Sky of dusk; twilight … the passing of day into night. I didn't need *Behel* to be rid of your father, Alere." He smiled as the elf tensed visibly. "I don't see why I'll need it for you either. Elves guard their minds better than most, but that is because they are often guarding the most terrible secrets. Fears and nightmares they have had too many centuries to accumulate. I realize you are young yet, hunter, but I know what scares you."

"You know nothing," Alere said.

"Give me *Aerkiren*," Vorhaven said. "And I will end your life quickly. It is more than I offered your friends."

"They are here, then," the elf replied, as if to confirm the matter to himself. Surely, he had seen them in the manor.

Vorhaven smiled as the elf's secret thoughts became his own. They were not his friends. Alere despised the Phoenix Elves, and all other elves, who had failed to assist their own kind during their direst hour. He needed someone to blame, unaware of how it was one of his own who had brought the shadows down upon the Verres mountains, through simple arrogance. As to humans, such as the young knight who had followed him here, Alere remained undecided. Vorhaven found that interesting, but it was too little, too late. This elf's changing perception of humans could not make up for the unfounded contempt of his ancestors.

"The fools came here almost more eagerly than you," Vorhaven finally said. "I'll have their weapons as well, when the berserker finishes with the elf woman, and when my pets have finished with him."

Alere foolishly tried to hide his concern by not displaying it. Vorhaven knew, however, that it was in his thoughts. Still, the elf continued with his bravado. "You haven't enough shadows here to deal with a man who feels only rage. If you have provoked him, you have only succeeded in drawing out Ilnon. A true berserker is the living embodiment of the god of rage and vengeance. He will tear this house apart, and everything in it."

"Even if that's true, it won't be your concern," Vorhaven told him. "Give my regards to your father if your wandering spirit should happen upon his at any time."

More shapes came out of the darkness that enshrouded the hall. Vorhaven watched them surge toward the lone white figure, then sat down upon his throne once again and closed his eyes, laughing to himself. He'd not been so entertained in years.

Let the berserker tear apart the house. Let him bury himself alive. He'll calm down quickly enough as he suffocates beneath the rubble and rebuilding the house will give me something to do. I will have four of the six Swords. I will have the strength to stamp out the elves of Yvaria at last. And then I will head south, claiming the cousins of the Verressi next.

The Eastern sorcerer had done well. The Blades came, as he believed they would, once Vorhaven concentrated his efforts on finding them. He had only to wait for the Moon Blade to be delivered. The Sun Blade would remain in Sheng Fan, but five would be enough—and he had only bargained with one dragon anyway. It would take more than one shadow beast—no matter how powerful it happened to be—to wrest a coveted treasure from a royal family's stubborn grip.

He heard Alere before him, introducing the shadows to *Aerkiren* before making his final stand against them. There were too many of them. Try as he might, he was only one elf, and he could not last forever.

"Bastien!"

The young knight's voice elsewhere in the house drew Vorhaven out of his thoughts. They must have found the gypsy. Evidently, his pets had finished with him and the others had come upon the remains.

How bothersome. Tristus Edainien should have been hacking Shirisae to pieces by now. That he wasn't, spoke well for his resolve ... something Vorhaven hadn't considered one of the knight's stronger aspects. Still, his young mind was so open ... .as easy to read as the pages of a book.

TRISTUS DIDN'T KNOW what to think as he looked upon the

gypsy. He believed the man dead long ago. To find his body here
made him wonder if this was also in his mind, part of the dreams the
master of this place used as a twisted form of entertainment for his
unwanted guests. He closed his eyes and opened them again, horrified to find the gypsy's broken, shredded body still lying on the floor
just inside the dark hall he and Shirisae had entered.

"Do you know him? He looks familiar."

Tristus shook his head as Shirisae arrived beside him. "His name
was Bastien. I ... didn't know him well. He traveled with us, but disappeared during a battle with men from Sheng Fan. We thought
he was dead. In fact, ..." Tristus swallowed with effort. "No one was
certain whether or not I had been the one to kill him ... in my..."

"In your psychotic rage?"

Tristus started, looking everywhere for the voice, that was not
Shirisae's. The lady elf had left him again, else he had left her, gone
once again into the dark recesses of his mind where the killer
waited behind a flimsy cage door to be let out. Tristus had barely
managed to maintain control throughout this ordeal of the mind.
Recently, he tried thinking of Xu Liang while he clutched *Dawnfire*.
The mystic was the only person who had been able to calm him,
and he'd felt blessed whenever the spear was in his possession. The
combination of two such strengthening forces proved to be just
enough. However, the past was also strong ... and the warmth and
security provided by the mystic and *Dawnfire* were slowly beginning to slip. Fortunately, there didn't seem to be anyone around to
be concerned with killing. Whoever had spoken to him seemed just
as suddenly to be gone.

And that was when Bastien rose from the floor, only it wasn't
the gypsy. The form that lifted from the red, pooling blood was no
battered corpse. The figure stood tall and moved with an ease and
grace that stole Tristus' breath. Dark, almond-shaped eyes regarded
him gently. Tristus knew better. He knew Xu Liang was not here,
but he stared helplessly at the image of the mystic, healthy again
and so beautiful.

Tristus felt weak in his shock, and took a step back to avoid
falling down.

Xu Liang hesitated, angling his lovely head thoughtfully. "Do I alarm you, Tristus Edainien?"

"Y-yes," Tristus stammered. Then he shook his head. "No. I mean ... I don't..."

The smallest of smiles formed on the mystic's lips. "I knew you were a person worthy of my trust. The others would have abandoned me, but you stayed."

Tristus wanted to speak on behalf of the others, but he couldn't bring himself to contradict Xu Liang at this moment. He was mystified in his presence, so relieved to see him well, to see that he wasn't angry with him.

The mystic came forward again, and Tristus stood frozen, seeing something in Xu Liang's eyes that frightened him as much as it thrilled him. Could Shirisae have been right? Was there some chance that Xu Liang could love him?

This can't be true, Tristus argued with himself. *This can't...*

Xu Liang came within an arm's reach. He took two more small steps, then stopped, standing so near that Tristus felt enveloped in his presence. His heart rattled and his breath faltered.

"You are alarmed," the mystic noted quietly, reaching out. He carefully touched Tristus' face, letting his cool fingers glide down to his chin. "I've seen the longing in your eyes," he whispered and Tristus began to tremble uncontrollably. "I know what is in your heart ... for it is in mine as well."

Tristus couldn't believe his ears, nor did he trust his aching body, filled with so much love and desire that he almost collapsed. Something wasn't right. Xu Liang was too proud to come to him like this. He wouldn't ...

The mystic interrupted the thought with his continued approach. Tristus closed his eyes, held by what he wanted, over what he believed to be possible. He could feel the warmth of Xu Liang's lips before they touched him, just before a sensation of wrong that was too great to ignore jolted him alert.

He snapped back, devastated by the shocked and angry look on Xu Liang's face as he did the unthinkable in rejecting him.

And then his world came to a horrifying halt, when he realized that the source of Xu Liang's anger was not his rejection, but an attack from Alere, who'd come out of nowhere and driven *Aerkiren* through the mystic's back. Tristus was screaming, even as the image shattered, revealing a young man with a scar across his left cheek in Xu Liang's place.

Tristus sank to the floor afterward, too confused to be angry—too horrified to be consumed by the fire within him. His condition only worsened when the stranger turned with Alere's blade still in him and seized the elf by the throat.

"It would seem that I underestimated you," the man said, his breath forming red bubbles through the blood on his lips. With his other hand he lifted his own black sword and braced the tip against Alere's chest.

Tristus moved without thinking. Lurching forward, he swung *Dawnfire* in a low arc and swept the man's feet out from under him. As the stranger fell, he dropped Alere, who managed not to fall on his opponent's sword, or his own, which now stuck farther out of the man's chest after he landed on his back.

Tristus rose quickly to pin the stranger, who refused death.

"He has the Night Blade!" the elf choked, and Tristus quickly lifted *Dawnfire* away from the man, who was raising his own weapon as if to display the fact Alere had given.

"Yes," he chuckled, sitting up.

An unseen force seemed to be pushing Tristus further off him while his attention was on keeping the Blades from coming against one another.

"And now … I have the Twilight Blade as well." The man rose slowly, keeping his opponents at bay with the black blade extended. "Give me the Dawn Blade, boy, and I will allow you to live out your days in a blissful dream state. Spend your last hours in arms that will never love you in life. If you force me to take the Blade, I will make certain your death is a long, miserable torture."

"Don't listen to him," Alere warned.

"I know," Tristus returned, unable to take offense at the elf's estimate of his resolve. He was too absorbed in wondering how to kill a man that wouldn't die, who was backing away from both of them slowly.

In the next instant, a dagger shot through the air, like a bolt of silver light.

The man lifted the Night Blade in front of him in response, and the eerie energy looming about the weapon caught the projectile, swiftly turning it about and sending it back to the elf who had thrown it.

Alere flinched aside, clutching his arm after the dagger glided past his shoulder. "If you are so confident, why don't you finish us now?"

The stranger laughed. "You cannot provoke me! I have you where I want you, elf! I know you will not leave here without your precious *Aerkiren*! Perhaps in a hundred years, I will let you look upon it again, as it does to you what it has done to me. I doubt, however, that you will survive that moment."

Tristus had heard and seen enough. He stood, dropped *Dawnfire* on the floor, and stepped confidently toward the stranger. While the man looked on in amusement, Tristus drew his sword of the Order, and held it calmly in front of him. He said evenly, "You are going nowhere. Your game has ended."

The man spat blood on him. "You have chosen a slow death, boy!"

Tristus wiped the spittle away from his cheek with his glove, keeping his eyes on the man … or whatever his state made him. He was expecting the attack that followed, but he was unprepared for the transformation that preceded it.

Within seconds, the form of the man peeled away, like a snake's shed skin, leaving the grotesque image of a demon with eyes that instantly terrified. He knew too well where he had seen those eyes before. He stared helplessly while the man stood straight, displaying his full height—which now easily matched Fu Ran's—then flexed leathery wings, snapping them out of their fold against his back and making the glowing blade that protruded from his chest more apparent.

The demon came forward in a rushed series of strokes that Tristus found himself hard-pressed to beat back. He felt the energy of each blow. He heard it strike a dull ring in his ears. The sound made his skull ache while the force of the attack soundly tested his endurance. The beast was driving him back with the Night Blade, and with its strength, and with the madness in its haunting yellow eyes.

Tristus passed beneath a doorway and became briefly aware of the outdoors as snowflakes landed on his face, but his concentration remained on the demon and the Night Blade, which struck chords of terror deep within him with every blow. He saw only the demon's hellish gaze, and acted with unconscious instinct when it dealt a blow that sent him reeling backward.

He reached out and grabbed hold of the demon's wing. It issued a soul-rending shriek, adding Tristus' heart to the rush of organs seeming to crowd in his throat, strangling his scream as he toppled over the balcony railing … toward the mist below, through a heavy orange haze, and into the dark, stinking water beneath it.

✦ ✦ ✦ ✦ ✦

ALERE STRUGGLED TO his feet, touching his aching throat, as if the contact would make it easier to swallow after Vorhaven's near crushing grip. He hadn't been expecting such strength, but now it was all clear. Vorhaven himself was a demon. He was different from the others, but he had not been unaffected by his own curse. Perhaps he had simply refused to accept it. Whatever the case, it hardly mattered now. The demon had just gone over the edge of the balcony with Tristus. It would surely kill the knight if the fall didn't.

Alere retrieved *Dawnfire* and hurried toward the balcony, emerging outside just as Shirisae did the same. He could not say where she had come from, where she had been while Tristus was being attacked by Vorhaven's mind tricks, but he had no time to question. Their surroundings altered again when they arrived at the balustrade.

They found themselves on a smaller balcony now, one overlooking the bog in front of the stone house in the Deepwood. Alere watched without displaying the apprehension he felt as the foul water stirred below. Shirisae appeared to be doing the same in the corner of his vision.

The knight eventually surfaced, but he was not alone.

✦ ✦ ✦ ✦ ✦

TRISTUS CLAWED HIS way to firmer ground ahead of the demon, gasping for air, grabbing up fistfuls of mud and snow. Something grabbed his leg. He turned over and kicked, shocked almost to stillness, seeing what his boot drove into. The giant serpent—eyeless and nearly without features—pulled back one of more than a dozen whip-like tendrils reflexively, then began flailing the many overlong limbs about in a blind search for its prey. A round mouth at the top end was open wide, displaying many circular rows of long, narrow teeth.

A strangled gasp of disbelief escaped Tristus, and he began to push himself away from the water's edge, horrified as the tendrils snaked onto land and wound about him. He found his dagger and began to slash at the slick black appendages, forcing the worm to moan when it bled, and eventually to recoil, but not before it successfully dragged him half into the bog again. Tristus dug his arms into the cold, soft earth and the worm ultimately submerged without its intended meal.

The surface of the water never quite stilled in the moment's respite that followed. Tristus thought for an instant that the worm had come back when a black form broke the slimy surface and shot into the sky. He realized as the lean, muscular shape came down on him that it was the demon. It landed hard, pinning him beneath its weight and one clawed hand, which clamped viciously around his throat. The other arm raised its obsidian blade above its head.

"Die!" the demon commanded, and Tristus thought that he might oblige it, before the creature's head suddenly flew off its shoulders.

The body slumped forward immediately afterward, driving the Night Blade into the wet earth beside Tristus' head while it retained its grip on the weapon, even in death. The tip of *Aerkiren* struck Tristus' breastplate, but did not penetrate.

Tristus was thanking God, even as the demon's reeking life fluid washed over his armor, staining it black. He realized when a shadow fell over him, that God was not who he needed to be thanking just at the moment—not God alone, at any rate.

Guang Ci stabbed his sword into the earth, jerked *Aerkiren* out of the demon's back with a determined twist, then placed the Blade down and silently began lifting the dead shadow beast off of Tristus.

Tristus helped when his limbs were free, and accepted the body-guard's assistance to his feet after they rolled the foul corpse into the bog. Something, presumably the worm, rolled just beneath the surface afterward, perhaps to claim the remains of the demon for itself.

Tristus bent over when his stomach protested the excitement along with the stench of the bog and of the demon. He braced his hands on his knees and concentrated strictly on breathing for several moments.

"Guang Ci," he said eventually. Even knowing the guard's under-standing ended there, he continued. "I owe you my life. Please accept my thanks."

The guard scarcely regarded him. The Fanese man swiftly picked up a sword and placed himself in front of Tristus while several dark shapes sank through the fiery haze that had been cast just above them by the torches.

Tristus straightened slowly, still finding it difficult to breathe normally. The fear that had never left him renewed itself full, though it was swiftly being overshadowed by utter exhaustion. "God ... have mercy."

God did not seem to be listening. In a heartbeat, the keirveshen were on them.

Tristus searched for a weapon. He was about to reach for *Aerkiren* when its rightful bearer hollered down at him from the balcony. Tristus looked in time to see *Dawnfire* soaring in his direction. He reached out and somehow managed to catch the weapon single-handedly. He considered returning the favor, but when he looked back to the balcony, he saw Alere vaulting over the railing.

The elf landed lightly, almost catlike, on his feet. Tristus threw Alere his Blade, just in time for him to wield it against an eager pair of winged demons. A quick glance let him know that Shirisae would be facing her opponents on the balcony. Tristus wished he could be up there to help her, but he realized quickly enough that she did not require his assistance—and he had his own troubles on the ground, besides.

The yard in front of the house quickly filled, as though every shadow cast by the flickering torches had suddenly come to life and all were bent on avenging their master's death. Tristus set to work surviving the upcoming moments, praying that his friends would be able to do the same.

◆ ◆ ◆ ◆ ◆

XU LIANG OPENED his eyes, but did not move. He clung to the dream as it left him, thinking of the details deliberately, storing them away before they could escape forever. Much of the nightmare had already fled, and gone to the deeper parts of his mind that he could not summon by will. He held onto what he could, even closing his eyes again to retrace his steps after his forcing back of the dark entity inside of Tristus, that had howled at his touch. He'd been drawn away in those moments the angry spirit had protested, by a vision that terrified him as much as it intrigued him.

Returning to those moments, Xu Liang found himself suddenly in a blackened chamber that felt cold and vast, like a cave. He could not tell if it was a cave. He saw no details beyond the torches just ahead of him, mounted on thick, coarse pillars, carved crudely from rock. He was drawn toward the dim light, toward the uneven surface it scarcely illuminated. It looked like a bed of round stones.

Xu Liang remembered kneeling before the peculiar rocks, placing his hand upon one, feeling heat ... and movement. He withdrew, staring with a curious frown. And then he took the object up in both hands and stood, carrying it the nearest torch. He held the stone—which was no stone at all, but a thin casing for something else—against the orange light and gazed upon the silhouette of a curled form within, moving.

"An egg?" he wondered, even as the figure within kicked, showing the claws on its tiny hands and feet, lashing its tail, and weakly flexing its wings. "The shadows are born from eggs?"

Something about that did not seem right. Xu Liang continued to stare at the creature, convinced that it was a demon. He recalled the bat-like keirveshen in the Hollowen. They may have been bat like; he hadn't really taken a close look at them. They may also have been ... dragon like? But those in the Hollowen had been so small. Perhaps they were bats once. And if bats were not immune to the dark affliction, as people were not ... then perhaps dragons ...

The thought terrified Xu Liang so greatly that he was unable to finish it. He dropped the egg, incidentally smashing it at his feet, where the incomplete form of an infant demon writhed a short time before expiring in a puddle of dark fluid and fragments of the egg's shell.

Xu Liang felt a presence suddenly behind him. Something great and terrible ... filled with so much anger, its body and soul in chaos. Slowly, calm in spite of his fear, Xu Liang turned to face the beast. The dragon bowed its sleek black head to look at Xu Liang through yellow eyes slit with a narrow pupil of utter blackness. From snout to crested forehead, the dragon's head was twice as tall as Xu Liang stood. Teeth as long and sharp as spears glistened in the torchlight.

Xu Liang should have been afraid, but somehow he was filled with a peculiar reverence—deference perhaps, as he looked upon this ancient and powerful creature, whose demonic eyes gleamed with intelligence. Overcome, Xu Liang pressed his hands together and bowed.

And then he heard a familiar voice, though the strangled tone was nothing he had heard before. "He has the Night Blade!"

The doors to his dreams slammed shut. Xu Liang opened his eyes. He felt sick. Sick with dread, sick with fear, sick with helplessness.

A peculiar sound in the room distracted him from the sudden onslaught. It sounded almost like growling, but then he realized where he had heard the sound before and reminded himself that the only fearsome noise a dwarf produced in his sleep was his snoring. Xu Liang sat up slowly, confirming his suspicions by seeking out Tarfan's shape in the darkness. He found the curled, squat frame sprawled at the distant foot of the bed and sighed with a helpless note of sentimentality for his small friend.

Shortly afterward, he frowned, noticing another shape closer to him. It was Taya, curled near the edge of the mattress to his right. Xu Liang could have expected the dwarf-maid's company along with Tarfan, but when he heard a deeper snore than the dwarf's, one which also sounded out of synch with Tarfan's breathing, he knew that circumstances were even stranger than he could have ever guessed.

Fu Ran appeared to be sitting on the floor to the left side of the bed, his back to the frame with his head fallen back over the mattress. Xu Liang didn't have to look to know that his bodyguards were probably nearby as well, sitting rigidly on the floor, sleeping in shifts. Xu Liang felt momentarily peeved at all of this uninvited, unannounced company and at the absurdity of it as well, but then, suddenly he felt touched by their deep concern. He took three of the excess pillows piled at the head of the bed and distributed them to the dwarves and Fu Ran.

Without waking them, he managed to convince them to accept the cushions. Taya moaned incoherently and simply hugged hers, while Tarfan rolled onto his stomach on top of his. In Fu Ran's case, Xu Liang simply nudged the pillow against the man's bald head until he lifted it enough for the cushion to be slid beneath, to support his neck, lest he awake with an immobilizing cramp.

Finally, Xu Liang lay himself back down, convinced even as he drifted into a dreamless slumber that he would be unable to sleep listening to Fu Ran and Tarfan's snoring.

TWENTY-SEVEN
Reunion

TRISTUS HAD NEVER considered himself proficient fighting with a halberd, or any other pole-mounted weapon, but somehow each strike he made with the platinum spear currently in his grasp came smoothly and almost naturally. He slid his grip nearly effortlessly from one part of the shaft to the next to compensate for the ever-changing reach required for each opponent as they came in droves, one immediately after the other with no pause between one's departure and another's arrival.

They swarmed at him, oblivious to fear, even as their fellows fell beneath the glowing blade. Tristus was aware of their nearness—their claws narrowly missing his face as they lashed out at him, their wings beating the air as they fluttered about for position—none willing to wait for the one before it to either die or claim victory. Somehow Tristus didn't panic. He fought with poise he'd never had in any battle prior to it, even as his heart thundered in his chest and his muscles ached with the effort required. He felt confident, not necessarily that he would live, but that he would fight well before he died. It was a strange, foreign sensation, but one he welcomed while he continued to fend off the demons.

And it was in this unnaturally collected state, that Tristus suddenly, finally came to understand *Dawnfire*. Almost as an instinctive reaction to the swarm of demons charging through an opening that was created in the melee, he lifted one hand off the shaft and spun it once in the other, creating a brief disk of energy with a circumference equal to the length of the spear. The spinning, golden light made a deep, ringing sound when several demons collided upon it and were promptly thrown back. In the freer space he'd created, Tristus was able to kill three of the beasts, rather than simply slicing at them without hope of delivering enough mortal blows. He felt his strength renew itself and added the newfound tactic to the battle wherever it seemed appropriate.

Above him, Shirisae sent bolts of crackling silver light racing toward the demons, burning holes through their wings and through their bodies, eliminating several opponents at once. The others were promptly dealt with on a closer level. Her phenomenal skill and careful balance between magical and physical attacks allowed no demon to touch her.

Alere typically had no trouble slicing through victims with blade as well as magic, though he was forced to cover more ground in his maneuvers in order to keep the demons away from him and to keep the projectile light flowing from *Aerkiren*.

Knowing both of them were there with him gave Tristus hope, as did recognizing the manner in which Guang Ci had taken up the weapon available to him. He fought as one inspired or guided by his master. It was probable that he was both.

◆ ◆ ◆ ◆ ◆

GUANG CI WAS scarcely aware of the weapon he had picked up, that he wielded with enthusiasm against multiple attackers. He was loosely alert to the fact that the blade was not his own, that it was heavier and that a bruised, vaporous light trailed each strike. He heard a voice in his mind, telling him that the demons were no match for him, that they feared him, and he believed that voice. He fought with more efficiency and accuracy than he'd ever exhibited in battle before, and when it was over, he felt a deep satisfaction course through him, a strength that troubled him as much as it had excited him during the battle. He contemplated this, staring at the strange weapon, and then at the dead bodies surrounding him.

He heard his name and looked away from the blanket of demon corpses at his feet, at the man with blue eyes, whom he currently protected as he would have Lord Xu Liang. He recalled the instructions his master had given the others, about protecting the dwarves as they would him, and he had carried those instructions through to each new ally Lord Xu Liang acquired, so long as they didn't threaten Lord Xu Liang.

Guang Ci assumed when the blue-eyed man began to speak, grinning with appreciation and praise, that he was commending him for carrying out his duties well and honorably. He bowed humbly.

◆ ◆ ◆ ◆ ◆

"HE DOESN'T understand you," Alere said in a quiet, irritated tone.

Tristus didn't believe anything was truly bothering the elf—after all, they'd won the battle against terrible odds after surviving horrendous manipulative nightmares within a haunted manor house—but he regarded him seriously, even as his own excitement scarcely kept the smile from his lips.

"You're wasting your breath when you should be recovering it," Alere continued.

"You realize he's taken up the Night Blade," Tristus said, disliking the elf's continued frown, but still managing to smile. He sighed patiently afterward. "Don't you understand? Not only have we discovered the Night Blade, but it appears that we've also discovered its bearer."

"To what purpose?" Alere asked, malcontent edging his voice. And then he turned, walking away while Tristus stared after him.

"Alere, what's the matter with you?" He glanced at Guang Ci apologetically, then followed the elf toward the horses, who were still huddled in the doorway of the manor. "Where are you going? We came here looking for you, to ask you to come back with us."

"To Vilciel?" Alere asked, wiping his blade with the edge of his stained cloak, apparently taking the pale garment for ruined after another gruesome battle. "I told you once already; I will not go there."

"You said more than that," Tristus reminded, frowning now at the elf's stubbornness. "Your words gave me hope that Xu Liang's quest would go on, even if he did not. That his purpose in uniting the Swords would not go unfulfilled. I thought you—"

"He is dead, then?" Alere asked, before Tristus had even finished speaking.

"What?"

The elf repeated himself. "The mystic has passed?"

Tristus glared, hurt now as well as angry. He had finally reached his limit with the elf's coldness. "You know his name, Alere. Don't speak of him as if he were a stranger, whom you care nothing for. And, damn you, look at me when I'm talking to you!"

The elf did not. He sheathed his blade and went about checking his gear that was strapped onto Breigh, readying to leave. He said, far too easily, "You have my condolences."

Tristus felt the entirety of the night's victory drain out of him with that statement. The loss was not apparent until just then. "I see now. You don't care. You don't care about anything, except your personal quest for vengeance. I suppose it's back to your mountain lair now that it's over." He felt tears stinging his eyes while Alere continued to ignore him, but he did not let them into his voice. "Keep your condolences. I am not the one who needs sympathy. My heart may bleed from time to time, but at least it has not turned to ice."

"Speak carefully," Alere warned. "You tread upon unfamiliar ground."

"Yes, I do," Tristus admitted bitterly. "And it is much to my regret. I had come to hope that we were friends, Alere. You were prepared to count me as such before you left. It grieves me that you would treat me with such disdain now. Have you no love in you at all, for any—"

Alere turned suddenly, and grabbed Tristus by the shoulders. He pushed him roughly into the shadows, against the wall just inside of the front hall, where he stood silently glaring at him for a long, confusing moment. At first Tristus was convinced the elf meant to attack him for aggravation. And then, not too quickly, Alere kissed him full on the mouth.

Tristus flushed and felt his heart thrumming in his ears, shocked beyond speech or movement at this discovery.

When the kiss ended, the elf's gray eyes searched Tristus' face, as if looking for something. And then he said angrily, "My heart has not become ice. It has become rebellious, and I would deal with it in my own way."

He moved as if he would step back, so Tristus grabbed his arm, detaining the elf because—Tristus believed—he was willing to be detained.

"You would deal with it by running away? Alere, I did not ... I could not have known how you feel, and knowing now doesn't change my mind. I seek your friendship and I appeal to your sense of honor and righteousness when I ask you to return with me, to complete this duty that was given to you when you took up *Aerkiren.*"

Alere continued to glare and slowly, Tristus released him.

He held the elf's smoldering gray gaze, and said quietly, "Xu Liang lives, but his faith is shattered. He believes he has failed. I..." Shame filled Tristus, strangling his words while they were forming. "I stole Blue Crane, and came to find you... to bring you back and prove to him that all hope is not lost."

Alere looked over his shoulder at the sleek gray steed, then back at Tristus. Then he turned and walked away. "You are a proficient thief," he said, and Tristus couldn't tell whether or not he was serious.

Tristus decided not to ask what he meant, following him at a distance. When he recovered his courage, he asked, "Will you come back, Alere?"

"Have you told him?" the elf asked suddenly, glancing at Shirisae when the lady elf finally made her way to the front hall from the upper floors, having decided against Alere's method of reaching the ground level.

"Told him what?" Tristus looked at Shirisae as well, knowing in spite of her apparent disinterest that she was listening.

"How you feel," Alere said bluntly.

Tristus went to Blue Crane and stood close to the animal, as if he could hide himself in its shadow. He suddenly felt very uncomfortable discussing this, particularly with the warmth of Alere's lips still fresh upon his own. "N-no."

Shirisae took her own horse by the bit, and led the black beast outside, casting Tristus a peculiar look of compassion when she walked by. He wanted to follow her, to not be left alone with the white elf, who was not only extremely bold, but also damned handsome. Of course, Tristus couldn't actually betray Xu Liang—there was nothing shared between them—but he felt somehow as if he had, and he didn't like the sensation. He didn't fully trust that he wouldn't allow it to happen again. He'd gone too long without affection. It felt good... too good. He wondered at the irony of his situation, that he should have the love of two of Dryth's most reclusive, elitist peoples and he could scarcely get a second thought from someone as understanding as Xu Liang seemed to be.

Finally, Alere said, "I will see the Blades united, but from there I cannot promise you anything. The master of the keirveshen has been destroyed, but the shadows themselves remain. I still feel that I must hunt them to be assured of the safety of my house and my family."

Tristus should have felt relieved, but instead he felt a weight sinking inside of him. Feeling depressed, he could only nod in response to Alere's words.

◆ ◆ ◆ ◆ ◆

THE DAYS PASSED slowly and silently. Awkwardly, Tristus thought as lay awake on his blankets, gazing into their dying campfire. Alere didn't actually ride with them, just as he hadn't throughout the previous journey through the Alabaster Mountains and across the Flatlands. The white elf scouted ahead and occasionally came back to report his findings, none of which had been much to worry about. Tristus found himself constantly thinking back to the start of his journey with Xu Liang and the others. He was sure that they had despised and distrusted him at first, all but Xu Liang and Taya. Xu Liang seemed to have no open opinion and treated him fairly while Taya was the only friend he could count among them for the first several days. Alere had scarcely looked at him, and Tristus could have counted the number of times he'd actually spoken to him on one hand.

How could he have known the elf's feelings? Where had such feelings come from? What did he mean when he said that his heart had become rebellious? Had he previously been in love with someone else? Why did he ask about Xu Liang—whether or not Tristus had confessed his feelings to the mystic? Why was Shirisae regarding him with such pity? What did she know that he did not?

It was becoming unbearable.

Someone touched him through the darkness, and he jumped involuntarily. In his sleeplessness, his eyes had long grown accustomed to the shifting darkness as the hours of night moved over him—across a moonless, starless sky—and he quickly realized that it was Shirisae kneeling beside him.

"It is your watch," the lady elf informed him. "You look tired. Have you not slept?"

"I'm fine," Tristus lied, aware that that wasn't what she had asked. He sat up and pushed both hands through his hair. Then he sighed and forced a polite smile. "It's your turn to rest, Shirisae. Sleep well."

Through the darkness he saw her red lips form a smile.

She touched his face with a sister's affection, then chastely planted a kiss on his forehead. "I fear that I have placed an unfair burden upon you," she said gently. "Please forgive me, and try not to think about it so much. I, of all people, should know that fate cannot be rushed or forced. Would you still offer me your heart in friendship, Tristus Edainien?"

"Shirisae," Tristus said, swallowing the emotions as they climbed his throat. "I gave my heart to you in that way long ago."

"Then I am content," she whispered, and hugged him briefly before slipping away into the darkness.

Tristus sighed and wiped his eyes, then rose to find a place to sit and keep an eye on the camp.

They had crossed Windra's Channel earlier in the day and traveled through gentle hills on their way back to the harsh, dark mountains along the upper edge of the Alabaster Range. They had at least another day's journey ahead of them, not including the hours it took to ascend to Vilciel. Perhaps there he could find a room to lock himself into and shut out the world for a span. He loved these people dearly, but he didn't know how to handle their loving him back, or their apparent inability to do so, in one particular case. He hadn't expected this when he set out from Andaria alone.

Tristus wandered a few yards from the campsite and held his cloak about him with one hand, feeling cold in his armor. Holding *Dawnfire* in his other hand, he stared south, envisioning the mountains he couldn't see through the darkness, recalling the city that had stolen his breath and the people he had left there. He missed Taya. Her kindness had come so automatic and unconditional, he felt like he could say anything to her. And he needed someone to talk to about now, someone who would just listen. Shirisae was lucky to have D'mitri. Tristus sometimes wished that he had siblings. He had cousins, but none that he felt particularly close to.

Sensing movement in the open darkness around him, Tristus tensed and took up *Dawnfire* in both hands. The action reminded him that the spear was the only significant weapon he had left. He'd lost his father's sword in the bog in front of Vorhaven's manor. He didn't think that he needed another weapon, but the sword of the Order had sentimental value.

"It's me," Alere announced, and Tristus was finally able to descry the elf's shape when he slipped down from Breigh's back.

Tristus relaxed his stance, but felt his insides knotting.

"Sleep if you like," the elf continued. "There isn't anything for miles to be concerned about."

"Thank you," Tristus said somewhat flatly, "but I've slept enough."

I've tried to, at any rate, he added in secret. He should have known better than to think that he could hide anything from Alere, however.

"You have been unable to sleep," the elf said, simply as a matter of fact.

He seemed as distant and imperturbable as ever, but Tristus would never be able to see him in the same light again. He knew now that there were multiple chambers within the elf's heart, and that not all of them were storage for vengeance.

Alere seemed to sense this and said, "I have made you uncomfortable."

"No," Tristus replied at once. "No, Alere, you haven't."

He felt the elf's clear eyes penetrating the darkness, cutting away the lie so that he could see clearly the truth hidden behind it.

Tristus sighed in defeat. "All right. I am a bit unhinged about this. I never expected ... I didn't think that..."

Alere said nothing, as if waiting for Tristus to finish. When Tristus failed to do so, he cast his own voice into the silence. "This is strange for me as well. I have cared for no one deeply, outside of my family."

Tristus waited, feeling somehow that the statement was incomplete, that the elf should say he hadn't loved anyone outside of his family since ... since some affair long past. But Alere didn't say anything more, and suddenly Tristus recalled what Shirisae had said about him, that he was young, even by elf standards. How young? Surely Alere wasn't ... surely he couldn't mean ...

Tristus was unable to finish the thought in his amaze that quickly became dismay. Maybe Alere didn't actually care for him in that way. Perhaps he was only confused. For an instant Tristus felt almost ten years younger, and then he suddenly felt very old and culpably insensitive to those around him while he was wrapped up in his concerns for himself.

"Alere," Tristus finally said, and then suddenly realized he didn't know what else to say. He'd been thinking of all that Gerrick had said to him, but none of it seemed to apply here. For Tristus it had already been established where his interests lay. His problems had stemmed in the past from shame and embarrassment, fear that he was not normal and, worst of all, immoral in the eyes of God.

Alere didn't know God as He would know the elf, regardless of his beliefs, and it wasn't clear whether or not Alere's current inclinations were ingrained or circumstantial.

At length, and more to himself, Tristus said, "I feel as if I know nothing about you."

"If you knew, it is likely that you would not understand," Alere replied quietly. "We are vastly different."

Tristus looked at him across the darkness, feeling leagues away from him. "Who is vastly different? You and I, or elves and humans?"

"Both," Alere answered. And in the next moment he said, "I cannot withdraw the statement made with my actions, but I will not force the subject."

Something in the elf's words irritated Tristus. "Indeed, you cannot withdraw such a statement, nor how boldly it was made. You cannot dismiss it either, Alere."

"Perhaps you should not have pressed for an answer you were not prepared to accept," Alere suggested in an even, reasonable tone that made Tristus rethink the elf's maturity, again. He seemed as far removed from boyhood as a man could get without having one foot in his grave.

"How was I to know you would deliver such an answer? You're closed tighter than a greedy merchant's purse and I had, after all, only recently crawled out of a slimy, reeking bog."

Alere laughed just then, and Tristus tried vainly to maintain his anger.

"What?" Tristus demanded. And then his lips rebelled, forming a smile when he continued. "What do you find so ... blasted amusing?"

"That I might be inclined to agree with a dwarf," Alere replied, still smiling, and it was a look that suited him, in spite of himself.

"What do you mean?"

"On reflection, you are more prone to trouble than any man—or elf, for that matter—that I have ever met."

"I don't agree with that," Tristus said, no longer amused. Thoughts of the past crept forward, along with those moments he had been forced to relive in Vorhaven's manor, under the influence of demon sorcery and the Night Blade.

"Do not take offense," Alere said, seriously now. "None was intended."

Tristus nodded, looking away from the elf. "No, I'm sure it wasn't." Then he shook his head. "I'm sorry, Alere. Perhaps I am wearier than I believed."

"You should rest," Alere advised, and Tristus didn't realize the elf had come closer until his hand became a gentle weight on his shoulder.

Again, Tristus nodded, avoiding Alere's pale gaze. "I'll be fine, Alere. Thank you... for your concern."

The elf hesitated, and Tristus began to feel pleasantly warm and unpleasantly awkward.

Don't, he begged in silence while Alere lingered near. *Please, don't.*

And then, as if hearing Tristus' pleas, Alere drew back and left him alone.

A relieved sigh escaped Tristus, and it was several moments before he was able to breathe normally again.

◆ ◆ ◆ ◆ ◆

VILCIEL HELD NO awe for Tristus this time. As he returned to Skytown, he felt a malignant terror swelling throughout his body. He had done what he set out to do, and been more successful than he seriously believed possible, finding not only Alere, but the Night Blade as well. However, now the time had finally come to face the consequences of just how he had gone about the deed.

He'd withheld his intentions from Xu Liang, allowed one of the mystic's guards to abandon his duty, stolen Blue Crane, and in effect stranded the mystic in a strange place with no recourse but to wait and to wonder. He kept thinking of Xu Liang's quiet anger, the soft tones of disapproval and the delicate frowns that chastened far better than any heated upbraiding Tristus had ever received within the Order. And such tones and expressions hadn't even been truly aimed at him yet. He could only anticipate the moment, and the remorse already filled his heart to the point of pain. He imagined the organ would burst when he actually beheld Xu Liang's wrath, as subtle and insidious as a slow-acting toxin.

Tristus would die of guilt. He resigned himself to his fate.

Their arrival was expected in Vilciel, just as before, but rather than griffins and strangers, friends were waiting for them this time. It was Taya's squeal of delight that brought Tristus somewhat out of his trance. He could not ignore the dwarf maiden when she ran across the snow-covered yard at the top of the final staircase to greet him. He crouched down to meet her, so that she could throw her short arms around his neck instead of his legs, and hugged her back with alacrity. He had indeed missed his little friend.

"What took you so long?" Taya demanded. "I thought something dreadful had happened!"

"Something dreadful did happen," Tristus replied, absorbing her generous warmth as she continued to hold him. "Thankfully, everyone came away all right."

"What happened?" Taya asked, deeply concerned. "You're not hurt?"

"No," Tristus answered, pulling gently away from her. "I'm all right. I'll tell you everything later." He stood to greet Fu Ran. He'd been expecting the large man's grin, but he was unprepared for the bear hug that came with it.

The Fanese giant stepped back to look at Tristus after nearly crushing him. "You look like you've been through all of the Infernal Regions at once."

"I feel like it," Tristus sighed.

Fu Ran laughed, folding his arms across his broad chest. He indicated Alere with a flickering glance. "I see you succeeded in recruiting him back into our camp."

Tristus looked over his shoulder at the stoic white elf, still mounted on Breigh, seeming completely removed from the occasion, except to return D'mitri's glare when the Phoenix Elf delivered one by way of welcoming his sister back.

"Yes," Tristus said absently, looking again at Fu Ran when something of more immediate concern suddenly came to mind. "There is something I have to tell you, Fu Ran... about the way Bastien..."

He didn't get the chance to finish. His attention was drawn, like water from a tipped glass on a canted table, toward the approaching figure of a man he'd last seen barely strong enough to sit up by himself. The mystic's recovery appeared incredible. He walked again with ease and elegance, his silken robes brushing the snow while he moved without haste. Xu Liang's hair was pulled back from his face once more, revealing not the beauty that Tristus recalled, but one greater, one earthlier, as his spiritual grace had retreated back within him. He was still thin, but he appeared less fragile and there was actually color in his cheeks, and a luster in his dark eyes that seemed to reflect life, rather than the magic that had been sustaining him before. His expression was tranquil, affirming his exquisite fairness and at the same time peeling apart Tristus' heart, relieving the pressure that had been building since he started up the mountain upon which Vilciel stood.

Xu Liang approached silently, trailed by Gai Ping and the other guards that had stayed in Vilciel. The Fanese warriors fell back just before the mystic reached Tristus, whereupon Xu Liang proceeded to bow, and said neutrally, "Welcome back, Tristus Edainien. I am pleased to see that you and the others have returned safely."

Tristus didn't know what to say, moved by the gesture and stunned by the lack of reproach. He said nothing, and was quickly distracted by Guang Ci, who came forward just when Xu Liang straightened from his bow.

The guard held the Night Blade flat in both hands and dropped onto one knee. He bowed his head and spoke respectfully in Fanese.

Xu Liang stared at the black sword as if it had no recognizable shape or form. A moment of silent study deciphered what was being held before him—what was being offered to him—and he finally gave Guang Ci his response. The words meant nothing to Tristus, but the guard's actions seemed to explain.

Guang Ci pulled the Night Blade closer to himself, then stood, bowing to his superior, and speaking in what seemed to be humble acceptance to the honor that had been bestowed upon him.

The mystic looked to Alere next, silently, then at Tristus again, and finally at all of them. "I request an audience with all of you indoors. Please come after you have sufficiently rested and refreshed yourselves."

And then he bowed once more and left.

The formality of the affair made Tristus wonder if he should expect anger after they'd gone in, out of the view of Vilciel's general public.

"How is he?" Tristus asked Fu Ran, watching the mystic depart.

"He seems normal," the former guard said, shrugging as if unconcerned.

Tristus frowned, confused until Tarfan stepped forward and explained. "The mage and the ox here aren't on speaking terms at the moment."

Tristus sighed heavily, wondering if the Swords truly represented order, having selected bearers in such turmoil as they happened to be. And when it wasn't the bearers directly, then it was the people they needed to support them.

"He's been having nightmares," Taya said gently. "He doesn't seem to remember them much when he wakes, but they make him feverish. He doesn't complain, but I've seen him clutching at his chest like there's a tightness or a burning inside, and I've heard him coughing. Not badly, but still it's clear that he isn't completely recovered from the aftermath of Ahjenta's Flame."

"Did you talk to the priestess?" Tristus asked, his concern deepening. He wondered if Xu Liang could still reject the Flame and die anyway, after all their efforts and his.

"Ahjenta talked to us," Tarfan informed peevishly. "She's more confusing to listen to than Xu Liang when he's speaking Fanese."

"He'll be all right," Fu Ran finally said, irritably. "He's stronger than he looks." He clapped Tristus on the shoulder. "Come on. It's a long walk back to the rooms. You can tell us all about your journey into Upper Yvaria along the way."

◆ ◆ ◆ ◆ ◆

XU LIANG STOOD upon the ledge of the enormous window of his borrowed dragon-sized room. He looked out at the cloud-layered horizon until he sensed the arrival of his guests. Shortly afterward, he heard them.

Shirisae had come first, leading D'mitri, Tristus, and the dwarves. Guang Ci arrived next, separated from his fellows—who guarded the entrance of the vast room—by the sacred Blade he now carried. Now Xu Liang understood why the young man found it so easy to disregard duty as he had when he left Vilciel with the knight. It was his destiny to come into possession of the Night Blade.

Fu Ran entered the room alone, as did Alere, whom Xu Liang had honestly not been expecting to see again in this lifetime. Perhaps the elf did not feel that his personal quest was over. Or perhaps he yet found himself drawn to his destiny as the bearer of the Twilight Blade.

When everyone had arrived, Xu Liang turned to face them. He gestured to the floor. "Please, bearers of the Celestial Blades, place your weapons here and then sit down, if you will. I must apologize, by the way, for this room's lack of accommodation."

Predictably, Tristus came forward first, and laid *Dawnfire* almost reverently upon the stone floor, as if in offering. Guang Ci followed, delayed only by Fu Ran's belated translation of Xu Liang's western words. The Dawn Blade and the Night Blade responded to each other, gleaming faintly, like familiar classmates whispering to one another while their tutor's back was turned.

Shirisae added the Storm Blade, whose crackling silver light reached eagerly for the gold-glowing spear beside it. Lastly, Alere presented his beloved *Aerkiren*, deigning to part with it by placing it upon the floor next to the aptly named *Behel*. Again the amount of light produced by the weapons was increased, confirming their relation.

Xu Liang waited for the others to be seated, forming a half circle before the Swords. Then he drew *Pearl Moon* from the scabbard tucked into his sash and lowered it slowly over the others. He watched the pale blue light rise and then drift off the slender blade like a fine, glowing mist, adding to the amalgamation of colors forming above the other Swords. It was fascinating to watch, but nothing spectacular. That would come, in time. For now, Xu Liang lowered to his knees and lay *Pearl Moon* down beside the others, noting to himself that one Blade was still missing—the Sun Blade— presumably still in possession of the Empress.

Xu Liang looked at the people huddled before him, regarding each of them separately but also equally. They waited patiently and eagerly, nervously as well as resignedly. Some of them were hopeful, others dubious or apprehensive. Whatever their concerns about the Swords and their capabilities, each of them believed that their coming together meant something, and that the man before them knew what. Xu Liang hoped that he would not disappoint them with his explanation.

"Regardless," he began, "of your past lives or your current beliefs, all of you have been summoned here by a single source, for a single purpose. It is not a task that can be forced upon you, but one which you must take up of your own free will with the understanding that you act not for yourself, but for the benefit of this world and all who would live peacefully upon it.

"This duty is not something that can be granted. It must be felt. Once felt—once accepted—it is nothing that can be abandoned without great consequence to the others involved. Here is where selfishness must end, where reliance begins, and where trust must be paramount. There can be no discord. No rebellion. Each must accept his or her own role with a willing soul and an open heart. Once entered into this bond, we must leave all others behind us, and treat this new union with absolute priority."

Xu Liang paused a moment, to be sure Fu Ran had time to speak the translation to Guang Ci. When he heard the large man's whispered echo cease, he continued. "There can be no glory in this task, for it is not a quest for personal gain or satisfaction. What those of us who continue on must do will seem at times mundane and at other times trying, even arduous and excruciating. Peace will come with success, though we may not recognize it once it is achieved. For the World will carry on, just as it ever has, but there will be less suffering, less despair, less darkness at the hands of evil forces that would seek to control us and to control our destinies. We will have restored a peace that most individuals go their entire lives scarcely aware of. A period of order will come to nature. The changes might seem subtle to us, but for those who can look beyond the physical world, knowledge will be granted. The knowledge that the Master, currently weakened by the constant struggle to contain Chaos, is well and at rest.

"When I speak of the Master, I refer to the world. When I speak of Chaos, I refer to the Dragon, which we have been asked to face by forces higher than ourselves. Already each of us has fought against this beast and realized victory, as well as defeat. We battle it now while we struggle within ourselves, wondering whether or not it is safe, or wise, or perhaps even right to go on to the next battle. That battle lies in Sheng Fan, farther from some of your homes than you have ever dared to travel, even in your dreams."

Xu Liang waited, allowing a lengthy period of silence, for all that he had said to be absorbed by his audience. Finally, he took up *Pearl Moon* and stood. He extended the Moon Blade outward, casting a veil of blue light over the people before him. And then he said, "I accept this calling. I place my life in the Heavens and offer my full trust and loyalty to those who would take this journey with me."

Silence filled the chamber as the darkness of eventide crept indoors. *Pearl Moon* glowed brilliantly in the gray air, but the Sword glowed alone. Even Guang Ci hesitated, perhaps unsure in this proposal of allegiance that seemed to contradict his sworn duty as servant to an imperial officer.

When the guard appeared to have sorted everything out in his mind, he stood and approached the Swords lying in front of Xu Liang. The younger Fanese man knelt down in a habitual display of respect, then slowly lifted the Night Blade and stood. He held the black sword out, so that the blade—now radiating with a strange, dark energy—touched the paler metal of the Moon Blade. It was not an act of aggression, but one of loyalty and trust, thus the Swords accepted the contact.

"Let us fight together on the battlefield, Lord Xu Liang," Guang Ci said in Fanese.

Xu Liang replied in his native tongue. "You honor me, Guang Ci. I know that I can expect great things."

The light between them grew suddenly stronger, blossoming with a lavish violet radiance. Xu Liang was quietly shocked, looking at Alere—who now stood beside Guang Ci—suddenly enough to reveal that shock through his calm expression. The elf's face was placid, completely unrevealing. Anything he might have said was held back by the arrival of the next Sword—Shirisae's *Firestorm*, whose energetic strands of light caressed and wound about its sibling Blades.

"This weapon was a gift to my people," the lady elf said. "I will repay the trust and generosity of the forces who bestowed it upon us with my life."

Most unexpectedly, Shirisae's joining left only Tristus to decide. The knight sat quietly on his knees, his hands clasped together and his head bowed. He seemed to be ... praying? When he was finished, he touched his brow with his fingertips, then his lips, and finally his armor, over his heart. He sat back upon completing the ritual and stared long at the Dawn Blade. Too many emotions passed over his gentle features for Xu Liang to begin to guess what was going through his mind.

Then the knight stood slowly. He came forward, retrieved the brilliant spear, and simply held it. "God, let me be worthy of this task," he whispered, then gently delivered the Blade to its siblings.

The golden light ignited the others, shooting beams of multicolored energy throughout the vast chamber. The power that radiated from the united weapons was magnificent, and Xu Liang could only imagine what it might feel and look like with the *Spear of Heaven* to add to the effect. For the first time since his journey had begun, he felt as if he would witness it. The Blades would be united. It had been decided.

TWENTY-EİGHT
Confrontations

AHJENTA APPROVED of her daughter's decision—even though her son did not—and decided to see the companions off well. She held a banquet in their honor, and to bless their departure. Music and lively conversation filled a grand hall that was fit for dragons and made functional for elves. Round tables dotted the vast floor, each one buried beneath mounds of unique elvish food that even Guang Ci found enticing. In particular, the guard seemed interested in a dish that consisted of layers of a tender white meat upon a bed of what seemed dark rice, though none of them could be certain, since they'd seen no land suitable for cultivation on any of the mountaintops of Vilciel. The spices were more potent than any of them expected, but it appeared they were to be tolerated in exchange for a texture that reminded them at least somewhat of home.

The Phoenix Elves had no fish, but they did have a curious recipe for noodles boiled in a thick and slightly sweet broth, which Xu Liang was willing to sample modestly. It would be the first truly solid food he'd eaten since coming out of fasting, so he decided to be cautious about how much he took in. He wondered for a moment how he might take it in at all—the bowl was too large to comfortably drink from and Guang Ci's decision to eat with his fingers seemed to be drawing the wrong kind of attention for a polite dinner occasion. Xu Liang eventually made the diplomatic choice and struggled with the peculiar elven utensils.

Fu Ran and Tarfan sat beside one another, each taking in their meal with alarming haste, as if in competition. Xu Liang would have guessed Fu Ran the natural victor in such a challenge, but Tarfan seemed to have an unnaturally large stomach for such a small individual.

"Are you boys tasting any of that?" Taya asked them.

Tarfan threw back a large gulp of elvish ale and promptly belched. "There's the flavor!"

"That's disgusting," the dwarf maiden said flatly.

Xu Liang agreed in silence, and noticed that he was not the only one at their table with nothing to say. He looked at Tristus, no longer able to justify the anger he'd felt toward him during the long days of awaiting his return to Vilciel. He had done what Xu Liang physically—and perhaps even mentally at the time—could not have done. He retrieved the final Sword and managed to bring back Alere, whom Xu Liang would have been inclined to let go. As to other concerns, Xu Liang would confront them when it became necessary ... if it became necessary.

"You're not eating?" he said to the knight.

Tristus looked at his plate, utterly disinterested, and showed nothing of a smile or any pleasant expression whatsoever when he lifted his gaze to look at Xu Liang. That was unlike him. Even if Tristus felt miserable, he always seemed to make an effort not to spread his misery to others, however useless those efforts tended to be. Now, however, he didn't even try.

"Excuse me," was all the knight said before leaving the table.

Other than Xu Liang, only Taya noticed—neither Alere nor Shiri-sae were even present at this particular table—and the young dwarf was about to go after him until Xu Liang stopped her. He touched her hand lightly, managing to summon her attention without having to shout over the combined volumes of music and chatter.

When she looked at him, he stood and said, "I will go."

◆ ◆ ◆ ◆ ◆

TRISTUS STOOD in the chill night air upon one of the smaller balconies that had been carved out of the vast stone walls by the elves and stared out across the grand city. It was lit with perpetual fires in many places, which the magic inherited by the previous inhabitants permitted. It was beautiful and frightening all at once, to think that such a marvelous place had been built by dragons, or at least for dragons.

Tristus still wished he could have found Eris. A city built for angels must have been something even more fantastic. He wondered why he stopped looking, why he ventured so far north to begin with.

You were scared. Not wandering, but running, like a...

"Something is troubling you," a familiar voice said, halting Tristus' thought before it finished.

Tristus didn't look back at Xu Liang, afraid to face him, still expecting retribution or at least reprimand. He didn't know why he should question the mystic's ability to forgive now, after worshipping him as a compassionate being before. Perhaps it had something to do with his own dishonesty. If Alere could be so brave, why couldn't he?

He'd been bold in the past when he needed to be, or just wanted to be. Why should he be so intimidated by Xu Liang?

Glumly, he answered his own question. *Because you know he'll reject you. He has his empress and you... you could have your pick of two very beautiful elves, but you stubbornly insist on the unobtainable. And because you've already chosen, you could never go to the preferred elf, even if you survived the inevitable rejection from Xu Liang and were inclined to do so. It wouldn't be fair to him. Your heart would still long for what it couldn't have, and what a terrible first relationship that would be for Alere; one that was untrue.*

Tristus wasn't terribly worried about Shirisae. She was strong. He felt that she could survive anything, and come away even stronger than before.

"I don't belong with the rest of you," he finally said. "I'm an exiled knight, running from my past, which is so much worse than any of you will ever know. What you saw... it was nothing in comparison to what I've done before. I... want to be with you—all of you." His face flushed as the words seem to come out of their own volition—and wrong—and he kept his gaze on the city, struggling to finish his statement. "I'm just ... having difficulty convincing myself that I have a right to."

"And your weaknesses that you would make strengths?" Xu Liang reminded.

"It's not working," Tristus was ashamed to admit. "You mustn't think that I don't want to change. I do..."

"Perhaps you do not need to change," Xu Liang suggested. "At least, not so drastically as you would attempt to. To strive to better oneself is natural and expected. To abandon oneself in an effort to attain a new self is foolish and unhealthy. For example, in your attempt to escape your misery by refusing to acknowledge it, you have only managed to consistently dwell on it and have made yourself even more miserable."

"You're right about that," Tristus sighed. "But I haven't been completely honest with you. My past isn't all that's troubling me. In fact, the only reason I've considered it tonight is because it brought me here, to..." He struggled for an instant with his courage, then threw himself upon the truth, as he might his own sword in a ritual attempt at suicide. "To you."

Strangely, Xu Liang had nothing to say. Perhaps he was uncertain as to precisely what was being said to him.

Tristus glanced back at him, but was unable to meet his gaze. He saw that the mystic's mouth formed a small frown and his heart slowed to a meandering plod, like an old man's as he lay upon his deathbed, awaiting the inevitable.

"Xu Liang..."

"Say nothing more," the mystic interrupted quietly.

"Why?" Tristus had to ask. Fearing that he already knew the answer, he didn't wait for it. He suddenly knew nothing of fear, thinking only that he loved the individual before him, deeply. "How long must I select my words to you with caution? How long must I steal glimpses of you, because I'm afraid to be caught gazing? I only want you to know how I feel."

"How you feel does not have to be spoken," Xu Liang replied, still quietly. Neither his words nor his tone revealed anything as to how he might feel himself, not one way or the other. "However, it is not only my awareness that concerns you, Tristus Edainien. I know what you would seek from me ... and it is something I am not capable of granting."

Tristus' heart broke instantaneously, far too quickly for tears to even form. He felt stunned and weak, and sought the balcony railing for support. Even expecting rejection, he could never have been truly braced for it. It hurt, like Hell itself. With a few simple words a dream was shattered, utterly destroyed—and he could already envision himself scrambling to collect the fragments, as if he had no dignity at all.

Xu Liang mistook his silence for confusion. "I am indebted to you, Tristus, for all that you have done, but I cannot return your—"

"I heard you," Tristus said quickly. "Please, don't embarrass me any further by sounding it out."

"Forgive me," Xu Liang said.

Tristus felt his blood rushing beneath his skin, his heart pounding mercilessly with pain, and with love that couldn't be quashed as easily as his hope.

"There's nothing to forgive," he muttered, and turned from the railing, doing all in his power to avoid so much as glancing at Xu Liang while he left the balcony.

He walked quickly through the grand dining hall, leaving the banquet without a word to any of the others, determined not to stop until he reached the guest suites. He made it halfway up the first stairwell before he collapsed in a heap of misery, curses, and tears.

◆ ◆ ◆ ◆ ◆

TAYA WAS BEGINNING to wonder what was taking Xu Liang and Tristus so long. Fu Ran and her uncle were rapidly becoming more irritating than humorous with their quaffing and gorging, and belching. She was growing so desperate for dignified company that she even welcomed the sight of Shirisae—beautiful and perfect as she happened to be in her long, flowing black gown with her flame-colored hair cascading down her back.

The daughter of the elven priestess sat down in Xu Liang's seat, perching on the edge as if she didn't plan to stay. A glance obviously told her that attempting to speak to either Fu Ran or Tarfan would be a waste of time, and so she asked Taya, "Have you seen Tristus?"

Taya mustered a quick smile over her automatic frown. "Not for a little while," she answered, wondering if she looked as jealous as she felt. And then she stupidly asked, "Why?"

Shirisae sat back and sighed, apparently without noticing the tone of Taya's interest. "I haven't seen him since the banquet started. He looked a bit glum. I thought maybe I could help cheer him up."

"No thanks," Taya said, then bit her tongue and quickly added, "We've already got plenty of help in that area. Uh ... Xu Liang just went to see if he's all right, in fact."

Shirisae rolled her golden eyes toward the ceiling, her red lips frowning. "I think that Xu Liang's attention is the last thing he needs."

Now Taya was curious, instead of simply jealous. "What do you mean?"

The lady elf glanced at Taya, then smiled too quickly. "Please don't take me wrong. I have the utmost respect for him. I just think that sometimes he can be a little … cold."

"Xu Liang?" Taya inquired, to be certain. Shirisae gave no indication, right or wrong, so Taya was forced to assume. Assuming that she was right, she lifted her chin haughtily and said, "He does have a lot on his mind, you know. I think it's understandable that he's a little detached after he nearly learned what it was to be on the stomped end of stomping a bug."

Shirisae, whose mind had clearly gone elsewhere, looked at Taya suddenly. "What about bugs?"

Taya sighed irritably. "The giant. Remember? It almost killed him."

"Oh," Shirisae responded, then waved the subject away with her hand, looking around the banquet hall, obviously for someone specific.

Taya groaned impatiently. "He's not here. What's the matter with you? Aren't there enough elf boys here that strike your fancy?"

The elf's yellow-pale skin turned almost as red as her lips. Her golden eyes widened, and for a moment her nostrils even flared. Taya wasn't sure if she should be prepared to dodge the lady elf's scathing words, or the back of her hand. She was surprised when neither came at her and Shirisae suddenly relaxed, and even smiled. Her tone was too sweet when she said, "My dear little Taya, I'm so sorry for being insensitive. This must be miserable for you, being so far away from home and all the dwarf boys."

Fu Ran and Tarfan both burst into laughter, of course choosing that very moment to pay attention to something other than their food and ale. Taya didn't have a comeback or a retort. She sat quietly and fumed.

"By the way," Shirisae said, drifting away from whatever satisfaction the previous moments may have brought her. "Has anyone seen my brother?"

Fu Ran lowered his recently refilled tumbler of ale and looked once around the room. "Come to think of it, has anyone seen Alere?"

Everyone looked at each other now. No one said anything. Fu Ran's question had given them their answer to both concerns.

◆ ◆ ◆ ◆ ◆

THERE WERE A great many vast and empty chambers within Vilciel's enormous structure. It proved a welcomed convenience for two who had quickly become bored with Ahjenta's banquet, and who didn't believe in delaying the inevitable.

Alere twirled *Aerkiren* once in his hand, testing the weight against the chill air around him. He wanted no disadvantages here ... for either of them. He eyed the Phoenix Elf across the large room they had selected. Shirisae's brother prepared himself and his weapon for the impending duel in his own way, appearing no less formidable in his current lack of armor. Alere, who had never worn armor greater than his soft leather tunic, watched the flames dancing off the other elf's curved sword and sent his voice across the empty distance. "Is that blade enchanted?"

"It is endowed," D'mitri called back, his tone suggesting that to answer his opponent was a waste of breath.

Alere did not give him the satisfaction of an irritated response and asked, "What do you mean by endowed? Try to be clear. I want this to be a fair match."

"It's a match, is it?" D'mitri wondered, smiling insolently. When it became apparent to him that Alere refused to be provoked, he said, "This sword was forged in the fiery breath of an elder dragon, and thus endowed with its power; an everlasting flame."

"Then the weapon itself is magical," Alere deduced. "That will do."

D'mitri did not hear him, or did not think it necessary to respond.

Alere sliced the air a few times with *Aerkiren*, then started toward his opponent. "Shall we begin?"

D'mitri unclasped his formal cloak, and threw it off to the side of their flat, featureless battleground. His teeth gleamed in the firelight cast down from huge braziers hanging high overhead. "I've been waiting for this. Don't expect any mercy. Nothing would please me more than to put a stop to my sister's plans for this ridiculous outing by killing you."

"Or by dying?" Alere offered.

That was all it took to incite D'mitri's temper. The Phoenix Elf charged, his flaming sword dragging low, informing Alere of his plan of attack.

Alere lifted *Aerkiren* high and halted the upward sweep, driving the fiery blade back down.

D'mitri swiftly broke away, leaping back and then lunging in again. He was an aggressive fighter, counting on the force of his frequent attacks to compensate for his lacking defense. Perhaps they were not so different after all.

For several moments, each of them tried to outdo the other's attack, pressing harder, striking faster. Fire and twilight danced erratically between the combatants, the two lights waxing with every connection and waning between blows. This was the only way they could understand and tolerate one another; in a contest of strength, speed, and cunning.

They were fated to be enemies somehow, their hatred coming as sudden and automatically as the attraction between two who were destined to become lovers. It went beyond Alere's resentment of his own kind, who failed to support the Verressi during the worst of the Shadow Wars. It extended far beneath the surface of D'mitri's arrogance and contempt. Neither of them could explain it, and neither of them cared to. They only knew that this battle between them felt comfortable, satisfying.

Their blades came together again and held. Neither of them would have admitted that they were resting, even as each tried to force the other back.

"You're better than I expected, for a child," D'mitri said through clenched teeth.

"You must be growing old," Alere replied. "I expected better."

The easily taunted Phoenix Elf growled and shoved Alere back, his anger feeding his strength. Their fight resumed. The clashing of their weapons resounded loudly throughout the chamber, adding to the intensity.

Alere could have gone on for hours and had no doubt that D'mitri could as well, but the sudden eruption of thunder indoors proved an adequate distraction for both of them. Great streaks of silver light scorched the icy air. As if it was rehearsed, D'mitri and Alere each took a last swing, they each batted the other away, and each of them stepped gracefully out of their deathly dance. In the forced pause, both elves realized they were winded.

The source of the thunder had been no mystery, and so it was no surprise when Shirisae glided across the floor in her flowing silk gown, carrying *Firestorm* in both hands after shooting multiple arcs of silver lightning into the hall.

The disapproval in her expression did not affect Alere—he welcomed a fight from her as well—but D'mitri actually displayed remorse beneath his mask of arrogance.

"What do you think you are doing?" Shirisae demanded.

Alere kept silent when he realized her words were aimed at her brother.

"How dare you to openly defy our mother?" She added in a harsh whisper, "How dare you defy me? We have formed an alliance with this elf, as well as with the humans. Whether or not you can appreciate that, you must recognize it."

D'mitri met his sister's gaze briefly, then decided not to argue. He sheathed his sword in a scabbard that enveloped the flame as well as the blade—and was presumably also an item of magic—then glared hatefully at Alere, and left.

Shirisae did not watch him leave, but listened to his heels clicking against the smooth stone floor. When he had gained sufficient distance, she looked at Alere and said, "I apologize for his uncouth behavior. He has always been ... difficult when it comes to outsiders."

"I require no explanation," Alere replied simply, putting away *Aerkiren*. "The decision to fight was mutual."

Shirisae's golden eyes glared, and she firmed her chin. "Well, it won't happen again in this house."

"No," Alere agreed. "There is scarcely time for it if we are to depart with the mystic, come sunrise."

Finally, the female elf said what she wanted to say. "You disgust me."

Alere issued no comment, knowing better than to provoke a fight after the last time. It would hardly be a fair contest while she was hampered by a dress, besides. He walked away from her and came upon Fu Ran, Tarfan, and Taya in the corridor outside of the enormous room.

"Damn," Fu Ran muttered. "It's over."

The faintest of smiles escaped Alere, as it amused him to think that the Fanese man had enough respect for either him or D'mitri to consider their battle worthy of an audience.

"I'm glad it is," Taya said haughtily. "Was anyone hurt?" she demanded of Alere. She added flatly, "I see you're not."

"It was a draw," Alere replied. "In every aspect. Where is everyone else?"

"The guards are in their places," Tarfan answered in his gruff manner. "Never too far from the mystic, who decided to retire early in preparation for tomorrow's journey."

"And the knight?" Alere inquired casually—disinterestedly, the others might have believed.

Taya shrugged irritably. "Moping in his room, I suppose. He's been acting unpleasant all evening and after Xu Liang went to talk with him, he didn't even come back to say goodnight. If Xu Liang can't reason with him, then..."

Alere was walking away before she finished, hearing nothing more of what she said, though her uncle's voice carried down the passageway.

"How's that for arrogance?" Tarfan blustered. "Not a care in the world, save for himself!"

◆ ◆ ◆ ◆ ◆

TRISTUS WAS FINISHED crying. There was no sense weeping over what he couldn't control. And he couldn't control life. It simply traveled its course, and those who tried to alter that course were fools.

Yes, you're a fool, he told himself. *You've always gone against the current. Time to join the others in the world. Time to walk the path that was given to you ... or what's left of it.*

He looked away from the fireplace—he'd been watching the modest blaze from the end of the bed for more than an hour—and glanced over his shoulder at *Dawnfire*, propped against the wall at the head of the bed, his armor resting nearby. Elven smiths had been kind enough to polish the white-gold plates and repair the dents. His father's sword was missing, but somehow the suit seemed in place beside the Dawn Blade. Tristus felt his emotions churning his blood again and sighed.

I don't feel that I'm worthy of this task, but I will see it through.

The faintest sweep of wood over stone drew Tristus' attention toward the door. Somehow he failed to be startled when his gaze settled on Alere.

The white elf hovered in the doorway, typically expressing nothing. He said simply, "The door was unlocked."

"I must have forgotten," Tristus replied, trying not to sound as miserable as he felt. Not only was his heart shattered, but his head had begun to hurt as well. Still, that was no reason for his deportment to suffer. "What can I do for you, my elven friend?"

Alere seemed to study him for a moment, then said, "I would ask for a moment of your time."

"And you would have it," Tristus said, standing. "Is anything the matter?"

Alere let himself into the room and closed the door behind him. In no particular hurry, he approached Tristus, and then stood quietly before him. His gray eyes flashed in the firelight while they moved over every detail of Tristus' face.

It did not take Tristus long to sort out what the matter was, and he was not oblivious to the lovely shape of the elf's nearly colorless eyes, nor was he unaffected by the secret warmth they offered. Before that warmth could ensnare him—something that would not be particularly difficult in his current state of susceptibility—he took a step back and used conversation to escape the dangerous silence.

"Have you eaten? I didn't see you at the banquet. I'm sure there are still plates out." He started to take steps around the elf. "If we go now, perhaps..."

Alere caught him by the arm.

His grip was gentle, easy for Tristus to escape. Tristus pulled free, but did not walk away. He looked at the floor. "We can talk elsewhere, Alere."

"I'm not going to force myself on you," Alere told him in a quiet, taut voice.

Depressed by the elf's timing, and afraid of the convenient escape he offered, Tristus waited several moments before finally whispering, "You wouldn't have to force yourself."

"Then why do you resist?"

Tristus frowned helplessly, angry with the elf for not leaving—angry with himself for not giving in. Why shouldn't he? He would be loved, at least. Wasn't that enough?

No, of course it couldn't be. Alere may not have known his own heart.

"Forgive me for saying this, Alere, but I honestly believe you're too young to understand. Your heart is, anyway."

"Inexperience," the elf said, not quite sounding mocking in his careful tone, "does not necessarily speak also of ignorance. I will admit that I am young by elven standards—perhaps by human standards as well—but I am not a child."

Tristus dared to look at him. By appearance, he was right.

"My people have changed as the elves of this region, and of others, can never comprehend," Alere furthered to say, as if sensing that more explanation was required to make Tristus understand. "The rapidity of the slaughter that took place during the war against the shadows changed us in order to save us as a race. Lifespans decreased. We still do not suffer decrepitude and the withering effects of aging, but our youth is nothing we take for granted anymore. Trust me when I say that my childhood ended long ago."

"I did not mean to offend you," Tristus replied in earnest. "I only ... don't want to see you hurt. I don't want to be the one to hurt you. And I would, Alere."

He finally summoned the courage to face the elf, but it didn't last. Alere was too composed, too patient as he waited to hear words that came to Tristus as laboriously as breath to a dying man. Tristus stalked toward the fireplace, casting his gaze into the fire, as if he could burn away the painful images that came to his mind.

"I did not come here to catch what has evidently been cast aside," Alere finally said, and if Tristus didn't happen to know that the elf wasn't as heartless as he seemed, he'd have told him to leave at once. Recalling the sparingly offered warmth he'd witnessed in the elf's eyes just a moment before, he waited and Alere continued. "I simply came to be assured that you were not suffering too greatly."

The elf spoke as if in reference to a wounded animal he had planned to put out of its misery, if its suffering had indeed turned out to be so great ... and Tristus couldn't help the smile that escaped him. It was difficult to believe that this outwardly dispassionate individual had even dreamt of expressing himself as meaningfully as he had in Upper Yvaria. Except Tristus doubted it was anything Alere had dreamed of. Alere had always been wondrously unplanned with his words, and in that instance, with his actions. He stated what seemed true to him automatically, and without reservation.

"When I arrived moments ago," Alere said, filling the silence Tristus had set between them, "you were more concerned with my peace of mind than with your own. I am constantly amazed by your generosity, and by your strength."

Tristus laughed now. The sound came out more bitter than he intended. "I wouldn't call it strength, my friend. Perhaps I am simply too stubborn—or too afraid—to back down. Anyway, we have our vows to uphold now. Our promise to see this mission through to its end, to trust and support one another." Warmth filled Tristus, a warmth that had nothing to do with the fire he stared at. After some length trying to form further words where none may have been required, he said, "I'm glad you decided to come, Alere."

Another brief silence trailed his words, and then the elf's hand came down gently on his shoulder. Tristus made the mistake of lifting his hand to Alere's. He meant to acknowledge his friend's concern, and found contact ... a physical warmth with connection that traveled quickly to the rest of his body, promising to fill the empty places, if he would allow it.

Alere gently squeezed his shoulder, and Tristus turned to face him slowly, more to blame for the kiss that followed than the elf was. Alere was guilty simply of being there, and of offering sympathy and love to someone who had gone too long without either. Tristus wanted it, desperately, but this was not the source from which he had hoped to gain it, even now. His mouth drank in Alere's sweet taste, but his mind was absent from the deed, his heart set on someone else.

Alere's affection was eager, but not forceful or possessive, and it enabled Tristus to pull away when he became aware of the dire wrong he was committing. He went to the mantle for support, feeling breathless, and held out his hand to ward off any further advance the elf might have made.

"Please, don't," Tristus said. "I could love you, Alere, but ... I could also betray you. I don't want that. I ... don't want to hurt you. I'm sorry."

"I understand," the elf said, as if he genuinely did understand, though his tone made it sound as if only a legitimate child would not. "It is not my ambition to harm you either. You said once before that you seek my friendship, Tristus. Know that you have it ... and that I will always welcome more if you are ever ready to give it. Goodnight."

With that said, the elf left. He was gone from the room before Tristus could do anything more than gape in his amaze at just how selfless and caring Alere actually happened to be. It saddened him to think that no one outside of himself and Alere's family might ever truly realize that hidden fact.

TWENTY-NINE
Leaving Skytown

THE MORNING BEGAN before the sun rose, with meditation and incense; a prayer to the Ancestors, that they would be permitted safe passage to Sheng Fan. In the light of early morning following the prayer, Xu Liang exercised his body that was still somewhat weak from the extreme spiritual effort he had made up until now, that had resulted in dire physical neglect. He performed a series of stretches first and felt the awakening of disused muscles. He had been too lax in his training, even before setting out on his journey to the West. Strength alone could not win wars. Xu Liang knew that well, but he was often forced to admit to himself that Xu Hong was right. Intelligence by itself would also fail to claim an ultimate victory. The mind and the body must work together. He had learned harshly that magic could assist in that effort, but it could not lead.

After stretching, he practiced various techniques with *Pearl Moon*. When he'd worked hard enough to feel winded, but not exhausted, and to feel the healthy ache of labored muscles, he stopped and proceeded to a silver basin further into the vast room, where recently heated water awaited. Originally, elven servants had kept the tub refreshed with clean, steaming water, and perfumed oils, but shortly after Xu Liang survived Ahjenta's fire healing, his own servants took up the task, along with all other duties required of them as his personal guards. There would not be much for them to do once they left Vilciel, with most of their equipment lost due to the ice giant's attack. They would be sleeping under the canopy of the Heavens. They may not even have enough bedrolls to lay out, let alone tents to set up.

Hoping for a swifter journey back to Sheng Fan than he'd endured leaving it, Xu Liang bathed, redressed in his layers of silk that had seen far better days, and set about the task of combing out his hair. The length of his hair—even apart from his beauty—was what distinguished him from other men. It was as symbolic and identifying to him as Fu Ran's dragon tattoos and his broad, sinister grin that gave him the title 'Laughing Devil'. On a more personal level, Xu Liang's ability to grow such a healthy length of hair set him apart from his brothers, all of whom followed Xu Hong by keeping their hair relatively short, tying up what couldn't be hidden beneath a helmet. Fang, his youngest brother in Du—Xiang Wei of Ying was actually the youngest of his half-siblings—had for some time been trying to grow a long beard, but he'd managed thus far only to achieve a bushier aspect to his broad countenance.

"I suppose that we can't all grow silk, brother," Fang would often say good-naturedly to Xu Liang, who smiled now, thinking positively for once about his family. It was difficult to honor them properly, living under Xu Hong's double standards. The Governor of Du could have adopted Xu Liang. Xu Mi was his wife. He had more right to her son than Xiang Wu, but pride overruled his sense of truth and honor. He chose to lie, and therefore to force that lie and the act of lying upon Xu Liang, while still expecting otherwise right and honorable behavior from him.

With the thought, a pain that had been lingering since his morning exercise stabbed suddenly behind his breast. It felt as if the muscles had suddenly pinched themselves together. Xu Liang placed his hand over the area of aggravation and breathed the kink out, then continued with his hair, tying and pinning it away from his face. He preferred it mostly freed.

Recognizing that in the past, Xu Hong thought to demonstrate during training what could happen to vain men on the battlefield by pulling Xu Liang's hair more than once. Xu Liang quickly learned how to evade the brutal maneuver, and Xu Hong naturally took it for defiance. Xu Liang narrowly escaped having his head shaved, so great was Xu Hong's anger at being outwitted by Xiang Wu's son. Quickly, it was decided that Xu Liang's hair be bound whenever he practiced his martial skills.

Eventually, Xu Liang's hair became more his own concern than anyone else's, particularly when he began spending more time in the academy town of Zhi Ping, where—as he suddenly recalled—he had first been introduced to Lord Ha Ming Jin, currently the Governor of Xun. The late Ha Sheng's son was best described, then and now, as ambitious.

Xu Liang thought about his former classmate and the man's current campaign against Ji, and wondered irresistibly how the troops he'd ordered to Fa Leng were faring. He'd left an even-tempered older general in command. The senior had the wisdom and planning of two notably versatile strategists to aid him, and the authority to summon more troops from the nearest city if necessary. Ha Ming Jin would not give in easily, but he should not have been able to advance against such resistance.

Gai Ping's approach interrupted the thought.

Xu Liang waited for the man to perform his ritual respect and to state his business.

"My lord, the others are ready to leave," the guard said. "The Lady Ahjenta awaits an audience with you as well."

Xu Liang nodded his acknowledgment. "I will be along shortly."

◆ ◆ ◆ ◆ ◆

"YOU'RE NOT coming?"

Tristus almost apologized for asking the question when D'mitri provided him with a sharp, golden glare.

When the Phoenix Elf seemed satisfied with the sting he'd inflicted upon his victim, he proceeded to oversee the saddling of a lovely steed, different from the other horses kept in Vilciel in that it was much smaller—built for speed rather than strength—and it was not black. Instead, its soft pelt was a reddish brown color, closer to the shade of the elves' hair rather than their armor.

Ahjenta—whom, according to Shirisae, was at first opposed to her leaving—had not only been kind enough to provide them with food and shelter during their time among her people, but now she extended her support and generosity even further by providing horses for those without. Tristus was too busy admiring the reddish steed before him to wonder why everyone else received a large black horse—except the dwarves, of course, who would be riding with others. He did, however, wonder why D'mitri had taken it upon himself to personally deliver this animal while Fu Ran and the guards were accommodated by strangers.

"My mother would have lent you griffins, if they were capable of long flights across oceans," the Phoenix Elf said, and he didn't have to mention his disagreement with such a notion. It was more than evident in his voice and on his face.

"This," he continued, gesturing at the russet steed, "is a gift from my sister. It is the offspring of wild horses. We discovered him abandoned as a colt in the forests of Gynth, wandered perhaps from the meadows of his birth."

"Gynth?" Tristus echoed, surprised. "Why, that's not far from the northernmost border of Andaria. You certainly cover a broad range in your wandering, don't you?"

"Yes," D'mitri replied. "So do you, knight. As I was saying, giving you this unique animal is my sister's idea, and you're fortunate that it is hers to give."

"I am grateful," Tristus said amicably. "Truly."

"And you should be." The elf glared at him again.

Tristus sighed, becoming impatient with D'mitri's supreme intolerance. "I understand that you dislike us. I regret it, but I do understand, D'mitri."

The flame-haired elf ignored his statement, stepping closer to Tristus, who felt in that moment as if he would have fit twice into the Phoenix Warrior's broad and supremely fit frame, even knowing that he himself did not happen to be a small person, not since a much younger man.

"I allow you to leave here alive, human," D'mitri said, "because I am confident that you will not return. Consider that when you think about Shirisae's childish affections. Consider also, that I would not welcome a half-breed niece or nephew … and that I would hunt you to the ends of this world, if necessary, to be sure you could never violate another elven woman for the remainder of your existence, should I even suspect that you dared so much as lay a finger on her."

For some reason, Tristus had always inspired the protective instincts of every man who was father or brother—or uncle, as it had recently turned out—to a female acquaintance of his since he was fourteen. It usually wasn't to this degree, but he wished someone could explain to him how a man who honestly wasn't interested could be so easily perceived as a threat to a lady's honor. Perhaps his heart had foreseen this trouble ahead of time, and that was why he was not interested.

Tristus held the Phoenix Elf's fiery gaze with equanimity that would have surprised himself if he considered it, and said, "D'mitri,

I've no intention of violating anyone, Shirisae least of all. I respect and care for her as I would my own sister. As to her affections, the matter has already been discussed and set aside. You may rest assured that no dishonor will be brought upon your sister by me."

D'mitri seemed to search him visually for evidence of honesty, then stepped back and proceeded to bully his fellow elves, unaware of the breath of relief that escaped Tristus. He glimpsed a white horse nearby and—almost as an afterthought—looked to her rider, quietly returning the smile that was in the pale elf's eyes.

Alere seemed to be commending his handling of the flame-haired tyrant. Tristus felt very near to having been 'handled' himself, and he could only wonder if Alere read that in his expression.

"You," D'mitri said to the white elf when he noticed him present, "I would invite back to this region for the occasion of your death upon my blade."

Alere scarcely dignified his animosity with a frown and said, "There are other foul things in this world that require my attention. You will have to wait."

D'mitri smiled wickedly and said something in elvish, words that Tristus could not begin to decipher, or perhaps he didn't care to, given the tone.

Alere scowled in response to whatever D'mitri had said, his hand suddenly hovering over the hilt of his sword.

Tristus spoke up quickly, "What is his name?"

Both elves looked at him, confused and irritated by the interruption.

Tristus had never dreamed to see the two of them united in anything, least of all annoyance with him. He cleared his throat and said, "This ... uh, this magnificent horse." He gestured toward the russet steed. "You didn't ... didn't tell me his name."

D'mitri looked at the animal briefly. "Sylvashen," he barked. And then he left, casting Alere a parting scowl.

"What does that mean?" Tristus wondered, relieved that the two elves were separated.

Alere came forward, looking the handsome beast over before giving Tristus his answer. "It means 'of the forest folk'."

Tristus walked toward Sylvashen and held his hand out to the animal's muzzle to introduce himself. The steed came forward, warming to its new master at once. "Well, he certainly is—hey, now, stop that." Tristus pulled the shoulder of his cloak out from between the steed's teeth, then patted him on the snout and smiled up at Alere. "He certainly is friendly."

"That's surprising," the white elf muttered. "Considering the source of the gift."

"Be nice, Alere," Tristus chided good-naturedly, stroking the red horse's neck, shrugging to keep his cloak out of its mouth. "I think that Sylvashen and I ... stop ... are going to become quite—stop it, Sylvashen—quite good friends."

Alere smiled. "He suits you."

Tristus smiled back, until his gaze strayed to a platform just above the snow-covered yard, where Xu Liang was issuing his ritualistically polite goodbyes to Ahjenta. He stared until the mystic turned from the priestess and started down the stairs. Blue Crane was near. That meant that soon Xu Liang would be as well. Tristus knew that the right thing to do was to apologize, but he didn't know exactly how to do so without seeming even more absurd than he must have seemed the night before.

The guards came first.

Tristus' heart began to hammer. All thought and any hope of forming rational words escaped him. He turned slowly, and led Sylvashen away.

◆ ◆ ◆ ◆ ◆

WHILE HUGGING HER twin goodbye, during a rare instance of displayed sentiment, Shirisae looked over D'mitri's shoulder and saw Tristus avoid Xu Liang. Several days ago, she would have liked to see nothing else more. In her determination to see her own desires satisfied, she would have encouraged him to walk away from the mystic and to forget about him. She knew better now. She knew Tristus was truly, deeply in love with Xu Liang, and that he would never forget him.

Somehow her own love had evolved beyond simple desires for herself. She wanted now, more than anything, to see Tristus happy. It saddened her to think that he couldn't be. And not because Xu Liang was too proud or not inclined to care deeply for another man. Shirisae had looked beyond the mystic's charm that he wore like cloaks of glamour cast upon him by the fae folk. She had used the insight given her by her mother and her grandmother—and so on, back to the beginnings of her family—and she had seen that Xu

Liang was afraid. His fear made him cold and, as she had tried to express to Tristus once before—then, for her own selfish reasons—it made him indifferent to the hearts that were offered to him. He knew they were in his keeping and he understood the hopes they represented, but he would not respond. He would rather watch them wilt and die in his hands, like plucked flowers, because to water them—to nurture them—would be the start to acknowledging them, and to maybe discovering that he wanted to continue caring for them. At times Shirisae pitied Xu Liang more than Tristus. At least Tristus confronted his feelings, whatever the consequences.

When she parted from her sibling, D'mitri looked over his own shoulder at the knight, then he gave his attention back to Shirisae. He was wearing his lecturing frown, rather than his scowl of disgust.

Shirisae smiled sadly when he lovingly touched her cheek, as he hadn't for many years. He spoke to her softly in elvish. "I know what you believe was told to you by the Flame, my sister, but I want you to put it out of your thoughts. Put *him* out of your thoughts, please, so that my mind and heart can be at ease while you are so very far away."

Shirisae took his hand in hers, and rested her face in his palm. "I wish you were coming with me."

"Though you know I cannot," D'mitri replied tenderly, accepting the change of subject. "I have been away too often and too long as it is. Come autumn I will be a father."

"And I will be an aunt," Shirisae reminded him, sighing wistfully, realizing that she was about to turn a second century and still had no children herself. Sudden tears threatened to make their parting sad, so she forced a smile for her brother's sake. "I know you will raise a brood of excellent warriors, D'mitri, just like their father. Though hopefully they will not all be as stubborn."

"Which brings me to what I've been meaning to say to you since last night, Shirisae." He withdrew his hand and looked down at the snow beneath their feet, drawing a long pause before he finally let out what was in his heart. "I apologize, sister, for the way I acted concerning the hunter. I know it is for my wife and the child not yet born to me that you spoke to me in such harsh tones. I am truly sorry."

"Sorry, but only for my sake," Shirisae said, and tried to give the words a light tone, as this would be their final conversation for an unspecified period of time—maybe forever, if the enemy awaiting in Sheng Fan was greater than the Swords, greater than what their unlikely assembly of warriors could make of them.

D'mitri smiled. Her brother said, "I apologized for your sake, yes." And then he recovered his frown. "For the orphaned Verressi, I would offer him only the satisfaction of dying a warrior's death. Though I would be sorely tempted to drag his bleeding and broken body to the darkest caves beneath our city, and watch the spiders make a feast of him."

"On that comforting thought, I will bid you farewell, then, D'mitri." She couldn't remember the last time she had honestly said farewell to him. She wasn't braced for the finality of the moment. Her smile quavered and then shattered, showing her sadness openly.

Her twin took her into his arms once more and held her tightly. "I await your safe return, my beloved sister. Remember that you are heiress to the Flame … and that nothing frightens you."

Shirisae laughed through her tears, recalling how, even as a small child, she had always tried to be as strong and fearless as her brother.

"I'll miss you," she whispered, then kissed his cheek and pulled away. He reached out to brush away her tears, but she wouldn't allow it. He would remember her strong, and therefore he would not spend precious thoughts that should all be for his son or daughter, worrying about her. In *Firestorm* as well as in her heart, she was bringing the Phoenix with her. The Flame would still protect her.

On that thought, Shirisae left her brother and didn't look back. At least she could be comforted in knowing that D'mitri had never cried a day of his long life.

◆ ◆ ◆ ◆ ◆

SOME HOURS AFTER its departure, the company arrived at the base of the mountain that housed Vilciel. The group huddled in the pass for only a few moments, perhaps to finalize the route they meant to take to the distant coast.

And then, suddenly, ten well-bred horses were spurred across the snow with their riders, heading north. It was likely that none of them noticed the griffin soaring overhead, seeing them off with D'mitri upon its back, who watched as his sister and twin was borne away from him.

EPİLOGUE

The Quest Ends ... A Journey Begins

IT HAD ONLY just occurred to Fu Ran, as he counted the days since leaving his ship, that the *Pride of Celestia* was due at the northeastern tip of Upper Yvaria in eighteen days. Their passage aboard the ship would be guaranteed, and their destination would be Aer, the country which directly preceded Sheng Fan on Dryth's eastern continent.

That was only if they could make it. They had less than twenty days to get to the port town of Willenthurn. If they made it in time, and the weather was agreeable for sailing, they would have only a matter of hours to locate the ship, whose captain didn't have a strong liking for long layovers where there wasn't a large profit in the loading or unloading of cargo to be made. It would not be easy, but it was possible.

Xu Liang silently thanked the priestess Ahjenta once more. They would not have had a chance if not for the horses she had provided for the others. For the first time since leaving Sheng Fan, it seemed that luck was truly on his side.

Hold strong, my empress. I am coming. And I have the Swords.

ABOUT THE
AU T H O R

T. A. MILES fell down a rabbit hole ages ago, and nothing more need be said about it.

T. A. MILES has been writing novels for nearly twenty years. She finally presented the results of her mental wanderings to readers in 2011 with the gothic-mystery Raventide, and has published six novels, five short stories, and one novella since.

WILL CURIOSITY pull you down the rabbit hole? Visit T. A. Miles at her blog, The Immarcescible Word, to experience her exclusive collection of snippets, extracts, grotesqueries, and more.

THEIMMARCESCIBLEWORD.COM

MORE FROM

· · · · · ·
RAVENTIDE BOOKS

THE BLOOD WARS TRILOGY

Blood Lilies
Blood Song
Blood Reign
The Blood Wars Trilogy Omnibus

CELESTIAL EMPIRE

Six Celestial Swords
Five Kingdoms
Four Barbarian Generals
Three Fates
Two Warring Dragons
One Empire

THE DREAMER SERIAL

A Bit(e) of Discretion, Please
A Little Night Magic
All the Tea in Chinatown
Four and Twenty Tengu
Man's Best Fiend
Djinn and Tonic

STAND ALONE STORIES

Raventide

Masque of Shadow

20748862R00229

Printed in Great Britain
by Amazon